WILD NIGHTS

WILD NIGHTS

A NOVEL BY

Janice Kaplan

St. Martin's Press

NEW YORK

Design by Robert Bull Design

Library of Congress Cataloging-in-Publication Data

Kaplan, Janice.
    Wild nights / Janice Kaplan.
      p. cm.
    ISBN 0-312-06492-6
    I. Title.
    PS3561.A5593W55   1991
    813'.54—dc20   91-20555
                                                     CIP

First Edition: September 1991

10 9 8 7 6 5 4 3 2 1

My husband is smart, funny, loving, kind, and handsome, and this is for him—again and always.

ACKNOWLEDGMENTS

I am grateful to Maureen Baron for her wonderful editing and her fine insights and instincts. I appreciate her talent as well as her attention to this book. My continued thanks to Esther Newberg for her support and enthusiasm. Thanks also to attorney Marcia Seibald for her legal information and to Vicky Smith and Robert Masello for their help, conversation, and advice. I'd finished writing this novel before I began working with Anthea Disney, but a note of thanks to her—because she makes it a pleasure to produce television shows. My parents, Libby and Stanley Kaplan, have offered wisdom and encouragement, and they have my deepest love.

In the years I've worked in television as a producer and writer, I have learned a lot from other producers, directors, and on-air personalities. I've enjoyed them all, but none of them appear in this book; it is strictly a work of fiction.

Wild Nights—Wild Nights!
Were I with thee
Wild Nights should be
Our luxury!

Futile—the Winds—
To a Heart in port—
Done with the Compass—
Done with the Chart!

Rowing in Eden—
Ah, the Sea!
Might I but moor—Tonight—
In Thee!

Emily Dickinson
c. 1861

CHAPTER ONE

STANDING in the middle of the control room, observing the chaos on the set, Keith Ross was so angry that he could have cried. But he managed instead to scream—at the stage manager, the director, and most of all, at his producer.

"Is this the first goddamn thing you've produced?" he roared, his face flushed with anger.

The producer, Josh Ambler, blanched under his Hollywood tan, the stress of the day causing crinkles around his cerulean-blue eyes. Confrontations with Keith Ross typically caused him to lose all composure, but this time he was determined to stand up for himself.

"If you'd quit interfering, I could do this show—but I can't work when you're always looking over my shoulder." His intention was to shout back at Keith, sounding strong and manly, but somehow the complaint came out more like a whine, which infuriated Keith even further.

"If you can't work, then quit. Or else I'll fire you." Outrage made Keith preternaturally loud, and his anger boomed through the control room; production assistants scattered off to Xerox scripts or pour coffee—anything to escape the fury that could easily settle next on them. When the executive producer was angry, the best idea was to get out of sight before he threw something. Not completely understanding that, Josh stood his ground.

1

"I'm an artist, Keith. I need creative control. You can't just come in and change everything I do."

"I can do whatever I damn well please, so you can take your fucking creative control and shove it. It happens to be my million dollars behind this production and my ass on the line."

The phone in the control room was ringing insistently, and when nobody picked it up, Keith hollered—"Don't we have any goddamn p.a.'s around here?"—then lunged for the receiver himself and barked, "Hello." The other line was also ringing; the director was waiting to talk to him because Josh's directives had seemed unwise; and the newest graphics for the special were in the monitors. Keith felt his temples throbbing. Don't have a stroke, it's not worth it, he told himself, but he wasn't sure how he could avoid it. The graphics were trite, stupid, and contrived—totally unlike the designs he had originally approved. Why had they been changed? He looked over at his egregious producer, the artiste, then sat down, all the anger suddenly drained from him. He wasn't giving in; he was simply calmed by the swift decision he had made.

"Josh, you're fired," he said. "Get out right now."

Josh's face registered a mix of confusion and panic. "We're in the middle of a production."

"I know that. And you're only making it worse. If I have to do everything myself, I'm not paying someone to put his name in the credits."

"For God's sakes, Keith, this is crazy. You can't do this."

"I can't? I just did. Get the fuck out."

The phones were ringing again, and since there were still no production assistants around, Keith grabbed a line and prepared to get the production back under control.

▬▬

"This is supposed to be an industry town. Aren't there any decent producers around?" Keith chomped on an ice cube, his frustration crunching across the table. He signaled the waitress to bring him another seltzer.

"Want anything?" he asked Barry Brunetti.

"Thanks, I'm fine." Barry, the handsome station manager of a network affiliate in Chicago, was proving how au courant he was by working his way through a frothy mixture of pear juice and champagne. The third man at the table, Armand Lopez, a narrow-eyed man of indeterminate ethnicity who had become a successful syndicator of other people's shows, pointed to his glass and ordered his third double whiskey. The men had run into each other at the broadcasters' convention—the one meeting of the year that everyone in the business attended—where the name of the game was making unexpected connections.

"Ambler didn't work out for you?" asked Barry Brunetti.

"Ambler was an ass, as were the last two producers I hired in L.A. and the three before that in New York. I'm sick and tired of having to do everything myself."

"You can't do everything," Lopez said, his words ever-so-slightly slurred. "Doesn't make business sense. A guy like you's got to be pouring out ideas that other people make work. That's how you're going to make the bucks in syndication."

"You're damn right I'm going to. Meanwhile, that special Ambler was supposed to be doing is in the can, but I spent the last week busting my ass over it."

"That's why we didn't see you much at the convention." Barry swirled his drink gently, sloshing the contents to the top of the glass, but not spilling a drop. "Tell me what you need. Maybe I can help."

"What do I need? A producer who goddamn knows how to produce. I'm sick of these people who have egos bigger than their talent. Ambler alienated half my sponsors because he considered it beneath him to talk to them. Sorry, pal, but a certain amount of sucking up is part of the game."

"Tell me about it." Barry grinned. "Don't mean to get personal, but when you were at the network, I always heard your name as part of a team. Ever think of getting back the other half?"

"Jillian van Dorne?" Keith looked up quickly. "I'd kill to get Jillian back. But I don't think she wants to work."

"You'd know better than I would, but I've heard her name tossed around a lot lately. She's done a couple of independent projects, and

3

there's some talk— Well, as I said, you'd know better than I about Jillian."

No, he didn't know anything about Jillian at all lately, but he wasn't going to admit that now. The rumor during the time they worked so closely together was that they were screwing, and the years of silence between them now might have suggested a deep well of ill feeling. But neither was correct, and they were still friends, even if in recent years they'd had no natural ambit for contact.

But maybe they would now.

Keith glanced at his watch. Almost midnight. Much too late to call the East Coast. But there was always the morning. And goddamn it, he was desperate.

▬▬▬

When the telephone rang, Eve jumped up from the table to answer it, knocking over her almost-empty cup of orange juice in the process. Offering a quick "Sorry, Mommy," she grabbed the phone.

"Hello, who's calling please?"

Jillian glanced at the morning's *New York Times* and didn't pay much attention to the call. Other mothers were always phoning their house in the mornings to arrange playdates or impromptu car pools. The effort to juggle children's schedules and adult lives was frequently complicated. Beams of sunlight glimmered off six-year-old Lila's golden hair and made a halo around three-year-old Eve's curls. The scent of newly blossoming lilacs crept in from one slightly opened window.

Eve seemed to be enjoying her phone conversation. There was a flush to her cheeks, and Jillian heard her reporting her name and her age then explaining that she had an older sister.

"Who is it, honey?" Jillian asked, looking up from the paper and wiping the spilled drops of juice with a napkin.

Eve held out the phone. "For you, Mommy. I forget what he said his name is."

Jillian took the phone and said hello.

"You didn't have that baby the last time we spoke."

The voice charged through her, bringing an immediate smile to her face. Keith Ross wasn't the only man in Hollywood whose English accent had been picked up in the Bronx rather than Trafalgar Square, but his voice boomed across any receiver with a gritty authority that few could match.

"I still don't have a baby," Jillian said, marveling that even after all this time, Keith wouldn't offer a normal "hello" or identify himself. "She's a big girl now. With an even bigger sister."

"That's why I'm calling. Do you have a few minutes?"

"Actually, I'm about to drive the girls to school."

"Then I'll be brief. There's a rumor around that Jillian van Dorne is ready to come back to television."

"Oh, really? Who told you that?"

"Not important. The point is that if it's true, I want to make the first offer."

From the hallway Jillian heard the grandfather clock striking eight o'clock. "I'm honored, Keith, but you're too late."

"Too late? Goddamn it, it's five o'clock in the morning here. I'm the first person awake in all of Los Angeles."

She laughed lightly, pleased to be parrying with him. It's what they had done for years, starting when she was almost a baby herself, just out of college, living in Los Angeles and ripping up the town.

"Are you based in L.A. again?" The last article she'd read in *Variety* said his independent production company was located in New York. Jillian hadn't seen Keith since they worked together at CBS, and that had been more than three years earlier. He hadn't bothered to send flowers when she had her second baby, and she hadn't thought to send the requisite congratulations each time he won another Emmy. But she liked him. Still and always.

"No, I'm just here at the broadcasters' convention—though I spent most of the week saving a special my company produced for the network. I'll be back in New York tomorrow morning. What time can you be at my office?"

"I don't know if tomorrow's a good day." She fumbled for the calendar that she kept near the phone, but before she could find it, Keith said, "Come on, Jillian, don't play games with me. You still shoot straight, don't you?"

The expression gave her a jolt, bringing back an image of herself

5

that she had almost forgotten. She was the one who used to say it all the time to directors and writers and nubile actresses: *I'm going to shoot straight with you.* And then she would. Knowing how to wield power gracefully had always been one of her greatest assets.

"How does eleven o'clock sound?" she asked.

"Eleven is perfect. See you then." Keith hung up without saying good-bye, and Jillian bit back a smile as she put the receiver on the hook.

"Who was that, Mommy?" Lila looked at Jillian curiously.

"Just an old friend of Mommy's."

"From when you were a television producer?"

"Yes, sweetie. Are you through with your breakfast? It's almost time for school."

Lila nodded but wasn't to be sidetracked. "Do you think you'll be a television producer again?"

Before Jillian could answer, Eve interrupted. "The man on the phone said I sound just like you, Mommy."

"You do, sweetheart. I don't know why, but you do. Now both of you find your schoolbags so we can get going." There was a clattering of chairs and another overturned cup, and despite the confusion of looking for schoolbags and sweaters, Jillian kept hearing Keith's voice—and she realized that she would be replaying the conversation for the rest of the day.

It was twenty minutes past eleven before Keith even got to his office, but since Jillian had been ushered in immediately and invited to sit in the inner sanctum rather than the lobby, she didn't mind at all. Keith's office was larger and more impressive than Jillian had remembered from earlier incarnations. A full wall of windows offered a view north to Central Park and that, combined with leather sofas in almost the same shade of tan as the thick carpet, made the room seem to go on forever. Keith had the same desk that Jillian remembered—a free-form, burled-wood sculpture that had been created for him by a craftsman he'd met on a shoot in Sonoma County. At least in this office the desk, which always reminded Jillian of a gargantuan tree stump, wasn't so overwhelming. Behind the desk stood two flowering lemon trees and a spindly avocado plant. Jillian realized that they had been placed there to make executives from L.A. feel at home—and to announce in a subtle way that Keith Ross was a bi-coastal force. Across from the vegetation sat a trophy case that at first glance seemed more appropriate for a football coach than a television producer. But Jillian didn't have to get up to know that at least three of the statues were Emmys. The rest were trophies from various organizations that awarded excellence in media.

"There she is. Jillian van Dorne. Alive and well and as gorgeous as ever."

Jillian turned quickly to the door, where Keith was standing eyeing her appreciatively. His face deeply tanned, his curly, sandy-colored hair brushed off his forehead, Keith was dressed casually in a rumpled Giorgio Armani suit and an open-necked white shirt. In place of a tie, he wore a thick gold chain—an L.A. look that Jillian had never much liked—and had a burgundy silk square crumpled into his breast pocket. Despite the efforts he always put into his personal style, Jillian had never been attracted to Keith. He was too short and abrasive to appeal to her taste. But she had always admired Keith's youthful quality, and when he came over to kiss her now, she decided that the new crinkles around his eyes were a sign of sun damage rather than of age.

"You look wonderful," she said.

"Thanks, so do you. You haven't changed one single bit."

She had wanted him to think that. As she was getting dressed this morning, she'd pulled out the clothes that had been her trademark in L.A.—a short slim skirt, Perry Ellis flats, a silk blouse, and a Gucci scarf. The flat shoes and short skirts had worked for years, serving the dual purpose of showing off her legs and allowing her to match strides with any male executive.

Keith crossed over to his desk, then thinking better of it, moved to the sofa next to Jillian and sat down.

"So give me a quick update on your life," Keith said. "How're things going?"

"Surprisingly well. It's been an interesting few years."

"I have regards for you from Barry Brunetti."

Jillian raised her eyebrows, trying to place the name. "You'll have to remind me," she said.

"He worked for you in L.A. Now he's the station manager at WOJ in Chicago."

It was a strong station known for its investigative reporting and its flashy anchormen. On the basis of WOJ stories, a Chicago Congressman had been voted out of office and indicted for having mob connections.

"Barry Brunetti?" She paused, unable to conjure a face to go with the name. Then an image flashed through her mind, and she said, "Is he that ambitious kid who worked as a unit manager on 'All My Love'?"

"Sounds right, but he's grown up. Still ambitious, but now he's very slick and a real ladies' man."

Smiling at the old-fashioned expression, Jillian said, "He always flirted with anyone in a skirt. I guess he was handsome enough, though it always seemed to me that he had more bluster and charm than taste. How did he end up as the station manager at WOJ?"

Keith reached into his pocket for a cigarette. "Television's changed in the last few years," he said, clenching the cigarette between his teeth and fumbling in his pockets until he found an oversized gold lighter. "You'd be amazed at how many Barry Brunettis there are in positions of power. By the way, I had a drink with him in L.A., and he's the one who told me that you were thinking of coming back to television."

Jillian gave a brief snort of surprise. "He's clearly well connected. Or else he's been tapping my telephone."

Leaning back into the plush leather sofa, Keith inhaled deeply on his cigarette and released the smoke in a long, smooth stream. He had quit smoking at least half-a-dozen times since Jillian had known him, and she considered his recidivism to be proof of the power of addiction. Keith was otherwise vain about both his health and his looks, spending hours working out at the gym and consulting nutritionists for New Age diets.

"Let's get back to you," Keith said, stubbing out the cigarette in a malachite ashtray. "May I be blunt?"

"You always are."

"You've been living in the suburbs and not working. Aren't you bored out of your mind?"

"Sometimes," she said honestly. "But I've taken a few free-lance projects. A couple of weeks or months of craziness, and then I'm back home."

"You worked on 'Requiem for the Homeless' last year, didn't you?"

"Sure did."

"Brilliant show." Keith lit another cigarette. "Problem with free-lancing is that there's no power. The show is never really yours. I can't imagine that Jillian van-Dorne is very happy doing that."

"It can be frustrating," Jillian admitted. "I was credited as supervising producer on the homeless show, but I did just about everything except put up the money."

"And all the critical acclaim landed on someone else's desk."

Jillian shrugged. "It doesn't matter very much. I can walk away from a project like that and then spend more time with my two beautiful daughters. I've discovered what it is to be a normal person."

"PTA meetings, suburban cocktail parties, and the youth soccer league?"

"Not exactly, but some version of that. And don't be scornful. I've enjoyed it."

Keith shrugged. "You're the smartest and most talented woman I've ever met in television, Jillian. Until you gave it up, I figured you were also the most ambitious."

"I probably was."

"So why did you give it up?" Keith asked.

The question hung in the air for a moment while Jillian glanced at her fingernails and smoothed an invisible crease in her skirt. "The long answer or the short one?"

"The short one now, the long one when I take you out to dinner."

"After I got married and had Lila, I took a three-week maternity leave and went back to work. I prided myself on being able to do everything. A couple of years later . . ." She paused. "Well, Eve was born when I was in Los Angeles by myself on a business trip. It was the ultimate Superwoman delivery—but instead of feeling satisfied, I felt incredibly lonely. Nothing cataclysmic happened—unless you put having a baby in that category—but that time I took a three-*month* maternity leave, and I still couldn't face going back. I was tired of traveling and working twenty-four hours a day. I had enough frequent flyer miles to go around the world a few times, but all the coupons sat in my desk because I had no time to take a vacation. I suddenly wanted to have a real life with my two babies."

"You had the whole town gossiping about you. The most powerful woman in television turns her back on the industry."

"I'm sure." Jillian grinned. "I also gave work to any number of magazine editors who decided this was a new trend. *Family Circle* and *New Woman* photographed me kissing my babies and wrote articles about executive women who toss in the towel to stay home. The articles were sufficiently nauseating that I began saying no to everyone else who called."

"Leading to even more rumors."

"So I've heard." Jillian grinned. "What did you hear—that I was dying or that my husband was leaving me?" When Keith didn't answer, she said, "None of it was true. I was just getting kicks from my babies instead of our ratings."

"But now that the girls are a little bigger, you've decided that it would be nice to have everything again, am I right? So you're coming back."

"Look, Keith, I haven't made any final decisions. There've been some feelers out from the networks, a couple of outright offers. That's probably what your Barry Brunetti heard about. I'm flattered, but I didn't say yes to anyone."

"Good thing, because I want you here."

Jillian leaned back and crossed her legs, an action guaranteed to win attention without a word being spoken. "Doing what?"

"What you do best. Creating programs. Producing shows. I've got a big business here, and I need someone I can trust to help me hold it up."

Jillian got up, walked over to the trophy case, and picked up one of the Emmys. For years she had been the hot executive at the network, presiding over the creation of Emmy-winning shows. Now, with Keith, she could win one herself. Turning the statue around in her hands, she realized how carefully she had repressed the part of herself that wanted one of these sitting on the mantel over her fireplace. She wanted to have it and own it.

And everyone knew she deserved it.

She put the Emmy back on the shelf and returned to Keith.

"Back up a step, okay?" She sat down on the sofa next to him. "All I know about Keith Ross Productions is what I've read. Fill me in."

"I left the network about the same time you did to form my own production company. I started with soft news specials—mini-documentaries, I called them—and we hit like gangbusters. The first was a report on divorce in America called 'Splitting.'"

"I saw it."

"And?"

"Good television. As I remember, you were talking high-minded sociological trends, but you had a layer of glitz and glamour on it an inch thick."

"That's it." Keith grinned. "We got everyone in Hollywood to talk to us. William Hurt. Steven Spielberg. Cher. Melanie Griffith." He glanced over at the trophy case. "The best way to start a production company is to win an Emmy your first time out."

"Pays off, I'm sure. Didn't I read in *Variety* that you're getting a few million dollars from one of the networks to produce a series of prime-time documentaries?"

He nodded. "Not bad, right? But to tell you the truth, Jillian, it's not the only thing I want to do. The networks aren't where it's at anymore. A few million doesn't mean anything to me right now. The big bucks are in syndication."

"Which you're also doing."

"Damn right." He banged his fist into the leather sofa. "And that's why I need you. Syndicate, syndicate, syndicate."

"I'm not a syndicator. How can I help?"

He looked abashed for a moment, then said, "I've had a revolving door of producers here. I get rid of all of them because I don't trust their judgment, and I end up doing everything myself, anyway. I keep looking for another Jillian van Dorne, and I can't find her."

He paused to look at Jillian, and their eyes locked. They had a history together, an understanding based on years of working together—frantically—at all hours, relying on each other, and publicly admitting their trust in a network world where the major form of diplomacy was backstabbing.

"Here's why I called, Jillian. I want you to take over my dealings with the networks. Produce the specials so I can turn my attention to syndicating new shows and making us all millions. The company's gotten too big for me. I can't handle it alone anymore."

Looking at him steely-eyed, she said, "You want a lot."

"And I'm willing to pay a lot." He leaned forward. "Care to negotiate?"

▬▬▬

At a few minutes after midnight, Jillian smoothed the silk coverlet tossed casually over her bed and thought briefly about how long it had taken her to select the pale blue moire fabric. Her decorator had insisted it should coordinate with—but not match—the bold chintz that covered the windows, and she had to admit that the total effect was just right.

The feel of the silk was therapeutic, calming her nerves, which the past hour's conversation with her husband Mark had managed to inflame. Mark was sitting rigidly at the edge of the bed now, watching the basketball play-offs on television. The game had been blaring throughout their argument, the cheers and hisses of the crowd lending a surreal effect to their conversation.

Jillian waited until a commercial for Heineken appeared on the screen, and as two happy couples clinked their glasses, she said, "I never expected you to react this way."

Mark swung around and glared at her. His face seemed puffed with anger, and a deep frown line cut across his forehead like a scar. His bushy eyebrows were knit together in tension.

"What did you expect—that I'd be thrilled?"

Jillian shrugged slightly and brushed her fingers through her silky hair. "You married me when I was a television executive. I thought that was the person you fell in love with."

"Things are different now. Our lives are working fine with you at home. Why should we change it?"

She sighed; they had been over this territory half-a-dozen times in the last hour. How could she explain what she had felt holding that Emmy in Keith's office? It was time for her to go back to work, release the ambitious soul that she had repressed these last three years. She loved being home with the girls, but she *could* do everything again. The old Jillian van Dorne was raring to be heard.

"Look, Mark, things worked out just fine those few times I took on projects. And now I want it all again. I mean, part of me *would* still like to stay home. . . ."

"Then stay home."

Jillian cupped her chin in her hands and shook her head in despair. Somehow battle lines had been drawn in the conversation, and as a result she had to defend her position with a vehemence she didn't necessarily feel. To Mark, emotional ambivalence was a sign of weakness.

She decided to try again. Taking a light tone, she said, "Come on, honey. I bet part of you misses that glamorous working wife you used to have."

"Wrong."

"How about that glamorous paycheck I used to bring home?"

His dark brown eyes were suddenly crowded with indignation. "Oh, so that's the real issue behind all this. You're not happy with how much I'm making."

"Frankly, I have no idea how much you're making. You've been rather secretive lately about your business." Excluding me on purpose, she wondered, or is that just what happens after a while? "We're married, and this is supposed to be a partnership. If you're having business problems, it would be nice if you let me in on them."

"Goddamn it!" He picked up one of the real-estate journals he had been flicking through earlier and threw it across the room. It thwacked against the wall and fell to the floor. "Just don't start with me about my business, okay?"

Startled, Jillian said quietly, "I have a feeling that there's something other than Keith Ross Productions that's upsetting you."

"Oh, you do?" Mark's voice seemed to contain a touch of hysteria. "Well, you're wrong again. The only thing upsetting me is

13

you." He stormed out of the room, kicking the journal on the floor and slamming the door.

Shaken, Jillian reached across the bed for the television remote control, and as she turned off the game, she realized she was trembling. She and Mark rarely had confrontations—in part because they were usually of one mind on important matters, but also because it wasn't either of their styles. Years ago, when she was used to dealing with the hot tempers and flaming passions of men in Hollywood, she had been drawn to Mark's ability to reason things out calmly. But he wasn't in a mood to be rational these days.

Jillian wandered through the bedroom, listening. She half-expected to hear the rumbling of the garage door from the other side of the house and the sounds of Mark's Jaguar taking off into the night. But instead she heard the creaking of the heavy oak door to the guest bedroom downstairs. Was he planning to spend the night there? At least he couldn't go too far in striped pajamas and a bathrobe.

What was wrong with Mark lately, anyway? He behaved as if he'd undergone a personality change in the last few months, turning into a man she hardly knew. He came home late almost every night, and he seemed distracted. There were phone calls at all hours, whispered conversations behind closed doors. When she wandered by his desk, she saw scribbled notes about tax abatements and Amendment 691-a. None of it sounded familiar to her, and it struck Jillian like a cold wind that, for the first time since they'd been married, Mark wasn't telling her about his work. Perhaps something else was going on in his life, too. When she asked a direct question, he answered, but he wasn't volunteering any information.

In the newly quiet bedroom, Jillian sighed. She wasn't going to go to sleep angry, and she wouldn't let Mark do that, either. Grabbing a terry bathrobe from the hook in the bathroom, Jillian pulled it on over her flimsy Christian Dior nightgown and headed down to the guest room. She knocked lightly, and when there was no answer, peeked in. The light was off, and Mark was already under the covers, so she went over to the edge of the bed and put a light hand on his shoulder.

"I wish I could convince you that this job isn't going to be bad for us," she said, stroking the soft material of his robe. Her fingers innocently grazed his chest, and in response Mark's body went rigid with tension, and the taut cords of his neck muscles bulged under his skin. He sat up abruptly, and a streak of light from the hallway cut across his face. She drew back, scorched by his physical rejection of her.

"It's not us that I'm worried about," he said. "It's the girls."

"The girls will be fine. They're not babies anymore."

"You were going to stay home until they both started school." Mark's tone was angry and accusatory.

Jillian folded her hands on her lap. It was all she could do not to stoop to his level, point out that technically the girls *were* both in school, even if, for Eve, it was nursery school. But she controlled herself, and said quietly, "I didn't come down here to start the argument again, Mark. We made a decision a few years ago based on what seemed right then, and we have to do the same thing now. Circumstances change."

"The circumstances haven't changed. You're just tired of being a mother. You don't even like being a mother. Why don't you admit it?"

"How dare you say that?" She asked it more in bewilderment than anger, her puzzlement itself an accusation. The joy she felt in motherhood was too obvious to be discussed; Mark was striking out, looking for a way to hurt her, and that fact was more upsetting than any meaningless comment he could make.

In the lingering silence, Mark swung his legs over the edge of the bed and dropped his head into his hands. "I'm sorry. That was uncalled for." He rubbed his eyes, then sat up straight, pulling his robe tightly around him. "I don't know what's gotten into me."

I don't either, Jillian thought.

"Should we go upstairs?" Mark asked.

Jillian nodded. "We can talk another time."

Upstairs she said good night to Mark and lay stiffly at the edge of the bed. It wasn't the first time that their bed seemed to have an invisible line down the middle. Lately Mark had been falling asleep before she came to bed or staying in his study until one or two in the morning. Ironic that he should claim to be concerned about the children, since his interest in family time seemed to have all but disappeared.

Jillian turned over in bed and plumped the pillow, thinking about the sequences in life. She had taken time out for her children—and she was grateful to have done that—but it was time to return to the career that had always mattered so much to her.

Jillian had a passion for television, a dedication to her work that was apparent when she was an undergraduate at UCLA and got her first job as a script reader at CBS. When she graduated, she was offered jobs at all three networks and chose to stay at CBS, which wooed her with promises of a bright future. Within a year she had been promoted three times, and network executives began to notice her. It was hard not to notice Jillian. Even at twenty-one, she had been flashy, sophisticated, and perfectly turned out, from her French-manicured nails to the thick blond hair that fell just below her chin.

Jillian's ambition was like a drum constantly beating in her ears. She knew that she was more creative and more talented than most of the people making decisions and set out to prove it. She had a flair for the unusual in programming; her formula was to ignore all formulas and go with her instincts. It worked, and at age twenty-five, she was declared a programming genius and put in charge of daytime programming at the network. Soap operas and game shows were her babies— sex and money, she joked. At a word from her, soap operas changed their storylines, killed or resurrected characters. Amid great controversy, she had a popular male game-show host fired and replaced him with a gray-haired, intellectual woman who became even more popular. Then, working with a cast of unknowns, she created a new soap that immediately became the biggest hit on the air.

With the job came a reputation for being ruthless and power hungry: she was too pretty, too successful, and too young to be well liked. Keith was one of the few people who understood that Jillian loved the power of her job only because it gave her a chance to be creative and find new directions in television. In a medium where successful ideas are copied and repeated, she insisted on originality. She gave young producers a chance, listened to new ideas, and refused to believe television's accepted wisdom.

Being constantly on the move suited Jillian, and she enjoyed leading the bi-coastal life her job demanded—spending half the week in New York, overseeing soap operas, and half in Los Angeles, dealing with programming decisions. She traveled first class and had limousines waiting on each coast. Never needing much sleep, she seemed to work a full week in each of her offices and invariably traveled on the overnight flight so she wouldn't spend a work day in the air.

For her days and nights in New York, the network leased her a suite at the Waldorf Towers, and it seemed more like home than the fabulously expensive house she rented on the other coast. In Brentwood, her name was on the door, but she'd never had time to unpack most of her boxes or buy any furniture. Instead, she worked constantly, entertained business associates at Ma Maison or Chasens, and rarely invited the men she dated to come home with her. It was easier to stay at a lover's house so she could leave before dawn and be at her desk by seven. Men wanted her, tried to impress her with their beachfront houses and Ferraris. Since she liked the sex and enjoyed being wanted, she often took what was offered and moved on.

For several years, she considered it an indulgence to work sixteen hours a day, seven days a week, and not worry about the responsibilities she had to anyone but herself. But eventually she began to think about the other needs in her life, and once she decided that she wanted marriage and a family after all, she acted quickly. When she met Mark Austin at a dinner party in New York, she was struck by how handsome he was—not tall, but gracefully compact with thick blond hair and compelling dark eyes. Back then, he had seemed charming and low-keyed—and he knew nothing about the television business.

"You're so different from the Hollywood moguls I'm used to dating," she admitted to him on their second date as they were having dinner at a small Indian restaurant in lower Manhattan.

"I hope a refreshing change," he said. "Like a taste of cool yogurt after too much hot curry."

She laughed. "I like that. It's how I'll think of you from now on."

The next morning, he sent a dozen roses to her office, and when she opened the box, she found two containers of vanilla yogurt tucked in at each end.

Without quite admitting that she was doing it, Jillian had gradually moved into Mark's apartment on Seventy-third Street, just around the corner from where his father lived with his third wife—a pleasantly gracious woman whom Jillian immediately liked. They welcomed her, and for the first time in years, she could share Christmas with a family. It seemed obvious that Jillian and Mark would get married, and they did—in a pretty ceremony at the Unitarian church a few blocks away, followed by a reception at the Explorer's Club, where Mark was a member. Jillian thought it romantic to eat canapés and wedding cake amidst the stuffed bears and antler trophies. They honeymooned in Paris, and when they came back, threw an extravagant bash for West Coast friends at the Beverly Hills Hotel.

She continued commuting and didn't mind it—she felt energized in Los Angeles, at home in New York. The best of both worlds. The time apart seemed to strengthen their marriage. After just a few months of marriage, they talked casually about having a family and Jillian decided to take a chance and see what would happen.

Barely a month later, she suspected she was pregnant. And she was glad. It was why she had married in the first place.

For several afternoons, Jillian had been feeling strangely light-headed and dizzy in the office. So, without mentioning it to Mark, she bought a home pregnancy test, woke up early in the morning to mix vials and urine, and watched the dipstick turn an unmistakable blue.

Slipping back into bed, she snuggled close to Mark. Half-asleep, he put his arm around her and stroked her shoulder. Feeling the sensuous silk of her nightgown, he drew her closer. They kissed, and she rolled halfway on top of him, flung a slim leg over his and murmured, "I'm going to make you happy this morning."

"Mmm, that's good," he whispered, misunderstanding.

As she kissed him, she felt the beginnings of his erection pressing against her hip. She laughed lightly and said, "It's too late for that. I'm already pregnant."

He didn't move, but the erection vanished as if she had dashed him with cold water. "Are you kidding?" he asked weakly.

"No. The proverbial rabbit died. Or in modern terms, the stick turned blue."

"My God." He sat up and looked at his gorgeous wife. "Are you happy?"

She nodded and asked, "Are you?"

"Mostly shocked. Do you think I'm ready to be a dad?"

"Maybe not today," she said, smiling, "but you have nine months to prepare."

Jillian was determined not to let the pregnancy interfere with the rest of her life. She exercised religiously and gained barely twenty pounds by her ninth month. She thought endlessly about the pregnancy but never talked about it, and most colleagues were happy to pretend that nothing had changed. Others seemed to soften toward her—men who had always fantasized about Jillian van Dorne seemed happy to realize that Jillian the untouchable had, quite obviously, been touched.

Always organized, she went into labor on her due date and labored in misery for twenty-four hours, then forgot the pain almost immediately when Lila was put into her arms. Cooing and cuddling with more energy than she knew she had left, Jillian gazed into her baby's eyes and melted.

Not one to waste time, Jillian checked out of the hospital the next morning and brought Lila home to their apartment. Mark's study had been converted into a nursery, and Jillian immediately decorated it with a brass crib from Lewis of London and a wood-and-brass dresser and changing table. She picked a rosy flower print from Marimekko for the quilts, crib bumpers, and curtains and placed two colorful mobiles over the crib for Lila to look at. By the time Lila was three days old, she was the owner of fourteen stuffed animals and two talking bears. If stimulation was important to a baby, Lila was not to be deprived. Her dresser lamp played "The Teddy Bears' Picnic," and she had a stuffed lamb that played a Mozart sonata when its tail was pulled. Inside the crib, Lila had a plastic mirror for discovering herself and educationally approved pictures. Despite it all, she was a happy baby.

Jillian hadn't felt the need for a baby nurse in those first days home—Lila was, after all, *her* baby—and her days suddenly moved to a new rhythm; they were a blur of feedings and changings, leisurely strolls by the river with Lila bundled into her blue English stroller. Inside, Lila nursed constantly at her breasts while Jillian watched afternoon soap operas. *Like any new mother*, she thought—with the twist that when Lila fell asleep, Jillian made calls to producers and scribbled down ideas for new shows. Her legendary energy seemed to return in days.

It took her two weeks to decide on a nanny. Eager as she was to get back to work, the thought of leaving Lila each morning gave her a chill. Quite simply, she would miss her. And worry about her. She interviewed thirty-two aspiring nannies before settling on Marguerite, an older woman with impeccable references who seemed sweet, competent, and caring. They agreed to try each other out for a day or two before making a long-term commitment.

On her first trial day, Marguerite got Lila ready for her walk and waved to Jillian as she rolled the carriage into the elevator. When the elevator door closed, Jillian felt a surge of panic, rushed to the living room window, and leaned out of her twentieth-floor window, as if she were in a tenement. She caught sight of Marguerite leaving the building, pushing the carriage toward the park. *What if she never returns? What if she steals my baby?* Jillian paced the apartment for an hour until Marguerite returned with a rosy-cheeked Lila. Overcome with relief, Jillian invited Marguerite to move in the next day.

The next week, Jillian resumed her regular work schedule. The bi-coastal commuting began again, and Jillian took Lila and Marguerite to Los Angeles with her whenever she could.

Though nothing obvious had changed, the birth had mellowed her, and some of the people who had always respected Jillian van Dorne actually began to like her. She was named vice-president of programming at the network, and nobody begrudged her the position. Her life seemed to be in perfect balance: the adrenaline-producing excitement of her work and the loving comfort of husband, baby, and nanny. For over a year, she was on top of the world.

Then she got pregnant again.

Though unwilling to slow down, Jillian found herself overwhelmed by exhaustion. The cross-country trips were torturous, and the spare moments she would have once spent sleeping or relaxing, she now spent playing with Lila. Without a moment for herself, she didn't have time for Mark, either.

Thinking about it now, Jillian sat up in bed and looked around the room. That's when everything had changed, of course. That's when everything had happened. The anguish built and built over those nine months, then tumbled down after Eve was born as unexpectedly as the Berlin Wall.

Thinking about Eve's birth still made her smile through tears. Four weeks before her due date, Jillian went to L.A. on business. After a day of meetings during which she felt fluish, she drove herself to Cedars-Sinai Hospital and announced that she was about to have her baby. An arrogant intern examined her and told her that she was only four centimeters dilated and should expect many hours of labor.

"You're wrong," she told him, breathing heavily and sweating profusely. "I've done this before. I know the pain. I must be in transition."

"You're not," he said dismissively. "It's going to get a lot worse than this."

He left the room, and thirty minutes later, Jillian rang for a nurse. Ten minutes later, nobody but Eve had arrived.

Jillian smiled to herself now at the memory of the crowd of residents, nurses, and doctors who had suddenly gathered in the labor room when they realized that the baby was being born.

Too restless to consider sleeping now, Jillian looked over at Mark. His back was to her, but his rhythmic breathing suggested he was in a deep sleep. Jillian got out of bed and walked down the hall to the girls' rooms. As usual, Lila had flung off her covers in her sleep, so Jillian pulled them back up and kissed her gently on the forehead. In the next room, Eve was almost hidden by stuffed animals and baby dolls.

"I love you, baby, " Jillian whispered, kissing Eve on the cheek. The child didn't stir, but Jillian continued stroking her soft hair . . . thoughtfully. . . .

CHAPTER TWO

ANNABELLE Fox woke up with her body throbbing and realized that she had been bad again last night. Bad, bad, bad. A crack of mid-afternoon sunlight broke through the edges of the closed shades and burst in her head like a thousand meteors—too bright and overwhelming to tolerate today. Last night was a blur. Sitting up in bed to assess the damage, she saw the usual array of tangled clothes tossed over the chairs. Her silver lamé bodystocking was on the floor, and the foxtail stole she wore over it had been thrown down on the edge of the filthy fireplace. Wasn't London supposed to be rife with chimney sweeps? None of them had ever made it to this flat. Next to the bed, the Formica table was a mess of dirty glasses and overflowing ashtrays. The sight of some well-sucked limes brought back a hazy memory and seemed to explain why her lips felt puckered and sore. Picking up a water glass which bore the unmistakable mark of her passionate purple lipstick, she sniffed the tequila and groaned.

Thinking of lying down again, Annabelle shifted the bedclothes and caught sight of a rusty streak smeared across the bottom sheet. Blood, no doubt. Her blood. Damnation, why did she have to *bleed*? Her body was always betraying her, embarrassing her when she most wanted to seem adult. Heck, she hadn't even started getting her monthlies until a couple of years ago, when she was sixteen. A late bloomer, her doctor had said when she'd gone for her first gynecological exam. Nothing to worry about. Not that she had been worried before the exam—not having her monthlies just meant she didn't have to be popping a birth-control pill every day like most of her friends. The exam had been worse than anything else. Feet up in stirrups and some doctor she'd never met before from National Health attacking her with freezing metal.

Denny would have been furious if he'd been around then. Another man looking at her was enough to drive him to distraction, and the thought of her spreading her legs for someone else, even a doctor, would make him want to kill. One of the stagehands at the club last night had given her some flowers after the show, and high on the adrenaline of the performance, she had given him a hug of thanks. That's why Denny had taken her so furiously when they got back to the flat, turning her over and slapping her bottom, then forcing himself into her that way, screaming that she was bad, bad, bad. It hurt—she couldn't make it stop hurting—and her screams mingled with his sent him to a wild climax that threatened to rip her apart.

Touching herself gently now, she determined that she was all right and definitely able to get out of bed. Did she have another show tonight? She couldn't begin to remember. Across the long, cluttered space of the loft, she noticed that the red power light was still glowing on the tape deck, evidence that nobody had remembered to turn it off last night. Maybe some music would blast away her fears and make the flat seem less lonely. With a whimper she scampered across the cold floor to the tape deck and, pushing the play button, heard her own voice crashing out of the speakers. Is this what they had been listening to last night? Goose bumps suddenly flecked her skin, and wrapping her arms around herself, she tried to rub them away.

"Louder, baby, let's hear you sing."

Startled, she spun around to see Denny bounding into the flat, a manilla envelope tucked under his arm. He looked paler and more worn than usual, his dirty-blond hair hanging almost to his shoulders which were hunched forward. But the demons she had seen last night lurking behind his eyes were gone, and he looked almost happy. Crack, ice, coke, hemp, pills? She never knew what sent him flying and sent his mood swinging. Nothing for her, thank you, except for the booze he made her drink.

Snapping his fingers to the music, Denny came over and picked her up, swung her around like a baby, and whooped with delight. Annabelle kicked her legs and giggled. This was a new mood for him.

"What is it? What's up?"

"You are, baby. You're what's up. You're platinum."

"Whoa! No joke?"

"No joke."

"I can't believe it. 'No More Teenage Virgins'?"

"What else. We're number one on every chart in England and America. And it gets better. 'Hips Wiggle, Girls Giggle' is about to turn gold." He put her down and, digging into the manilla envelope, found a press release from CBS Records. "Take a look at this." He held it up for her, and she saw a picture of herself under the thick black headline, HOTTEST SINGER ON TWO CONTINENTS.

"Me?" she asked.

"You, dolly. Hottest singer on two continents, and I'm the one who's made you that way." Grabbing her arms, he kissed her squarely on the lips, and she tossed back her head and laughed.

"Oh, Denny, isn't this the best? I must be rich now." She turned around, preening, then jumped up and down like a small child. "Come on, Denny, let's go buy something wonderful this afternoon. I have money, don't I? I'll buy you a car. Or let's get a cottage in Hampstead Heath. Please, Denny? Someplace with trees and a little brook. What do you say?"

"I say shut up!"

Annabelle stopped in mid-pirouette, startled by the reaction. She looked up to find that Denny's eyes were blazing. The demons were back. Oh God, how had she done *that*? Anger seethed from his body, tumbling past the satisfaction that had been there just a moment ago.

"Your money, is it?" He grabbed her wrists so tightly that she flinched. "I'm working like a madman all day to get things going for us and you're lying around in bed. Why the hell aren't you dressed?"

"I just got up and I didn't know what to put on. I don't even know if we have a show tonight. When I got up, you weren't here, and I was all alone." Her lower lip trembled and she didn't try to stop it. That's why she had Denny—he'd promised long ago that he'd always be there to take care of her and tell her what to do so she would never again be left alone. He'd promised. That was their deal.

24

"Of course we have a show tonight." Letting go of her wrists, he glared at her and pushed a finger at her chest. "But get this straight—we're not going on any fucking buying spree. So get your ass in gear."

Whimpering again, she leaned close to him and said, "Come on, Denny, don't be mean to me."

He shook his arm, flicking her away like a pesky mosquito. "I'm never mean to you, but I don't want to hear about *your* money. I'm the one making the music happen here and I'm not going to let you throw it all away."

"I perform every night and then you keep me up until morning," she whispered, raising clenched fists to her mouth, afraid to say the words. "I have to sleep sometime."

"And what about me?" Denny stuck his thumbs inside the edges of his black leather pants and kicked the manilla envelope that had fallen to the ground. "It's okay if I work round the clock, right? You get a little publicity and a little good news and all of a sudden I'm hearing star shit from you? I won't stand for that, you hear me? I'll walk out right now and you can watch your career disappear faster than the ten lines of coke I gave to the boys in your band last night."

Her body began shaking, maybe because her feet were bare against the cold stone floor. "Don't walk out, Denny. All I want is to have some fun and buy things for you. Not for me, for you. I need you."

"You're damn right you do, so why are you giving me lip? You didn't go platinum just because of your voice, dolly, and don't forget that. There are a lot of little whores in Piccadilly Square who sing just like you do, and you could go back to being one of them at any time."

"I'm sorry, Denny." She felt herself folding, terrified that he would walk out the door again. "It's just that you promised you wouldn't leave me, but when I woke up, I was all alone. I get scared without you."

Lacing his fingers tightly around her waist, he marveled that his encircling thumbs almost touched. Her skinny body trembled, collapsing in his hands, so he changed his tone, and suddenly crooning said, "Don't be scared. I'm not going to leave you as long as you're a good dolly. Want to show me that you're a good dolly?"

When she didn't answer, he said, "I've got more news for you. Show me how good you are while I tell you the news."

Still shaking, she dropped to her knees and rubbed her hands over the leather at his thighs, his hips, his crotch.

"What's your news?"

"Be a good dolly first."

Her fingers released the snaps at his crotch, and when she lowered his leather pants, she found him waiting but not ready. Easy to arouse my Denny, she thought, easy to get him where he wants to be. The stone floor seemed to cut through the soft skin of her knees, but she paid no attention. If she made him happy enough, maybe she could be Denny's drug, the only drug he'd ever need.

"You like having my dick in your mouth, don't you? You like it as much as I do?" The voice seemed to be disembodied, coming from a different part of the room; or maybe it was just that she was trying to tune out all sensation and let herself float. Not thinking. Just grinding her face against his hardness the way he liked it.

"This is where my dolly belongs. On her knees in front of me. It's why you want your big Denny here, right? So you can have me in your mouth." His own words excited him and he began gyrating his hips, pushing her head so she would take him deeper. Then suddenly he grabbed her thin shoulders and shook her frantically while he released himself into her.

There was quiet for a moment while they both recovered and Annabelle rose unsteadily to her feet.

"Was that okay?" she asked softly.

"Good, dolly." He didn't touch her or stroke her, and she sank into the sofa while he lit one of the foul-smelling brown cigarettes he favored lately. Funny how it never felt like sex when they did it that way. More like a job. Despite the bitter taste in her mouth, she wondered how Denny could really be satisfied when sex was so quick and cold. For the hundredth time, she resolved to try harder to keep Denny happy.

Turning her head slightly to avoid the stinging smoke of the Turkish cigarette, she asked, "What's the other good news?"

"You want more?" He adjusted the leather pants around his

too-thin hips, snapping the crotch she had left open. "Here it is. We're going to the States."

"Really?" Her instinct was to leap off the sofa and hug him in delight, but remembering how he had responded to her last burst of excitement, she sat tight. "I thought you didn't want us to go again."

"No choice, we're going. But it won't be like last time with all those dumpy cities. We're big-time now, and we've got two incredible gigs. First stop is New York. A gig at a Broadway theatre. Then you're booked at the Rumn Club in L.A. for two weeks. There might be a television deal attached, but I'm trying to decide."

Arms crossed, she forced herself to stay on the sofa rather than dance around the room. This time in America she'd be careful what she said and not make Denny angry. Funny how things worked out. Sitting all day in grimy hotel rooms, she used to watch hour after hour of television and think how it looked like fun—more fun than most of the other things she did. Then on her first trip to the States, she'd been invited on one of those local chat shows. What was it called? "A.M. Toledo" or "A.M. Des Moines." Something like that. When the interviewer asked her personal questions, she answered them honestly because it didn't occur to her that she could do otherwise. But Denny had been watching on a huge monitor while he sat waiting for her in the green room, and the moment she stepped off the air, his fury devoured her like a bonfire.

"Just chat show prattle," she had explained, but he dragged her back to the hotel to beat into her the message that she did not, *did not*, talk about him that way anywhere. Their story was their secret. The world would know only the tale they chose to tell. She withstood the punishment that afternoon because she knew that Denny was right and she was wrong and she would never talk that freely again. But he didn't trust her, despite her getting on her knees and doing every trick she knew to beg forgiveness.

They had flown back to Heathrow Airport that very night, and Denny banned all interviews. That was when they both discovered the first law of media—reporters always want what they can't get. Once it was clear that Annabelle Fox was unavailable to talk, offers came in from every network, magazine, and talk show in two countries. But Denny said no to all of them and he meant it, so the speculation began. The publicist for the record company leaked out stories as to why Annabelle insisted on privacy, and though none were true, each one was more intriguing than the last. The press began labeling her the Mysterious Annabelle and the Hidden Fox.

"What kind of television deal?" she asked now, trying to keep any excitement out of her voice.

"Doesn't matter."

"I'll say the right things this time, Denny, I swear I will. You tell me what to say and I'll say it."

"Forget it. I haven't decided yet if we'll do it. In fact, we probably won't."

Pouting, she stood up. "You can trust me, Denny. You've got to trust me."

"Bullshit." But he wasn't looking at her anymore or even following the conversation because he was fiddling with the locked drawer of his rolltop desk, removing the small brass pillbox that she knew didn't contain vitamins. So it was going to be coke today. Probably already had been. If only she were better at recognizing the signs, she'd know what was coming.

"What the fuck are you looking at?" He snorted one line, then another, and reached over to whack her away. But she scooted off before he could touch her. There was a show to do, and she had to get dressed.

Keith Ross maneuvered his silver Maserati into the left-hand lane of the Henry Hudson Parkway, less out of necessity than to have some sense of actually driving. As usual on Friday evening, the highway was heavy with traffic—New Yorkers fleeing the city, suburbanites eager to get home, Wall Street executives heading for their weekend houses in Connecticut. But tonight was worse than usual. He hadn't moved more than a hundred yards in the last twenty minutes, and the cacophony of horns combined with the acrid fumes of idling cars gave him a blazing headache.

Keith adjusted the volume on the tape deck so Beethoven's Seventh would fill all the empty space in the car. The sound system was about the only part of the Maserati that Keith still found pleasurable. Four years ago when he lived in L.A., he had bought the car to use every day—both for transportation and as a declaration of success. But now it sat in a Kinney garage on East Fifty-seventh Street all week, in one of the monitored spots near the front that allowed poorer patrons a chance to fantasize while they waited at the cashier's booth to reclaim their Rabbits, Novas, and Volkswagen Jettas. Each time he went to get the car, he could feel the accumulated stares, and before he got in, he brushed off a week's worth of grime, envy, and desire. Just that day, a curvaceous young woman who was watching him get his car purred, "Only studs drive Maseratis." Since she was clinging seductively to her football player–sized escort, Keith couldn't decide which of them the suggestive comment was meant to inflame.

Reaching over the stick shift now, which seemed permanently locked in first gear this trip, Keith quickly dialed a familiar number. From the speaker over his left ear, he heard the ringing and then a slightly breathless "Hello?"

"It's Keith. I'm stuck in traffic. But if I ever get moving, I'm just a few minutes away."

"Don't worry about it. Barney called, too. He just left his office."

"We should be there at about the same time, then."

"I can wait. Just drive carefully. The chicken is still cooking, anyway."

He pushed the button to disconnect and found himself smiling. Of all the women in New York, Lotte Rossman was the only one who could get him to drive to Riverdale on a Friday night to eat overdone chicken and sodden potato latkes.

Half an hour later, Keith left the Maserati in the circular driveway in front of Lotte's building, slipped one of the young doormen twenty dollars, and asked him to watch the car.

"May I move it if it's necessary, sir?"

"Absolutely."

The young man grinned, making it clear that the chance to drive the car was more satisfying than the money.

The apartment building was a reasonably modern structure that copied—badly—some of the more luxurious apartments in Manhattan. A too-large crystal chandelier dominated the lobby, which was also adorned with smoked-glass mirrors and a round concierge desk. In Riverdale, the concierge's main duties were to collect deliveries from dry cleaners and Chinese restaurants. The apartments themselves were comfortably large with fake marble bathrooms and spacious kitchens, amenities that appealed to young couples who moved from Manhattan and to other tenants like Lotte—elderly Jews who had lived in the Bronx all their lives and moved up to Riverdale in retirement.

Lotte opened the door on the first buzz. At the sight of her, Keith put down the bouquet of spring flowers he had brought and hugged her tightly. Stepping back, he said, "You look great. Better than ever."

She brushed aside the compliment with a wave of her hand, but her fingers fluttered to the careful bun at the nape of her neck and nimbly adjusted the white bobby pins holding it in place.

"You're always flattering me. How come you're so tan?"

"I'm just back from L.A."

"You enjoyed yourself?"

"It was business, Mom."

"Some business. You work and you get tan."

He laughed and went into the dining room in search of a vase. The table was set carefully for Shabbat with a white embroidered tablecloth and Lotte Rossman's best silver and crystal. A well-worn challah cloth covered the plate in the center of the table, and three silver winecups surrounded it. Keith noted with a pang that the winecups were badly tarnished, blotches of dull gray obliterating some of the finely engraved Jewish prayers that adorned the cups. Lotte would never knowingly allow such a travesty on Shabbat, but her eyesight was weakening, and Keith knew that she had simply failed to see it.

"What do you think, Chaim? Everything look nice?" Lotte had followed him into the room.

"Great, Mom. I haven't had a real Shabbat in too long." Lotte clucked knowingly but didn't ask any questions, so Keith added, "And nobody has called me Chaim in even longer."

"Only your mother knows who you really are."

"And you'll never tell," he said affectionately. He leaned over and kissed her on the top of the head. At age seventy-nine, Lotte Rossman was several inches shy of five feet tall. Her spine had bent only slightly with age, and her children still thought of her as the woman with the steel backbone. Over fifty years ago, she had left her hometown of Rauchberg, Germany, with her four tiny children, to escape the thundering Nazi footsteps she heard gathering outside. Her husband never made it out. Against all odds she had made a new life for herself in America, and ten years later, she had remarried and started yet another family, giving birth to the babies she named Chaim and Avram—and who now, grown and assimilated, were Keith and Barney.

"Mom, I have a great idea," Keith said, opening the glass-fronted cabinet that housed most of Lotte's decorative treasures and taking out an antique Baccarat vase.

"Tell me your great idea, but come to the kitchen so I can turn down the oven."

He dropped the flowers into the vase, made a vague attempt at arranging them, and followed Lotte into the kitchen. The rich aromas of German-Jewish cooking filled the apartment, evoking memories of other Friday nights, years of celebrations and sorrows. For years after his father died, Keith thought that Lotte would never be happy again; but for the second time in her life, she overcame the guilt of being the survivor and pressed forward.

Keith filled the vase of flowers with water and watched his mother checking the oven.

"Here's the idea, Mom. I'm thinking about doing a documentary on survivors. People who've made it through plane crashes. Terrorist attacks. Fighting in wars. I want you to be part of it. Next time I come up here, I'm going to bring a camera crew and sit you down right here in the kitchen and have you tell your life story."

"Everyone who'd be interested in my life story has already heard it."

"Not so, Mom. This is a way of preserving history. You're a witness. Even now there are people trying to say that the Holocaust never happened, that Jews exaggerated the whole thing. History demands that you be seen and heard."

Behind them a door closed, and from the hall, a voice called out, "Did I hear something about a witness?"

Keith and Lotte exchanged a glance and looked up as Barney sauntered into the kitchen. He was wearing a beige trench coat over a conservative blue suit and carrying the well-worn briefcase that spoke of hard-earned power. Several inches taller than Keith, Barney had the same fine features and sandy-colored hair, but his was straight and cut too long in the front, so it dropped down over his forehead, and the gesture of flicking it away had become second nature to him.

Barney pecked his mother on the cheek and leaned over to give Keith a half hug.

"How did you get in?" Lotte asked.

"The door wasn't locked. I guess you forgot after Keith came in."

"I must be getting old—as if we needed any more proof," Lotte said with a shrug.

"You'll never be old, Mom." Barney leaned on the counter where Lotte had left a plate of pastries for dessert and popped an apricot kugel into his mouth. "My Glenda sends her regrets for not being able to make it tonight. She's working late again." Glenda had spent eight years as an associate at a large midtown law firm, and there were intimations that she was about to be made a partner. Having a husband who was the District Attorney certainly improved her chances, but she was determined to prove that she was worthy in her own right.

"Two lawyers in one family should be against the law," Keith said. "Do you newlyweds ever get to see each other?"

"Not exactly newlyweds—it's been almost two years. But it's tough. What's that expression about two-career couples with no children?" Barney took another kugel for inspiration, then answered his own question. "DINKS. Double-income, no kids. That's what we are. We're working on the kids, but it's hard to make babies when you never see each other. Our schedules are lousy and it doesn't seem to be getting any better."

"Everything gets better with time," Lotte said.

"We're running out of time, Mom. Glenda's thirty-five."

"I was over forty when you were born," Lotte said firmly.

Keith reached across the table and patted her hand. "Just the point I was trying to make before about this documentary. Yuppies always think they're inventing everything in life. Babies. Late childbirth. Family tragedy. We need witnesses like you to remind us about the cycles of life. You could give twenty million television viewers a new perspective on their own existence."

"We have enough stars in this family. Now are you boys ready for Shabbat?" To change the subject, she gestured her sons toward the dining room table and followed them to their seats. "Matches?" she asked, and when Keith produced a package, she draped a lace kerchief over her head and lit the Shabbat candles, covering her eyes to recite the blessing. They sang the kiddush together and each took a sip of the too-sweet kosher wine. Lotte blessed the challah and lifting the cloth, broke off a piece for each of them. Challah was the bread of peace. She wouldn't take a knife to it.

Rituals complete, Lotte went to the kitchen and let her sons help her get the meal to the table.

"So," she said, once everyone was eating, "I have both of my famous sons tonight. When I say 'What's new?' to you two, I expect real news." They both laughed and Lotte turned to Barney and asked, "How's the life of the District Attorney?"

"Satisfying, though our office lost a couple of big cases this week."

"Can we hear the gory details?" Keith dunked his challah into his chicken soup, something he wouldn't dream of doing at any other table, and watched as Barney did the same.

"It's not really *Shabbos* table talk."

"Go ahead," Lotte said encouragingly. "God doesn't get offended at hearing about the real world."

Barney smiled at the casual relationship his mother had with God and realized how comforting it was to think of a power higher than judges and juries. "As I said, not the best week when you lose two cases that seemed like sure things. First a decision came in on a kid who shot a cop. We thought we had an open-and-shut case of murder, but the jury came back saying it was self-defense. Turned it into an issue of a poor Hispanic kid protecting himself against a racist society. Clever defense, but the fact is that he killed a good cop in cold blood and is walking free."

"Not walking too far, I imagine," Keith said.

"He'll be back in a few weeks on another case—this one manslaughter. We've got a strong case there, but who knows any-more?" Barney pushed his soup bowl to the side and began moving chicken and dumplings from the serving dish to his plate.

"What does this mean, Barney?" Lotte asked. "Are juries believing in the underdog again?"

"You'd think so from this case. But one thing I've learned is that when it comes to juries, rules don't hold. Same courthouse, same week, we brought a criminal case against a big real-estate firm—and this time they were the ones who got away with murder. Seems they were involved with a development project in lower Manhattan, and halfway through the job one of the construction cranes broke and dropped a shower of cement from four stories up. Killed one of the workers, a young black guy about twenty-two years old named Terence Owens. Crane operator was working without a license, so we brought charges. Sounds pretty cut-and-dried, right?"

"Right," said Lotte, following the story carefully.

"Bad news is that we lost."

"Incredible." Keith finished his matzoh ball and put down his spoon. "How do you lose a case like that?"

"Pretty lousy work on the part of the D.A., huh? Thanks for the support, brother."

"Come on, I didn't mean that personally. But it seems that if a construction crane drops a cement block on a worker's head, someone's made a mistake."

"Agreed." Barney spoke in the calm, authoritative tone that allowed him to win more cases in the courtroom than he lost. "They wheedled out of our charges on a lot of legal technicalities and settled a civil suit with the family for pocket change." He shook his head. "I haven't yet figured out who they bought off—but as far as they know now, it's cheaper to kill a black kid than to pay for a licensed construction company."

"Will the vindictive D.A. at least try to get the company on something else?"

"There've been some rumors about financial irregularities, so we'll investigate. I'm not on any campaign against them, though." He smiled, then added, "Of course, the way things look lately, I'm beginning to believe that if I have *any* company investigated—or any individual for that matter—I'll come up with possible corruption charges."

"I didn't cheat on my tax returns last year," Keith said. "You can investigate me."

"Just don't go back another year, right?" Barney grinned good-naturedly at his brother. "But what's going on in the glamorous world of television?"

"Ah, the glamour." Keith yawned. *If it's so glamorous, why am I having Friday night dinner with my mother?* "I think I hired a new producer this week to handle the network specials we're doing. We're negotiating a deal now, and if all goes well, we might end up as partners."

Barney looked surprised but said only, "I assume you're not giving away the store."

"You don't have to worry about that." It was a sore spot with Barney that Keith didn't use Glenda's law firm for his legal contracts, but Keith was insistent on keeping family and business separate.

"So who's the lucky man?" Lotte asked.

"Lucky lady," Keith corrected. "A woman I worked with for years in Los Angeles. She's known as a programming genius. Jillian van Dorne."

"The name sounds familiar," Barney said.

"You might have met her when I worked with her before. A classy-looking WASP with the kind of gorgeous, long legs that are distinctly missing from the Jewish gene pool."

"Not nice talk but I know who you mean." Lotte's water glass clattered against the side of her plate as she tried to put it down on the table. "I met her one time when I visited you in L.A." With a twinkle in her eye, she added, "I could never decide if you were dating her or not."

"Neither could I." Keith smiled. "But all indications are that I wasn't."

"Is she married?"

"For years now. And they've got two little daughters." Keith turned to Barney, whose brow was still puckered with the concentrated strain of trying to remember the woman. "If you saw her, you'd remember her."

Barney broke off another piece of challah and put it thoughtfully to his mouth. "I never met her, but I think I just placed the name. What a coincidence."

"What is?"

"Jillian van Dorne is married to Mark Austin, isn't she?"

"I think so. They live up in Melrose. You know him?"

Barney gave his brother a disconcerted glance. "Mark Austin is the manager of Austin Realty. His father owns it and is trying to keep it a family business." Keith looked at him blankly, so Barney took a sip of wine and continued. "Austin Realty is the company I was just telling you about. The ones involved in the crane case that killed the Owens boy."

Keith sat back and tapped the edges of his fingertips together. "So, Mr. D.A., what do I do with that information?"

"Nothing at all," Barney said with a shrug. "Just a coincidence that it came up tonight."

"Yes, quite a coincidence." Lotte looked around the table with determined cheerfulness. "Are you gentlemen ready for dessert?"

■

Mark Austin pulled back the white louvered blind and, from the window on the fourth floor, looked down at the security guard posted at Thirty-eighth Street and Park Avenue. The street was quiet, and the guard, locked in a four-foot-square booth that seemed to make him more prisoner than watchman, was reading the newspaper. Mark dropped the blind back in place and turned to Cynthia Reilly, the smartest lawyer at Austin Realty. She had a dagger-sharp mind that whipped effortlessly through legal intricacies.

Right now she was perched at the edge of a sofa, her elbows planted on knees that were spread wide apart, her navy-blue flowered Natori robe draping over her slim thighs. Leaning forward, a cigarette clamped in her mouth, Cynthia ran her fingers through her thick reddish-brown hair.

"Anything interesting out there?" she asked.

"Nothing. Not a gun in sight." He smiled feebly, trying not to notice the lace-edged camisole she was wearing under the robe that barely covered her plentiful breasts. The first time he had seen those breasts, succumbed to them in this very apartment, he had buried himself in the warmth of her cleavage, like a baby seeking sustenance. Her body was rapturous to him, as succulent as spring fruits dripping with juicy pleasure at every taste. He had indulged—oh, how he had indulged that night—and then risen, dazed, from the bed near midnight, realizing that he had to stumble back to his real life. That first night, feeling guilty but deliriously sated, he had also drawn back the blinds—and found M-16 rifles pointed at him.

"What's going on across the street?" he had asked.

"That's the Cuban embassy," Cynthia had called sleepily from bed. "Maybe Fidel is in town for the U.N."

The roof of the building where the embassy was housed happened to be on the same level as Cynthia's window, and four uniformed soldiers were protecting the building with the armaments of modern warfare.

Since then Mark had come to enjoy the delicious irony of committing adultery under the watchful eye of Fidel Castro's sharpshooters.

But now that was all coming to an end. Just a few minutes ago Mark had explained to Cynthia that their affair had to stop, and instead of screaming or crying or begging him to stay, she was sitting seductively on the velvet sofa.

"You're a good man." Cynthia flicked the long ash from her cigarette into a sculpted brass ashtray that looked like a wave. "You broke up before we fucked today, not after. That's classy."

"Come on, Cynthia . . ."

"No, I mean it. Most men fuck first and give the bad news after. But not Mark Austin. The problem is that I'm horny today. I was ready for you. Any way we can forget what you said for an hour?"

"Cynthia, I was serious. This has to be over. I can't go on."

"I'm serious, too. But you can break up with me in an hour, and it will be just as finished." Her breasts lured him, heaving under the lace. "Come here, boss. At least give me a final hug before you go." She rose and walked over to him, swaying her narrow hips with the gentle twist that he loved to feel under him in bed, the sinuousness that always told him she was on the verge of gratifying herself.

"Aren't you going to miss me?" She draped her arms around his neck and pushed her body close to his. Her breasts crushed against his white shirt, and as he groped under the camisole, she uttered a low moan of desire. "Come here," she whispered, taking his hand and leading him into the bedroom. The blinds were already drawn, and the quilt had been pulled back from the bed. Mark undressed quickly, eager for her serpentine body to be wrapped around him. Sliding under the sheets, they made love hungrily, not talking, the moans of their satisfaction the only sounds in the room.

"That wasn't so bad, was it?" Cynthia asked when their lovemaking was over. She strolled to the bathroom, unembarrassed by her nakedness, and came back to sit on the edge of the bed. "I like fond farewells."

"You know I'm fond of you. I always will be." He stroked her thigh and sat up, aware that he had spent too much time in the apartment already without completing what he had come to do. "I'm going to take a quick shower," he said.

The water pulsated from the shower massage in rhythmic vibrations, and Mark turned the shower head to produce, instead, a smooth, steady stream. Cynthia's lavender soap was in the soap dish, and Mark wondered if he should use it to wash or if the lavender scent would be too obvious and make Jillian suspicious. Days when he anticipated a sexual encounter, he usually prepared by slipping a bar of Safeguard into his briefcase, but today it just held papers. The pounding water and an unsoaped washcloth should be enough to rinse off the lingering smell of his sinning.

While Mark dressed, Cynthia disappeared from the bedroom. He found her lying gracefully on the sofa in the living room, a thick book propped against her knees.

"So our affair is over now?" she asked brightly.

"You don't make it easy."

"Thank goodness for that."

"We need to have a professional conversation, too."

"Oh?" She tucked one leg under her robe, and Mark thought briefly of how different she looked in the office, her thick hair pulled back, the curves of her body hidden by a gray worsted-wool suit. But even that sedate attire couldn't hide her sensuality; it was evident in the seductive swing of her walk and in the way her skirts were always slit just a little too high in the back so any man standing behind her would be tempted to slip his hand onto her firm ass. Mark wondered how many other men in the office knew that beneath the proper suits was hidden a red Victorian corset with lace-up straps and garters.

Probably too many. Maybe that was why his father had insisted— no, suggested—that the affair end. Mark and his father were peers in the business; Mark made a point of never calling him "Dad," only a cavalier "Bill." If Bill had an opinion, Mark listened to it, then made his own decisions.

He had decided himself that propriety demanded an end to their affair. He had to keep telling himself that.

Without sitting down, Mark said, "We're going through with that deal in London with the Wright Company. Bill wants to put you in charge of the opening stages. Get it negotiated and off the ground."

"My thanks for saving his balls on the Owens crane case?"

Mark shrugged. "We're grateful on that one, no doubt about it. No criminal charges, pennies in the civil suit, and almost no publicity. When that damn crane broke, I thought it was going to turn into a cause célèbre in the papers. But there was nothing. I read one article buried in the back of the *Times*. Care to tell me how you pulled that off?"

Cynthia smiled enigmatically. "Not right now. Tell me more about the Wright project."

Knowing he wouldn't get a better answer, Mark said, "It's the first time we've done a joint venture with them, though my father's known Kingsley Wright for years. They've come up with some financing plans that could be a windfall for all of us. We bring our joint expertise into buying real estate and developing projects in Eastern Europe. Wright apparently has his eyes on Hungary and Czechoslovakia, but we need you to oversee the planning and make sure it's all aboveboard. We don't want to end up arguing this one in court, too."

"Got it. Your dad had figured out that next time he goes before a jury, he might lose his balls, after all. Not something Mark Junior has to worry about, right, darling? Given my inexplicable fondness for your anatomy, my legal skills will continue to save the day."

"My personal feelings aside, Cynthia, you're as good as it gets in this business. The Wright project could be the biggest one we've done, and we trust you with it. It will mean relocating to London for two or three months. We have an apartment in Mayfair that you're welcome to use."

Cynthia tossed her book aside and uttered a deep, throaty laugh. "So that's it, is it? Son of the owner gets to end his torrid affair by sending the correspondent off to London for a few months to cool off. Why did you bother telling me it was over? You could have been completely cowardly and just let us drift apart without any words at all."

"Your reassignment has nothing to do with our affair. I'm sorry if the timing was unfortunate."

"God, you're a liar. How can you say these things to me with a straight face?"

"It happens to be true, Cynthia. In all these months, we haven't let our relationship get in the way of work, and that's not going to change now."

"Forget it." Cynthia shook her mane of hair and stood up. "I'll be in the office of William Mark Austin, Senior, better known as Bill, tomorrow morning at nine o'clock to discuss the Wright assignment. Tell him I'm looking forward to it." She reached her hand out to Mark, waited for him to take it, and squeezed it gently. "Good-bye, Mark. I'm glad we'll still be working together."

Handing him his coat, she led him to the door and watched him struggling to find something to say. Failing, he kissed her on the cheek and disappeared into the hall.

After Cynthia locked and bolted the door behind him, she observed him for a moment through a peephole that made it look like he was walking down an endless tunnel to Wonderland. When he was finally gone, her eyes turned hard and she slumped against the door. So much for the glorious, no-strings affair with the boss's son. She was proud of herself for maintaining control and not telling him what she really thought. There were some things she just had to put up with to make sure life went on as it should. Mark would come back to her, no doubt about that. This was just one of those temporary setbacks. She wondered if it was his wife or his father who was making him break up with her now. Probably his father, who knew how important she'd become to the company. But it didn't matter. Tomorrow in Bill's office she'd be completely professional and thank him for the reassignment to London. Then she'd just wait for Mark to come begging back.

"He's a lousy fuck anyway," she murmured to herself as she headed toward the bathroom. "A really lousy fuck."

CHAPTER THREE

IN the bottom of the third inning, Lila van Dorne Austin came up to bat at the Melrose playing field and smacked the softball so hard that it went soaring over the head of the little boy playing second base and deep into the outfield, where two other six-year-olds scrambled to retrieve it. By the time they did, Lila was safely on third base. The throw back to the pitcher was so far off target that Lila watched the ball bounce away and then galloped gleefully to home plate.

"Nice hit, Lila." The team coach, the father of one of the other little girls, met her at the plate and patted her on the back. "But you should go on back to third base. No stealing bases in this game."

"That wasn't stealing. It was fair." Lila grinned, then trotted back to the base, unconcerned. It was a warm Saturday afternoon, and the stands around the field were dotted with parents, happy to turn the children's game into a family outing. Most had come with picnic baskets and coolers. They cheered good-naturedly for each other's children and made it clear that they were sophisticated enough not to care who played best. Scorning the "Little League parents" who made children's games into arenas of adult competitiveness, they tried to offer little more than an ironic smile when their child turned out to be the star of the game. Most of the fathers in Melrose didn't need to live their competitive urges through their children—they had quite enough competitiveness all week in their offices on Wall Street and in midtown

Manhattan. They had to win enough games there to support the half-million-dollar homes that were standard in town.

The next child at bat struck out, despite the gentle throws offered by the father who was pitching. Stuck on third base, Lila made a face and called out encouragement to her best friend, Kelsey, who was now coming up to bat. Kelsey hit a pop fly that the shortstop caught, staring at his glove in disbelief. Lila tagged third and then raced for home where Kelsey hugged her.

"Sacrifice fly!" she explained delightedly.

The coach didn't have the heart to dampen their enthusiasm.

Lila turned around to wave to her mother, who had stationed herself halfway between the softball field and the toddler playground, where Eve had joined a group of younger brothers and sisters intent on building the largest sand castle ever.

"No husband today?" Jillian's neighbor and good friend Valerie Beasley sidled up to her, her hands resting on her stomach.

"Mark is working. And your husband?"

"Same. Want me to watch Eve for you so you can concentrate on softball?"

"That's okay, I'm fine here." She glanced over at the sandbox, where Eve was digging happily with Val's three-year-old daughter, Cara. Turning back to Valerie, Jillian asked, "How are you feeling?"

"Pretty good. I'm tired of being pregnant, but the doctor says I've got at least another six weeks to go." She stroked her stomach. "This baby must know it's softball season, because he's practicing his hits."

They turned to the field, where Lila had just made two outs in a row, the last by catching the line drive of a little boy.

"She's good," Valerie said.

Jillian watched the boy who had just been put out walk disconsolately back to the bench. "Softball really shouldn't be co-ed at this age. The girls are so much better coordinated than the boys."

"Amazing, isn't it?" Valerie brushed back her hair, which was blowing in the light breeze. "The boys think they're supposed to be the hotshot athletes, but the girls can run rings around them. I don't feel too sorry for them, though. Puberty comes along soon enough, the boys get stronger, and they spend the rest of their lives getting revenge on the girls who humiliated them on the playground."

"Is that what happens?" Jillian smiled and tucked her hands into the pockets of her suede jacket. "A new view of the origins of sexism. I like it."

"But it's true," Valerie persisted. "My happiest memory is of taking a hiking trip with the Outing Club when I was eleven. Two weeks later I got my period, my mother started talking about the responsibilities of womanhood, and all of a sudden I was supposed to wear dresses and be nice to the boys I was used to beating up."

On the field, Lila caught yet another throw, her third put-out of the inning, and from the shouting of her teammates, it was clear that the game was over. Flushed with victory, Lila raced over to her mother to collect her postgame congratulations.

"Nice game," Jillian said, hugging her. "Today was your day."

"It was fun. Can I go play with Evie?"

"Go ahead."

Lila raced ahead, and Jillian and Valerie moved closer to the swing sets, keeping an eye on the girls.

"So it's been all downhill since age eleven?" Jillian asked.

"Not really. But let's be honest. When you were a kid, dreaming your dreams about the future, did they include all this?" Her gesture took in the fathers who had gathered by the backstop on the softball field to talk business, the children playing on the playground equipment, and the mothers who stood by, waiting to be needed.

"Nope. All I thought about was being a success in my career. Even then I wanted to be in television. But all this, as you put it, hasn't diminished my life—it's made it richer."

Valerie grimaced. "All I can say is that my tenth college reunion is coming up next month. Waddling in, pushing Cara in a stroller, isn't exactly the triumphant return to campus I imagined when I graduated."

"Where did you go to school?"

"MIT. Long way from there to here, isn't it? The boys there don't understand that girl engineers will have a different life than they will. In fact, MIT guys aren't so good at the differences between girls and boys at all. There's a joke that when an MIT boy wants to get fresh with a girl, he rubs his crotch and says, 'Want to see my thing? Come on, want to see my thing?' Then he reaches down and pulls out his slide rule."

Jillian laughed generously. "We went to school a long time ago. Even MIT guys don't use slide rules anymore."

"Trust me, the ones I knew still use them."

"And you don't think they'll look kindly on what you've done with your MIT degree?" Valerie had been an executive at an international engineering company in the years before she got married. Now she seemed content to be a full-time mother, devoting herself to her child and to the huge 1920s brick Tudor house she was refurbishing. Recalling previous conversations, Jillian said, "I thought you didn't miss working."

"I don't miss work. I had enough experience with backstabbing, politicking, and men who hate working with women to last quite a long time. Work is highly overrated, thank you. I think that's where the women's movement went wrong. Betty Friedan convinced us that a job would be a great fulfillment, but most jobs are just jobs."

"Maybe, but they provide us with *something*, don't you think? A sense of identity apart from husband and kids. A way of boosting self-esteem. Those things count for something."

"Of course, but you should get your identity and sense of self-esteem from things that *matter*—and when you come right down to it, most jobs *don't* matter. They're just games men play. Sure, women can play just as well, but do they really want to?" Valerie shook her head. "Tell the truth, Jillian. Do you miss your job?"

Jillian dug the toe of her moccasin into the soft ground and made a pattern of concentric circles. "Confession time. I'm thinking of going back to work. Full-time." Valerie raised her eyebrows but didn't ask anything, so Jillian said, "It's not totally out of the blue. I'd been making some discreet phone calls and the offers started. The one I'm negotiating right now is just about perfect, but I'm still torn." She looked at the pattern she'd made in the ground and realized it mimicked her thoughts—endless circles leading nowhere. "Sometimes I feel guilty about abandoning the girls, and sometimes I feel even guiltier about giving up the career I spent so long building."

Valerie rubbed her stomach, then smiled self-consciously. "Ignore everything I just said about work, okay? Your experience was different than mine. You got fulfillment from your job. You loved it." Out of the corner of her eye, Valerie noticed Cara attempting to climb up the ladder to the slide, and excusing herself—from both need and embarrassment—ambled over to help.

Looking around the playground, it occurred to Jillian that most of the mothers who were now idling on benches, pushing their toddlers on the swings, and giving bottles to babies had been ambitious once, fighting for the right to decide their own fates. But babies had intervened on their march for equality, and ambivalence had replaced determination. How many years of education at Briarcliff and Radcliffe and Mount Holyoke were accumulated here? How many regrets were buried under the sand castles?

Jillian had often heard the other mothers talk about being bored—but in truth it wasn't boredom she felt as much as a sense of diminishment—of being less than she could be. For the last few nights, she had slipped into the girls' rooms while they were sleeping, and watching them, wondered if she were really doing them a favor by not working. What good was it to tell children over and over that girls can do anything if there were no role models to prove it?

Valerie helped Cara up the ladder and cheered as she whooshed down the slide with a shriek of delight. Coming back to Jillian, she said, "What you just said about abandoning the girls is silly, you know. If you're not working and you're resentful, your kids are going to suffer a lot more than if you *are* working and you're happy about it."

Jillian smiled at Valerie's efforts to make amends by reciting the working mothers' mantra: It wasn't whether or not you worked that affected your children, but how satisfied you felt. "Do any of us really believe that, or is it what we tell ourselves in the morning when we leave crying children behind?"

Valerie shrugged. "My mother sacrificed her life to bring up her kids, and I don't think any of us benefited. We sensed the holes in her life, and we felt guilty because we couldn't fill them."

"There are a lot of holes in my life right now," Jillian admitted slowly, "and I think that going back to television could start filling them."

"Then you have your answer."

46

"Mark hated the idea when I first brought it up, but I think he's coming around."

"It won't be that different for him. You've always gone off to do your glamorous projects. You never quite joined the ranks of us mothers who haven't put on panty hose in three years."

Jillian smiled, remembering the few television specials she had produced over the past few years, the four- or six-week projects she would take occasionally to get out of the house and flex her producer's muscles. No, she had never really given it up. And maybe being back at work, doing what she loved, would strengthen her marriage, give it the spark that had been missing for so long now. It would be nice to have Mark again. Working with Keith Ross, she would once again be the ambitious, successful woman Mark had married—and maybe that would help renew the pleasure they had felt in each other those many years before.

■

Mark Austin struck a match against the side of the elegant green-and-white box that he had found on the mantelpiece and held the flame to the newspapers crumpled on the bottom of the fireplace. The paper immediately flared and Mark sat back on his heels, waiting to see if the kindling would catch. In a moment, he heard the crisp popping sounds of dried wood burning, and he silently thanked the innkeepers who had arranged the wood so precisely before they arrived. The kindling would blaze wildly for a few minutes, then once the fire was hot enough, the shooting flames would settle down and the big logs would burn slowly and deliberately for hours. Sort of like a relationship, he thought. The late spring weather was far too warm for a fire, but Jillian thought it romantic and he didn't want to argue.

Behind him Jillian was curled up on the four-poster bed, reading a novel. He could sense her glancing up at him from time to time and was gratified that he had succeeded in getting the fire going.

"That fire smells wonderful." She came up behind him and rested her fingers on his shoulders. "Do you think there's something special about New Hampshire wood?"

"Maybe the sap in it. Listen, you can hear it hissing."

They were quiet for a moment, then Jillian said, "I never realized it was sap that made a fire sound like that."

"I seem to remember that from Boy Scout days."

"I'm sure you're right."

Jillian was being ingratiating, and he appreciated it. Better than the cold silence that had filled the car for much of the ride there. This was their weekend to make up, but he was having trouble getting into a conciliatory spirit.

Jillian settled into the rocking chair next to the fire and looked around the room. "Is this the way you remember it?" she asked.

"Sort of. I think the last time I saw you sitting in that chair, you were pregnant with Eve."

"I remember that." She leaned her head against the soft padding on the chair. "I was exhausted from all the traveling I was doing, and we came up here for my birthday. It was our first overnight away from Lila."

"Yup. And you had a much harder time of it than she did."

Mark poked at the fire with the long-handled tongs, then pulled the screen grating closed.

"I think that was the time I mentioned wanting to take a very long maternity leave, and you said that I should get back as soon as I could. Just pregnancy hormones, you said. As soon as the baby was born, I'd be raring to go back."

"But you weren't."

"No, I guess those pregnancy hormones lasted a few years."

Mark moved away, feeling that he'd been set up. So that's why she had suggested the Greenfield Inn for this weekend—to dredge up old memories and remind him of the person he had once been. Well, that person was gone; his needs had changed. No weekend in an antique-filled inn could bring it back.

In the face of his silence, she persisted. "We were also here when I was pregnant with Lila. Remember that? We figured it was the last time we'd ever be alone. We weren't so far off."

"Well, you're not pregnant now, so you can drink." He opened the eighteenth-century painted birch cabinet that was always well stocked. "We've got sherry and red wine. But I'm sure one of the Greenfields will bring you up anything you want from the bar."

"Sherry is fine."

He opened the bottle and poured the amber liquid into two gold-rimmed wineglasses, wondering as he did if the gold flakes would end up clinging to his lips. He never trusted antique stemware.

They clicked glasses and drank quietly, then she reached for his hand. He wanted to pull his hand back and move away from her gaze, but he couldn't do that. "We haven't talked in such a long time, Mark. I don't want us to drift apart. Tell me what's been going on with you."

Cynthia is what's been going on with me, he thought, and he realized suddenly just what it was that an affair did to a marriage: it undermined your ability to talk honestly to each other. The real danger wasn't the sex or the diminished desire for your partner—it was holding a secret that you couldn't share.

He shrugged lamely and said, "I don't mean to be unavailable, but it's been a busy time." Struggling for an answer he could share, he added, "At least that court case we were concerned about is over. Turns out that it wasn't worth the worry. We were all cleared on all fronts."

She hesitated, then just said, "Good," and took a sip of sherry. Something about her deliberate calm made Mark wonder if she knew more about the case than they had ever discussed. That would be like Jillian, he thought. She wasn't easily deceived.

Silence fell between them, and Mark moved away to stir the wood in the fireplace again. Though the big log had caught and was burning white hot, he couldn't get it to flare. The heat wasn't enough—he wanted flames and magic and drama right now. Damn this room and its cursedly happy memories.

"What can I do?" From across the room, Jillian's normally sultry voice had a hard edge that made Mark turn around in surprise. She put down the sherry and gave a small, ironic smile. "Sorry, that sounds awfully B-movieish, doesn't it. But this was our weekend to get back on track, and I have a feeling that we're not doing a very good job of it. Maybe we should talk about my job so we can get that out of the way."

"Goddamn it, Jillian." He put down the fire tongs and paced around the room, feeling all his tension focusing onto the subject on which he was *allowed* to explode. In a voice louder than he'd planned, he asked, "What do you want—for me to tell you how happy I am about your job? Is that why we came here this weekend? So you could get me to say that everything is fine and then you can sign a contract on Monday without feeling guilty?"

Taking a deep breath, she controlled her mild exasperation. "I'm just trying to figure out what the problem is. You used to love my working. What do you think is going to happen if I join up with Keith?"

"That's a good question." Her rationality took the edge off his anger, and he looked out the window at the hilly field where some black angus cows were grazing. Here they were, at the bucolic getaway that had always seemed so perfect. Why did it seem a little silly today?

Jillian looked at him inquisitively, and since she was waiting for an answer, he ran the question through his head. Just what *was* bothering him? Jillian had been so strong and independent when he first met her, and that—along with the long legs, slim body, and golden-girl face—was what had attracted him. He never really understood why she had fallen for him in return, but those early years of marrying, buying a house and having babies, had been exhilarating. There was always a project for them to do together and a reason why she needed him. But after Eve was born and they decided that their family was complete, his life had taken off in its own direction. Jillian was right that he hadn't wanted her to leave her powerful position at the network, but once she had done it, he felt a certain security in having her at home. At least she wasn't subject to the same temptations that he was.

"Maybe I don't want to have to compete with you," he said, and his own honesty surprised him.

"But we didn't feel competitive in the early days," she said, and he just nodded lamely. There was no way to admit to her how devoted he had been back then without acknowledging what had changed. When he had felt committed to her, he didn't worry about such things. Now, because of Cynthia, he knew he could get along without her.

But he couldn't explain that.

Switching tactics, he said, "I'm sorry, Jillian. I've been overworked and overreacting. I know you're not going to abandon the girls, but I worry about being able to fill in. Things are busier for me than they were when Lila was tiny and I could always be home early if you had to be late."

"I remember those days," Jillian said simply. "You help me and I'll help you. It was nice, wasn't it? Two careers that both mattered a lot and a family that mattered more than anything. It was easy for me to run off to Los Angeles when I had to or for you to spend all night in union negotiations because we backed each other up. We didn't count chips, but the score stayed pretty even because we each respected what the other was doing."

"You're the one who changed it," Mark said accusingly. "And now the economic reality is different. I know Keith is promising you a nice hunk of change, but I can't afford to risk the investment we've got in Austin Realty. I've got to be available. Take the job if you want, go back to your career—but realize that you're making it hard on both of us."

"I won't ask for you to make things easier."

The words, said with neither ice nor anger, hit their target. "I mean, I'll help when I can." The effort to amend his position fell flat even to his own ears, and Mark added, "But I don't want you to count on me to make dinner."

"I wouldn't dream of it anymore." She let it sink it, then said, "Marguerite has agreed to come back full-time. She'll move in with us on a Monday-through-Friday basis, if that's what we want."

After Eve was born and Jillian was home more, Marguerite began working for them on a part-time basis. She was in her late fifties now and used the extra time to take care of her own grandchildren, who had recently come with their parents from Ireland. But she loved Jillian and the children and was happy to get her old job back. Even Mark had to admit that he felt comfortable having Marguerite around.

"So everything is worked out," Mark said, sarcasm snapping with his words. "Hooray."

"Hooray, indeed." Jillian stood up and paced the length of the room, then stopped in front of the fireplace, her arms folded, and turned to him with a small smile. "I'd say our weekend is turning out to be as romantic as labor pains, wouldn't you?"

Glancing up, he saw the smile that had wooed him so many years earlier and said, "The shittiest romantic weekend on record, I'd imagine."

She laughed. "I share the sentiment, if not the language. Would

51

you like to take a walk before dinner? Gazing at some cows might put things in perspective."

"We'll have to jump over dung patties, I'm afraid."

"I've been doing it all day."

He allowed himself to share her laughter, and they went down the narrow staircase to the front hall, where Butch Greenfield, the owner of the inn, was just coming in. Dressed in denim overalls and a flannel shirt with the sleeves rolled up, his past as a Wall Street executive was well hidden, and he looked every inch the country innkeeper.

"Everything okay in your room, folks?" he asked, in the laconic, New Hampshire drawl he'd managed to acquire after fifteen years of being a genuine New Englander.

"As lovely as always," Jillian said.

"Glad you're back. Lots has happened since the last time I saw you." He filled them in on stories about his children and grandchildren, most of whom worked at the inn. One of his daughters had checked them in when they arrived, and Butch said his oldest daughter would be hostess in the dining room at dinner—even though her two-month-old baby had to sleep in a basket under the maître d's desk. It was a busy time, and the whole family had pitched in with vigor.

Mark and Jillian promised to be back from their walk well before dinner, and Butch held the door open for them as they stepped out into the cool dusk. The encounter with Butch gave them something to talk about other than themselves, and they discussed the Greenfield family as they wended their way through the cow pasture.

"Maybe we should give up all our ambitious driving and come open an inn in New Hampshire," Jillian said at one point, stepping carefully on the soft, rain-soaked ground.

"Nope," Mark replied. "Wouldn't suit us at all."

"Can't be all that bad living happily in the country with your family working with you."

"Yeah, it's just great working with your family," Mark said coldly. He shoved his hands into the pockets of his leather jacket and began walking a little faster.

"I'm sorry. Maybe that was insensitive. Are things not going well with you and your dad lately?"

"Everything is fine." Mark's demeanor belied the words and, realizing it, he added brusquely, "My father is strong-willed, in case you hadn't noticed. He promises to relinquish authority, but he's not good at letting go of the reins."

Mark had been at odds with his father for years, but they had reached a truce of sorts several years earlier when Mark, tired of being in his father's shadow, talked about leaving the business. He took a three-month leave to explore other options but went back when he realized that being on his own wouldn't pay him the kind of salary he received for being William Austin's son. It was worth putting up with some hurt pride. And he'd finally begun to make a difference in the business: the deal they were doing right now was his brainchild. Then there was the setup his father didn't even know about. Sure the project was wild and maybe even dangerous, but it was his way of making a mark.

Leaving wasn't really an issue anymore. Too much else was pressing on him to consider running away. He thought briefly about how nice it would be to spill out the whole story to Jillian, let her know the complexities and problems that were stabbing at him on an almost daily basis. But he couldn't do it. Her response would be sympathetic and businesslike, but he'd be able to see the contempt on her face—and he couldn't cope with that right now.

"You went in to see Keith a couple of times this week," Mark said instead, hoping his effort to change the subject wasn't too obvious. "Are you pleased with the projects he's got going?"

Jillian smiled. "Is that question a peace offering or curiosity?"

"Both."

"Twice as good." She slipped her fingers through the crook in his elbow and leaned into the steep hill they were climbing. "The newest excitement is that Wink Cola is sponsoring a rock concert at the Princess Theatre on Broadway, featuring the hottest musical stars of four decades. It's called something like 'Decades . . . In Concert.' They've got an incredible lineup, and Keith is negotiating to get exclusive TV rights to it for one of our specials."

"Sounds good. What's the special?"

"Keith sold the network on a series of three documentaries called 'The Secret Life.' The idea is to get behind-the-scenes with a big celebrity. The first one is going to be 'The Secret Life of Rock and Roll.' This show at the Princess seems tailor-made for us, because Keith's just heard that Annabelle Fox is going to be there, and he's desperate to get her."

"Why?"

"She's one of the biggest rock stars right now, and nobody knows much about her. Unfortunately, she's not real eager to change that. Keith keeps running into a brick wall by the name of Lenny. No, Denny. Keith says he's the most insolent manager he's ever encountered. And the rumors are that he's her live-in boyfriend, too."

"He is," Mark said.

Jillian laughed. "Do you read the same gossip columns Keith does?"

"No, but I happen to know Denny."

Jillian stopped dead in her tracks and stared at Mark through the gathering dusk. "You *know* Denny?"

"Not well, but I've met him a few times. Keith's right—he's insolent and obnoxious. But he sure has made a killing with Annabelle."

Barely hearing what Mark said, Jillian continued to look at him with astonishment. "How do you know Denny?"

"Why are you so surprised? I do know a few people." He tried not to show how inexplicably pleased he was with himself for astounding her.

"From what I've heard, the guy is a long-haired druggie who lives in a dirty flat outside London. Not exactly your circle of friends, I shouldn't think."

"You're looking for behind-the-scenes? I'll tell you behind-the-scenes. The boy went to Eton. True, he got thrown out when he was about sixteen, nonetheless he is Eton educated. I think he got sent to a military academy after that, but he ran away. He surfaced again when he was about twenty-one, and his parents started giving him money—partly out of guilt and partly because he had trust funds coming to him."

"How do you *know* all this?"

Enjoying himself, Mark smiled enigmatically. "For some reason, it hasn't occurred to anybody that penurious druggies don't turn unknown singers—even if they have a voice like Annabelle Fox—into big stars. It takes money. Underneath his scuzzy veneer, Denny is one wealthy, albeit mixed-up, young man."

Jillian shook her head. "Maybe we'll just interview you for the documentary."

"Not necessary." Mark laughed shortly. "But if you'd like, I could make a couple of phone calls and see if I can help you."

"If I'd *like*? You don't understand. Keith would probably double my salary if he heard this conversation. Why didn't you ever tell me this before?"

"It never came up. Anyway, I haven't known either Denny or his story for very long. The reason I know him is that he happens to be the son of one of the biggest real-estate lords in London. Guy named Kingsley Wright. We've just gotten involved in a major building project with him." .

"I don't know what to say. Whatever you can do would be wonderful."

"Fine." Mark looked up at the sky, which had turned from the mysterious opalescence of dusk to a deepening gray. In the growing darkness, stars were bursting out, and the lights from the inn seemed very far away. "We'd better get back, or we won't be able to see well enough to avoid these cow patties."

They turned around and started down the hill to the inn.

"I don't know how we're doing on romance, but at least you're getting my business on track," Jillian said.

"Glad to help with the business," Mark said. And though Jillian recognized it as a giant concession, almost an acceptance of her working with Keith, she felt a strange chill when he didn't say anything about the other half of the equation.

CHAPTER FOUR

AT WOJ-TV headquarters in downtown Chicago, Barry Brunetti took his morning cup of coffee and the current issues of several magazines and closed his office door. It was his chance to find out the things he *really* needed to know in the world. At the other end of the building, the newsroom was bustling with reporters, camera crews, and teletype machines, but theirs wasn't the news he found particularly compelling.

A few weeks ago, a Chicago magazine had named Barry one of the ten most eligible bachelors in the city, and though he had scoffed at it in public, he was proud of the designation. "Handsome . . . successful . . . young . . . clever . . ."—the writer had found all the best adjectives to describe him.

And all he'd done was take her out for coffee. She didn't even know how good he was in bed.

As always when he walked into his office, Barry stopped to check the grids hanging on the far wall. They were directly across from the large windows that looked out on Lake Michigan. He didn't know which wall bore the more impressive sight. The good view gave the suggestion of power—but the grids were the *real* power. The entire far wall was covered with a giant board made out of a shiny material that allowed him to write each programming decision conclusively in thick black marker—then wipe it away when he changed his mind. As he had once explained to a gullible date—he wrote and Chicago watched.

His grids were his pride and joy, reflecting on a half-hour by half-hour basis the shows on WOJ versus the shows on the other top stations in Chicago. Because they were a network affiliate, some of the decisions were made for him, but otherwise, his programming power still surprised him. When he had wanted to give a local show featuring young comics a chance, he'd written it in for 9 A.M. But Chicago wasn't interested, and the show floundered; so with a swipe of his marking pen, he moved it to 4 P.M., and suddenly it found an audience. In his world, audience translated into big bucks from advertising dollars.

He juggled the blocks on the grids regularly, since his job was not only to find the shows people wanted to watch but to schedule them so that his station got the highest ratings possible. It was his judgment against that of the other station managers in town, and he loved playing the game. That manager's news magazine show versus my rerun sitcom on Wednesday nights at 7:30. He gets two-tenths of a rating point higher, so commands more advertising dollars. He wins. But my show costs half the amount to produce, so my bottom line is better. I win.

Barry loved the gamesmanship of it. And he loved cutting deals. Years ago station managers bought whatever programming was available and paid dearly for it. Now it worked the other way. Syndicators were desperate for airtime; they needed to be on stations in New York, Los Angeles, and Chicago as surely as birds need air and fish need water. It was the only way they could collect their big advertising dollars. Sure, the most successful shows still commanded a healthy price in station licensing fees, but often now the bargaining power was in his court.

Barry settled into the overstuffed high-backed executive chair he'd bought from a company that usually furnished movie sets. Not for him the ergonomically correct chairs that other executives at the station used. He was the boss, and he wanted everyone who walked in to realize it immediately. The station was a success and so was he. The only problem in his life right now was that he needed a big show that was all his. Something he could show the network boys that would make them want him. Chicago wasn't bad, but he was aiming higher. President of NBC Entertainment sounded like a nice title. A couple of million dollars in salary and a house in Malibu.

Flipping the pages of *Electronic Media*, he was so surprised by the headline on page five that he lurched forward to read the article and sloshed his coffee over the very story he wanted to study. Instinctively, he pulled a neatly pressed handkerchief out of his pocket to dab at the puddle of coffee. Then he picked up the phone to call Keith Ross.

"You just cost me a brand-new linen handkerchief," he said when Keith got on the line.

"How did I do that?"

"Reading about you made me spill my coffee. All of a sudden it's Keith Ross, ladies' man, hmm?"

"What the hell are you reading?"

Barry laughed and took a sip of the remaining coffee, which was now barely lukewarm. "I see you've snagged Annabelle Fox and Jillian van Dorne. Two hot ladies. How'd you get 'em?"

"Hey, you're way behind the times," Keith said. "Jillian has been with me for a couple of months now. She came aboard just after I saw you in Los Angeles. And Jillian got me Annabelle. Don't ask how."

He wondered if Keith had known about Jillian when they'd talked about her in L.A. or had he put them together? Should he try to take credit for that right now? Deciding it wasn't worth the discussion, Barry asked instead, "That rock-and-roll special is definitely going to the network?"

"Deal's tied up tight as a drum. Why, would you have been interested in it?"

"Of course. You don't need me to tell you that show's going to be a winner. But the shocker for me is the other show you're working on. Keith Ross, the network man, is planning a syndicated late-night show?"

"You bet, and it's going to be dynamite."

Barry paused for a moment, realizing that he should have thought more carefully about what he was going to say before he dialed the number. Keith Ross was one of the few men in the industry whose name on a show almost guaranteed success, and now that he was teamed with Jillian, Barry had a sense that he should try to get in on the ground floor. This could be what he needed: attaching his name to a winner and grabbing some of the credit for it. Barry often said that it wasn't his job to be a genius—only to pretend that he was.

"Well, I'm always interested in new hot properties," Barry said carefully, "and from what I've read, you've got a wild show cooked up. I don't know what you've worked out in terms of co-production deals, but when the time is right, we should talk."

"That we'll definitely do," Keith said.

"Jillian was always a terrific gal to work with," Barry said, deciding to press the point of his connection to them a little further. "I have great memories of that soap we did together in L.A."

"Yes, Jillian certainly remembers you from that show, too."

Uncertain about the tone in Keith's voice, Barry said, "Of course, we were both kids then, and I was even more of a kid than she was. How far we've both come, hmm?"

"Far, indeed," Keith said jovially.

"Give Jillian my best, would you? Tell her I'd love to see her."

"I'll pass it along," Keith said.

Hanging up, Barry felt a surge of satisfaction. Part of his success was always knowing the right thing to say at the right time. A few well-placed phone calls and a little playing with his connections and before too long he'd be the king of television.

■

"*Who* sends his best?"

"Barry Brunetti. Station manager of WOJ in Chicago."

"Oh, God, yes." Jillian put down her purse and wondered if Keith had been waiting at his office door for her to arrive. "You mentioned him once before. Why were you talking to him?"

"Beats the hell out of me. He called this morning. Saw the piece about us in *Electronic Media*. It doesn't hurt to have a station manager in Chicago call about our soon-to-be-syndicated show before we've even got a minute of it on tape."

"He has good instincts," Jillian said. "I always found his ambition excessive but his business sense intact. It's cool that he's responding so early."

"Cool?"

Jillian laughed slightly. "I'm sorry, you caught me just as I was getting in, so I'm still talking like my six-year-old. Give me five minutes and I'll have made the transition to full-fledged grown-up."

"Don't bother. It's kind of cute."

Keith walked out before Jillian could retort that there was no word in the English language that she hated more than "cute." Cute girls became cheerleaders and prom queens, but they did not become network executives. Jillian van Dorne had never been cute, and at this point in her life, she was grateful for that.

Still standing, Jillian flipped through the phone messages on her desk. There weren't many. Most of the people she dealt with knew not to try reaching her in the office before ten o'clock. Since she'd started with Keith two months earlier, she'd been catching the 9:07 train from Melrose each morning, arriving at Grand Central Station at 9:36. The crush of the early-morning commute was over by then, which meant that she could get a seat on the train and walk to her office without fighting legions of male executives who wouldn't dream of catching anything later than the 7:10.

Mornings were hectic, but at least she got to eat breakfast with the girls and deliver them to school before heading into the city. Now that it was summer, she drove the girls to day camp before she caught the train. That started the day right. The girls wouldn't mind having Marguerite take them, but it made Jillian feel unsettled if she didn't connect with her daughters in the morning.

Keith, an early riser, liked to be at his desk by eight, but he understood Jillian's schedule and made no comments on those mornings when Jillian stayed to chat with a camp counselor and took a later train. It was one of the concessions he'd made to get her and keep her.

Looking around her office, a sunny enclave just down the hall from Keith's, Jillian was at peace with the choices she'd made. Lila and Eve had accepted her working with scarcely a blink, and after just a couple of weeks of settling in, Jillian felt as if she'd never left television. Reactions to her return amused her. Some people who just recognized her name didn't seem at all surprised to have Jillian van Dorne calling again. Those who knew her better wouldn't talk business until they got an answer to the constant question, "What have you been up to?" After a few conversations in which she seemed to spend too long explaining and apologizing, Jillian managed to trim the answer down to two witty sentences.

They'd gone into pre-production on "The Secret Life of Rock and Roll," and Jillian had hired an additional staff to get it going. It surprised her how many talented producers and writers were floating around New York, looking for work.

"It's this new market," Keith had explained when she mentioned it. "Used to be that everyone was coddled by the networks and shuffled from show to show. Now with syndication there are a lot of independent companies. They get a big show with big money, so they hire a big staff. Then *poof*. It goes off the air and a lot of people are out of work."

"We'll keep everyone employed for a long time," Jillian had said confidently.

Jillian buzzed her assistant Liz, a shapely young blonde who had announced to Keith on her initial interview that she was willing to do *anything* to break into television production.

"All you have to do is work hard," Keith had told her sternly.

"That's all I had in mind," a flustered Liz had responded.

Embarrassed to have misunderstood, Keith hired Liz immediately and told the story to Jillian, who laughed uproariously and said that maybe it would be best to have Liz assigned to her.

"Everything okay this morning?" Jillian asked when Liz answered the buzz and came into her office, looking eager and alert.

"Fine," Liz said. "You're supposed to have lunch with that director Emil Luvic, and he called about half an hour ago."

"I hope he didn't cancel." Jillian was looking forward to seeing Emil again. Thoughts of his dark good looks had been on her mind this morning as she dressed, and she spent a little more time than usual selecting her outfit and putting on her makeup.

"No, but he's not reachable the rest of the morning, and he wanted to know where to meet you. So I made a reservation for one o'clock at Auberge d'Argent."

Jillian made a face. "One of my least favorite spots."

"Oh, no." Liz looked stricken. "You weren't in yet, and Emil said he'd be out shooting all morning, so I had to come up with someplace.

I thought you and Keith took people to Auberge d'Argent all the time."

"Only when we're trying to impress out-of-town advertisers, which we do a lot lately."

"You want to impress Emil, too, don't you?"

Jillian looked at her with surprise and, stammering slightly, Liz explained, "I heard you and Keith talking about how good he is. I'm sorry."

"Don't apologize. It's fine to pay attention to what everyone's saying. That's how you learn what's going on." It amazed Jillian how maternal she felt toward the young production assistants in the office. They clearly revered her, and Liz had already adopted Jillian's signature style of dressing, including the flat shoes and the short skirts. Liz's blouses were rayon rather than silk and her scarves weren't Gucci, but Jillian was nonetheless flattered.

"Why don't you like Auberge d'Argent?" Liz asked. Her tone was intense, and Jillian had the impression that she was looking for a lesson in taste.

"It's a place for businessmen with large expense accounts and larger egos. It's horribly stuffy and has an insufferable gilt-and-brocade decor. I would have picked someplace less pretentious. Emil is the most brilliant director in television, but he's Hungarian and has his own style. He's as likely to wear blue jeans to lunch as anything else." Liz was listening with rapt attention, so Jillian added, "The scoop on Emil is that he's the best director on either coast. Half the shows on the air get offered to him, and he's choosy about what he takes. We want him because he has an artistic sensibility—but he knows how to shoot for high ratings."

"I hope he'll do it," Liz said, distraught, "but I don't know what to do at this point about the restaurant."

"Not a thing," Jillian said. "And stop worrying. It's only lunch."

At a few minutes after one, Jillian watched a doorman swing open the heavy brass doors at Auberge d'Argent and smile obsequiously at her. The maître d', his face lined and sallow, looked up from his podium at Jillian's entrance with the hint of a welcoming smile. He recognized her as the classy woman who came in sometimes with the television crowd, and he thought her a nice addition to his luncheon ensemble. Many of the executives at the white-clothed tables always seemed to know her, and the others could at least have something pleasant to look at between their pâté and duck flambé.

"May I help you?"

"Jillian van Dorne. Has my guest arrived?"

"Ah. Ms. van Dorne." The maître d' looked down at his reservation book, then back at her, a rush of embarrassment crossing his usually implacable demeanor. It was obvious that he knew her face but hadn't known her name.

"Your guest . . . I somehow didn't realize . . ." He glanced toward the back of the restaurant, and through the dimness, Jillian thought she glimpsed Emil.

"Perhaps I could . . ." began the maître d'.

Suddenly understanding the situation, Jillian laughed. The maître d' had seated Emil—a casually dressed foreigner whom he didn't recognize—at a table in the back. Now connecting him to Jillian, he wanted to rectify the error, move them to a more desirable spot.

But it was too late. Emil spotted her from across the room and stood up. God, he's gorgeous, thought Jillian, leaving the maître d' and approaching him. Emil was about six feet tall, a slim, broad-shouldered man with rippling muscles and an aura of power. His handsome face was partly hidden by shaded Porsche sunglasses, making his expression impenetrable, but he sported a sexy stubble of beard and the curl of his lips revealed his pleasure in seeing her. Always stylishly hip in his own fashion, Emil was wearing a V-necked linen sweater with no shirt and a leather aviator jacket. Outside, it was too hot for leather, but the restaurant was chilly—the temperature set to accommodate men in three-piece suits.

Emil took a few steps forward to greet her—shoulders erect, a confident swagger to his walk—and kissed her on the cheek.

"You're here," he said simply.

"Sorry to be late." The maître d' rushed over to pull out her chair, but Jillian waved him away and sat down. "There was an investor in our office this morning who didn't want to leave."

"You're worth waiting for," Emil said, his rich Hungarian accent making the words sing. "Are you aware that all the men in a restaurant stare as you walk by?"

She had been aware of it for years, but said, "I didn't notice anybody but you."

"That's because mine was the most intent stare."

They smiled at each other, Jillian realizing that Emil was as practiced in the fine art of executive flirtation as she. Maybe it's why we're both so successful in television, she thought. Surface means everything.

"I've been reading a lot about Keith Ross Productions in *Variety*," Emil said, on more neutral ground. "Is the deal as good as it sounds?"

"Better. Keith got a hunk of money and virtual carte blanche from the network to produce three prime-time documentaries." She chose the word carefully, knowing that Emil had higher aspirations than most TV directors and was attracted to serious projects.

"Keith also got you, the lucky man."

"And my first mission is to get you."

"That should be easy."

The comment made her pause, but knowing that Emil had already told Keith that he wasn't likely to be available for the project, Jillian plunged right in. "We're calling the first show 'The Secret Life of Rock and Roll.' It's a backstage documentary on how a star is made, and the star we're following around town is Annabelle Fox."

"I'm impressed." Emil sat back. "How did you get her?"

"Hard work," Jillian said, not bothering to mention the three visits she and Keith had made to London in the last month. Thank heavens for school vacation, which meant that the children and Marguerite had been able to come with her on the last trip. They had traipsed happily to Buckingham Palace and gone rowing in Hyde Park while Jillian sat in smoky rooms with Annabelle's manager, Denny Wright, convincing him that he should trust them to make a documentary that wouldn't tarnish Annabelle's image. He seemed to hate Jillian at first sight, looking right through her and directing all his comments to Keith.

Mark had bowed out of the talks once he'd put Jillian and Denny in touch, and not much was ever said about Kingsley Wright. Denny seemed to have a curious relationship to the company—he scorned his father but was privy to most of the company's inside information.

"It should be a powerful show, Emil," Jillian said now. "We want to take a serious look at rock and roll and what it's like being an international celebrity at the age of eighteen. We're shooting behind-the-scenes as well as out front at a couple of rock concerts. You can pick the crews and get as many cameras as you need." She paused and drummed her fingers on the table and added ingenuously, "Now tell me what I have to do to get you."

"You have me, baby."

She laughed. "Come on, I'm serious, Emil. We really want you for this show."

"And I want you, too." He gave a low chuckle, and Jillian felt a faint blush creep up her neck. Harmless flirtation, Jillian reminded herself, but as she looked at him, Emil leaned forward, took off his dark glasses, and gazed at her contemplatively. Jillian wondered if he were thinking about the last show they had done together, the "Requiem for the Homeless." He had directed the show with such emotion that one critic called it the most eloquent cry for help in the history of television. They'd spent long hours together editing it, and after it was done, they'd gone to the Rainbow Room for a late-night drink. Watching the stars and sipping their cognac, Emil had told her that she had to come back to television. "You can't keep doing wonderful projects and leaving," he'd said.

But she was glad to flee back to Melrose after that project, because she didn't want to imagine what it would be like to have many more late-night drinks with Emil.

"It's been nearly a year since I've seen you," Jillian said now, keeping her tone even.

"There were reasons I didn't call." From across the table, Emil reached out his hand and stroked her wrist with his thumb. "I'm glad you're working again and I'm glad you want me to work with you. Keith's a genius, of course, but I have so much right now that I said no. He forgot to tell me you're involved. That sweetens the package."

She looked carefully at him, trying to decide what tone to take to get back in control of the situation. "I'm glad, but it's a strictly professional package, Emil. We have to understand each other on that."

He released her wrist and sat back in his chair, his eyes twinkling with amusement. Jillian felt suddenly embarrassed, aware that she had taken his casual banter too seriously. What's happened to my sense of humor? she wondered. Amused seduction was the currency of TV negotiation, and she had tried to buy too much with Emil's coins.

But he put her at ease immediately.

"Professionally speaking, the last show I did with you was such a pleasure, I'd like to repeat the experience." His voice had a tone of warm acceptance that made Jillian feel better.

"This show will be even better."

"I wouldn't object." He took out a small pocket calendar. "What days are you shooting, and when will you need me?"

Taking out her own calendar, Jillian flipped the pages quickly and ran through the schedule. "There's a live concert in New York six weeks from now, on the tenth of September. It's a double whammy— we're using footage for the special, but we're also shooting the whole concert live."

"Whatever for?"

Jillian smiled. "One of Keith's clever ideas. He sold it to the Entertainment Channel on cable, fully sponsored by Wink Cola. Anyway, that makes it a bit more complicated, so we'll need you available that entire week. Then three days of remote shoots on the fifteenth, sixteenth, and seventeenth in New York. We fly to L.A. and shoot there the eighteenth through the twenty-first. After that, about three days in London. The dates are flexible. I anticipate at least a full week of editing at the end of it all, and I'll want you there for that."

Emil nodded and looking up from his calendar, said, "Not as bad as I thought. There's only one day I'd have to be in two places at the same time. L.A. for you and New Orleans for a special I'm shooting for ABC."

"Can you manage it?"

"Only if you promise to be in both places with me." He laughed, and she smiled slightly as she played with the straw in her drink.

"I'll work it out and call you in your office tomorrow," Emil said. Then changing the subject abruptly, he asked, "How are your kids?"

"Terrific, thanks."

"And your husband? I forget the good man's name."

"Mark. Also fine."

"Glad to hear it. Are you hungry?"

"Not the slightest bit."

"Good, let's get out of here. It's a gorgeous day, and I'm flying back to L.A. this afternoon, which means five hours on a plane. Let me walk you to your office." He stood up and steered her easily toward the door, where the maître d' intercepted them, looking anxiously from one to the other. "Is there a problem, madame? Monsieur?"

Emil slowly shrugged his shoulders. "The lady doesn't like sitting next to the men's room—though I, of course, am used to it."

"My apologies, monsieur. I will arrange for a different table."

"Not now," Emil said with an exaggerated sigh. "Too much time eating means too little time for love." The maître d' dropped his mouth in shock as Emil pushed open the door for Jillian, and outside on the sidewalk, in the bright July sunshine, she burst into happy laughter.

"You know I can never go back there now," she said as they turned to walk up Park Avenue.

"I'm sorry."

"Don't worry—it's never been my favorite spot."

"Well, I spoke only the truth," Emil said. "I don't like to be scorned at a restaurant. And I do like to be in love."

■

Keith buzzed Jillian in the middle of the afternoon, asking if she had a few minutes to talk. She said she did, and when she came into his office a moment later, he looked up with a cigarette in his mouth and asked, "What's the word on Emil?"

"He'll let me know tomorrow, but I'd say it's ninety percent certain."

"Good. How much did you offer him?"

"We didn't negotiate."

Keith raised an eyebrow but didn't question her. Jillian had her ways. Toughest broad in broadcasting, people used to say. As far as Keith could tell, though, the real problem was that all the men in the industry wanted to fuck her but couldn't get near. She was one cool lady. Years ago, he used to watch her walking around the sets at CBS in Television City, her sophisticated glamour more appealing than the big breasts and skinny legs of any of the starlets. But the starlets could be manipulated and Jillian was always in control. Back then, nobody worked harder or was more single-minded about success. His buddies called Jillian a ball-buster, a tough cunt, but Keith had always liked her. Now she seemed to have a more balanced life, and it made her work even better. Getting her into his production company had been a stroke of luck.

"You have plans for tonight?" Keith asked.

"Why?"

"Henry Munroe is in town and we're having dinner at Twenty-One. I'd like you to be there."

Munroe was the chief executive of Wink Cola, the big soft-drink company that was sponsoring both the concert and the documentaries. Getting Wink for the documentary had been Keith's coup, and in the world of television, where deals were made on barter and trade-offs, having the sponsor's money up front had made everything else easier.

"Any problems?" Jillian asked.

"He wants to talk about editorial control, and I think you should be in on those discussions early. Since Wink Cola is aimed at a youth market, they're thinking about using Annabelle Fox in future commercials. They want to make sure we're not revealing anything that will conflict with the image they have in mind."

"There certainly are a lot of people trying to create Annabelle Fox," Jillian said cuttingly. "I guess it's the latest game in town—create an image for the cipher. But it's going to be a problem, Keith. I've promised Emil a free hand and told him we're looking for cinema verité."

"It's not a problem," Keith said. "You can explain it to Munroe in a way that he'll buy it."

"When are you meeting tonight?"

"Seven-thirty."

Jillian bit her lip, not wanting another night where she couldn't put the girls to bed.

Reading her mind, Keith said, "Come in a little later in the morning tomorrow if you need to."

"You can't catch fireflies in the morning."

"Pardon?"

"The joys of a summer night, Keith. I promised the girls we'd catch fireflies tonight. They have the bottles all ready."

"There'll still be fireflies tomorrow night."

"I'll tell you what. You explain to two small girls about 'tomorrow night,' and I'll straighten things out with Henry Munroe."

"Your job sounds easier."

"My point exactly. How about if you have dinner with Mr. Munroe tonight, and I'll take him out for breakfast tomorrow? I'll get in a little early, and we'll have oat bran muffins and fruit yogurt at the Royalton. We'll feel very virtuous as we sip herbal tea and discuss Annabelle Fox."

"I can probably sell him on that." He picked up the phone to track down Henry Munroe and tried not to smile as Jillian walked out of the office.

■

"Mommy, can I come to your concert?" Lila turned her wide eyes on Jillian.

"No, sweetie, I'm afraid you're a little too young for that."

"But everybody is talking about it."

"Really? What are they saying?" Jillian was surprised that a rock concert in New York City would have aroused the interest of six-year-olds in Melrose. But she had been too busy the last few weeks to know what her daughters and their friends were talking about. *I'll make it up to you,* she silently promised. *I really will.*

"Everybody is talking about it because if you buy three six-packs of Wink Cola, you can send away and get a T-shirt with a picture of five rock stars on it. It's really nice. Cara already has it, but I told her we don't drink soda at our house." She looked plaintively at her mother.

"I can probably get you the T-shirt, sweetie, even without sending away for it."

"You can?" Lila brightened and came over to give her mother a hug. "Gosh, Mommy, you're so important."

"Absolutely," Jillian said, laughing. "Anytime you need a T-shirt, you ask me about it first."

▬▬

"This is a bigger pain in the ass than you promised."

Pacing the stage of the empty Princess Theatre, Emil Luvic looked down at Jillian, who was sitting in the front row.

Sure that Emil was just letting off steam, Jillian refolded her arms and looked to the back of the theatre, wondering when the lighting and audio men would arrive. She'd never dealt with anything like this before. The concert promoters were going to have a hit on their hands—they'd known that since the day they'd opened the box office and found a line stretched down the block—but they were damned uncooperative. All she'd been hearing from the promoters lately was how they wanted to maintain the integrity of the concert and not turn it into a made-for-television product. Jillian wanted to know just how it was that a rock concert had more intrinsic integrity than a television show, but she bit her tongue and didn't ask.

"Are you ignoring me?" Emil walked to the edge of the stage and stared down at her.

"Of course not. But there's nothing I can do to mediate your audio problems until their technical director arrives."

"Then you are ignoring me." With a leap that made Jillian gasp, he flung himself off the edge of the stage and landed as gracefully as a cat. While she gawked, he sat down next to her.

"What are you studying?" he asked, gesturing toward the Filofax in her lap.

"My schedule. It's really impossible these next few days."

"And I'm making it worse, demanding that you be here for my discussions."

"I don't mind at all. It's just that I have only the haziest understanding of the technical problems. Kensuki could help you more than I can." Ken Kensuki was the production coordinator Jillian had hired.

"He's doing a fine job," Emil said. "But we're at a point now where your sexy smile will get us further than his computer."

"It only goes further with you," Jillian said.

"That's true. One smile from you and I'm willing to do anything."

Jillian heard voices coming from the back of the cavernous theatre, and turned around to see four or five burly men dressed in blue jeans and workshirts walking down the center aisle. Two of them were shaggy-haired and scruffy, and one husky man sported a braid that reached halfway down his back. Kensuki, small and considerably more conservatively dressed, was with them.

"See what I mean?" whispered Emil. "They're the chief technicians for the concert."

For the next half-hour, Jillian listened as they talked about amps and reverb and bass tonality. The key problem seemed to be that the set designer had created a revolving stage with two levels on each side and large platforms studded with neon footlights. To keep wires from showing or getting loose while the set revolved, all electrical wiring had to go through a central board created in a small space beneath one of the lower platforms. The engineers were concerned about the additional wiring Emil had requested so that the sound would track directly onto his tapes. There were also concerns about lighting and where Emil wanted to place his cameras.

At one point the husky man with the braid, the stage manager, tossed up his hands and growled, "This is a real bummer. I don't know how the fuck we're supposed to put on a show if you're interfering with every damn step we take."

"Hey, it's your reputation we're protecting," Emil said. "Big as this theatre is, a few million more people will be watching at home on television. If it looks like shit to them, they're going to assume you put out a shit concert."

Once they thought about that, they started making some progress. An hour later, after they had shaken hands all around, Emil asked Kensuki to check on the availability of outlets backstage. Alone together in the theatre again, Jillian said to Emil, "I never heard you swear before. I thought you were the only director without any curse words in his vocabulary."

"You're right, it's not my usual style."

"But I suppose there's something about reaching people on their own level," Jillian said.

"And just what level do you think these rock techies are at?"

"The lowest. But we're bedfellows at the moment."

"I'll spare you the obvious comment," Emil said, smiling. He took her hand for a moment and then dropped it. "For all your sophistication, Ms. van Dorne, you have an innocence about you that I find most appealing."

She started to respond, but just then Kensuki came back, so she didn't bother.

"I've made some revisions on the number of cameras I need," Emil said, reaching into his briefcase to pull out his notes. "I can get away with four out front, but I really need two handhelds backstage."

Taking the paper, Kensuki turned to Jillian and said, "I'll run the cost estimates on this and get to you this afternoon."

"Fine," Jillian said. "But consider it approved. If I have to start second-guessing my director's decisions, I'm sunk."

Kensuki looked at her in surprise, but Jillian looked at her watch and stood up. "I have to get back to the office, gentlemen. Why don't you two stay and make sure you're agreed on all the details."

"Maybe you should stay, too," said Kensuki. "I understand that Annabelle's manager and backup band will be here in a few minutes for a technical rehearsal."

"I think you can do it without me." Jillian picked up the Louis Vuitton bag that she carried instead of a briefcase and flung her linen blazer over her arm. She didn't have any desire to see Denny more often than she had to. "Everything will be fine, Kensuki. Just make sure you give Emil whatever he needs. I trust him totally."

Waiting outside the theatre for an empty taxi to come along, Jillian told herself that the technical matters were well under control. Having Emil involved made her feel calmer. Though he'd made his reputation by being creative and always getting the shot that nobody else saw, she knew that he also had a cool efficiency, an ability to stay in command of any situation. If he were fretting now, it was only so that he could give his full attention to the creative side of things later. He simply wouldn't let anything go wrong.

She just wished she could say the same about the star. Here it was, three days before the concert, and she still hadn't met the woman who was going to be standing in the spotlight—the focal point of all this wild expenditure of money and effort. According to Denny, Annabelle Fox had arrived in New York a few days earlier. She was staying at the Westview Hotel and didn't want to be disturbed. When Jillian had called the hotel, she was told that no calls could be put through to the room.

"Have Annabelle call me if she'd like to chat about the show," Jillian had suggested to Denny.

"She won't want to," Denny said irritably. "She leaves all that to me."

Denny's guidelines about what they could and couldn't shoot were rigid, but Jillian was counting on Annabelle's being more amenable to interviews than Denny said. Jillian had been through enough celebrity shows to know that the stars were usually far more agreeable than their managers. Over the years, she'd been surprised to find that some of the sweetest stars had the nastiest front men. Once you got by them, the stars themselves were a piece of cake. Jillian and Emil would be spending so much time with Annabelle over the next couple of weeks that maybe she would start to trust them and open up.

She had to if "The Secret Life of Rock and Roll" was going to be more than a piece of fluff.

Eager to get back to the office now, Jillian waved her hand impatiently at a cab whizzing down Seventh Avenue. As it got closer, she saw that the off-duty light was on and the driver had no intention of stopping. Damn. The drizzly weather was distinctly uncomfortable, and she'd left her raincoat in the office. Glancing at the sky, she decided that there was about to be an all-out downpour. Maybe she should walk over to one of the hotels where cabs congregated before more rain came and totally extinguished her chances of finding one.

When the light turned red, Jillian crossed Seventh Avenue, heading east toward one of the big, flashy hotels nearby. Halfway across the street, she stopped and suddenly spun around, retracing her steps. Hotels near the theatre. The Westview. When Jillian had expressed surprise that Annabelle was staying at such an unlikely location, Denny had snarled over the phone that it was near the theatre, and that was all that mattered.

Stopping at a phone booth, Jillian called information and asked for the number of the Westview Hotel. "And please confirm the address before giving me the number," she told the operator. After a brief pause, the operator offered an address on Ninth Avenue, and Jillian thanked her, then hung up. The hotel was just a few blocks away, but since she was walking toward unknown territory, Jillian readjusted her shoulder bag across her body, from left shoulder to right hip. Most savvy women in New York wouldn't dream of carrying a bag otherwise. It was the most basic protection against purse snatching.

Getting to the Westview, Jillian was grateful for the precautions she had taken. The block before the hotel was unfriendly, dotted with hawkers for peep shows and neon signs boasting *Naked Girls! $1*. Several homeless men were sleeping on a grating across from the hotel. The awning of the hotel was torn and hanging dangerously over the door, and the letters were peeling off. Given its appearance from the outside, Jillian wondered why the hottest rock singer on two continents would be staying there.

Inside, the hotel was at least presentable, and the lobby was crammed with Spanish-speaking visitors waiting to check in. Jillian surmised that they had just stepped off the tour bus parked outside and, excusing herself, she moved past several of them to get to the front desk.

"Could you ring one of your guests for me?" she asked.

The clerk pointed across the lobby. "House phone," he said.

On the phone, the operator explained that no calls could go through to that room, and Jillian said, "I know that, but I just need to let her know that I'm waiting in the lobby."

After a pause the operator said, "I'll turn on her message light. If she calls me, I'll give her the message."

"I'll stay right here by the phone," Jillian said.

Barely two minutes later, the house phone rang back, and when Jillian picked it up, a high-pitched, familiar-sounding voice asked, "Is this Jillian van Dorne from the television show?"

"The same. I was just coming from the theatre, and since we haven't met, I thought I'd take a chance on coming by to say hello."

"I'm glad you did," Annabelle said.

Charging ahead, Jillian said, "If you're not busy right now, maybe we could go out for an early lunch?"

There was a hesitation on the other end. "I'm not dressed yet, and Denny said he'd be back soon so I shouldn't go out."

"How disappointing."

There was a moment of silence, then Annabelle blurted, "Would you like to come up for a moment?"

"Absolutely." Jillian got the room number, and a few minutes later was knocking on the door of Room 918. The door opened a crack, the chain still on, and through the opening, Jillian caught sight of the face made famous on millions of record covers and music videos.

"Hi. You looking for me?" Annabelle's voice had a curious tone, somewhere between eager and hostile. Jillian decided that Annabelle's reported months on the streets as a fifteen-year-old, just before Denny found her, made her leery of doorway encounters.

"Yes, we just spoke on the phone. I'm Jillian van Dorne."

"Just a sec." The door closed for the chain to be removed, then opened again. Jillian stepped in quickly, and when the door slammed behind her, she extended a hand. "It's so nice to meet you, Annabelle."

"You too."

Shaking hands, Jillian was struck with how tiny Annabelle Fox was in person. Her narrow shoulders and slight frame made her look like a child, but there was a hardness to her eyes that belied any suggestion of innocence. With no makeup on now, her skin looked creamy and soft, and the pouty lips she'd made famous in her hit song "Kissables" were hardly noticeable. She was absurdly dressed in baby-doll pajamas, and her long spindly legs and wild bushy hair made Jillian think of nothing so much as a young colt. In one hand, she was holding a bottle of nail polish, and the object of her attention had clearly been her toenails, which were now lavishly striped in various shades of pink and purple.

Though not meaning to stare, Jillian noticed that the hotel suite was in striking disarray. The living room where they were standing was a mess of overturned glasses and crumpled papers. Cushions from the sofa were tossed on the floor, and Jillian wondered if the boys in the band had been romping with Annabelle the previous night. Then she noticed a distinctive pair of black suede shoes flung near the television set and realized that Denny shared living quarters with his star. Seeing the shoes made her shudder. How often had she stared at them during negotiations in London, when Denny had been so verbally abusive toward her that she refused to look at his face?

"I've just come from the theatre," Jillian said, "and I couldn't be more excited. The set looks fabulous, and we're thrilled to be working with you."

"Oh, good." Annabelle looked like a little girl who'd just been handed a lollipop. "I haven't seen it yet. Denny and the band should be over there now. Did you see them?"

"I must have just missed them."

"He didn't want me to go. We were partying late last night, and I'm supposed to rest up for a bit."

"He's very protective of you," Jillian said gently.

"Yes." She smiled sweetly, and since she seemed mostly pleased with how well she was being protected, Jillian didn't press it. Instead she asked, "Have you had the chance to see much of New York?"

"No. Denny's been busy, and he says I'll get mobbed if I go out myself. But I really wanted to go shopping. I've heard a lot about American shopping malls."

"There aren't a lot of malls in New York," Jillian said, smiling, "but I'd love to take you shopping."

"You would?" Annabelle looked surprised. "How could we manage it?"

Thinking quickly, Jillian said, "I'll arrange for a limo, and you'll hardly be seen. We'll start at Maxie's on Columbus Avenue—it's New York trendy and has just your kind of clothes. Then we'll zip down to SoHo because there's a store behind the Margot Galleries that has wearable museum art. All one-of-a-kind pieces."

"Oooh, it sounds wonderful!" Annabelle squealed.

"Go get dressed," Jillian urged, heading over to the phone to call for the car.

Annabelle ran over to the bedroom, kicking her legs, then stopped short in the doorway. Turning back to Jillian, she said disconsolately, "I can't do it. Denny's not here, and I don't have any money."

Jillian thought for barely a moment, then hoping she wasn't making a mistake, said, "Don't worry, this one's on me."

CHAPTER FIVE

FOR the second day in a row, it was raining in London, a cold driving rain that seemed to penetrate straight to the bones, and as he walked down Kenilton Lane in Mayfair, Mark Austin wished for the hundredth time that he had remembered to bring along his Burberry. New York had been so sunny when he left that he had gone to the plane in shirtsleeves, carrying his blue blazer, and it hadn't occurred to him that he might need something more. Buying a new raincoat wouldn't be a problem on an early September day in London—he had already seen half-a-dozen window displays for Aquascutum coats and Burberrys—but his coat at home was in perfectly fine condition, and he wasn't in the mood to spend six hundred dollars on sheer forgetfulness.

At a sudden gust of wind, Mark lowered his umbrella, hoping that it wouldn't break. He had left the hotel during a brief pause in the rain and, ever-optimistic, decided to walk. When the downpour started again, there wasn't a cab in sight, so he had ducked into the corner tobacco store and purchased the only available umbrella; still he was going to arrive at his meeting drenched to the skin. He cursed the weather and his bad luck. This was one day he wanted to make a good impression.

Finally arriving at a building that looked more like a cozy home than an office, Mark dashed up the outside stairway and went inside, not bothering to admire the elaborate grillwork on the heavy front door. He shook out the soaking umbrella and jammed it into an already well-stuffed umbrella stand. Patting vainly at his hair, he looked around to see if anybody was watching and, deciding that they weren't, he whipped out a comb from his pocket and smoothed his sodden hair.

Since there was nobody at the front desk to greet him, Mark made his way down the corridor and found what he wanted.

Cynthia Reilly.

She was sitting ramrod straight behind a desk at an end office, writing furiously in a thick notebook. Seeing her, Mark stopped and caught his breath. Though they spoke regularly on the phone about business, they hadn't seen each other in two or three months now, since the day Mark told her about her reassignment to London. Despite the gray day and the fluorescent lighting, there was an unmistakable glow to Cynthia. A puddle of sunshine in the midst of dreary London, Mark thought. He knocked lightly on her opened door, and Cynthia looked up sharply, only a flicker of surprise crossing her face.

"I'm a little early," Mark said.

Cynthia ran her tongue across her upper lip, the only indication that she, too, might be feeling some emotion at seeing him again. "It doesn't matter. I've gone through all the documents. Come in."

As he walked in, he noticed the vase on her desk was filled with wilting roses, and documents and legal books were piled messily on a windowsill. A sweet smell permeated the room from a basket of potpourri that sat next to an overflowing ashtray. The contrasts pleased him because they were so typical of Cynthia: her contradictions had always charmed him. He stood at the edge of her desk and smiled fondly at her. She caught the look, but instead of offering any social niceties, she turned a page in the notebook and said, "My opinion is that this addendum to the proposal is a scam. Probably illegal, though we may be able to find enough loopholes so it's not going to put you in jail immediately. But anybody who looks closely enough will know what's up."

Mark sank into the chair across from her desk and tried to decide how to respond. Of the million personal comments that drifted through his head, none seemed a proper way to begin. He realized why

Cynthia stuck to business, picking up their last phone conversation as if several hours and his presence hadn't intervened.

Rather than trying to work out his feelings, he asked, "Would you say we should go ahead with the deal?"

"If you're trying to preserve the name and integrity of Austin Realty, no. For the amount of money you might be able to make—" She looked at him and shrugged. "Maybe."

Trying to concentrate on what Cynthia was saying meant not looking too deeply into her flashing green eyes, framed today in emerald-green eyeglasses that he'd never seen before. The primmer she tries to look, the more seductive she is, he thought. More contrasts. Her luscious body was hidden by a brown plaid suit. But when she crossed her legs, Mark saw that the skirt was slit almost to the middle of her thigh, and her silky hose made a seductive whooshing sound as her thighs rubbed together. He had the feeling that in a different era, Cynthia would have been a perfect concubine, a piece of sugar candy kept in a sultan's indulgent hideaway. She was a woman born to give pleasure, and that instinct couldn't be hidden by her efforts to dress so she would be taken seriously as a professional. Intelligence and advanced schooling were no match for a body that made a man want to weep.

Cynthia was so perfect now that he could barely imagine what she had been like when she was younger and that smoldering sexuality was still untouched. She had told him so much about her youth that Mark had a vivid image of her standing on the shooting range with a cocked pistol in her hand. All around her, young uniformed men stopped their target practice to admire her determination and—what the hell—her teenage breasts.

After her parents' divorce when she was five, Cynthia lived with her father, a strict and ambitious military man who had retained custody of Cynthia and kept her out of the clutches of her alcoholic mother. Her childhood was a tangle of conflicting messages. Her father rewarded her for achievement and high aspirations; other men seemed interested in different attributes. Through most of her teenage years, she flounced around military bases in Alabama and North Carolina wearing halter tops and short shorts and learning to wield men's weapons. Her father wanted her versed in pistols and rifles so she would have the skills of a man; she enjoyed the practice ranges because there was always someone offering to help—which meant standing behind her and steadying her hands while rubbing his uniformed body against her nubile skin.

It was thrillingly easy to win the attention of young men in uniform. The hugging and kissing and pawing made her feel well loved in a way that her father's cold judgments did not. At sixteen she had sex for the first time with a twenty-year-old cadet who was so overcome by her soft flesh and virgin thighs that he promised undying loyalty. For four months, they slipped off whenever they could, finding unseemly places on the base to bless with their lovemaking. The intrigue was somewhat more exciting to her than the sex, but she liked the way beads of perspiration popped out on Kyle's forehead when he begged her to spread her legs. Lust made his whole body tremble, and she sometimes imagined that if she said no to him, he would quite literally explode, the force of his erection sending him into space like some crazed satellite.

After sex Kyle would hold her tightly, and sometimes their bodies would stick together, the semen he spilled on her bare belly sealing them like an adhesive. The closeness pleased her; after his first orgasm, he would kiss her breasts and moan softly while he whispered her name. The back of his neck felt damp when she touched it and sensing his excitement caused a warm rush of pleasure between her legs. This was love, and unlike what her father offered, she didn't have to pass a test or give a speech to get it.

The day Kyle told her that he was being transferred to California, Cynthia went home and pulled out a large suitcase. Love mattered more than anything—certainly more than school and family—and she decided she would go with him. For two weeks the suitcase sat open in her bedroom while she tossed in books and underwear and shorts. If her father wondered why it was there, he didn't say anything. Nor did he say anything the night Cynthia came home from a date with Kyle and stayed up all night sobbing. The day Kyle left for California— without her, as he insisted it had to be—she stayed tearfully in her room, removing each item from the suitcase which, finally empty, she put back in the basement. Without saying a word, her father had won.

He was still there, and Kyle was gone. Mark could picture both her pain and her father's silent satisfaction.

And now I was foolish enough to reject her, Mark thought. Cynthia was not a woman who easily accepted wavering in a man. If she takes me back, I'll give her all the comfort she needs. He had been able to resist the lure of her body more easily than the seduction of her mind. She was handling the company's deal brilliantly. But that wasn't all; she had come up with a scheme that would bind them forever, something to make him big money that wasn't under the control of his father.

He wondered if he dare do it and accept the risk that was involved. It had never been his style in the past, but it was Cynthia's style. And that's what mattered.

Cynthia reached into her desk drawer and pulled out a sealed brown envelope, and handed it to Mark. "You'll find two memos in there regarding the Austin-Wright deal. One is for your eyes only—my personal opinion on the deal and how you should handle it. The other is my official legal opinion. I'll begin circulating it tomorrow, unless you have any comments or changes that you need to make."

"I'll get back to you on it this afternoon," he said, taking the envelope.

There was silence between them for a moment, then she asked quietly, "Have you thought about the idea I mentioned on the phone?"

"Yes." He swallowed. "I want to do it. An offshore company . . ."

"The Cayman Islands," she said with authority. "I think it's the safest at the moment. The least easily traced." She must have seen the concern on his face because she added, "We don't really have to worry, because there are legal loopholes that will make this okay. You're not setting it up for investment purposes but as a legitimate supply company. Let me play. I think I can make it work."

And make me rich, he thought. Money that wouldn't have anything to do with his father—and that would make him feel equal to Jillian again. "I want to do it," he repeated, wetting his lips.

"Fine, I'll work it out." She nodded briskly, as if it were an ordinary business undertaking they were discussing, not a scheme that made his heart pound just to think of it. "We'll discuss it in a few days."

Feeling dismissed and looking for a middle ground of intimacy, he changed the subject and asked solicitously, "How do you like working here?"

"Quite lovely," Cynthia said, with the twinge of an English accent. "It's very civilized. A maid in a black uniform and a white ruffled apron comes by every day at four with a cart of tea, and we all stop and indulge. And then, of course, I had the pleasure of meeting the beauteous Jillian a couple of weeks ago."

"You did?" He heard the edge of panic in his voice, and at Cynthia's laughter, he tried to sound calm as he asked, "How did that happen?"

"Very innocently, so you don't need to look as if an earthquake just hit. Your dad's been working in the office down the hall, and Jillian was apparently in London for a few days, so she stopped by with the girls. It was very sweet. Two little angels you have there—and they were so excited about seeing Grandpa Bill in London."

Mark swallowed hard, trying to decide how much sarcasm Cynthia intended with her comment. Then, feeling an overwhelming need to explain himself, he said, "Jillian was in London on business, and I couldn't leave the office in New York to join her." When she didn't say anything, he added, "I mean, with Bill spending so much time here, one of us had to control things at home."

"Yes, Bill has been spending a lot of time here. We're getting along splendidly. I can see it's best that the two of you aren't here at the same time."

Too preoccupied to think what she might mean, Mark asked, "Where did you and Jillian meet?"

"At the water cooler. It was just by chance, which is lucky since I don't think Bill would have done the introductions. But your wife didn't seem to have a flicker of interest at hearing my name. Which I found curious."

His anxiety making him restless, Mark stood up and crossed to the window. Rain poured off the old-fashioned awning outside in sheets.

"Why is it curious that she wouldn't know your name?"

"I just assumed it had come up at some point between the two of you. I used to imagine that you'd had a horrible fight, and she'd threatened to kill herself if you didn't end our affair immediately. But seeing her, I figure it's more likely that she wrote you a polite note, asking you to break up with your lover and devote more time to the family."

She was being outrageous, and he knew it, but it appealed to him all the same. Turning from the window, he said, "Jillian never even suspected our affair."

"Not as smart as she looks, hmm? What happened, then? Did Bill demand you end it?"

"Of course not." So he was lying. Bill wasn't exactly trying to control Mark's life, but he had laid out such a good explanation for why the affair with Cynthia had to end that Mark had bought it. But no more. He was stepping out from Bill's shadow now. Doing what he wanted. And if that included having Cynthia and setting up an illegal company that would make him rich, so be it.

Cynthia looked as if she didn't believe his denial about Bill's influence, but instead of pursuing the subject, she switched gears and said, "I certainly don't want to interfere in your marital bliss, but I'm wondering if there's any chance you asked your wife to indemnify you against lawsuits arising from her television show."

"Why in hell would I have done that?"

"I heard a good deal about the business she was conducting here. Making contacts with Denny Wright, who manages Annabelle Fox. An entire television show is being planned around Annabelle—and you introduced Jillian to Denny, didn't you?"

"I plead guilty there, yes."

"Next point is that they met in the conference room just down the hall—the site of the negotiating headquarters of Wright-Austin Realty. I mention all this as your lawyer, by the way. Denny Wright might have taken all this as an implicit agreement that the show coming out of it would be favorable to him. I don't know that Jillian feels the same way."

Mark found it strange to be discussing Jillian with Cynthia, particularly since his lust for the woman across the desk was rising by the moment.

"I have no idea what Jillian intends to do with the show."

"My point exactly. We have been negotiating in good faith with Wright Management, of which Denny Wright happens to be the vice-president of record. You and I know that his name is there only for tax and compensation purposes, but that's strictly beside the point. Jillian's dealings with him, coming at this time, could end up troublesome for us."

From his place at the window, Mark wondered at the twisted reasoning required of a clever lawyer. Cynthia's razor-sharp legal mind took turns that would never have occurred to him in a million years.

And her body took turns that made him want to shiver. She had slid her chair sideways to the desk to talk to him, and he could see her bosom straining under the confines of the suit, noticed the wide belt that emphasized the nipped contour of her waist. Examining the outfit, he realized that she wasn't wearing a blouse under the suit jacket; her cleavage was hidden only by the flimsy chiffon scarf she had tied loosely around her collar. She had crossed her legs, left knee over right, and while she talked, she made circles with her left ankle, causing her spiked heel to vibrate up and down like some strangely eroticized machine.

Purposefully crossing the room, Mark placed his fingertips on the edge of her desk and leaned over the wilting roses until his face was so close to Cynthia's that he could see the specks of glowing powder that contributed to the creamy whiteness of her skin.

"I made a mistake," he said softly.

"It can be rectified," she said with a shrug. "If it's all right with you, I'll write an indemnification for her to sign immediately. If you find that too awkward, just tell me, and I'll find another way around it."

"Do whatever you want, because that's not how I made a mistake." His voice was still soft, and Cynthia seemed to notice all at once his proximity to her. When she didn't pull back, he said, "The mistake I made is that I shouldn't have ended our affair. I've missed you desperately."

"I'm sorry about that," she said coolly, "but I'm sure things have been going much better for you and Jillian without me around."

"I wish you'd forget about Jillian." He stood up abruptly and began moving around the room again, aware of her gaze following him. At the doorway he asked, "Mind if I close it?"

"Not at all."

The door closed with a satisfying thud, the hallmark of an English building that was sturdy enough to have survived bombings and war. He posed against the door, eyeing Cynthia with a steady, steely gaze.

"The fact is that I have no desire left for Jillian. The marriage is stale, and we have nothing to say to each other anymore."

"Strange to hear you say that when she spoke so warmly of you."

Again he had to decide whether or not the comment was meant sarcastically. Uncertain, he said, "I didn't realize what stability you gave to my life. Is there a way I can apologize and have you again?" He wanted her body so much that he could almost feel it heaving against him.

"You don't really want me, I shouldn't think. You have your family. Now that I've seen them, I know you'll never leave them."

"Did I ever say I would? What you and I have is something different, Cynthia. I can't explain to you right now why I thought I had to throw it away, but it was a terrible, terrible mistake."

"I can't correct that one quite so easily," she said, sliding back her chair. "No predated indemnifications I can think of to fit this bill. Now, should we get on with our business?"

Her coldness startled him, but there seemed no way around it. He wondered if she were just giving him a taste of his own rejection. Once assured of his remorse, would she return?

"Listen, why don't I go over all these papers and come back later. I'll take you out to lunch. Or we could have a drink at the end of the day."

"I'll be working late. Let's make it lunch."

"Fine."

"Are you working this morning in Bill's office?"

The thought hadn't really occurred to him. He kept his distance from Bill, didn't sit in Daddy's chair just because he was away. But the thought of going back out into the rain was even more unappealing than accepting the role of boss's son.

"Yes, I'll be there. Why don't you find me when you're ready for lunch."

They'd have lunch in a little pub, Mark thought, leaving Cynthia and making his way to Bill's office. A few beers and some apologies and they'd be holding hands under the table again. Maybe they'd stop in his hotel room on the way back to the office. No, damn it, he'd scheduled all those meetings this afternoon. He'd have to hold the mood until tonight, get her back into his bed then. Whether he liked it or not, it was going to be necessary to deal with the conflicts of honor and lechery. Cynthia had to understand that the terms hadn't changed, and he wasn't leaving Jillian. Strange that she had even said such a thing today. It had never come up before.

At Bill's incredibly neat desk, Mark unloaded his briefcase and checked his own pocket calendar. A penciled notation reminded him that tonight was the big concert in New York. Jillian was surely too busy to talk to him now, but he should call nonetheless. That way he could leave a message with her assistant to say he was thinking of her—and he never actually had to connect.

To his surprise, he got through immediately.

"I'm so glad you called," Jillian said, sounding genuinely pleased to hear from him.

"I didn't want to bother you. I just wanted to say good luck."

"Thanks. That means a lot. How's London? Are you unbearably busy?"

"Um, no. Well, yes." He paused to collect himself, wondering why the simplest question from Jillian left him nonplussed. "You're the one with the big night coming up. You must be nervous."

"No reason to be nervous at this point. Everything's been worked out, and if there are going to be any surprises, they'll happen behind-the-scenes tonight. I'll be with the cameramen backstage, and we'll see what we get."

"What are you expecting?" Cynthia's warning about the indemnification resounded in his head, but this was obviously not the time to ask about it.

"I'm not sure. Annabelle Fox is a bit of a mystery. She's scared to death of something, though I haven't figured out what. You'd think a kid her age who's such a hot star would be bouncing off the walls, but she doesn't even seem to understand how big she is. And she has wild mood swings. We had a great shopping trip a couple of days ago where she giggled and hugged me and told me I was her new best friend—just the way a child might. Then I brought her back to her sleazy hotel, and since then, she hasn't even been taking my telephone calls."

"Oh." Mark was at a loss for how to respond. His wife's fascination with the intricacies of human nature left him cold. But Jillian changed the subject herself.

"The girls are fine, but they miss you," she said.

"I'll call them tonight. I couldn't reach them this morning because of the time difference."

"Tonight would be good. I won't be home because of the concert, and Lila got very grouchy this morning when she realized it."

"Won't Marguerite be there?"

"Of course, but Lila announced that she likes to have a parent at night."

"I'm sorry I'm not there."

"Yes, me too." Jillian sounded more sad than angry. Before he'd left, she'd asked, "You really have to go to London this particular week?" with a mixture of bewilderment and hurt. And he'd responded, "Yes, this week is crucial." Now he wondered if it had been a mistake. The trip could have been rescheduled easily; it was tied to nothing except the appointments he'd made and the dates he'd made them.

He hadn't really stopped to think why he'd wanted to go away when Jillian was so immersed in this new project. Maybe it was the absorption that irked him, the eagerness with which she went off to work each day. On top of that, she was so intent on being Supermom that he could hardly bear it. One morning a few weeks ago, she'd stayed home from work to go to the swim show at Lila's camp. "I wouldn't miss that for anything," she'd insisted. It wasn't as if Lila could really swim, either. Some random kicking and windmilling of arms propelled her from one end of the pool to the other, but Jillian came home as enthusiastic that day as if she'd just witnessed the return of Mark Spitz. Two days later, she'd left work early to take Eve swimming at a pond just outside Melrose, explaining that it wasn't fair for Lila to have special mommy-time and not Eve.

If she were so good at managing everything—well, let her go ahead and manage.

The phone line from London to New York crackled, and Mark thought of how Lila had once asked him if there were phone cables buried under the Atlantic Ocean. He had responded with a lengthy explanation about satellite communication but realized when he was finished that her explanation seemed far more realistic than his. He had an image now of a colorful fish nibbling at the wire, interrupting his conversation.

"Having any problems with Denny?" Mark asked.

"Oh, he'll be fine," Jillian said.

His own abruptness seemed to have cooled some of her enthusiasm for talking with him, but nonetheless he was irritated. He didn't expect gratitude for setting her up with Denny Wright, but maybe a few words of thanks. Some recognition that she couldn't have done any of this without him.

There was some noise in the background, the sounds of people coming into her office, and Jillian said, "Hold on a second, would you?"

Put on hold on a transatlantic call. There was a time that would have bothered him. Now he counted the seconds not because they were costing him money, but because his wife had something more important to do than speak to him. It was satisfying to be angry with her.

The line was silent only briefly, and when Jillian came back a few moments later, he said, "You're busy I guess."

"No, it's fine. Just a quick problem that needed attention."

But the interruption had left him without anything more to say, and he made an excuse about his other phone ringing, wished her good luck with the evening's shoot, and hung up.

■

Jillian stared at the phone for a moment after the line from London went dead, trying to pinpoint the vague discomfort she felt. It was too bad that Mark had decided to be away this week, though it was probably for the best. If he were in New York, she would have wanted him to come to the concert, and she would have been insulted when he had produced a reason why he couldn't make it. As a second choice, she would have expected him to spend the evening with the girls, and he would have agreed but something would have intervened.

Too much work. An unexpected meeting at the office. Many apologies and explanations, but still no daddy available to put the girls to sleep. And no husband available to share her pleasure in being back in the thick of television.

So this is where eight years of marriage brings us, she thought disgruntledly. A wonderful job and a husband who doesn't want to be around. Even this phone call. She had felt like chatting with him, and he'd felt like hanging up as quickly as he could.

Before she'd gone back to television, Mark had made it clear that he wasn't going to let her schedule inconvenience his, and while she hadn't objected at the time, she wondered what he was trying to prove. Didn't he realize that he was the one missing out? He scorned her efforts to be with the girls and also work hard, but to her that's what life was all about. Finding room for everything.

Jillian swung her chair around to the antique cabinet behind her desk. Flipping through the files in one drawer, she found the notes she needed for tonight's concert and slipped them into her pocketbook. It was time to get to the theatre. She glanced into the gold oval mirror she kept in her pocketbook and decided her makeup needed touching up. Propping the mirror on the top of the cabinet, she carefully framed her lips with a pale pink pencil then dabbed on lipstick in a similar shade. With a light hand, she applied a quick brush of blusher and clipped on the mabe pearl earrings she'd taken off to use the telephone. The mirror and cosmetics went back into her pocketbook. Now she was ready, and she wouldn't have to think about how she looked for the rest of the night.

Spinning the chair back around, she looked up into Emil's handsome, tanned face.

"I feel we've just shared an intimate moment," he said.

Torn between surprise at seeing him and embarrassment at his having watched her primping, Jillian said, "That's about as intimate as I get."

"Then I'm pleased to have been a part of it. Still, I apologize for walking in on you. It's just that there was nobody to stop me."

"My best assistant Liz is already over at the theatre. I told her to hang out there today and make herself useful to anybody who needs her. I figured somebody would need an extra hand, whether Keith or you—" She paused and looked questioningly at Emil.

"Ah, you're wondering why somebody as important as your director isn't at the theatre this very minute?"

"It does occur to me that we're shooting a show across town in just a few hours." Sounding calmer than she felt, Jillian locked her top drawer and stood up, straightening out some random papers left behind on her desk.

"The engineering setup is complete, and there's nothing to do now except wait for the screaming crowd to arrive so we can turn on our cameras. But since it's time for you to be heading over to the theatre, I thought I'd provide an escort. I have a limousine downstairs."

They went down in the elevator, and Emil ushered Jillian into a waiting car.

"Your timing is perfect," Jillian said, settling into the soft leather seat next to Emil. "Do I dare ask how this happened?"

"I'd like to take credit for anticipating your every desire," Emil said, popping open a bottle of Evian water from the bar next to his seat, "but in fact, I heard the driver at the theatre telling Keith that he was coming over to get you. I decided to hitch a ride and come get you myself. It's the only chance you and I will have to talk about the last-minute details. The moment you get to the theatre, you're going to be too busy to look at me."

"That could never happen," Jillian said with more vehemence than she intended. Then noticing Emil's small smile, she quickly asked, "How did the rehearsal go after I left last night?"

"Fair, I guess. The show is going to be hot. A lot of the performances are incredible. The idea of three generations of rock and roll is a good one, but tempers were flaring at the rehearsal, and Annabelle spent most of her time looking terrified. Her band members tell me that happens all the time—but once the show starts and the lights are on, she's suddenly a star."

"Maybe we should have gotten some footage backstage during the rehearsal," Jillian said. "My fault for missing it."

"I guess you had no choice. You heard the story about Jonah, didn't you?"

90

"No, what happened?" Jonah was one of Emil's favorite camera-men.

"All we did after you left was a walk-through so the cameramen could set shots, but just to make sure everything was in order, I asked Jonah to roll tape on one of the handhelds for a few minutes. He left camera two and went backstage, and the next thing I knew I heard screaming and yelling. Denny stomped onto the stage in the middle of one of Annabelle's numbers and hollered that he had assurances from you that there'd be no shooting during the rehearsal."

"Assurances from me?" Jillian looked astonished. "We never discussed any such thing."

"Ah. Very interesting. That doesn't explain why he knocked the camera out of Jonah's hand and smashed the lens."

"I'm not kidding, Emil. It never even came up."

"So Jonah was thrown to the whales for no particular reason."

"I'm afraid so. Nothing at all evil about what he was doing."

"I'll keep that in mind," Emil said, tight-lipped. He pulled a sheaf of yellow papers from his pocket. "Let's make sure that there are no misunderstandings between us. I'm shooting the full concert tape for the Entertainment Channel as if it were going out live, with no editing. Of course, if you want to change the package and edit in any backstage material or shots from the iso reels, you can do that later."

"Agreed," Jillian said. An iso reel included the untouched, isolated shots from one of the cameras and made editing a far easier proposition.

"Now, as far as the 'Secret Life' special goes, the line feed will have all the concert footage you need. But since I'm shooting two iso cameras, the real question is whether I'm looking for anything special on those."

"I'd love to have one reel that's close-ups of Annabelle perform-ing."

"That's just what I was planning."

"Good. I'll leave the other iso to you."

"I'm also planning to use star filters on all the cameras except camera three, which is the establishing wide shot. Any problem with that?"

"Of course not, I like that look. It's glitzy. And if Annabelle is wearing that gold-sequined miniskirt she had on last night, you'll *need* star filters."

Emil mentioned two other special effects he was planning to use, and after giving her opinion, Jillian said, "You really should clear all of this with Keith, though. You know the division of labor—I'm executive producer on the 'Secret Life' special, and Keith gets top billing on the cable concert."

"I know, Keith already mentioned it. But he asked me to get your opinions. I'm not supposed to tell you that he thinks you have a better eye for these things than he does."

Jillian laughed and looking out the window, realized that they were almost at the theatre.

"Anything else?" she asked.

"Just one more thing. Are you shooting at the party after the concert?"

"Of course." Wink Cola was throwing a post-concert party at Chopsticks, a chic, new restaurant near the theatre district that featured California-style nouvelle Chinese food. The stars of the concert had all promised to come, and Keith was planning to escort Annabelle. The party would no doubt make it into all the gossip and society columns, and getting Keith's name right next to Annabelle's would provide some early publicity for their special. "You'll be there, won't you?"

"Probably, but knowing that you're shooting makes it signifi-cantly less appealing. If you're working, it means you can't be my date."

"Your date?" Jillian smiled. "Such a charmingly old-fashioned word."

"Then I'll try again. Would you like to be my lover, my amourette, my Dulcinea, my inamorata? Will you play Heloise to my Abelard, Chloe to my Daphnis, and Melisande to my Pelleas? What I want from you has been described by Montaigne as the insatiate thirst of enjoying a greedily desired object and is more simply put in the Bible as the fulfilling of the law. Would you be gracious enough to help me fulfill the law tonight?"

Jillian laughed. "You've moved a far way from a simple date."

"It's what happens when a man sits next to a beautiful woman in the backseat of a limousine. His whole body moves in ways that I will spare you."

Jillian blushed slightly, then embarrassed by her reaction said, "We're almost at the theatre. Shouldn't we be thinking about the concert?"

"I can think about more than one thing at a time, which is valuable when I'm working with you."

"Unfortunately I am easily distracted." Turning away from Emil, Jillian looked out the smoked-glass window and saw that they were stuck in traffic. The limousine so insulated her from the city that until that moment she hadn't been aware of the cacophony of car horns and the ominous rumble of power tools slamming through concrete. All around them on Broadway, a crush of cars merged chaotically around men in hard hats lodged in the middle of the street, their bodies trembling under the force of their jackhammers. Digging up the streets was a daily occurrence in Manhattan. What was going on now? Sewer repair? A deteriorating water main? Con Ed? And why did it have to occur at four o'clock in the afternoon on a warm Friday, when traffic was guaranteed to be overwhelming anyway?

After several minutes of not moving, Jillian said, "Why don't we just get out and walk? We're just a couple of blocks away."

"Relax for another minute." Emil leaned his head against the glove leather seat and smiled affectionately at her impatience. "Enjoy it; this is the last chance you'll get to relax for hours."

When they finally pulled up in front of the theatre, the driver got out of the car to open Emil's door, then dashed around to Jillian's side—but she had already stepped out.

"Bad habit of mine," Jillian said. "I never wait."

Taking her arm, Emil propelled her through a throng of double-parked cars. On the sidewalk in front of the theatre, a knot of burly men were arguing loudly. They stopped abruptly when they saw Emil, and one of them—a threatening figure with a thick black beard who was wearing a sweat-soaked bandanna around his neck—raised a hand and called out, "Yo, boss!"

"What can I do for you?" Emil asked.

"Some little girl with a clipboard came by to get the spellings on all our names. You planning to run our names in the credits?"

"We thought it'd be nice, yes."

"Thanks, boss. Appreciate it."

"Anything else I can help with?" Emil asked. "Seem to be a lot of loud voices."

"Nah. We'll kill each other and get it settled."

"Wait until after the concert, if you wouldn't mind. I hate to do a show shorthanded."

The man with the bandanna laughed gruffly. "Whatever you say, boss."

They left the men and walked into the theatre, and Jillian said, "Boss?"

"They're stagehands for the concert."

"Are they part of our crew?"

"No, they're on the concert payroll, but I guess I've been controlling a lot of things this afternoon."

"So you're boss to everyone." For some reason, the fact pleased her, confirming her image of Emil as the man always in control.

They walked through the theatre to the alleyway outside the stage door, where a trailer was serving as a temporary control room. Emil leaped up the three rickety metal steps to the trailer and with a sharp tug, pulled open the door. Turning back again, he offered a hand to Jillian as she stretched to reach the first step. Inside, the trailer was crammed with control panels, small monitors, and four stools where Emil, his assistant director, the technical director, and the audio engineer would sit during the show. There was no space left to enter and Jillian stood in the doorway until, putting his arm around her waist, Emil said, "Come squeeze in." With some shifting of bodies, she managed to jam herself in next to Emil's seat. The audio engineer who was smoking a cigar ground it out quickly as Jillian entered, but the smell of tobacco lingered in the air.

"Did you get the board straightened out?" Emil asked his technical director, a lanky dark-skinned man named Darryn who was busy testing the complicated control panel.

"Everything's fine, boss." At the appellation, Emil glanced at Jillian, and they both smiled.

"Good. Why don't you show Jillian some of the effects we've worked out."

94

Darryn nodded without looking up and pointed to one of the monitors that carried the logo DECADES . . . IN CONCERT! "Watch that one," he said to Jillian. He spun some dials, and in a moment, the logo seemed to explode from the screen, dissolving into a shower of stars that resolved into a graphic outline of a rock singer holding a microphone. From the left corner of the screen, the DECADES . . . IN CONCERT! logo reappeared and floated down over the stars, stopping just below the star picture.

The whole effect took barely five seconds, and when Jillian didn't comment immediately, Darryn said, "Watch it again."

This time Jillian was ready. "It's terrific. I'm just stunned that you did that here." Elaborate effects usually required sophisticated machines—toys, the technical guys called them—and expensive time in a post-production facility.

"Darryn is very creative," Emil said. "He makes that toy sing."

"Keep it singing," Jillian advised. "Any more I can see?"

Darryn flipped several more images onto the screen, and Jillian expressed satisfaction with each one.

"I've got to get going now," Jillian said, patting Darryn lightly on the back. "I'm so pleased with what you've done. Nice work."

Emil followed Jillian out of the trailer.

"Did you really like all those effects?" he asked.

"More or less. The first one is terrific. You should use it for a bumper out of the first commercial break and at the midbreak."

"The last one he showed you was dreadful. It made me dizzy just to look at it."

"It wasn't great," Jillian agreed, "but it's up to you whether or not to call for it. If you use it and we all later decide we don't like it, we can fix it in post." Everything could be fixed in post-production. Back when she was still at the network, Jillian had heard a story about the director on a weekly detective series who had forgotten to shoot the last scene of a show. It wasn't as bizarre as it sounded; shows were almost always taped out of sequence, so missing a scene wasn't blatant stupidity—it was a simple oversight. By the time anyone realized it, though, it was too late to reshoot. The quandary landed in the hands of the post-production supervisor who, using outtakes from earlier shows, special effects, and video mixing, managed to fashion a final scene. The night that it aired, it garnered a twenty-two share, which meant that some twenty million people were watching, and not one called in to complain about the ending.

"If you didn't like an effect, why didn't you say anything to Darryn?" Emil asked.

"There's no sense discouraging him. Let him get the best pictures he can, and we'll make our judgments later."

Emil ran a finger down Jillian's arm. "You're devious. I didn't realize that about you."

"Not devious, just practical." Before he could respond, Jillian said, "I want to get started shooting some pre-show material. Are you having Jonah work with me backstage, or is he on camera two for the show?"

"After what happened at the rehearsal, I think we'd better keep him away from backstage. Can you work with Nathan?"

"He'll be fine." Inside the theatre her assistant Liz was standing by, making herself available, as Jillian had requested. Jillian motioned her over and asked her to find Nathan. "Tell him that I need him to head over to the Westview Hotel with me," Jillian explained. "This is a good time to set up some before-the-big-show shots of Annabelle."

As Liz walked away, a group of writers, segment producers, and assistants seemed to appear from nowhere, slowly encircling Jillian with their questions. Another group of technicians—both from the TV crew and the floor staff—surrounded Emil. From the midst of the circles they inhabited, they smiled dolefully at each other. Emil answered the questions quickly, and people began to move away, back to work. Jillian did the same, and slowly they drifted back to each other.

"A deluge," Emil said.

Halfway across the theatre there was shouting, and Jillian and Emil turned quickly to see Denny stumbling toward them. An ashen-faced Liz scuttled along next to him, and it was hard to tell if she were escorting him or being held captive. Even from a distance, Denny looked disheveled, his long hair hanging in greasy streaks around his face, his shirt crumpled around the edge of his pants.

"Like hell you'll go to the hotel!" Denny hollered when he was barely within shouting distance of Jillian. "Like hell you will."

Jillian waited until he got closer.

"What's wrong, Denny?"

He lurched toward them.

"I heard this little Girl Guide here giving instructions to your cameraman." Denny spat out the words. "Listen, Missus Bitch Producer, I never invited you to the hotel, and you'll stay the fuck away."

Jillian glanced over at Liz, who looked stricken, her eyes open wide in shock.

Controlling herself, Jillian said, "There's no reason for you to listen to this abuse, Liz. Why don't you find Keith and see if he needs any help with the press before show time."

Liz turned quickly and left the small group.

"Like hell you'll go to the hotel," Denny repeated loudly.

His eyes were wild, and he looked so wired that Jillian realized he must be on something, flying before the concert.

"I'm not sure what your problem is, Denny. Everything's been worked out."

"I'm not the one with the fucking problem. All I need from you, lady, is that you keep your fucking cameras out of my girl's face, you understand?"

"No, I don't understand at all." Her voice was high-pitched and loud, a sign of anxiety. "We're doing a behind-the-scenes documentary on Annabelle. We've agreed to that, and it's all in writing. Why are you trying to change the rules?"

"I don't care about any fucking papers we have. You kidnapped my bitch when I had told her to stay the fuck inside the hotel room. I don't trust you anymore, lady."

"Well, you damn well have to trust me." Her voice shook with anger and outrage.

"I don't damn well have to do anything. I can't stand having you bitch girls around me anymore. Where the fuck are all the men? Do I have to deal with women the rest of my life?"

He leaned over her threateningly, then staggered forward, his body lurching against hers so awkwardly that when Jillian grabbed him, she wasn't sure if she were fighting him or protecting him from a fall.

97

Emil, who had been standing back, lunged toward them; Denny jerked backward, and Emil was suddenly standing between Jillian and Denny, his intervention so smooth that it seemed like he had been there all along.

"You okay?" he asked Jillian, grabbing her elbow with a protectiveness she appreciated but was too riled to accept.

"Of course." She took in a breath.

Emil turned to Denny. Next to him, Emil seemed massive and sure, his muscles throbbing under the rolled-up sleeves of his white shirt, his sturdy strength undisturbed by Denny's agitation.

"You want to deal man-to-man?" Emil asked. "Okay, deal with me."

Denny rolled back onto the heels of his black leather sneakers, jamming his hands into his pockets.

"These asshole women are trying to fuck me. I swear they are."

"All Jillian is doing is making you rich, man. See all those candy concession stands in the front of the theatre? Next time you're in New York those stands will be selling Annabelle Fox T-shirts and Annabelle Fox key rings. Every teenybopper is going to want a memento that says Annabelle Fox because they've seen her on television. And in America, it's being on television that makes you a star. That's what Jillian's doing for you."

"Oh yeah?" Instead of calming him, the speech seemed to push Denny's anger in new directions. "I'm the one making Annabelle a star. All these bitches need *me*. I don't need them. And I won't put up with any shit from any of them."

Emil looked from Denny to Jillian, trying to decide how to continue. In a moment, he unclenched his fist, and, clamping a friendly hand on Denny's shoulder, said, "Come on, Denny, man-to-man, as you said. There's no room for hurt feelings."

"No room for nasty interfering either." Denny pointed a finger at Jillian. "She interferes and fucks things up and I swear I'll get my little bitch on the first flight back to London. I've done it before."

"But you won't have to do it again. I had the cameras turned off last night when you wanted me to, didn't I? I'm directing this project, which means I'm controlling it. We're doing this right or we're not doing it at all."

98

For some reason that seemed to calm Denny down. He looked distrustfully from Jillian back to Emil, then, planting himself shakily in front of Emil, said, "Okay, I'll talk to you, nobody else."

"Fine. Now, what do we have to get settled right now?"

"I don't want any fucking cameras in my girl's hotel room."

"Then let's make a deal. No cameras at the hotel as long as Jillian and the crew have access to Annabelle's dressing room backstage during the whole concert?"

Denny seemed to deflate. "Yeah, I'll do that. Just make sure that it happens, okay? I'll trust you to take care of *her*."

He walked away then, and Jillian watched him, open-mouthed, then turned quickly, heading off in the other direction.

"Hey!" Emil called. "Wait a minute. Where are you going?"

Jillian stopped. "I'm going off to calm down so the entire theatre doesn't hear the producer and director squabbling."

Emil wrinkled his eyebrows, and Jillian tried not to notice his broad shoulders leaning toward her protectively. "Are you angry at Denny or me?"

"You, frankly. We'll handle this man-to-man, hmm? Thank you very much, Emil, but I don't need that kind of help. And since when is it your decision that I won't shoot in the hotel but I will have access backstage? I don't recall our making you the senior producer on this project."

"Hey, listen. That guy was wired on something. High as a kite. Reasoning with him wasn't going to get you anything. All I wanted to do was get him back on track so he didn't blow everything for us two hours before the show. If that took more appeasing than you like, I'm sorry."

"You don't seem to have much faith in my abilities to get things on track. I'm the one who negotiated with him in the first place."

"And I'm amazed. He hates women. Didn't you get that?"

"Yes, I got that. We're bitches and assholes and he thinks we're all out to get him. So he needs a few years in psychotherapy to work it through. That doesn't mean you had to side with him."

"I wasn't siding with him, and once again, I'm sorry if I offended you. But once in a while brute masculinity has a role in life."

"Fine."

"Fine? That's it?"

"Yes. I'm not going to argue with you about this. You know how I feel, but I also appreciate your diffusing the situation with Denny. So, fine. Enjoy your brute masculinity and let's move on."

She started to walk away again, but he put a strong hand on her shoulder, and she stopped—unwilling to scuffle with him—but didn't turn around. Standing behind her, he said in a low voice, "You don't have to hide your anger from me—it's part of life. Lovers' quarrels should end with passion—the terrifying bang of a gun or the overwhelming embrace of a kiss. It shouldn't end with your stalking away from me in a snit."

"I'm not in a snit, and we're not lovers."

"That could change."

"It won't," Jillian said, finally shaking off his hand. "Trust me, it won't."

CHAPTER SIX

THE dressing room in the theatre was dank and cramped, but all Annabelle Fox noticed when she opened the door was a big bouquet of flowers that filled her nostrils with their pungent sweetness. The flowers had been propped in a corner of the dressing table, angled between two mirrors so reflections of the reflections flickered across the room. The tension in her chest melted at the sight of the flowers and, skipping across the small space, Annabelle flung down the large bag of clothes and cosmetics she was carrying and carefully disentangled the ribbon from the stems. A few yellow petals fell to the floor as she tried to get to the card. Denny loves me after all, she thought, struggling with a knot in the ribbon. He really does. Eager for affirmation, she pulled at the ribbon, beheading a red tulip in the process, and tore open the card.

Good luck with the show! We're behind you all the way! Best from Jillian and Keith.

Disappointment coursed through her like a gulp of tequila, making her chest pound and sending a rush of warmth to her face. If the flowers weren't from Denny, then nothing had changed and he still . . . Still what? she wondered. Still hated her? No, he said he loved her and that must be right—despite the way he'd been acting the last few days. Maybe he was as nervous about her New York opening as she was. He wanted what was best, he *knew* what was best, and when he got angry, it was only because she didn't listen to him. Denny had to take care of her, like a good man should.

Only the vaguest memories lingered of her own father—and she couldn't be sure that the fearsome figure she remembered was *really* her father and not just the man her mother was living with then. Rather than picturing him, she sometimes sensed him in her bones: he was huge and menacing and always smelled of beer and sweat. When he came home at night, he would gather her in his big arms to hug her, but more often than not, the night ended with a spanking. A spanking that she *deserved*. Though she was tiny and frail then, she was always doing something wrong. Sometimes she would beg him not to hit her, but that just made him angrier and made the beatings more severe. Her mother would send her to her room, and then she would lie in bed, trembling, waiting for his heavy footsteps. But he *loved* her. That's what had mattered. He had *loved* her. When he raised his hand to her, he growled, "I'm hitting you because I love you. I don't want you to grow up bad." His giant hand would smash down on her bottom, and even then she didn't cry because he wanted her to be a brave girl, and if she cried, he would hit her harder.

When he left for good, Annabelle couldn't have been more than five years old. Her mother was too sad to think of hitting her, but Annabelle wished she would, because his leaving was all her fault. If she had been a better child, he would have stayed, and they wouldn't have become so poor.

That's why she would be good with Denny—so he would never leave her.

She busied herself removing the makeup from her bag and setting it up on her dressing table. She wished Denny were with her right now because coming to the theatre all by herself had filled her with panic. There she was, walking in the stage door by herself, and Bruce Springsteen had come over and said hello. It could have been a wonderful moment, but she was too scared to appreciate it. What was she supposed to say to Bruce Springsteen? Why were they even on the same program? She had scampered off to find her dressing room and thought she caught sight of Diana Ross—God, she was gorgeous in person—standing inside the spacious star's dressing room right next door. Half-a-dozen people were bustling around Diana, but she had waved when Annabelle walked by. Annabelle opened her mouth to say hello, and only the silliest croak emerged.

What if that happened to her tonight, when she opened her mouth onstage? The boys in the band always talked about how she came alive the moment she began to perform, and it was true—hitting the spotlight seemed to turn her into a different person. She thought of it like a switch in the back of her brain that flicked on when exposed to bright lights and cheering fans. All her fears went away; she wasn't a scaredy-cat anymore. But she lived in terror that the switch would break and one day she'd wind up onstage and still be herself. She'd start groping for the switch, but the truth was, she wouldn't know where to find it. Denny wanted her to take a few snorts of coke before she went on, but she put her foot down on that. No. Absolutely not. Until the switch turned off by itself, she wasn't going to fool with it.

The signs in front of the theatre said SOLD OUT, but she was sure no one was coming to see her. The lines were for Bruce Springsteen and Diana Ross and all the other big names. Compared to them, Annabelle Fox was nobody. The seats would probably be empty when she walked onstage, everyone out buying popcorn or smoking joints. Four decades of rock and roll, and hers was the voice that nobody cared about. If this were just a regular concert, she would have been the opening act on the program—the least important coming first. But television had its own rules, and the producers had insisted on hitting with the big guns at the top. Keep people from switching channels. Annabelle was to be like the last guest on Johnny Carson—an oddity that was slipped in at the end, for whatever time was left. Come to think of it, maybe she wouldn't have to perform at all.

From the dressing room next door, she heard noise and laughter, which made the silence in her own room even more stunning. She looked around for a radio or television—her constant companions these days in the hotel—but didn't find one. There wasn't even a clock, so she couldn't judge how much more time she had to get ready. Probably too much.

When she heard a knock on the door, Annabelle opened it eagerly. The burst of pleasure she felt at seeing Jillian standing there was immediately replaced by dread. Denny didn't like Jillian. Didn't trust her. And he had been so angry the last time they'd been together.

"Did you just arrive?" Jillian asked.

"Few minutes ago." She kept her hand on the doorknob, not sure if she should let Jillian in or not. How was she supposed to know who to trust anymore? Jillian had been nicer to her than anyone in ages, and they'd had so much fun going shopping. It was almost like having a girlfriend again. Jillian marched into the shops in SoHo as if she owned them, and Annabelle felt free with her—freer than she had in ages. When Annabelle tried on skintight leopard-print pants, Jillian teased her about whether or not she should walk around the New York jungle looking like that. So Annabelle went to put them back, but Jillian said, "Don't you dare. This is probably the only chance I'll have in my whole life to buy something like that." Jillian tossed her American Express Gold Card at the salesclerk, and while she was ringing it up, Jillian found some green rubber-framed sunglasses that Annabelle fell in love with immediately. Looking at the two of them, you'd think their tastes couldn't be more different, but Jillian just seemed to understand.

"I wanted to start shooting some before-the-show candids, if you don't mind," Jillian said. "My cameraman's around the corner, but you let me know if you're ready for him."

Annabelle looked around helplessly. How was she to know whether or not she was ready? She tried to remember everything Denny had told her about what to say on television. She was going to do it right this time and make Denny proud.

"We just want to get shots of you preparing for the concert," Jillian said, filling in Annabelle's silence. "Putting on your makeup and your stage clothes—all that."

"I guess it's okay."

"Good." But instead of going off to get her cameraman, Jillian said, "Can I come in and talk to you for a moment?"

"Sure." Annabelle stepped out of the doorway, realizing that she had been blocking it. Jillian slipped by her and half-shut the door.

"I just wanted to make sure that everything is okay with you. You've been hard to reach the last couple of days."

"Yes, well . . ." She paused, remembering what Denny said. *Don't confide in anyone. These people aren't your friends.* "It's just been busy."

Jillian nodded. "I sure understand about being busy. But if there's anything troubling you, I want you to let me know. We're going to be spending a lot of time together in the next couple of weeks, and I don't want you to be at all uncomfortable."

"Oh, I'm comfortable with you," Annabelle said ingenuously. "I had fun shopping the other day."

"Me too. You should know, though, that I had a bit of a run in with Denny a little while ago. I think we've straightened it out. I don't want there to be any bad feelings."

Annabelle nodded mutely.

"Everything good between you and Denny?"

Denny had warned her about that. People like Jillian could be tricky. Try to get her to say things she didn't mean and didn't want to say. *Never* ever *say anything bad about me. They'll screw you to the wall for it.* "Everything's fine with Denny," Annabelle said. Trying not to sound too anxious, she asked, "Do you know where he is?"

"He's floating around the theatre somewhere. I'm sure he'll be here in a few minutes." Jillian checked her watch. "Why don't I grab my cameraman Nathan and come right back. Try to ignore us when we're shooting, by the way. Just do what you normally would before a show."

A moment after Jillian left, Annabelle sat down on the floor to do some stretching exercises—legs astraddle, trying to touch her chest to the floor. The ritual always made it easier for her to breathe when she felt nervous. Funny, it was something she'd stumbled on herself, and just the other day on one of those American chat shows on television, she'd seen some bouncy exercise expert talking about it. Exercise released the diaphragm, the woman said. Allowed you to breathe deeply and ease your nerves. Of course, Annabelle wouldn't have bothered to try it on that woman's advice, because she had already figured out that those chat shows were full of malarkey. Like the one she'd been watching yesterday when Denny walked in—the one that made him so mad. It wasn't like she was really paying attention to it—just background noise so she didn't feel so alone in the hotel. The host of the show was a big black lady who walked around the audience with a microphone, and people just stood up and said personal things about their lives. Most of the women who got up talked about their sex lives and their husbands, and the black lady was saying that no man had a right to humiliate you for any reason. One lady looked straight into the camera and said that anyone who was being abused at home should drop whatever she was doing, put aside all her excuses, and *leave right then*. That's when Denny walked in and started hollering about the trash on American television. He wanted to know why the fuck Annabelle was sitting around when she should be rehearsing. And, of course, that wasn't fair, because she had just been waiting for *him* to go to the rehearsal studio. It wasn't her fault that he was two hours late.

The dressing room door opened, and Annabelle, her back to the door, didn't bother to turn around until she heard the lock click and realized that it wasn't Jillian and the cameraman who had come in.

"Well, look at my dolly," Denny said leeringly. "Knew I was coming and got your legs spread for me already, eh?"

"Just doing exercises." She snapped her legs closed and spun around on her bottom to face him. "So glad you're here. They're going to start filming in a minute, and I didn't want to do it alone."

"They'll wait," Denny said. He got on his knees next to her, his rough hands on her shoulders. "We've got something to do first, don't we? Get ready for the show and all. Lie down, love."

"Not now, Denny." She looked at him pleadingly and braced herself with one arm firmly planted on the gritty carpet. "Really, Jillian's going to be back in a minute."

"Since when do I give a fuck about Jillian?" His position on his knees gave him enough leverage to push her down; her arm gave way and she was lying flat on her back.

"Please, Denny, I don't want to." She lay almost frozen, knowing that if she squirmed to get away, it would just excite him more. What was it that black lady had said? Anybody who takes you against your will is raping you. Even if it's your husband.

How about if it was your manager, the man who controlled your life?

"You don't have a right to do this," she said boldly. Heck, Diana Ross had just said hello to her. She was *someone*.

"I have a right to do whatever I want. You're mine, remember?" He was pulling down his jeans with one hand, keeping his full weight on her so she couldn't escape. Skinny as he was, she couldn't push him off her. It was impossible to do *anything* when you were lying on your back. His rough, bony knees pressed against her smooth thighs, forcing her to spread her legs. The day was so warm that she had come out bare-legged, wearing a flouncy denim skirt with ankle socks and sneakers. Denny pushed the skirt up so that the layers of denim were flung over her face, and she felt herself choking against the material covering her mouth. She spluttered and coughed, and Denny moved his hand just enough for her to shake loose of the material.

"You've got to stop," she said, gasping for breath. Denny's taking her had always been a game she didn't much enjoy, but suddenly now it was worse than that.

"No way I'm going to stop. I want your cunt." His rough fingers scratched at her thighs, finding the little scrap of material that was her only protection. "Pick up your ass," he growled, trying to tug off the panties. But she wouldn't. "Your ass," he repeated, and this time he pulled at the panties with such force that the string of material connecting the front and back panels ripped, and there was no way left to resist him. As he thrust himself inside her, she gave a small yelp of pain. Her body was dry and unwelcoming, but he didn't care, and he pounded himself in and out while she closed her eyes and made tight fists at her side against the insult. He cursed softly, and growled, "That's my bitch. My own bitch! I take her when I want." When he ground himself into her, his hipbone seemed to pierce the soft skin at her waist, and she cried, "Stop, Denny, it hurts!"

But to him, the pain was a sign of his manhood, and he muttered, "It hurts because I'm big and I fuck you deep." She didn't contradict him, just waited for the heaving that meant he had come.

When he finally rolled off her, breathing heavily, they both heard the gentle knocking on the door. Denny stood and zipped his jeans, then pulled her up. Shaking, she tried to get back on her feet, and when she stood up, she felt his semen already beginning to trickle down her inner thighs. So he thought he had a big cock, did he? Not as far as she was concerned. Maybe it was the drugs—coke today, again, wasn't it?—that made him seem so shriveled. Sure he could hurt her when he shoved himself inside because even after all she'd done, she was tight down there. But he left his come an inch from her opening, so her body could reject it the moment she stood. *Small dick, small dick, Denny has a small dick.* It sounded like a nursery rhyme in her head and made her giggle when she looked at him. Somehow that made her feel much, much better.

When the concert started, Jillian was in the control room, pressed against the wall, without even enough room to pace.

"I want this to be good," Emil had whispered. "I think of it as your comeback show."

Suddenly, she realized just how nervous she was. For a few years now, the baby years, she had been resting on her laurels, impressing people in Melrose with all that she had accomplished in television. The tales of her success had made her different and special, which is what she wanted to be, but they were wearing thin. Now it was time to start accomplishing again.

Emil settled into his seat, joking with his cameramen over the headsets. Tits and ass time, Jillian thought, remembering the crude comments that usually passed for humor when a crew was getting ready for a show. It was part of the weird ritual of male bonding. Prove how macho you all are, and then you're ready to work together. The increased number of women operating cameras hadn't changed the ritual; a woman was welcome as long as she was willing to be one of the boys. Jillian had learned simply to stay away when the boys' games were going on and assert herself when professionalism had returned.

Given the tight quarters, she couldn't help overhearing Emil's banter—and realized that it was different. No jokes about women or directions to camera two to take all tight shots of breasts. He gave his instructions calmly and pleasantly, and when he was comfortable with the angles they were giving him and convinced that all the cameramen were ready, he flicked off the talk switch on his microphone and turned to Jillian.

"Get everything you need backstage?" he asked.

"For the moment. We're done in the dressing room, and Nathan is just shooting some generic footage. I'll go back as soon as the show starts."

There was no particular reason for her to be in the control room just then—other than that she found it comforting. Something strange had been going on in Annabelle's dressing room when Jillian first went back with Nathan. Annabelle had looked positively teary-eyed when she'd opened the door. At her request, they'd given her ten minutes to pull herself together, but once Jillian and Nathan went in to start shooting, everything was fine. Denny sat on a stool crooning words of encouragement while Annabelle put on her makeup, and she warbled a few uncertain notes, warming up.

Emil turned back to the monitors, and a few moments later, the assistant director began counting down for the show to begin. Even though there was nothing much left for her to do, Jillian felt a thudding in her chest—more excitement than nerves. She wanted to stay and watch from the security of the control room, but it wasn't fair to abandon Nathan, so she slipped out just as she heard Emil calling into his microphone, "Let's do it, everybody."

The electricity from the audience coursed through the theatre, making its way backstage to where Jillian found Annabelle cowering, her face a mask of anxiety. She wouldn't appear for well over an hour, but she was staring into the mirror, putting a final swirl into her hair and piercing glittery gold dangling earrings through her earlobes. In her dressing room, the roar of the crowd was muted, a distant rumble impinging on the strained silence that seemed to reverberate between Annabelle and Denny. He sat slouched and unmoving in a chair, eyes half-closed, thoroughly indifferent to what was going on.

"How do I look?" Annabelle asked Jillian uncertainly.

"Terrific." The quiet in the room surprised her. Though Annabelle Fox was a big star making her New York debut, there were no hairdressers or makeup artists around to help her out. She'd have to remember to ask her about that on-camera sometime.

Jillian was bursting to see what was happening onstage, but she sat quietly with Annabelle, chatting perfunctorily, through most of the first half of the concert. When Springsteen came onstage, Annabelle stood up.

"I wanna go see him," she said. "I'll watch from the wings. That okay, Denny?"

"I already gave you permission for that," he said, sounding irritated, but he got up anyway to follow her out.

Annabelle found a spot at the edge of the stage where she was well hidden by pulleys and curtains—and almost immediately became engrossed by the star. Jillian gestured to Nathan to join them, and he got a shot of Annabelle looking wide-eyed out at the stage, then jumping up and down like a teenybopper when Springsteen broke into "Born to Run." The audience was jubilant at Springsteen's performance, and Annabelle was a woman transformed by delight.

Springsteen was sweating when he finally stepped off the stage, and whether it was because he saw the camera or felt the high of the moment, he gave Annabelle a big hug that literally lifted her off her feet, then rushed back to the spotlight to acknowledge the crowd that was stomping and whistling and screaming.

Nathan went to change batteries in the camera, and Jillian made her way over to the control room to find Keith standing outside the trailer, smoking a cigarette.

"What do you think?" Jillian asked.

"It's a winner." Keith threw the cigarette to the ground and stepped on it. "The concert's great, and Emil is shooting the hell out of it. That man's talented."

Jillian went into the trailer where, even though it was intermission, the monitors were glowing with the images of the show. Emil was replaying the Springsteen number, and watching on tape what she had seen moments earlier live gave Jillian a strange sensation. The camera had been in tight on Springsteen's face when he finished the song, then pulled back as he ran offstage. The next image was a shot from a low angle, catching Annabelle full face and Springsteen from behind, their double silhouette in the lower corner of the screen almost overpowered by the bursting brightness of the stage lights that filled the rest. As Springsteen picked up Annabelle, she tossed back her head and kicked up her legs; for a split second, hair and toes almost met in an arc behind her. "Freeze it there!" Emil called. The technical director pushed a button, and the fleeting image that Emil had noticed was now caught forever. Emil nodded in satisfaction. "Use that as the bumper going into commercial," he said to his assistant. "Have chyron add a line that says 'Still to come . . . Annabelle Fox!'" He leaned back in his chair—nearly knocking over Jillian as he did so.

110

"Whoa, I'm sorry!" Instinctively, he spun around and grabbed her around the waist. "I didn't even realize you were there."

"My fault. I was so intent on watching that I didn't realize I was hanging on to the back of your chair."

"No problem. Are you okay?"

"I'm fine. Sorry I was too close."

"You could never be too close."

Jillian started to respond, but noticing that the technical director was listening avidly, she let it drop.

"I think I'll go outside for a breath of air," Emil said.

Stepping outside the trailer, Emil reached up to help Jillian on the stairs again. As their hands touched, she realized hers were cold and damp. "You concentrate so intently during a shoot," Emil said. He touched the furrowed space between her brows. "Such intensity in your eyes. I love looking at them."

"I worry a lot," Jillian admitted, "but watching what you do certainly makes me calmer."

"Does that mean you've forgiven me for intervening with Denny?"

"Hardly." Jillian felt herself bristling again. "But if you'd like to be assigned the responsibility of keeping Denny Wright from going over the edge, I'm glad to give it to you. The man strikes me as a full-fledged psychopath."

"I worry about your being around him. Can I ask you to do me a favor? Don't get yourself into any situations where you're alone with him." When Jillian tossed her head coltishly, Emil touched her hair. "I know you can handle yourself in any situation, and that you *will* handle yourself. But I want to protect you. Is that such a terrible thing?"

"You ask questions that are too difficult to answer during an intermission."

"Well, then, let's save the conversation. Intermission is almost over anyway." Emil looked at her reflectively, then headed back to the control room, and after hesitating for a moment, Jillian went backstage to await Annabelle's performance.

It was worth waiting for. From the moment she stepped onstage in her skintight, gold-sequined bodysuit, the audience went wild. Her first song was "No More Teenage Virgins," and Annabelle pranced around the stage, pouting and posing. The young fans in the audience screamed in delight, and those who had come to see the older stars still cheered appreciatively.

"She's amazing," Nathan said to Jillian. He started to swing his camera around to Denny, who was just a few feet away from them, but Jillian whispered, "Keep focused on stage." She wasn't interested in any more shots of the glowering manager. Annabelle lurched into her next song, "Kissables," and the audience began applauding at almost the first note: the hit song was as familiar as a road sign. For the last year, Annabelle Fox's music had been in the air; you didn't have to listen for it to hear it. How many times had Jillian heard snatches of these songs as she switched stations on the car radio? For a long time, she hadn't linked the music with the name, and she imagined people at home watching the concert who didn't know Annabelle Fox turning to each other and saying, "That's her song?" and then, "That's her song, *too.*" To anybody who hadn't been living in a cave for the last year, the music would be familiar. Disc jockeys seemed to love Annabelle's tunes; they played them over and over. And her music crossed all lines. Jillian had heard it on rock stations, Top Ten stations, light listening . . . In an amazingly short time, Annabelle Fox had gone from being unknown to being one of the biggest stars in the business.

Where had she come from, anyway? Jillian was glad to be doing the special, because she wanted to find out.

Annabelle finished her song, and long before the audience finished cheering, the band hit the music for the next number. The applause, just starting to die down from "Kissables," rolled in again like a wave, and Annabelle's voice soared above it. Jillian felt her own heart thudding in excitement, the energy from Annabelle's performance reaching out to her in the wings.

"Hey. There's been a misunderstanding."

Jillian jumped, hearing Denny's voice. He was standing right next to her. He moved like a cat burglar, and she immediately flashed on Emil's warning about being alone with him. It was silly, of course, and even sillier for the thought to occur to her now, when there were hundreds of people just a few feet away from them. Strange that he should choose now to talk. Wasn't he interested in seeing Annabelle's performance?

"What's the misunderstanding?" She didn't really want to talk to him, but he was impossible to ignore.

"Annabelle won't be at the party after the concert. We don't do that. And I don't want you asking her about it—you hear?"

Her instinct was to tell him that it was a free country and she'd ask Annabelle anything she chose, but instead she bit back the petulance and, staying in character as a producer, asked, "Where will you be going instead?"

"Back to the hotel. That's what we do. And there'll be no cameras."

Onstage the band was cooking, and Annabelle's clear voice cut through the music. As the lyrics got suggestive, Annabelle's lithe body contorted in pleasure, and her open mouth suggested nothing so much as a woman in the throes of orgasm. "No celebrating," Denny hissed. "Nothing!" He swaggered away, and Jillian felt a sheet of fear momentarily wrapping itself around her. Her first impression—that he was a crazed but harmless druggie—had been replaced by something more ominous. He was a thug. A con man. His very presence frightened her.

Annabelle's number was over, and she took her bows, breathless and glowing. When she ran out to the wings to hug Denny, her energy was like an overcharged burst of electricity. A moment later, she joined the other performers for a finale that had been written just for the concert, and the disparate voices, representing forty years of rock and roll, broke into a song called "Decades." Jillian had expected it to be tacky, but instead it was glorious. Three of the cameramen were taking shots of the audience, and Jillian knew just what Emil was doing—intercutting close-ups of the stars with shots of people of all ages in the audience. There was a father in the second row who had his arm around his preteen son. A girl who looked about fourteen leaned on her mother's shoulder. The idea worked. Music reaching across the generations.

As the show ended and the curtain fell, hugs and congratulations were scattered around the stage. Nathan got a few shots of Annabelle being hugged and patted by some of the other stars, but after just a few minutes, Denny put his hands on Annabelle's shoulders and started to pull her away. Even from a distance, Jillian could see that they were exchanging words—Annabelle was trying to shake him off, but he was holding her tightly and soon whisked her away from the pack of stars. Jillian tried to follow them, but by the time she got back to Annabelle's dressing room, Denny was standing outside like a mastiff protecting the entrance.

"No admittance this time," he growled. "That's the end of the night. Good-fucking-bye."

"I just wanted to congratulate Annabelle. She was terrific."

"She's heard how terrific she is. That's enough."

"There must be some way I can convince you to come to the party." She tried to keep her voice light, so he wouldn't take it as a threat.

"No way. Good-bye. You hear me? Good-bye."

■

"But I *want* to go to the party." Looking at Denny in her dressing room mirror, Annabelle stabbed at her eyelid with a cotton pad soaked in makeup remover, leaving an angry streak in the thick gold grease that she had applied so carefully. As she continued to dab at the eyelid, her face took on a strange, masklike appearance. Remnants of the heavy makeup remained smeared above her eye; below it smudges of mascara and eyeliner formed a black half-circle that made her face seem puffy and weathered.

"I have every right to go to that party if I want." The night's success made her defiant, willing even to forget the consequences of standing up to Denny. Bruce Springsteen had *hugged* her. And after the concert, when the heavy curtain had fallen for the last time, Diana Ross had told her she was going to be a big, big star. The audience loved her. How could Denny Wright tell her not to go to the party? "It's not the right career move," he had told her a few minutes ago, onstage. She was known as the girl who didn't party. Yes, they were letting Jillian shoot that show about her, but she shouldn't get too much publicity yet. No use changing her image right now when the

114

old image had gotten her so far. Besides, she wasn't ready for a party like that, he insisted. She might fuck it up.

But she had done everything right so far. Been a good girl in New York. Had a smash debut. When was she supposed to be rewarded for it and have a little fun?

"I've been working my bones off, Denny Wright, and I don't think you care." She waved the makeup-covered pad like a bloody bandage of war, a symbol of her courage. "I get so scared before a concert, but I do it. I step out onstage, and I'm not trembling anymore, and everyone *loved* me. You saw it, Denny, didn't you? Everyone wants to congratulate me and kiss me, but I come back here when you say, and now you tell me that's the end—I can't even celebrate. It's not fair, Denny. I don't even know anymore if you want me to be happy." A few tears mixed into the smeared eye makeup, and she swatted at the whole mess with her gold-sequined sleeve. Her own words surprised her; they first caught in her throat, then tumbled out, her momentary indignation stronger than her fear.

She was prepared for Denny to yell at her, to hit her, to smash her into the wall and call her an ungrateful bitch, as he so often did. But even though it had been a while tonight since he took a hit of coke, she wasn't prepared to see his eyes soften. When he came over to her, it wasn't to menace her, but to put his arms around her shoulders and pull her close to him.

"My dolly did a great job," he said, rocking her gently, almost like a baby. "Denny loves his Annabelle. Of course we're going to celebrate, but it will be you and me celebrating. Just like it's always been. We're the ones who made it, and nobody can take that away from us. I won't let them. They're all going to try, dolly, you don't understand that. Everyone else wants to hurt you and knock you down, but Denny is here to protect you. I won't let anyone get near you because I love you and I'm going to take care of you."

"Do you really love me, Denny?"

"Jesus, I love you more than anything. Would I go through all this if I didn't? You gotta trust me. Denny knows best. And Denny loves you." He kissed the back of her neck, then unzipped the gold-sequined bodysuit and pulled it down until her small nipples popped out; he covered then with wet kisses, his tongue drawing circles which excited her. Getting down on his knees, he pulled off the costume, so she was standing naked in front of him.

"We're going to have two bottles of champagne at the hotel and celebrate ourselves. Denny's going to make you feel good tonight. Anything you want." He picked her up as he liked to do, a small bare bundle in his arms. "How does that sound, love? Anything you want."

"I like it, Denny." She kissed his lips, trying not to notice that they were hard and puckered. So the night was going to be a triumph to the end, after all. Denny loved her again.

That's all she really wanted.

■

"There was no way you could convince her to come?" Keith stood outside Chopsticks, in brief consultation with Jillian. Limousines clogged the street in front of the restaurant, but Jillian was convinced that Annabelle wouldn't be stepping out of one of them.

"No way at all. I thought Annabelle looked upset when Denny dragged her off after the show, so I waited for her at the backstage door for close to an hour. By the time she came out, she and Denny were strolling hand-in-hand, and they both seemed perfectly content. She said she was sorry to miss the party, but she'll see us in a few days in Los Angeles. There was a big crowd waiting at the stage door, and she stopped to give autographs." Denny had kept his hand on her elbow all the while, and Annabelle signed the concert programs and scraps of paper that were thrust in her face. With her makeup off, she seemed too young to be out so late at night.

"Shit." Keith looked out at the street, where two chauffeurs were leaning against a long white limousine chatting as casually as two co-workers at the office water fountain. The fact that it was late at night and cars behind them were furiously honking their horns didn't seem to disturb them.

"I don't think it matters much for the show," Jillian said. She took a deep breath, still trying to clear the smoky tension of the theatre from her lungs. The air was unusually crisp and fresh for New York. "Nathan's inside right now shooting the other stars, and we'll use the footage. It might be even more effective since Annabelle's not with them. You see rock stars at parties all the time, but we'll have the footage of this fabulous party going on, and maybe get a voice-over from her explaining why she wasn't interested. Sort of like Marlon Brando not coming to the Academy Awards. It's news."

Keith eyed her dubiously, then kicked at a crack in the sidewalk with the soft leather toe of his Italian moccasins. "You're right it will work in the show, but for now it kills all the p.r. value."

He turned to go into the restaurant and Jillian, suddenly feeling weary, was pleased to see Emil sauntering over to her.

"Are you partying tonight?" he asked.

"I think I'd rather just stand quietly on the sidewalk," Jillian said. "My head is spinning. I'm sure you've heard that Annabelle isn't coming?"

"Yes, I heard. So I was wondering if I could buy you a drink and finish that conversation we started at intermission."

"That sounds wonderful. Let's go someplace quiet and far away from all this. Nathan has almost finished shooting, and I've quite had it."

"I'm with you, if that's what you'd like."

In an instant, Jillian reconsidered. "Oh gosh, I really shouldn't. There are all those executives from Wink Cola inside, and they shouldn't be ignored, since they happen to be our sponsors. Could you bear to stay here for a little bit?"

Emil laughed. "I've never seen you ambivalent before. The decisive Jillian van Dorne can't decide where to have her drink. Let me make a suggestion. I'd like to disappear, too, but you'll be angry at yourself if you do. Let's go inside, and when you've finished playing the crowd and doing your business socializing, we'll go wherever you'd like."

"It's a deal." Inside, Jillian put on her business face again. She mingled and chatted, squeezing the arm of an Entertainment Channel executive named Dick Slavin and accepting a peck on the cheek from Henry Munroe, the president of Wink Cola. Emil stayed close to Jillian's side, shaking hands with the businessmen and frequently leaning over to whisper someone's name to her or share a funny insight on the scene. Jillian found herself giggling and leaning close to him.

"You two are quite a team," Henry Munroe commented at one

117

point, taking the glass of champagne that a waitress proferred on a black lacquer tray. "When we put out this much money on a project, it's nice to know that we're working with the best."

A p.r. flack from Wink came over then and excused himself for interrupting. "But it's time to get some pictures," he said. "The press is here."

Jillian watched him expertly position Munroe near the biggest stars, so they would be talking casually when the photographers' flashbulbs went off. The pictures would appear in various newspapers and magazine celebrity columns. Good publicity, though not exactly free, Jillian thought, noticing how quickly the champagne was disappearing. Her own glass was almost full, and she looked over at Emil's glass and noticed that he, too, had taken only a few sips. What was this attraction she felt for him tonight? Simple relief that he had brought in such a gorgeous show? She took another sip of champagne and realized that the attraction was mixed with a physical longing, a pleasure at being so close to him tonight, sensing his attentive presence.

"When can we get out of here?" he whispered when they were briefly alone.

"Soon, I hope."

"I'd invite you to my hotel to have a drink, but I'm afraid you'd say no."

She *would* say no, of course, but she didn't want to. Emil's powerful, sexy body attracted her as the devil's own temptation. Lurking inside her was the Jillian van Dorne of long ago, an original woman not bound by the constraints of family. Even for a night, it would be nice to live as if she had no responsibilities except to her own desires.

But she couldn't.

When she hesitated, he said, "Isn't there an American expression about 'Don't say no, say maybe'?"

She smiled. "I'm not sure, but 'maybe' sounds like a reasonable answer one way or another."

He sighed heavily. "Your friend Mr. Munroe is right, you know. We *do* make a good team. We understand each other and have the same rhythms and needs."

118

"Professionally, of course."

"Of course."

Across the room, somebody tapped a glass for attention, and Henry Munroe took a microphone and made a brief, ingratiating speech. Then several other people at the party got up to say words of praise and thanks, and more champagne flowed. By the time it was all over, it was early morning, and Jillian had no choice—it was time to go home.

Emil walked her to the limousine that would take her home and said good-bye. When the driver closed the door, Jillian opened the window, expecting Emil to lean over and kiss her. But he stayed politely on the curb, and as the car pulled away, she lost him immediately in the darkness.

CHAPTER SEVEN

WHEN Mark arrived home from London, Jillian confronted him—almost out of the blue, he thought—and told him she was frightened that they were letting their family fall apart. He thought at first that she knew, or at least had surmised, about Cynthia, but she made no mention of it, and her concerns seemed more generic.

"I don't want a divorce," she said—and her even using the word stunned him. "We're both too smart and insightful to stop talking and allow our family to disintegrate."

"It's not disintegrating. But, hey, you've gone back to work and the rules have changed." Knowing how she would respond even before she started, he added, "I don't mean it's all your fault. It's just that life goes on and things aren't always the same. Look, maybe we're not as passionate as we were eight years ago, but it's not worth getting crazy about it."

"I'm just not sure what we're protecting anymore," she said. "We're both so careful not to shake things up, and you're keeping everything locked in. Maybe I am, too, because I don't tell you how much it hurts when you make no effort at all to support my career. You just resent it, for whatever your reasons. You go off to London at the one time it would be nice to have you home, and then you don't even want to talk to me on the phone when you're there. It hurts to be talking to your husband and know that he can't wait to hang up."

Mark said nothing, just looked at his fingers and used the back of his thumb to worry an overgrown cuticle on his ring finger. Jillian seemed close to tears but kept her voice soft and her emotions in check when she went on. "We've been married for eight years, and I trust you. But I also know that we're human. I don't expect you never to look at another woman again, but if something is going on with you, it doesn't have to kill the marriage. Let's work on it like grown-ups and figure out something that will keep both of us satisfied."

So maybe she *did* know about Cynthia. Know that they had tumbled back into bed in London, after all. Overcome by the bliss of her soft skin and her womanly scent, he had forgotten his plan to remind her that theirs was just an affair; and as he drank in her loveliness for hour after hour, he began to wonder if his forgetfulness was caused by desires even deeper than lust.

But Jillian couldn't know about that. She was only guessing from his distracted behavior. She tried to get him to talk, but Mark knew when to remain silent. Why discuss something that could do nothing but hurt her more? He didn't see what he had to gain by being honest with Jillian. His concession to her entreaties was to promise to try harder at home.

And he did that. Every night for a week he came home early enough to have dinner with the children and help put them to sleep. If he had to read *Goodnight Moon* to Eve one more time, he was going to scream. Eve had no interest in any of the dozens of other books on her shelves, and getting her to sleep demanded endless readings about the goddamn great green room with its telephone and red balloon and picture of the cow jumping over the moon. He could recite that book backward and forward, but he hadn't had the chance to look at a newspaper in days. Lila, at least, had varied tastes. Despite a certain fondness for *Chicken Little*, she was perfectly happy to read the books Mark bought her about construction and skyscrapers and architecture. Her studying books, Lila called them, and despite his suspicion that she was reading them only to please him, Mark had to admit a certain pride in his elder daughter's willingness to learn.

Juggling both children at bedtime was a chore Mark had never learned to manage, and when Jillian called one night to say she would be late, he cursed himself for having already given Marguerite the night off. He skipped giving the girls a bath because he couldn't stand cleaning up the water they always splashed onto the floor; still, there were hands to wash and teeth and hair to brush and pajamas to find. Eve would not put on her teddy bear pajamas and insisted on her Care Bear nightgown, which he couldn't locate anywhere. She whined endlessly while he searched through drawers, finding enough outfits to clothe the children in an entire Third World country but no Care Bear nightgown. Eve tossed herself to the ground, announcing that if she couldn't have the nightgown she wanted, she wouldn't put on anything.

"Then you can sleep naked, for all I care!" he shouted. His roaring made her burst into tears, and he had to spend the next twenty minutes calming her down. He wondered how Jillian had done it when both girls were smaller and he was always late.

By Saturday morning, Mark announced that he had to spend some time at the office, and though he caught Jillian's look of hurt and bewilderment, he was unmoved. She had arranged for the family to spend the day together at a farm upstate—all of them together outdoors, she told Mark, and they would remember the family joy they were trying to preserve.

Mark liked family weekends but enough was enough; he had been making the sacrifices all week, and it was time for Jillian to pick up some of the slack. He didn't consider it vengeance exactly, though he did wonder sometimes if it was absolutely necessary for Jillian to be working so hard. What did they *do* at those production meetings, anyway? Having met Keith Ross on a few social occasions, Mark at least knew he didn't have to be jealous of him. Keith was a talented man and a very rich one but not someone his classy wife would consider in anything other than business terms. Of course, there were other people around, too, but Mark trusted Jillian, at least trusted her commitment to their marriage. And as far as he was concerned, there was nothing hypocritical about assuring himself of that just before going off to call Cynthia.

When Mark announced his intention to go to the office, he expected Jillian to cancel the farm trip, but by nine o'clock, she had the children piled into the car and ready for their excursion. Although it was September, the weather hadn't really turned to fall yet, and they wore short-sleeves and overalls and talked eagerly about what was in the large picnic basket that Jillian had put in the trunk.

"It will be at least an hour before we get there," Jillian warned the children as she turned on the motor. "Anyone want to go to the bathroom again?"

Mark came to the side of the car to say good-bye and looked to the backseat, where the girls were safely strapped in, Eve in a booster seat, Lila with a seatbelt. Each girl clutched a book or puzzle and a box of apple juice. Secrets for getting through a trip. Mark was impressed that Jillian had thought of everything, and as he looked at his wife in the car, her thick hair curling over the neck of a white cotton sweater, her face glowing with the anticipation of a day outside, he felt a momentary pang of regret at not joining her. But the children were already waving and throwing him good-bye kisses, so it was too late to change his mind without losing face.

"Have a good time!" he called.

"We will, Daddy! Wish you could come!"

Driving to his office, he tried to decide what would happen to the family if he were to go away for good. Not much, probably. Now that Jillian was making money again, she didn't really need him at all. Surely Jillian had doubts about her life, her vulnerabilities, but he had never really observed them. She made major life decisions without a moment's anguish that he could see. When she'd wanted to have her babies, she did; when she was ready to go back to her career, she did that, too. Her strength was attractive but at times overwhelming.

Jillian had asked him if he still loved her, and he said yes, but the truth was that he wasn't really sure. What was love supposed to mean anymore? It was Cynthia who aroused him sexually. Cynthia he dreamed about. But Jillian was right: divorce was messy, and they were somehow *above* that. Keep the surfaces smooth, and everything would be fine. He liked the idea of being married. Having a home base actually made it easier to wander—a truth he had come to one Sunday when he took Eve to the park and noticed that every few minutes she would run to him and hold his hand for a moment, sit on his lap, then go off again to the swings and the seesaw. He was a touchstone for her needs—and sometimes he felt that Jillian filled that role for him.

The moment Mark arrived at the office, he called Cynthia in

London, and they talked for over an hour. There was always something to say to Cynthia, even though most of the conversation today was recounting the great sex they'd had the last night they were together. Just talking to her made him so excited that he felt an erection pressing against his trousers.

"I hope this line isn't bugged," Cynthia whispered loudly after reporting in vivid detail how much she liked it when Mark stood behind her while she perched on all fours on the bed. Mark didn't admit that the position had been all Cynthia's inspiration; he had never done that before.

"If it is bugged, I hope the agents are having a good time," he said heartily.

"Any reason it should be bugged?" Cynthia sounded more curious than wary.

"No," Mark said, speaking loudly, pretending that there was indeed a third person who could hear. "We may be a construction company, but we're not involved with the Mafia. Our hands are clean. All our businesses are legal."

"Which won't be true next week," Cynthia said with a girlish giggle.

After he hung up, Mark tried to work, but he found himself reading the newspaper and picking up a magazine from the pile of mail. Maybe he should have gone to the farm with the family, after all. Better that than sitting here, wishing he were in London with Cynthia and dreaming about her fine, lush body moistening his with her passion.

He called home from the office several times during the day, getting no answer until almost five, when Jillian picked up the phone and explained that they had just walked in the door.

"We had a wonderful day in the country," Jillian said, sounding a bit breathless.

"How are the girls?"

"Fine, now. Eve threw up in the car on the way home—but I don't think she's sick. She just ate too much. It was a wonderful farm with a big apple orchard. The girls climbed the trees and picked every apple they could reach. They were ecstatic."

"How many did they get?"

"A little under two bushels." Jillian laughed. "I'm thinking of hiring them out for the season. They'd make great laborers."

"*Two bushels?*"

"Lots of apple pies and applesauce and apple pancakes," Jillian said cheerfully.

"I assume you all had fun, at least."

"It was terrific. You should have seen the girls climbing up the trees. They loved it. Lila was absolutely fearless. She climbs like a monkey."

In the background, Mark heard Eve calling to Jillian to help her in the bathroom.

"I'm going to run," Jillian said. "Don't forget we have the Robertsons' party tonight."

"Damn, I did forget."

"You'll make it, won't you?"

"Of course," he said, hanging up. The upscale couples in Melrose were constantly having dinner parties, and while Jillian turned down most of the invitations, she had eagerly accepted this one, since Sam Robertson was an investment banker who worked closely with the networks. Mark would have preferred staying home. It would probably be another party where he wouldn't know anyone and would spend the evening watching Jillian shine, feeling intimidated by his own wife. He felt a brief flash of irrational anger at Jillian for the fine family day she'd had without him.

■

Mark got home in time to kiss the girls good night and change into the gray suit Jillian had hung on the door of his closet. The Robertsons lived in a sprawling Spanish-style estate on the edge of the water in Melrose. By the time Jillian and Mark drove up, the circular driveway was crowded with the toys of the suburban rich: Jaguars, Porsches, and Ferraris. Two chauffeur-driven limousines, obviously bringing guests from the city, were double-parked in front of the house. After a tuxedoed butler let them in and took their coats, Jillian put her hand on Mark's arm and walked with him into the living room.

Waiters carrying silver trays immediately offered champagne, and as Jillian reached for a glass, Mark noticed several men in the room looking at her. She was wearing a simple black satin Valentino dress, the scalloped neckline showing off her silky pale skin. Her thick hair was pulled back elegantly with a satin bow, and Mark thought there was a rightness about her style, a confidence in her simplicity that was more appealing than the poufs and diamonds of the other women in the room. Across their champagne glasses he looked at her carefully and decided, as he had hundreds of times before, that the real source of her beauty was the character and intelligence of her flashing eyes.

"Jillian! What a pleasure to see you." A tall, heavyset man with thick gray hair came up behind them and kissed Jillian on the cheek. He introduced himself to Mark as Sam Robertson.

"I hope you won't mind my taking your wife for a bit," he said, a bit too heartily. "Several of my guests have been looking forward to meeting her."

Obviously excluded from the invitation, Mark watched Sam and Jillian move across the room, stopping several times for handshakes and introductions. Finishing his champagne, Mark went to the bar which had been set up in a corner of the dining room and asked for a double Dewar's straight up. Not normally a drinking man, he was in a mood to drink. Back in the living room, Mark noticed that a group of three or four men had gathered around Jillian. He recognized one of them as a past president of ABC News and assumed the others had similar posts. From the animated exchange going on, it was impossible to tell who was trying to impress whom, though all of the men were leaning close to Jillian, touching her arm to make a point, talking eagerly. She, at least, stood coolly still, enjoying the conversation.

He must have been staring across the room for too long because a small, dark-haired woman wearing a purple crushed-velvet suit with a diamond broach at the neck sidled up to him and said, "Ever wonder what they find to talk about?"

"Pardon?"

"Your wife and all our husbands. Don't worry, it has to be business. My husband hasn't had a personal conversation in the last ten years."

Mark wondered if the woman was drunk, but she seemed

126

pleasantly controlled, so he introduced himself and she extended a warm hand and said, "A pleasure to meet you. I'm Lydia Homestead. My husband is the slightly paunchy man gazing at your wife's breasts."

At a loss for how to respond, Mark offered his name, then asked, "What does your husband do?"

"He makes money. Officially, he's a lawyer, but really he's a dealmaker for the networks. Entertainment-type things. He gets everybody to sign the papers that they wanted to sign anyway, and they pay him huge amounts for that."

"And what do you do?"

"I work at home, as they say. That's supposed to be respectable again, but you and I both know that it's not. I was a social worker before I started having babies, but I couldn't figure out why my little ones should stay with a teenager baby-sitter while I helped other people's children deal with their problems."

"Sounds reasonable."

She shrugged. "That's what my husband Walter says, but I don't believe it. I'm sure he'd much rather be married to your Superwoman wife." She glanced over at the group around Jillian and saw that the conversation hadn't slowed. Turning back to Mark, she said, "I'm glad I met you, because now I don't have to be jealous. Walter may have designs on Jillian, but if she's got you at home, she wouldn't look twice at him."

Mark laughed. There was something innocent and charming about Lydia Homestead, despite her blunt talk. She continued to look over Mark's shoulder at the group across the room, where her husband was flirting wildly with Jillian. Catching the hurt look in her eye, Mark finally quipped, "Let me know if Walter and Jillian leave together. Then you and I can go out for a drink."

"I'd love it."

Mark took a long drag of his Dewar's, thinking how nice it would be to do that.

"So tell me," Lydia said, "is it wonderful having Superwoman for a wife?"

"Not particularly. I'd much rather have a wife who stayed home."

He was surprised to hear himself saying that. He knew it wasn't the staying at home that mattered so much as the taking care of him. Cynthia took care of him.

"How are your children?" Lydia asked.

"My children?" He looked at her quizzically, and she smiled.

"Our children go to nursery school together. I've admired your wife from afar for a long time, and I hear about you from my son."

Just then, Jillian appeared at Mark's side and slipped her arm through his. "Sam asks that we find our dinner partners and head to the tables," she said sweetly.

"Sounds good," Mark said. "By the way, honey, this is Lydia Homestead. Our children apparently go to school together."

"Nice to meet you," Jillian said.

He thought of leaving them together and going off to Sam's bedroom to call Cynthia. So what if it was two in the morning in London. She'd get a kick out of hearing a quick hello from him. Deciding against it, he walked with Jillian to the indoor courtyard where dinner was being served. They found their seats at a round table set with antique china and crystal; the courtyard was dim, and the soft glow from the candelabra in the center of the table seemed to reflect off Jillian's creamy skin and create a halo around her honeyed hair. My wife the angel, thought Mark, but when he turned to talk to her, he found that she had already struck up a conversation with the man on her left. What the hell. He *would* call Cynthia. Excusing himself from the table, he walked away quickly, and as he stepped back into the living room, he encountered Lydia Homestead and her husband coming in to dinner. Lydia smiled pleasantly at him but didn't stop to talk.

When they arrived home shortly after one in the morning, Mark flicked on the bedroom television set, switching channels until he got to a football game on the all-sports cable network. Jillian, who was taking off her jewelry in their dressing alcove, glanced at the television and noticed that the players seemed small and that the signs in the stadium were in Japanese. A taped game from the Japanese Football League? Amazing what got on TV lately.

Football wasn't one of Mark's great interests, so she knew the television was just a source of noise, a way of making it less obvious that they had nothing to say to each other. It was often like that on Saturday nights. After an evening of socializing with other couples, they felt embarrassed; they didn't quite know how to end the night once they were alone together. Too many years had passed for them to feel the thrill of desire, the heart-pounding passion they knew before they were married that would drive them to bed, grateful the formal evening activity was over.

"Did you enjoy talking to Lydia?" Jillian asked, slipping off her dress, barely turning around.

"She was pleasant enough." There was a hesitancy in his voice, a slight reluctance to press on. "Had you met her husband Walter before?"

"I'd seen him once or twice. He's quite influential at the networks, you know."

"So I heard."

She turned her back again, hunching over to pull off her slip and panty hose. There was no graceful way to do that, no way to make the act sensual rather than clumsy. Out of nowhere, she thought what it would be like to undress in front of Emil and suddenly understood the appeal of garter belts and silk panties; anything that would bring some grace to the interim stages before nakedness.

"Lydia was nicer than most of the other snobby types there," Mark said. "That wasn't exactly my crowd." He flicked off the television, and they faced each other: Mark bare to the chest, his trousers still on, she naked at last, pulling on her Christian Dior robe.

"I made some important contacts tonight, but I'm sorry if you had a miserable time. At least the dinner was good."

Mark shrugged, headed to the bathroom, and got out his toothbrush. Jillian walked in and began brushing her hair. "What did you and Walter talk about?" Mark asked.

"Network business, mostly," Jillian said. "I'm not sure you realized, but that was quite a powerful group of men there tonight. A lot of the network's big-money boys. But I meant to ask you—do Walter and Lydia have a son named Adam?"

Mark held up a finger to tell her to hold on a moment while he finished brushing his teeth. He spat the foam into the sink, and they both watched it curling lazily down the drain—until Mark turned the water on high, splashed his face, and rinsed the sink. He glanced at the toilet and Jillian left the bathroom unasked so he could urinate. They maintained a certain delicacy about bathroom functions, more his discreetness than hers, but she had learned to respect it. From behind the partly closed door, she heard the rush of his peeing, and his voice rising over it.

"I think the youngest one's name was Adam. They have three boys, and she said her youngest is in school with one of ours."

"Eve told me a few days ago that she was marrying Adam Homestead. I thought it was cute—Adam and Eve getting married."

"Getting married? She's not even four."

"Oh, you know what kids do." Jillian gestured vaguely, suddenly aware that he didn't know at all. "They're just beginning to understand the difference between boys and girls, so they crawl under the slide in the playground together and say they're married. It's all very cute and harmless."

The toilet flushed, and Mark opened the door, out of his trousers now, wearing only pajama bottoms.

Jillian took his place in the bathroom, ignoring her own image in the mirrors that circled the large room. But a reflection of the exercise bicycle in the corner caught her eye, and she felt a momentary pang of guilt, trying to remember the last time she had used it. There simply wasn't time anymore. She thought of the women like Walter's wife who spent one hundred percent of their time on husband, children, family, and self—the things that filled maybe ten percent of her time now. But she was going to make this complicated life of hers work.

The long marble counter next to the sink was decorated with baskets of scented soaps and embroidered linen towels, but Jillian washed with a bar of Ivory soap and patted her face dry with a white terry cloth. She tried to decide if she should slip in her diaphragm before getting into bed and decided not to bother. Saturday night or not, Mark would reject her if she approached him. She had tried too many times lately and been hurt too often to want to risk it again.

Mark was already under the covers, reading a magazine, when

she curled in beside him. He turned off the light, and she asked, "Are you going to work tomorrow?"

"No, I don't think so." Then he amended it. "Maybe for an hour or so in the morning."

"Don't forget I'm going to L.A. on Monday."

"I know." He felt awkward. "It's going to be hard for me to be home, so—"

"Don't worry," she said, interrupting him. "It's all arranged with Marguerite. She won't leave you for a minute."

"Well, good."

Jillian was feeling mellow, and she decided to excuse Mark all over again for distancing himself from the family and from her. It wasn't worth destroying the family over whatever was bothering him. Even if he's having an affair, she thought. Full of forgiveness, she was about to tell Mark that she loved him when he turned over so sharply that the only thing left to talk to was his back.

CHAPTER EIGHT

AT a little after nine o'clock at night, Barney Rossman called his wife Glenda on the speakerphone in his office to tell her that he was on his way home. He pressed the button that would dial their home number, and the sound of the ringing phone filled his otherwise quiet office. After a dozen or more rings, he hit the button to disconnect, and another button that would dial her office. At that number she picked up almost immediately.

"Glenda Petruski."

"Hello, Ms. Petruski. It's your husband."

"Hi, honey. Where are you calling from? You sound far away."

Calling on the speakerphone was an instinct with him, but now he picked up the receiver. "That better?" he asked.

"Much. You're still in the office?"

"Yup, but I was coming home. How are you doing?"

"Oh, honey, I'm sorry. I've got a brief that has to be done by eight o'clock tomorrow morning. I shouldn't be all night, but I'll be at least another couple of hours."

"That's okay. Maybe I'll stay here and finish up some work, too." He paused. "How is— I mean, are you feeling okay?"

Knowing exactly what he meant, she sniffled slightly and said, "It was a false alarm. I mean a false hope. Just one day late, as it turns out. I got my period this afternoon."

"Oh. Don't be upset. There's always next month." He eyed the brown paper bag from the pharmacy that he had left out on his desk so he wouldn't forget to take it home. The pharmacist had assured him that the at-home pregnancy tests were so reliable now that they could predict pregnancy with ninety-eight percent accuracy when the woman's period was just one day late. It was going to be Barney's little surprise for Glenda tonight. Oh well. He'd put it back in his drawer until next month. Nothing like a period to predict nonpregnancy with one hundred percent accuracy.

"Have you eaten dinner?" Glenda asked.

"Not yet. I was hoping we'd have it together, so—"

"I feel so bad about this," she said, interrupting. "This came up unexpectedly, and the partner in charge is insistent that I stay to see it through."

"I didn't mean to make you feel guilty," Barney said. "In fact, if it would make you feel less guilty, why don't you call the Chinese restaurant and order me some dinner to have while I work? It's the next best thing to eating together."

She giggled. "Gosh, that's romantic. And you'll call to order for me?"

"That's the kind of guy I am."

"I love that guy."

"I love you, too."

He hung up smiling to himself and, unlocking his desk, took out the thick folder on Austin Realty that one of the young prosecutors had given to him that afternoon. The District Attorney's office had acquired such prestige lately that he seemed to have his pick of the brightest law school graduates in the country. His staff was bright, no doubt about that, but not quite as good-looking as the television depictions of lawyers would have you believe. Margery Warren, the assistant D.A. who had put together the Austin file, was one of the smartest women he knew, but she was barely five feet tall and stocky. She wore thick wire-rimmed glasses, no makeup, and pulled her thin brown hair back in a ponytail. He hoped his brother Keith would never have the chance to meet her. Keith wouldn't hire someone like that if she were the last woman on earth. Not quite the Jillian van Dorne type that Keith liked to install in his office.

Barney opened the folder and started reading. He'd run into

Jillian just once, a few weeks ago in Keith's office, and the encounter had disturbed him. For the first time since he'd become District Attorney, he was feeling a conflict of interest. It wasn't a conflict that the media would pick up on or even one that would hurt his image, because the relationships were too distant. He was investigating his brother's partner's husband. Big deal. Funny thing was that he didn't even know how the connection would affect his opinion of the case. Even if he decided to move against Austin Realty, it wouldn't reflect back to Keith, would it? The situation wasn't clear, but it made him uncomfortable, nonetheless.

Well over an hour later, he finished reading the folder and sat back to ponder what was there. The company had been dancing on the edge of the law for years, apparently, and if he wanted to make a case, he probably could. The business they had pulled with the tax breaks for low-income housing really crossed the line, and even if he didn't get them on it, the IRS probably would. But he had to be careful in prosecuting high-profile cases that weren't related to drugs or murder; if he hit too hard on white-collar crime, the media would accuse him of grandstanding, following the lead of the former Manhattan D.A. who had taken a little too much pleasure in leading millionaire Wall Street executives away in handcuffs.

The most interesting part of the Austin report was the end. Assistant D.A. Warren had been stung when they lost the Owens crane case, so he had to remember that maybe she carried some personal vendetta against Austin Realty. In fact, she had gone well beyond any standard report here and done some serious investigating that couldn't be made public. She'd put a little too much of her speculation on paper—he'd have to warn her against doing that in the future—but he had to admit that it made compelling reading. For example, there were her queries as to why Austin Realty was getting involved with Kingsley Wright in England. Everything about it smelled wrong. And even more ominous was her suspicion about a certain offshore company in the Cayman Islands that she had reason to believe was being set up as a front for Austin Realty.

He swung his chair around to his old IBM Selectric typewriter and rolled in a piece of paper, labeling it as a confidential memo to Assistant D.A. Warren. He had insisted on keeping the typewriter just for moments like these when he didn't want to dictate a message but certainly didn't want to struggle with the computers and electronic typewriters that everyone else had mastered. He typed quickly, thanking her for the file and for all her hard work and asking her to keep him personally apprised of any developments she heard about in the deal between Austin Realty and Wright Construction. *I suspect we'll both know when is the right time to act,* he wrote in conclusion. Pulling the paper out of the typewriter, he realized that Assistant D.A. Warren seemed privy to a surprising amount of inside dope on Austin Realty, and he wondered who was dealing her information.

■

"So how's it going with that new syndicated talk show?" Barry Brunetti twirled the swizzle stick around his gin and tonic and raised his voice just loud enough so it could be heard above the din at the bar. He tried to keep his attention focused on Keith Ross—nobody liked a man with a wandering eye—but it wasn't easy. Leave it to Keith to find a restaurant with the best-looking chicks in Manhattan. Barry had always figured New York broads as being a distant second to the good-looking numbers in Los Angeles, but from what he'd seen so far tonight, he could be persuaded to change his mind. A models' hangout, Keith had called this place, and at least half-a-dozen women had walked by with bodies to die for. Whether or not they were cover-girl types, he couldn't really say. He hadn't spent much time looking at their faces.

"I think the show is going to happen," Keith said. "We're still a few steps away from shooting a pilot, but most of the pieces are falling into place."

"From what I've heard it's brilliant. Late nights are tough, but your formula has leaked out. I've heard it and I like it."

"Well, thanks."

Keith sounded distant—maybe surprised that Barry knew so much. Trying to back off, Barry said, "Of course, this is just one of many for you. You're probably too busy right now with the rock-and-roll special to give it full attention."

"Not really. Jillian's handling the special so well that whenever I step in I feel as if I'm interfering. It's working out exactly as I'd hoped. I spend my time being creative—getting ideas and selling them—then she takes over and is brilliant at executing them."

"Sounds perfect," Barry said. "I really wish I'd managed to see Jillian this trip."

"I'm sure she would have liked that, too," Keith said vaguely. Actually, Jillian's exact words when Keith extended the invitation were that she would have loved to join them, but she had to go home and feed Lila's pet gerbil. Keith had thought about that for a minute, then asked, "Is that anything like telling a guy you can't go out on a date with him because you have to wash your hair?"

"Almost identical," Jillian said, laughing. "Barry Brunetti is not high on my list for socializing."

Barry gulped at his drink and caught the eye of a young woman a couple of seats down at the bar—a stunningly exotic creature who, he guessed, probably had some Vietnamese blood in her. If they'd been in Chicago, he'd have swaggered over, introduced himself as the general manager of WOJ-TV, and told her that a woman as beautiful as she had to appear on his station. Somewhere in the conversation, he'd work in about being named one of Chicago's most-eligible men. Not one of the women he'd approached that way had ever told him to go to hell, and some of them had even ended up in his bed. Just the thought of having this Oriental beauty in bed with him made his crotch tingle, and he had to force himself to return to business with Keith.

"Let me put my cards on the table," Barry said. "I'd like to have you shoot the pilot at our studios. I can't quote you numbers or prices, of course, until we can sit down and talk specifics, but I'll guarantee you a much better deal than you could get anywhere. I mean *much* better."

Keith picked through the dish of salted nuts in front of him until he found two cashews, and he placed one of them thoughtfully in his mouth. "It's nice to have that offer, Barry, and I wouldn't dream of saying no right now. But Chicago isn't the best place for us to shoot. We're a New York–based production company, and it would be pretty hard to pick up and move."

"WOJ is a good station," Barry said. "A feather in any syndicator's cap. Even if you can't do it for the life of the show, think about it for the pilot. There are deals that can make it worthwhile for both of us in the long run. Remember, you don't want to lose Chicago."

Keith chewed the second cashew, trying to decide what Barry was telling him. Would he buy the show only if Keith shot it at his facility—and blackball him otherwise? Given the current state of television syndication, it wasn't clear who was bribing whom. Keith needed to air on a station like WOJ, but WOJ also needed a hit. The real question was whether Keith's show could be a hit right off the mark. Barry obviously thought that it would be.

"Are you looking for a co-production deal?" Keith asked bluntly. "Do you want to put some money up front and then be cut in on the show?"

"How much are you talking about?"

"I'm going to try to do the pilot for two hundred fifty thousand, and I've budgeted a year's worth of shows at about three million."

"I figured it would be even higher, given your performance costs. Doing music is expensive, and I'll bet your star is going to cost a mint."

"We haven't settled on a star yet," Keith said.

"Good party line. No use talking about her too soon." Barry winked at him, and it suddenly occurred to Keith that announcing the talk show and the special at the same time had somehow linked the two in Barry's mind. *He probably thinks we've got Annabelle Fox to host the late-night syndicated show.*

Damn if that wasn't a good idea.

"I'm not going to make some of these decisions final until we're a little further along," Keith said.

"Understood," Barry said. "And you and I will be talking on a regular basis until then."

Keith nodded, pleased that the ground was set and knowing that all the points had been made. Time to turn to other matters. "So tell me, Barry, are you happy there in Chicago?" Keith asked.

"I've got other ambitions," Barry admitted. "But I guess you've figured that out by now." Then, lowering his voice, he said, "My ambition for tonight is to get my hands on that gorgeous Oriental number sitting a few seats down from you. I've had my eye on her all night."

Keith turned slightly and saw the dark-eyed innocent who had aroused Barry's lust. "Probably one of the Elite models," Keith said, turning back to Barry. "I don't know her, but one of the girls she's talking to is an acquaintance of mine. Excuse me a minute." Slipping off the bar stool, he pushed through the crowd of gorgeous women and wealthy men at the bar and went over to his friend, who introduced him to Ming Lu. They exchanged a few words, and when Keith told Ming Lu that there was an important television executive sitting at the bar who was dying to meet her, she stood up immediately.

From the look on Barry's face when he brought Ming Lu over, Keith knew that he was going to be able to cut any kind of deal with Barry that he wanted.

CHAPTER NINE

JILLIAN walked quickly down Santa Monica Boulevard, the only person headed for the Rumn Club at nine-thirty in the morning. In another few hours, her camera crew would be arriving, and later tonight, as always, there would be hundreds of people crowded into the tables at the club and a throng standing at the door waiting to get in. With its black walls, funky music, and tequila-mixed drinks, it was the hottest rock club in Los Angeles at the moment. For the young, hip crowd that swarmed in every night, the big-name stars on stage and the loud music reverberating around the room were the first notes of a mating call—and as Jillian thought about it, that more than anything was probably the appeal of the club.

The front door of the club was still locked, so Jillian walked around and gave her name to the sleepy-looking guard she'd had stationed at the side entrance for the day—a standard precaution when they were shooting. Not knowing that the attractive woman requesting entrance was the person who would be signing his paycheck, the guard simply nodded and watched her walk in. Nice legs, he thought. Nice legs.

The Rumn Club was dim at that hour and smelled faintly of stale cigarette smoke. The neon lights were off and the small, high windows blocked more sun than they let through, so it was almost impossible to see the much-talked-about mural on the far wall. Jillian had seen it before, though—an eighteen-foot close-up of the inside of a flower, pseudo–Georgia O'Keeffe, that most people considered more anatomical than botanical. When an otherwise glowing review of the Rumn Club in the *L.A. Times* gently rebuked the owners of the club for installing the mural, the artist indignantly paraphrased O'Keeffe in replying that anybody who saw vaginas in her flowers was looking too hard. Jillian found it amusing that the mural could arouse such controversy when a few blocks away on Sunset Boulevard, people walked by peep shows, strip joints, and triple-X-rated movies without a second thought.

Jillian moved quickly through the very long bar area into the club proper—which for a moment seemed dark and quiet. Then she heard a strange, animalistic sound, and as her eyes adjusted to the light, she realized that it was coming from Annabelle Fox, who sat alone at a small table. The young singer's shoulders were shaking, and her thick hair spewed from her face like some untamed Gorgon. Dressed in a fuchsia bodysuit and black leather miniskirt, she made no effort to hide her sobbing, and the sound echoed strangely through the dim room. Sitting straight in her chair, her legs spread apart, her face was tilted slightly upward, and she cried into the open space of the club.

Even more surprising to Jillian was the fact that coming toward Annabelle, holding a mug in his hand, was Emil.

In a few long strides, he was at Annabelle's side, and his presence seemed to ease her hysterical sobs. Putting a comforting hand on her shaking shoulders, he said, "Some tea with milk for you," and held the cup steady while Annabelle reached for it.

She managed to sip the tea, then put the mug on the table and, clutching Emil's hand with both of hers, cried, "I need you." Her voice, strained from the sobbing, was strangely high-pitched, and she clung to Emil like a lifeline. Jillian stopped where she was, sensing that this wasn't the moment to intrude.

Emil pulled up a chair next to Annabelle and, sitting down, said, "I know it all seems very frightening now, but we're going to work it out. And we—"

He couldn't continue because Annabelle stood up suddenly, knocking over her chair, and in a single motion flung her tiny form onto his knees.

"Don't leave me!" she begged.

Emil seemed momentarily stunned, then rocked her gently, patting her back. "I'm not leaving," Emil said softly. "I'm right here."

Annabelle's harsh sobs began again, then turned into sniffles and hiccups, and she grabbed for the crisp, white handkerchief that Emil pulled out of his back pocket. She wiped her nose, then looked at him longingly. Emil made no move. Annabelle leaned close against his chest, and said, "I'll do anything you want me to," and when he still didn't respond, she tossed her arms around his neck and pressed her mouth hard against his.

Jillian felt her heart beating too hard, anger and disbelief making her body react on its own. She turned away, not wanting to know what would follow, but she heard Emil's chair squeak against the wooden floor, and unable to resist, looked over again in time to see Emil had pulled away and was standing up, looming over the chair where Annabelle still sat.

"Please stop it," he said. His tone was firm and slightly angry.

"But you have to help me," she said, moaning slightly.

"I *will* help you. I've said I'll help you. But I'm not looking for sexual favors in return."

"That's the only way people have helped me before," Annabelle said, and she began sobbing again. Emil stood close, not leaving her, but not touching her, either. At that point, Jillian said loudly, "Good morning."

Emil looked up sharply and, spotting Jillian in the darkness of the club, said, "Good morning to you. I didn't hear you come in."

"I've just been here a minute."

"Well, I'm glad you're here. Maybe you can help us."

Moving closer to their scene, Jillian asked, "What's going on?"

Emil gestured toward Annabelle, suggesting that Jillian should ask her herself.

"Annabelle?" Jillian ventured closer. "What's happened?"

But the girl buried her head in her hands so her words were strangely muffled. "Go away, Jillian. I'm not supposed to trust you."

Baffled, Jillian looked at Emil, but he just shrugged, so she said, "Of course you can trust me, Annabelle. I'd never do anything to hurt you. Who said not to trust me?"

"*He* said it. *Don't trust Jillian.* Denny said that if I tell you the

141

truth, you'll use it to destroy me. Or he will destroy me, or—" The other possibilities were lost in choking sobs.

"Whoever said that is wrong," Jillian said gently, but Annabelle kept her face hidden in her hands and just offered a weak cry of "Please go away! Go away!"

Jillian looked helplessly at Emil, and he crouched down gracefully, balancing on the balls of his feet so his face was level with Annabelle's. "I'm not going to leave you," he said to Annabelle, "and I'm not going to betray you. But I have to talk to Jillian. Is that all right?"

Annabelle slowly lifted her face from her hands and, looking into Emil's eyes, whispered, "I don't know who to trust."

Jillian saw that Annabelle's face was more than just tearstained: an ugly purple bruise that started just above her left eyebrow had seeped down through the tender skin around her eye; the eyelid was mottled and swollen, and there was a frightening black gash under the eye.

"I've already promised that I won't let anything more happen to you," Emil said.

The comment seemed to satisfy Annabelle, who hid her face again as Emil stood up. Putting a hand on Jillian's elbow, he propelled her back toward the bar and helped her onto a bar stool. Jillian noticed they could still see Annabelle but were clearly out of earshot.

"What in heaven's name is going on?" Jillian asked.

"The secret life of rock and roll," Emil said grimly. "I'm afraid we've stumbled on Annabelle's secret, and it's an ugly one."

Still not understanding, Jillian said, "What is it? What's upset her so much?"

"In a word—Denny."

A sudden insight flashed through Jillian like a bolt, and she said with certainty, "He's beating her up."

"You've got it. As far as I can tell, he's brutalizing her and keeping her so thoroughly terrorized that she won't move without his permission."

"The poor girl." Memories of Annabelle's strange behavior in New York crowded Jillian's mind and, shaking her head, Jillian said,

"All the signs were there, weren't they? But I missed them. God, I feel awful about that."

"They've been clever at keeping it hidden. I have the feeling that he controls her like a master puppeteer. Just nice enough sometimes to keep her off balance and just brutal enough to have her in a state of perpetual fear. Even staring out of a black eye, she's afraid to say anything bad about him."

"What's she doing here this morning? What are *you* doing here this morning?"

"I woke up very early—mostly because I was thinking about you, but that's another story—and came over here to look around. It was about seven o'clock, and I found Annabelle in a little hole of a dressing room upstairs. She started screaming hysterically when I first opened the door because she thought I was Denny. Once she realized it was me, she turned almost comatose, and all I could get her to say was that she'd been drinking a lot of tequila after the late show last night and then was too wiped out to leave. Her face told a more frightening story, but I didn't ask. For about an hour, she followed me around like a puppy dog, watching me set up, and when I was done and told her I was going back home, she fell apart. That's when the sobbing started, and she said she would never go back to Denny. Before long, she was pleading to come home with me."

"I don't blame her," Jillian said. There was something comforting about Emil's powerful presence and his quiet strength. She could imagine that to Annabelle he appeared as savior, bodyguard, and hero. Just the person to trust with her story.

"Annabelle is scared to death," Emil continued, "but she can't decide whether to be more afraid of going home to Denny and having him kill her or leaving him for good and having him kill her career. Denny's managed to convince her that she's nothing without him— and that if she walks out on him, he'll destroy her."

"Well, there must be something we can do." Jillian stood up and paced briefly by the bar, wondering how to help Annabelle without hurting the show. I shouldn't be thinking about the show at a time like this, she thought, but her professional instincts were strong. Looking at Emil, she said, "You've obviously won her trust, anyway. What does she want from you?"

Emil thought about the question, then with an enigmatic smile, asked, "If I say security, physical comfort, and a bed in my house, will you be jealous?"

"Of course I'll be jealous." One of Annabelle's long hairs was clinging to Emil's black polo shirt; reaching over, Jillian picked it off and looked at it contemplatively for a moment before releasing it into the air. "My first thought when I walked in on your scene was that you'd had a brief fling with Annabelle these last couple of days in Los Angeles and were trying to escape—but that she wanted you forever."

"Not a chance of that." Emil removed his shaded gray glasses and wiped them with a napkin from the bar. "I don't have brief flings. When I'm interested in a woman, I treat it seriously, because I don't get interested very often. You can consider yourself a special case." He put the glasses back on, and Jillian realized that he was standing very close to her, talking in a low, husky voice. "You have an effect on me like no woman I've met. I'd much rather spend my time thinking about you than having sex with Annabelle."

"I'd rather not even think about the effect you have on me."

"Think about it." He brushed the back of his hand against hers.

Jillian tossed her head. "If I do, we'll never take care of Annabelle." She glanced over at the young singer, who had put her head down on the table and seemed to be asleep. "We're supposed to start shooting with her tonight. What do you say we get her into a hotel, let her sleep for a bit, and then figure out what to do?"

"Fine. Her backup group is staying at a place on Manhattan Beach, but I don't want her going over there. She'll just drink more tequila and be totally trashed by tonight."

"Where's Denny?"

"Some unimpressive hotel down the street. Fortunately, Annabelle has all her makeup and stage clothes in the dressing room here, so there's no need for anyone to go by the hotel. I do think someone should spend the day with her, though. Not necessarily a bodyguard—just someone levelheaded who can be with her and call for help if it becomes necessary."

"You've thought of everything," Jillian said. "Why don't you go back to Annabelle and let me see what I can arrange."

At the back of the club, Jillian noticed a long, gloomy staircase leading down to the basement, where restrooms and phones were invariably located. Downstairs, three pay telephones jutted out of a wall, which was painted stark white as if to accommodate the various telephone numbers scrawled on it. There was a strange artistry to the designs, a giant mural created by callers who had pencil but no pad when they dialed information. One of the numbers, written on the wall in black Magic Marker, belonged to an L.A. talent agency. How many aspiring actors and actresses came down here each night to call an agent and find out if there was an audition for them the next day—or if they should go back upstairs and find hope and encouragement at the bar?

Jillian dialed the Beverly Hills Hotel and when there was no answer in Keith's room asked for Rob Daly, one of the production assistants she had hired for this shoot. Barely twenty-five, Rob was a smart, good-looking kid who had produced exceptional films as a student at UCLA film school and was now working as gofer and boy Friday to get experience in the real world of moviemaking. Because he had grown up in Laguna Beach and looked like a surfer, he was always fighting to be taken seriously. Jillian found that amusing and trusted him implicitly.

Though he sounded as if he had been asleep, Rob listened alertly to an abbreviated telling of Annabelle's story and had Jillian hold on while he checked with the manager to make sure there was a room available for Annabelle.

Rob is the perfect person for this job, Jillian thought while she held the phone. He knows his way around L.A. and he's very kind.

In a few minutes, Rob got breathlessly back on the phone to say that the manager would take care of it. "I'll have a limo at the club in fifteen minutes to pick her up," Rob said.

"Thanks. But before you get in the car, would you try to track down Keith? He's not in his room, so you might try the pool first, the coffee shop second, and the steam room third."

The limo arrived twenty minutes later with just Rob in the backseat.

"Keith was swimming, but he'll be along in a few minutes," Rob explained.

Emil introduced him to Annabelle, and if Rob felt at all

overwhelmed about having one of the biggest rock stars in the world as his charge for the day, he didn't show it.

Annabelle looked calmer now that everyone had rallied around her, and she climbed eagerly into the car with Rob.

"Rob will be close to you all day," Emil promised her, "and if there are any problems, he'll call us immediately."

"Good," Annabelle said. Then she added bravely, "I'm still going to do my show tonight. Tell everyone they can count on me."

As they watched the car pull away, Emil stroked his cheek, rubbing at it like sandpaper on a stone. "Americans have strange ideas about relationships, you know that? They always accuse Eastern Europeans of chauvinism—our men are too macho and our women too feminine. But where I come from, the men don't beat the women. They respect them. It's not a bad thing for people to respect each other."

Jillian sighed. "True enough, Emil, but may I remind you that Denny and Annabelle are English? Using and abusing women is hardly just an American hobby."

"How about admiring and desiring them?" Emil asked, turning his full attention to her.

Standing on the sidewalk with Emil next to her and the Hollywood sun shining warmly down, Jillian felt surprisingly relaxed. The fact that Annabelle's troubles could bring down their million-dollar special hadn't yet sunk in. She'd turned tragedy to advantage before and she'd do it again.

When Keith arrived at the Rumn Club a few minutes later and heard the story, he wasn't quite so sanguine.

"This is shit," he said, pacing across the floor as Emil explained the situation. "We've already spent about ten thousand dollars on this L.A. shoot, and I don't want it down the toilet."

"We can still shoot her show tonight," Emil said, "but you can forget about a sit-down interview that's anything but fluff. No way that girl is going to talk about Denny yet."

"We don't air this show for another month," Keith said. "If the story about the boyfriend breaks in the press before that, we'll look like idiots for having missed it."

Jillian, sitting at a table with her forehead resting against her

146

fingertips, asked, "Where's Annabelle going to live after this? I mean, she can't go back to Denny, and as far as I can tell she doesn't have any friends or family to turn to."

"Who the hell cares at the moment?" Keith blew some smoke out of the corner of his mouth, trying to avoid Jillian's face. "I hate to be hard-hearted, but we've got to take care of the show right now. We'll worry about the humanitarian angles another time, okay?"

"No," Jillian said. "Annabelle may be worth a few million dollars, but she's a scared little kid who needs some support. She trusts Emil, and I think she'll start trusting me again, which means we have a responsibility toward her. When I spent the day with her, she told me how much she loves the United States, and I wouldn't be surprised if she wanted to move here. Now, that would be a good soap-opera story, wouldn't it? Young cockney singer makes it so big that she breaks away from her Machiavellian manager and starts a new life in Hollywood. Black eyes and all. He comes after her and—well, who knows what could happen?" She paused to take a sip of coffee, then said, "If Annabelle needs a new home, I'd like to find it for her right away. Get her settled away from Denny immediately."

Keith, suddenly understanding exactly what Jillian was aiming at, looked at her admiringly. "Jeez, it pays to have a partner who knows her way around soaps. In other words, you want to throw out what we'd planned to shoot and get footage of her packing her bags and breaking away from the malevolent manager, right? That way even if she won't talk about it, we can show it."

Jillian nodded. "When I first got to the club this morning, I asked Emil what was going on, and he said, 'The secret life of rock and roll.' I don't think we've got a problem here, Keith. I think we've got an incredible story handed to us that's going to make this special more explosive than we could have dreamed. We just have to make sure we capture the drama and play it right. I agree with you that it's not what we planned to shoot, but it could be a heck of a lot better."

Keith lit another cigarette almost before the first one was out. "Do it," he said. "I'm with you all the way."

Jillian excused herself to make some phone calls, and ten minutes later came back with the news that a realtor she knew was leasing a furnished house in Laurel Canyon. It was small but had gorgeous views. "Six thousand a month, but it's probably worth it. Annabelle can move in immediately, and we can get our at-home shots today and tomorrow. Maybe Annabelle will have a confrontation with Denny there. Even if we pay for the whole damn thing, it'll be cheaper than rescheduling the shoot."

The cigarette drooped from Keith's mouth. "Only thing I'm concerned about is whether we're going to be sliced and diced for setting this up. This is supposed to be a real-life documentary. People find out that we set it up as carefully as if it were a scene out of 'General Hospital,' and there's going to be hollering about our being unethical."

"Unethical?" Jillian shrugged. "I don't see that at all. Emil promised Annabelle we'd help her out, and now we're doing just that. No more, no less."

Keith ground out the cigarette and didn't light another one. "Okay, I'm sold. Move her into the house in Laurel Canyon, but see if you can keep our names off the checks."

"Will do."

Suddenly lighthearted, Keith added, "Emil's got a great house out here, from what I've heard. Of course, I've never been invited to it. I don't know why Annabelle can't just move in with him. Probably be cheaper."

"No, thank you," Emil said.

"She too young for you or too sexy?"

"Both."

"I don't know about you Hungarians," Keith said, shaking his head with mock concern. "What do you do with yourselves at night?"

"Work. Read. Think."

"Bullshit. I've heard the stories about you."

"None of them true."

"Too bad. Maybe you should do something about that undying loyalty of yours to Erin. Keeps getting in the way of a good time. Eighteen years is enough, don't you think?"

Emil rocked gently on the balls of his feet, not answering, and Jillian walked away briskly to get the details of Annabelle's move under way. She wouldn't ask who Erin was. It wasn't her business.

148

Annabelle was awed by both the house Jillian showed her and with her recommendation that Artie Glenn of Artists Management take over for Denny.

"At least for the short term," Jillian said as they sat on Annabelle's new terrace, waiting for the realtor to arrive with the papers to sign.

"Would Artie Glenn really take me on?" Annabelle asked, sounding uncertain.

"Of course. I spoke to him an hour ago, and he'll come to the Rumn Club tonight so you can meet him."

Annabelle looked dubious, and Jillian said gently, "Artie's a professional, and he'll treat you like a professional. No manager has the right to control your life, Annabelle. And nobody has the right to hurt you. You're too good for that."

She'd been repeating that message to Annabelle all afternoon, and she hoped that it was starting to get through. This morning Annabelle had reacted out of fear: some deep instinct for survival had told her that she had to break away; but now, faced with the reality of being on her own, she might start to slip back. Jillian didn't want her to hesitate and start finding excuses for Denny's behavior.

The realtor arrived, a very blond woman wearing bright pink sunglasses and an Ellesse running suit. Jillian reluctantly co-signed all the papers, since Annabelle was underage.

"We almost never rent a house like this for just a month," the realtor said to Annabelle, "but it happened to be available, and Jillian said you were in a jam."

"A short-term jam," Annabelle said lamely.

"We usually consider six months to a year as short-term," the realtor said.

When Annabelle looked worried and said, "I couldn't imagine staying anyplace that long," the realtor just laughed and collected her papers. Once the woman had bustled away, Annabelle looked around, as if she were trying to take in the fact that one record-breaking album and two hit singles in two months won you a fabulous house and the most renowned manager in the business. The innocence in her eyes reminded Jillian of an expression of Lila's when someone gave her an unexpected present or told her that she was the best reader in the whole first grade. It was pleasure mixed with surprise.

"Wonderful that everything is under control, isn't it?" Jillian asked cheerfully. "This house is probably yours for as long as you want it."

Annabelle didn't say anything, and Jillian wondered briefly what her own daughters would be like when they were teenagers. If only there were a formula for giving girls confidence in themselves and making them realize that it was all right to be the center of their own universe. Rock stars or not, teenage girls seemed to hold themselves in particular disdain, which made them targets for every kind of exploitation. It was something understood as implicitly by the makers of cosmetics—who knew that young women needed lipstick and eyeliner and blusher to make themselves feel pretty—as it was by the pimps on Forty-second Street who waited at the bus terminals for runaways from Minnesota.

"I guess these last twenty-four hours have been hard for you," Jillian said sympathetically. "But you've done everything right. What a great example you're setting for all your young fans."

"Maybe," Annabelle said, blinking back some tears. "But it's just been awful, you know? I thought Denny was such a lovable bloke, but now it turns out he's just bad."

Having learned that among American teenagers "bad" meant good, Jillian duly noted that with a cockney accent, bad still meant bad.

"At least you're turning a new leaf now," Jillian said. "You can forget about Denny."

"I'd rather kill him." Annabelle's eyes seemed dull, and the lack of passion in her voice gave the words a startling impact. She really would like to kill him, Jillian thought. Not as a crime of passion, but because she's coming to her senses.

"I'm not sure what the best way is for you to deal with Denny right now," Jillian said truthfully. "Maybe we should sit down with our lawyer and discuss whether she thinks you should press charges."

Annabelle closed her eyes, as if she were thinking about it, but Jillian realized that the girl was exhausted and about to fall asleep.

150

Since she didn't relish the thought of carrying her into her bed, she reached down and shook her arm gently. "You still haven't gotten any rest," Jillian said. "Want to sleep now?"

"Will you stay with me? I don't want to be alone."

There was a whimper in her voice, so Jillian said, "How about if Rob stays with you again?"

Annabelle suddenly perked up. "Oh yes! He wasn't supposed to leave my side, was he?" She looked around, expecting him to materialize.

"He went off to do some errands for us, but I'll get him back." UCLA film school couldn't have prepared Rob for this part of the job.

"In that case, I will get into bed," Annabelle said. "Tell Rob to find me there, would you?"

■

The Rumn Club was bustling with cameramen, lighting men, and their equipment when Jillian got back, but everything seemed under control, so Jillian took Emil aside to give him a brief rundown on where they stood with Annabelle.

"So the day is saved," Emil said.

"Not quite. I'm now wondering if Annabelle needs more protection than she'll get from Rob."

"Sounds to me like it's Rob who needs the protection."

Jillian laughed. "If he steps into her bedroom, probably. But I'm worried about Denny and whether he's going to come looking for her." She ran her tongue along her upper lip and added, "Because if he does, someone should be there."

"With a camera?"

Jillian flicked back a strand of hair. "I'm not that hard-hearted, you know."

"Good to hear," Emil said.

"In fact, I'm beginning to think of Annabelle as my third daughter. But there's no reason we can't help her *and* do a terrific show."

The lights were on and the cameras in position when Annabelle arrived at the Rumn Club at six o'clock—pulling up in a small van

151

driven by the boys in the band rather than the limo that they had ordered for her. Annabelle sat in the front seat, sandwiched between her drummer, who was at the wheel, and Rob, who smiled sheepishly out the window. Annabelle's face looked slightly puffy around the eyes, but the bruises were hidden by thick pancake makeup.

The band members jumped out of the van, helped Annabelle down, and swaggered into the club. Rob lingered at the door after they went in.

"They stopped by the house and she insisted on coming with them," he whispered to Jillian. "I'm sorry I didn't call to warn you, but there was no time."

"No problem. In fact it's great. Makes her seem more down-home. The unpretentious rock star. I like it."

With the documentary cameras on, Annabelle's teenage confusion and despair vanished. She preened for the cameras, practicing her vocals as she changed into stage clothes in her dressing room, performing a few leg kicks and pelvic thrusts as she peered into the mirror to fix her hair. "Look like a tart, don't I?" she giggled, turning to the camera at one point, holding up her comb.

"Who turned her on?" muttered Keith, who was standing in the back of the room.

A slow blush crept up Rob's neck. Keith, noticing it, shook his head slowly. "As long as it's a natural high, I don't mind," he said.

The natural high continued as Annabelle stepped onstage for her eight o'clock show. The crowd, even larger than expected, was with her, and she tossed herself gleefully around the stage as the cameras recorded it all.

"I think we've got everything we need," Emil told Jillian, after Annabelle had finished her second encore and the fans at the tables were starting to retreat to the bar. "Should we wrap for the night?"

"No way. I want to shoot the ten o'clock show."

"Isn't it supposed to be the same?" Emil asked.

"Supposed to be, but who knows? Maybe we'll get some unusual cuts out of it."

When Annabelle came back onstage at ten-twenty, the new audience, slightly drunker and more raucous, gave lusty roars of approval as she launched into "No More Teenage Virgins." In answer, she flipped her short skirt up in the back and wiggled like a teenage Betty Boop.

"Jillian?"

It was Rob, suddenly at her side, talking loudly to be heard over the music and rowdy audience.

Jillian turned to him, about to make a comment about Annabelle's onstage undulations, but checked herself when she noticed Rob's face contorted with worry.

"I need to talk to you," he said, gesturing to be understood even as his words were drowned out by the music blasting from one of the most celebrated sound systems in L.A.

She motioned him to follow her to the back, but finding that it wasn't any quieter there, she led him to the staircase.

"What is it?" she asked as they stood on the second step, protected from the din.

"Denny just came in, and I've been watching him. At least I think it's him. The face is right, and he's got a diamond stud in his left ear. From here, it looks like he's drunk or stoned and mumbling to himself."

"Well, hallelujah," Jillian said. "The dice are falling our way."

Rob looked at her in horror. "What do you mean?"

"We'll get a camera on him right away. We have permission to shoot everyone in the club. There's a notice of general release as people walked in."

"I'm telling you this so someone can protect Annabelle, not exploit her even more," Rob said.

Jillian shrugged. "Welcome to the real world of television, Rob. We're all trying to protect Annabelle, but we have a story to report, too."

Going quickly back into the club, which was still reverberating with Annabelle's music, Jillian found Emil and mouthed the single word "Denny." Emil looked across the room and nodded. "Just tell camera three to turn around and get the audience instead of the stage," Jillian said, her mouth close to Emil's ear so he could hear her above the din. "I'm sure we have enough of his angles from the first show."

"Thanks for the advice, but I'll direct, if that's okay."

Jillian looked away, not sure whether to be angry or embarrassed, and Emil put an arm around her slim waist. "I didn't mean to snap," he said, pushing her hair away from her ear. "You can tell me anything you want. I love the way it feels when you whisper in my ear."

Still feeling rebuked, Jillian nonetheless stayed next to him, her eye on Denny. Just watching him made her tense, as if she were staring at a loaded cannon. A few minutes later, while Annabelle was singing "Hips Wiggle, Girls Giggle," Denny abruptly pushed back his chair, upsetting the glass of beer on the table in front of him. The amber contents splashed over the edge of the table, and a moment later the glass rolled through the puddle and crashed onto the floor. The accident might have gone unheeded if Denny, now standing, hadn't roared "Fuck it!" during a break in the music and stormed over to the cameraman who was taking the audience shots. Noticing the uproar, Emil sidled over to Denny and asked if something was wrong.

"You're damn right something's wrong!" yelled Denny, his voice rising over the music that had started again. "I remember you, you're the fucking director, right? Well, that punk is pointing his camera at me, and I want to know why."

"Just some audience shots," Emil said.

"Tell him to shoot someone else in the fucking audience or he'll have his camera over his head."

"I don't like threats," Emil said, looking at Denny, who was nearly his height but thin and slightly hunched, his dirty-blond hair hanging almost to the shoulders of his well-worn leather biker's jacket. His skin was sallow and he looked pale and unhealthy, but he stepped menacingly toward Emil. Without thinking about it, Emil assumed a casual fighter's stance, feet planted broadly apart, shoulders squared in readiness.

It was enough. Denny took a step backward. "Don't fuck with me," Denny said, the threat lingering in his words but not in his tone. "You don't like threats, and I don't like fucking commie assholes. Go back to Red country."

Denny was already walking away as he tossed the provocation over his shoulder, the words almost lost to the music. Still, Emil felt his muscles flexing for the kill and had to hold himself in check, his body rigid, to keep from responding as he would have liked. When he felt a hand on his shoulder, he spun around tensely, startling Jillian, whose long, slim fingers were left suspended in midair.

"Just me," she said weakly.

He took a deep breath, noticing from the corner of his eye that Denny had left the club, and checked to see that Luke on camera three had picked up the entire exchange.

"What is it?" Emil asked Jillian.

"First, are you all right?" Her voice was hoarse from shouting over the music.

"Of course."

"Good. The crew can wrap at the end of the set. Then I need you and Keith to come with me to my hotel for a meeting."

■

Keith Ross couldn't stop eating cashew nuts. From the minute they got back to the hotel at just after one A.M., he had been sipping tonic water and devouring cashew nuts. Maybe his body needed the salt. Or maybe he was just hungry. Emil sat silently while Jillian did all the talking and planning. As far as Keith was concerned, they had a hit special even if they did nothing more. Jillian didn't see it that way. She was pushing and pushing, saying that there was sure to be a confrontation between Annabelle and Denny at some point: he wasn't just walking away from his gold mine. Maybe they should arrange the confrontation so Annabelle had some security—and so they could shoot it.

Keith shifted in his seat. "Is it too trashy?" he asked.

"Oh, for heaven's sakes, Keith." Jillian, working at the edge of fatigue and frustration, shook her head impatiently. "This is the music business we're looking at, and rock and roll stars aren't exactly God's little angels. Half the music videos I see lately are about sadism and violence and sex. It's doubtful that anybody will be shocked to discover that the young girls involved—whether they're stars or not—are being exploited."

Keith took another fistful of cashews and stood up. "Fine. If you want my approval, you've got it. But I don't have a feel for this one, so you two work out the details."

155

"You're going to bed?"

"I am. Back to my own hotel. Good night, team." He strolled away.

Nearly one in the morning, and Jillian and Emil were alone in an otherwise empty lounge. For the second time that night, Emil had to restrain himself, but this time it was an urge to lean over and devour Jillian, taste the woman, luxuriate in her until she begged him to stop.

Or begged him for more.

Instead he just looked at her. "So let's work out the details for the confrontation," he said.

She already had them in her mind, and as she outlined her ideas for the next day, he nodded, made a few suggestions, and scratched notes on a yellow legal pad.

"Sounds fine to me," Emil said when they were finished. "I'd run it by your legal department to make sure you're not getting in over your head, but it looks good."

She nodded, and they sat still for a moment, each aware that the night's work was officially over. Jillian made a move to leave, but Emil put out a hand and touched her arm, and she sat back in her chair, closing her eyes. "Everything suddenly aches," she said, dropping her head. "The adrenaline has been pumping through me since early this morning, and now I feel as if it's all just drained through the soles of my feet."

Emil got up, moved behind her chair, and gently pushing her hair to one side, said, "You need to relax. Let me give you a back rub." He put his thumbs high on her shoulder blades and let his fingers roam across to the tension in her neck muscles.

"I can feel the knots," he said, massaging.

She hadn't moved since he came over; just kept her head dropped forward and her eyes closed. Emil massaged thoughtfully. Often when he was directing, he felt a tightness spreading across his shoulder blades and he would turn his head in circles to relieve it, shrug his shoulders to loosen up. Invariably someone would come over to offer a back rub. Sometimes he wouldn't even turn around; he'd keep calling shots, aware for a moment or two of firm hands easing away the knots in his neck muscles. "The director's rub," his assistant director used to joke; it was something that people in television just *did* for each other, almost a trademark of their profession. Which, of course, was why Jillian accepted his hands on her so casually, didn't mind his thumbs pressing down her backbone, his fingers easing her tension. And he, of course, didn't notice the sweet curve of her waist or the gentle drift of perfume he sensed at her neck.

"Oh, that's good." Jillian sat up straight now, shrugging away his hands and rolling her shoulders. "Thank you. Can I return the favor?"

"Not now." He gave a final squeeze to her shoulders and pulled over a chair, spinning it around so he straddled the seat and faced her, his elbows on the chair back.

"You have long days," he said. "And it must be hard for you to be away from home."

"I don't like being away from the children." She looked at him frankly, and he knew better than to ask if she minded being away from her husband. "How about you?" she asked. "Who do you miss when you're working?"

He shrugged. "Nobody, really. My life isn't set up that way."

"Even after eighteen years with Erin?"

He looked up sharply and saw that she was teasing him—and had no idea who Erin was.

"I love Erin deeply, it's true. But we're used to being apart."

"Oh." She wanted information but wouldn't ask it directly. "I heard Keith mention your loyalty to her this morning."

"Loyalty, yes, but why assume Erin is a 'her'?" He was enjoying himself now—pleased to be one up on Jillian and also to know that she was curious abut him, wanting to know more before she committed any part of herself. A sexy woman but one who obviously wasn't out there playing around at random. He liked that.

She sighed. "All right, I shouldn't be prying, but I'm interested. Is Erin your lover? Your dog?"

"Erin is my son. Eighteen and a senior in high school."

"Honestly?" Jillian's voice squeaked with surprise, and she seemed to cast about, trying to find something to say. "He lives with you?"

"Always has. His mother and I split when he was a year old, and he's been with me ever since. She doesn't see him very much, but I've devoted a lot to him. Over the years I've turned down a lot of big projects—including a few that Keith offered—because they required too much travel, and I didn't want to leave Erin behind. And, as Keith also knows, my son always seemed more important to me than the various women who flitted in and out of my life."

Ignoring that, Jillian said, "You were a single parent before it was chic."

"I suppose. It's paid off. Erin's a smart, dedicated boy. I'm proud of him."

"How could you possibly have a son who's eighteen? You look like a kid yourself."

"No, I've put in my years. But I did start early. Erin came along when I was barely twenty."

They chatted for a few more minutes; Emil could see Jillian struggling to change her picture of him, to put Erin in perspective. When they said good night, he wanted desperately to kiss her, hold her tightly in his arms and carry her away, but he didn't dare. Not in a public spot, however deserted it was at this hour. She was married and deserved his discretion. Someday it might matter that they hadn't kissed in the hotel lounge.

■

As Emil maneuvered his Porsche out to the freeway, he realized that he enjoyed the car, but not with the passion that he would have expected in the first years after he left Hungary. Back then, he wanted everything; craved success like a mistress. Was that always the way in life? The feeling that accompanied fulfilling a desire was never as intense, never even as gratifying, as the sensation of desire itself.

The focus of his desire right now was Jillian, and he wondered if the reality of Jillian in his arms would measure up to the expectation.

It would. He knew it would.

That's why he was moving slowly, continuing the dance. The more they knew about each other, the better it would be. Soon he would tell her the rest of the story about Erin.

Emil had grown up in one of Hungary's more privileged families. His parents ran a large hotel in Budapest, and as a child he would wander through the Buda Castle District, intoxicated by the medieval

158

atmosphere that made him yearn for his own place in history. Because he had been so young during the terror of 1956, he had only fleeting images of the rebellion, and his recollection of the bloody slaughter that occurred when Russian troops rolled in was probably based more on family telling than on actual memory.

Once he was old enough to help out in the hotel, he would give guests directions to the city's historic spots, and as he did so he began to realize that Hungarians had been fighting for independence since the Middle Ages—and still hadn't achieved it. The guests visited Szentharomsag Ter, where they could see an assemblage of saints carved in stone, and the famous Matthias Church. In the sixteenth century, after the Turks had slashed their way to power, the church was converted to a mosque. The Austrians finally helped drive the Turks out of the country in 1699, and Matthias Church was the site of the 1867 coronation of Franz Joseph—the Emperor of Austria—as King of Hungary. But Franz Joseph was not the hero in Hungary that he was in Austria. The leaders whose names were on the squares and streets of Budapest—Kossuth, Szechenyi, Rakoczi—had fought against him for Hungarian self-determination.

"We have always done what we believed, no matter what the government or the guns or the royalty said," Emil's father told him over and over.

His father believed in God, not Communism.

His hero was Cardinal Mindszenty, the martyr who was jailed and exiled for his beliefs when Emil was young. Because his parents were devout Catholics, Emil spent his youth in fear that they would be taken from him. Slowly he came to understand that his parents prospered by having the proper politics in public; they made up for their hypocrisy by doubling their devotion to their religion at home.

His parents spoke to him often of hell and damnation and the penalty for spilling your seed in vain. By the time he was fourteen, his hormones were stirring, but he was afraid even to take himself in hand to ease the tension. The boys in school didn't talk about sex, and the teachers lectured harshly only on dedication and hard work. His parents had a priest visit frequently, and Emil began to wonder how the world had propagated itself if sex were so evil. He tried to talk to his father about it, and his father told him to have a cigarette whenever he started to think about sex. It would distract him. He smoked a lot until he was seventeen.

Then Marina Porter arrived.

Emil was working at the front desk of the hotel one cold Saturday when he first saw Marina. He was strappingly handsome by then, his muscular body already that of a man. He had a square jaw and powerful chin; his rugged features made him look like he should be out mountain climbing, not standing behind a chilly hotel desk. Marina's father had business in Pest, and she and her mother had come along and were going on to Innsbruck to ski. Emil had never seen a girl quite like Marina. The girls he lusted after in his school wore coarse wool skirts in drab colors that reached almost to their ankles. When they dressed up, it was often in traditional peasant costumes. Most were quiet and submissive, understanding that men should be men, and that a man's role was to dominate.

Marina Porter didn't understand that at all.

Also seventeen, she was a California girl who dressed in the short skirts and garish colors that were so popular among Americans in the late Sixties. Her hair was teased high on her head, and from the first time she met him, she talked to him as if he were an old friend. The second night of her stay, she told him that her parents had an official function to attend that night, and she would be alone. Would he like to show her around a little? It was like asking a starving man if he wanted to eat.

He took her to Old Buda, walking through the cobblestone streets where no traffic was allowed, showing her the thick medieval walls that circumscribed the city and the tower of the Church of St. Mary Magdalene, the thirteenth-century holy site that had been destroyed by the Germans in the Second World War. He spoke in halting English of the sites they passed, and she listened avidly.

"You know so much," she said to him.

He shrugged. "It is my home."

"Will it always be?" she asked.

"What do you mean?"

"I don't know. Everything's so old here. It's interesting and all that, but you should see California. It's not gray like this."

As they walked down Orszaghaz utca, where rows of fifteenth-century buildings had been declared national monuments, she took his hand, and he silently vowed that he would go to California where everything wasn't old.

They spent as much time together as they could in the next week, and she explained that she was studying to be an actress. She told him over and over how handsome he was and how well he would do in California. Before she left, she kissed him and let him fondle her breasts.

He made up his mind immediately. He would leave Budapest and go to college in California.

He applied for visas and transfers and the right to leave and the right to enter, and miraculously they were all granted to him. He left Budapest on a rainy June day and after several flights, delays, and stopovers, arrived in California two days later to find the most glorious sunshine he had ever experienced. So far Marina had been right about everything.

As a foreign student at the University of Southern California, he spent the summer studying English and getting acclimated. He decided to study film, and the professors were encouraging. When school started in September, he was ready for everything. His only shock was that Marina moved in with him.

That first night when she took off her clothes and slipped into his bed, he decided that there really was a God after all. Hell be damned, he was going to enjoy heaven on earth. Her body was smooth, like fine silk, and she moved in bed like a graceful dancer. Naked, she put her tongue on his lips, then let her mouth slide to his chest, moaning when she felt his muscles and his power beneath her. He remained in control, unflinching, but when she moved her tongue to his most delicate flesh, he was totally at her mercy. He succumbed almost immediately to her pleasuring, then minutes later found himself ready for more and eager to give her pleasure.

Instinct made him a good lover, and Marina's eagerness for novelty made him even better. They made love four or five times a day. He had endless stamina for sex, and it seemed that they couldn't walk by each other without lust intervening.

When he could bother to think about them, his studies were going well. At school in Hungary, where memorization and drills were

161

the order, he was considered a good student; here professors spoke of creativity and originality—and considered him brilliant.

He spent his time making movies and making love.

This was America, where life was free and open, but he found himself feeling guilty about Marina. He didn't want to be living in sin for too much longer. This heaven on earth was all very well, but his father's verbal pictures of the licking flames of hell were hard to forget. He was also terrified of losing Marina. Finally he decided that a wedding was in order, and they were married in the church on campus on his nineteenth birthday.

He was thoroughly devoted to Marina and too inexperienced to recognize her wandering eye. Now that she had this sexy, gorgeous foreigner all for her own, she had other plans. Emil's new American friends tried to warn him, but he didn't understand. In his third year at school, he made a documentary on American romance that won a prize as the best student film of the year, and suddenly he was a celebrity on campus.

Just as suddenly Marina became pregnant.

"I don't know what happened," she told him, crying softly. "I almost never forget to take the pill."

He stroked her back, embarrassed to tell her that the pregnancy thrilled him. It was the way of life for men and women, what should be done. He lived in California now, but his soul was Hungarian—and there pregnancy was seen as a fulfillment.

Marina, still striving to be an actress, saw it as a disaster and wanted an abortion.

Emil was horrified: he begged and cajoled, touched her swelling stomach while they made love to show that it excited him, would not interfere with their passion. What finally convinced her, though, were not his entreaties but her own error. Because it had taken her a long time to realize that she was pregnant, she had misjudged the dates; so when she secretly went to a doctor she knew to have the pregnancy terminated, he told her it was too late.

Emil worried about finances and his ability to finish school, but he was entranced by the idea of a child. Marina didn't want to talk about it and refused to read the books on pregnancy and child care that he brought home from the library.

When Erin was born, Emil stayed in school but took two jobs on campus to meet their new expenses. Rushing home between classes to play with his new son, he would find that Marina had left the infant with a baby-sitter and rushed off to a dance class or audition.

Or someplace that he didn't know about.

She seemed to be ignoring both him and the baby.

"You only think that because you're a chauvinistic European," she told him when he tried to broach the subject. "Maybe your mother hung around in peasant clothes, but I have better things to do."

He didn't understand her growing animosity, couldn't recognize that she blamed him and the baby for all her own failings and inadequacies. Erin was a glorious baby, but Marina didn't want him around and told that to Emil over and over. One day, when Erin was just over a year old, Emil came home at noon and heard a strange sound from the bathroom. Walking in quietly, he saw the bathroom door ajar and his wife naked on the floor, rhythmically sucking the cock of Professor Jackson, the chairman of the Department of Communications and Film.

Her academic major.

Professor Jackson must have been close to sixty, and his mottled flesh hung loosely on him. His pubic hair was gray and grizzly, and when Marina, surprised at Emil's arrival, pulled away from him, his flaccid penis flopped from her mouth and bobbed at his sagging balls like a limp tadpole out of water.

It wasn't lust that had inspired Marina.

Stunned, Emil walked back to the living room, where Erin had been left in front of the television set, and scooped him out of the playpen. There was nothing to say; he just took his child and left. That night he stayed with friends who tried to reassure him that Marina was an aspiring actress, and it was not unheard of in that profession to use one's sexual wiles to get ahead. But he wasn't appeased by the thought that his wife was whoring to advance her career. What was wrong with American women? Gray, medieval Hungary, where men and women knew their place, began to seem appealing again. One week after graduation, he flew back to Budapest with Erin, entering as an American citizen. They moved in with his parents at the hotel, and he tried to make a life for himself as a filmmaker.

But four years in America had changed him.

He couldn't be in Budapest now without seeing the politics and social structure in a new light. His parents thought it demeaning for a strong Eastern European man to change diapers and were embarrassed to have him there with a baby and no wife. They tried to introduce him to agreeable young women, but he had no interest in the confining life that young Hungarian girls welcomed. He spent all his time working on a documentary, and when it was done, he knew it was brilliant. Filmed from the point of view of a child living through the 1956 revolt, it was called *Two Thousand Dead*.

His father watched it in silence when Emil played it for him.

"My son, you have a choice," his father said quietly when the last frame had flicked from the screen. "Burn the film or leave the country forever."

Emil understood but waited to leave until the film had been chosen by the New York Film Festival. Then he said good-bye to his homeland, packed clothes, cameras, books, and Erin, and flew all night and part of the day to start yet another new life in America.

And the life has been good, he thought now, pulling the Porsche into his driveway. He missed his country and his parents even more, but he had been able to see them in Vienna and Berlin and once even in Rome, so he no longer agonized every day about having left to come to America. Now that Eastern Europe had been turned on its head, he held out great hopes that his parents would come to visit him and that he would even see Budapest again. He even wondered if his film would someday be shown there. Given the new openness that was supposedly occurring, maybe he would eventually be a hero in his own land.

But it didn't really matter anymore. Over the years he had devoted himself to child and career, and both had flourished. He allowed himself some amusements, dated many women, and finally had the experiences that he had missed as a teenager. He was now a discriminating connoisseur, knowing what he wanted and what he liked in a woman. A good body, a strong sense of self, stability, brains, talent—he insisted on the whole package.

Having glimpsed it in Jillian, he wondered how strenuously he should go about trying to get it.

CHAPTER TEN

"CYNTHIA, do you think you can get a flight back to New York tonight?" Mark tried to keep his voice calm, but he sensed an edge of panic creeping in that he hoped Cynthia didn't notice.

"If you really want, I suppose I could, but I'm not sure I understand the urgency."

"I just explained it," he said, irrational anger rising. The letter from the D.A.'s office was on his desk, and he picked it up again with trembling fingers. A friendly letter, or at least not outwardly menacing, but it sure asked a lot of questions. And he wanted Cynthia sitting right next to him to answer them. He also wanted her lying next to him to comfort him with her hot tongue and her eager body. "Why the hell do you think we're being investigated?"

"Probably because the crane case brought you to the D.A.'s attention. Nothing much more or less than that."

"Not because of the . . ."

He paused, interrupted by Cynthia's piercing laugh. "Your problem, darling, is that you can't remember anymore what's legal and what's not."

It was true. Just holding the letter made him sweat because he couldn't decide which of the recent dealings of Wright Realty would stand up to scrutiny. Or if the D.A. had discovered the one activity that he knew wouldn't stand up at all.

"Oh, I've come up with an interesting little tidbit that might bear on that letter," Cynthia said. "The Manhattan D.A., Barney Rossman, is the brother of your wife's partner. What's his name? Keith Ross."

"Say that again?" His mind wasn't in any condition to handle complicated equations.

She repeated the relationship, and he said, "So what does that get us?"

"Really nothing at all. I just thought it was interesting. It does raise the possibility of your whispering a few too many things to your wife during a moment of passion in bed and her passing them on. Something you should be aware of, maybe."

"I don't whisper anything to my wife in bed, and we don't have moments of passion anymore."

"It's all right, Mark. You don't have to tell me that."

"I know I don't have to, but it happens to be true. You're all I want anymore, Cynthia."

"If you're trying to convince me to sleep with you tonight, you've done a good job. Can your secretary get me into a hotel near your office?"

"I'll fire her if she doesn't. Should we take care of the plane flight, too?"

"I'll arrange it from here. Just meet me at the hotel with the papers from the D.A. and a bottle of champagne. Then we'll take one thing at a time."

■

Jillian sat on Annabelle's new terrace, sipping an iced tea and contemplating Emil's firm bottom. Standing just a few feet away, Emil had his back to her as he talked to a cameraman and made some final checks on the sound equipment. What was it about Emil that was so sexually exciting? She used to think his talent and confidence were the great stimulants, but looking at him now from behind, his bottom accentuated by the tight jeans he was wearing, his muscular arms and shoulders outlined by the white Lacoste sweatshirt that also accented his glowing tanned skin, she had to admit that his pure physical appeal was almost overwhelming.

Emil spun around, looking for Jillian, caught her staring, and said simply, "Jillian, come over here for a second, would you? We've got some questions."

They all had some questions about the afternoon's shoot.

A raving Denny had waited for Annabelle outside the Rumn Club the night before, but protected by Rob, she had refused to talk to him, and he didn't yet know where she was living.

"If I never tell him, he'll never find me," Annabelle had suggested hopefully to Jillian that morning.

"Nice try, but it won't work. You have to make it clear to Denny that your abusive relationship is over. If you don't straighten things out right away, he'll be forever harassing you. It's time to get on with your life without him."

"But what could I say to him?" Annabelle asked in the little-girl voice she sometimes took on that always threatened to turn to tears. "He's all I've got."

"No, you've got Emil and Keith and Rob and me for moral support, and loads of fans who aren't going to leave you no matter what. And don't forget you've got Artie Glenn to work with now. You can bet he'll treat you like a professional."

"He didn't sound sure that he even wanted me last night," Annabelle said.

"Don't be silly—he was just being cautious." Jillian decided not to mention that Artie Glenn had called her very early that morning, worried that if Denny didn't sign release forms, they'd be sitting ducks for lawsuits. But now wasn't the time to stress the importance of Denny's signature, Jillian decided, and she just said, "Denny's been trying to keep you as his slave, and it's time you broke free."

Tears popped into Annabelle's eyes. "I guess I'm a little scared to leave. Denny says I'd be nothing without him, you know. That's one reason I've stayed so long."

"Oh, come on, you're not that naïve, are you?" Jillian took a breath, trying to decide if Annabelle was strong enough to hear the truth. The bruises and black eye, expertly hidden last night by makeup, were apparent in the pale day's sun, and the girl looked frail. Rob Daly, torn between discretion and his job, told Jillian that Annabelle had clung to him all night in bed, sobbing and wanting to be held. It was no mystery that Rob and Annabelle had gotten together—she was like a free-floating particle, ready to bind to anything that bumped into her path.

"Denny's very rich, you know," Annabelle said, and Jillian wasn't sure if it was meant as explanation or pride.

"You're rich, too. Or at least you should be."

"Denny takes care of all my money." There was a hesitancy in her voice—again the pride at being taken care of by Denny clashing with the painful awareness that all was not what it should have been. "He only gives me spending money."

"Look," Jillian said gently, "there's nothing wrong with relying on someone else, and there's certainly nothing wrong with loving someone. But I have the feeling that Denny spent a lot of time crushing your ego so you'd stay with him. You stayed because you didn't see any other options. But now you do, and Denny's going to have to learn that he can't intimidate you into loving him."

"But I do love him," Annabelle said, wide-eyed. "Or at least I thought I did. Do you think he loves me?"

"People have different ways of showing love. But I don't think you hit someone you love, and I don't think you hurt someone you love. Ever."

Annabelle offered her famous pout, then with a proud toss of her head said, "He gets wildly jealous if he thinks I'm sleeping around."

"I can understand that, because Denny seems obsessed with dominating you and holding on to you. But jealousy isn't necessarily love."

"I want to be loved," Annabelle said simply.

Jillian nodded. "We all do, but the question is how much we'll put up with for it. How many compromises we're willing to make."

"Have you had to make compromises for love?" Annabelle asked.

"I've never had to deal with being physically abused," Jillian said, "but if it ever happened, that would be the end. Immediately. As for other compromises . . ." She paused, wanting to be a tower of strength for Annabelle, the proof she needed that love should be a pleasure and never a burden. But how much would she herself put up with to keep Mark? Far more than she wanted to admit. There would be no difficulty in tallying the recent rejections and the blows to her ego that she had chosen to overlook; lately Mark had tried to make her feel that her life was less important than his. It was subtler than bruises and beatings but still damaging. Telling Annabelle what to do seemed so easy. *If Denny loved you, he wouldn't treat you that way.* But who would give her the same advice about Mark?

"You have to decide where you'll draw the line," Jillian said finally. "Love is never perfect, but it should at least enhance your life. Once it starts destroying it, you have to take steps."

"So what should I do?" Annabelle's small voice sounded frightened.

"Call Denny and have him come over this afternoon. You'll be on your own turf, so you'll feel some measure of control. See if you can talk to him rationally about what's going on."

Annabelle looked at her helplessly, and said, "You can't talk rationally to Denny. He goes into rages. If I don't appease him and say just the right thing at just the right time, he becomes a madman."

"I'm sure you're very good at saying just the right thing, but your life can't go on that way." Jillian said it firmly, leaving no room this time for questioning. "This time you set the rules for the relationship, and if he doesn't want to follow them, it's over. I know it's hard, but you won't be alone."

Annabelle called Denny and arranged for him to come over late that afternoon. She didn't mind Jillian's idea of putting the whole meeting on tape, either. "Seeing how you handle the situation is going to help millions of women to deal with similar problems," Jillian said to encourage her. And though it was both true and convincing to Annabelle, the words sounded strangely hollow to Jillian.

Now Jillian, still drinking her iced tea, joined Emil and the cameraman, Luke, and listened to their questions about propriety. Denny knew about the documentary, but he certainly wasn't going to want this meeting taped. What if things got nasty and he demanded that the cameras be turned off?

"He can't order us to leave, because it's Annabelle's house," Jillian said. "Anyway, let's not worry about it too much. We'll try to stay out of the way, and maybe he'll forget about us."

"I've got a long-range lens and a handheld," Luke said. "I assumed you want to do this without taking any time to reset?"

"You got it. Don't get anxious about the quality of the shots—just get them. For the moment this is cinema verité."

Emil decided to stay inside, afraid that his presence would be a red flag for Denny.

Denny didn't need any red flags. Jillian and Luke were on the terrace, mostly out of sight, when Denny arrived, and his anger flared as soon as he walked around to the back of the house and saw Annabelle emerging from the swimming pool.

Her house. Her yard. Denny wasn't expected for another half-hour. She was wearing the bottom of a neon-green string bikini and nothing else.

As Annabelle stepped off the pool ladder, she saw Denny and, after hesitating a moment, lifted a hand and tentatively waved to him.

"Hi," she called weakly. "Weren't expecting you yet."

She scampered over to the chaise lounge where she'd left her towel and T-shirt. Denny strode purposefully toward her, his heavy leather boots pounding like hammers against the blue-and-white ceramic tile. As Annabelle reached for her towel, Denny grabbed her wrist so forcefully that she gave a little yelp of pain.

Annabelle's back was to the camera, and Denny was holding her wrist at such an odd angle that a chill went through Jillian; she wondered if the wrist were broken. Luke moved in tighter on Denny's face. His pupils seemed dilated, and his mouth was contorted in fury.

Annabelle broke loose from Denny's grasp and pulled a T-shirt over her head. As she wriggled into it, Denny grabbed for the scanty bathing-suit material at her crotch.

"I came here to find out who's been fucking with your brain, but now I want to know who's been fucking the rest of you!" he hollered.

"Hands off me, please," Annabelle said, pushing him away and covering herself. "I don't want you here if you're going to be an animal." She looked triumphant, as if her first moment of standing up for herself felt better than she could have imagined.

But it wasn't enough.

Denny pushed away the chaise separating them and leaned his face menacingly close to her. "You better want me however you find me, little cunt. If not for me, you'd still be lickin' dick in Piccadilly Square."

Annabelle shook her head and looked around for an ally to restore her resolve. On the porch, Jillian felt a sinking sensation in her stomach. Annabelle was looking for her, wanted her there for support—but she was going to have to handle this herself.

Annabelle and Denny were arguing now in loud voices—he threatening and overbearing, she, the big star, cowering and on the verge of tears. Several times she repeated phrases that Jillian had used earlier in the day, but the prim words about needing to have some control over her own life sounded absurd in the face of Denny's mad rantings. Annabelle seemed to be folding.

On the terrace, Luke turned to Jillian and snarled, "You got her into this. Shouldn't you go help her out?"

Jillian shook her head slightly. "She's doing fine."

As if she sensed the encouragement, Annabelle pulled out the papers that Artie Glenn had dropped off, a standard agreement putting her bookings under the control of Artists Management.

"I think I need services other than just yours at this point," Annabelle said in a high, strained voice. "I'd like you to help me make an easy transition."

The words sounded stilted coming from Annabelle's mouth, and instead of having the calming effect Jillian had intended when she offered them to Annabelle, they sent Denny into a new fit of temper. He grabbed the papers from Annabelle's hand and with a roar of anger, threw them into the swimming pool.

"Don't do that!" Annabelle shrieked, running toward him. He stopped her with an elbow to her stomach, then reared back and slapped her across the face with such force that she went reeling, stumbling against the side of the pool, catching herself against the ladder.

On the terrace Luke said, "Oh, shit," and continued shooting.

Denny was gesturing wildly, shouting obscenities at Annabelle, who sat slumped against the edge of the pool, dissolved in tears.

Jillian heard the door between the living room and terrace open quietly and saw Emil step out, unable to resist the lure of the shoot any longer.

It took Emil barely a moment to sum up the situation in the yard. A burning anger rose to his cheeks, flushing beneath his tanned skin,

171

that seemed to set the whole terrace on fire. Lips set in fury, Emil jumped off the terrace and ran toward the pool.

"Get away from her!" he called.

Denny ignored him and shook his fist at Annabelle. "You'll sink without me, you little bitch. You'll be eating shit off the floor, which is what you deserve. You know you have no talent and so do I, and without me everyone else in the fucking world is going to know it, too." He kicked her in the shoulder, and because her hysteria had already made her limp and helpless, the kick sent her sprawling headfirst into the pool.

Emil grabbed Denny around the waist and with barely controlled rage jerked one arm behind his back. He dragged him away from the pool and with stormy authority called, "Stay away from her!" Without waiting for a response, he bounded back to the swimming pool and reached in to help Annabelle, who was crying too hard to find the edge. His strong arms pulled her toward the ladder, and as he was leaning over, vulnerable to attack, Denny came staggering back toward them. But Emil stood up abruptly and, swinging around, caught Denny with a fist to the jaw. Denny fell to his knees, then furious, got up and tried to return the blow. But he was an uncoordinated mass of surging adrenaline, too stoned and out of control to hold his own in a real fight. In a moment Emil had Denny's arms pinned behind his back and was pushing him toward the front yard.

"Get the hell out of here," Emil called, "or I'll have the police on you in ten seconds!"

Emil shoved Denny beyond the high fence, slammed it decisively, and moved back yet again to the pool, where Annabelle, wailing and alone, was pulling herself shakily up the ladder.

Luke's camera recorded Annabelle in close-up as she emerged from the pool in her clinging, sopping-wet T-shirt.

■

It took over an hour for Annabelle to calm down, but once she did, Jillian managed to convince her that she had won the round.

"He knows he can't manipulate you anymore," Jillian said, "and he's raging in frustration."

Annabelle didn't want to talk about it. All she wanted to do was have a drink and go to sleep. As usual she wanted Rob as her baby-sitter. Jillian and Emil stayed with her talking about how strong she had been, what she had proved to Denny and herself.

When Rob arrived Jillian and Emil conferred briefly on their evening's plans and left. Jillian thought she sensed a smoldering anger in Emil as they got into the Porsche and drove to a small Italian restaurant for an early dinner. She wanted him to talk about it, but he seemed resistant. He tuned the Porsche's stereo to a classical music station and listened intently to the Mozart.

In the restaurant Emil ordered a bottle of a good Chianti and buttered a hunk of warm Italian bread while they glanced at the menus and listened to an excessively agreeable waiter discuss the evening's specials.

Finally left to themselves again, Emil said, "Are you finished with Annabelle?"

Aware of the slant he'd put on the question, Jillian said, "Personally, I'm not going to abandon her, if that's what you mean. But in terms of the shoot, I think we have just about everything we need. A lot of good footage. It's a powerful story, and we're going to have to make sure we tell it right."

Emil tossed down his bread and looked at her steadily.

Jillian admired the glacial luster of his eyes for a moment and then sighed. "You're angry at me, and I'm not sure why."

He shook his head. "Not angry. Just trying to understand you."

"I'm very simple to understand today. I'm just trying to produce an interesting show."

"But I know you too well to think you'd do that at the expense of everything else."

She shrugged and leaned her elbows on the table, her fingers clasped at her chin. "Go ahead, Emil. I know you want to give me a lecture on how ruthless I am and how I exploited Annabelle, just watching from behind a camera while the poor girl was being knocked around. If you hadn't stepped out to the terrace when you did, nobody would have intervened."

"Is that true?"

"I don't know," she admitted with a sigh.

He shrugged. "I'm not lecturing, but yes, I think the day could have been handled better."

"Tell me how."

He shrugged. "It's a fine line when you're making a documentary. You can't show a whole life, so you pick and choose pieces, hoping it gives some semblance of a complete story. Then when you're shooting, you have to be there and not be there at the same time. All in the search for truth."

"And what do you think? Did we find truth?"

Before he could answer, a waiter appeared at the table to display the bottle of Chianti Emil had ordered and to comment on what a fine choice it was. He opened it with a flourish and offered a splash to Emil, who tasted it, nodded briefly, and watched as the waiter filled Jillian's glass, then completed filling his own. When the waiter finally walked away, Emil swirled his glass and said to Jillian, "Let's not dissemble, you and I. Tell the rest of the world whatever you like, and I'll stand behind it, but we know that you manipulated the situation from the start. Every 'behind-the-scenes' shot we have of Annabelle bears your imprint."

He spoke in a calm tone, but still Jillian felt stung.

"That's not fair. I gave some advice, but I didn't create the story. You were the one who found out the truth about Denny. It was clear that Annabelle had to leave him, and we just helped her. We didn't arrange for that scene with Denny shouting at you at the Rumn Club last night."

"But you arranged for the scenes today."

"I'm not a fortune teller, so I couldn't know what would happen. I arranged all the elements, yes, but that's not the same as arranging the outcome."

"Elements behave in a fairly stable manner, Jillian. You mix hydrogen and oxygen in certain conditions and you get water. Oxygen and methane and you get an explosion."

"Were everything in science so certain, Emil, nobody would bother doing any experiments anymore." Jillian picked up her fork and began stabbing at the basil-and-arugula salad that had been put in front of her.

"Then I'll change my metaphor. You weren't playing scientist, you were playing puppeteer, making your characters dance when you needed them. But this isn't just a stage show, it's life."

"I'm aware of that."

"Are you? Then I'm not sure where we draw the line between your behavior and Denny's. Each of you think you know what's best for Annabelle, and you just plow ahead with your own agenda in mind."

"God, you're unfair." The fork tumbled from her fingers, and her eyes blazed at him from across the table. "I happen to believe that there is such a thing as good and bad in this world. If you can't distinguish my actions from Denny's, it's because you're refusing to make moral judgments, and I don't know what more to say."

"Why don't you just explain your actions to me."

She gulped at her water, trying to swallow her resentment; her throat felt tight from the effort of holding back her indignation, and suddenly she realized that there were tears gathering behind her eyes. But she wouldn't give in to them; she was determined to stay in control, not be overwhelmed by Emil's icy anger. "All right, let me try. Annabelle doesn't need either me or Denny to tell her what to do. She needs to do what she wants. But sometimes saying that is easier than doing it. If I set up anything, it was for her to fight for her own freedom." She looked at Emil closely. "You should know about *that*, at least."

Some of his coldness seemed to melt. Returning her gaze, he said, "Yes, I do know about that. And you're right. Sometimes you don't really know what you want until you have to put yourself on the line to get it."

"When Annabelle was at the pool, she was confronting herself as much as she was confronting Denny. I guess I should be angry at you for deciding to rescue her when she really needed to rescue herself."

Emil took a sip of wine. "All right, I'll forgive your efforts at manipulation if you'll forgive mine at rescuing."

"Forgiven." She picked up the fork again, finishing the salad that was still on her plate. "The other point to remember is that Annabelle will be in a better position after we're through with our show than she was before, and that counts for something."

"Yes, it counts for a lot." Emil smiled. "It was interesting for me to watch you work today. You're smart, and that has always attracted me. But now I understand just how smart—and why you're so in demand in this business. I suspect you can finesse any situation to your own advantage."

"Why do I have the feeling that I'm not supposed to say thank you?"

He laughed, and this time when their eyes met it was in affection, not anger.

They moved on to more general topics, and Emil, who generally preferred listening to talking, succumbed to Jillian's charm and began to tell her about the work he had been doing, the serious films he was trying to make in between his lucrative television work. It was difficult because the lure of television in America was so great—not just the money he earned for it, but the power he felt.

"It's the ultimate democratic medium," he told Jillian. "You can enter people's homes and reveal your personal vision. Television executives always complain about the tyranny of ratings, but I don't believe greatness has to be sacrificed to mass appeal. There's nothing wrong with offering truths and moral education in stories that people like to hear."

"And nothing wrong with finding a palatable way of presenting one of those moral truths—which is really all we were trying to do today," Jillian said, deciding to defend herself one more time. "If we put this show together right, we'll be showing women both the dangers and triumphs of standing up for themselves."

Emil picked up an asparagus between his fingers and looking at it contemplatively, said, "Okay, I'll buy that. And I'll also say that for most of the day today, you were a true friend to Annabelle. Probably a better friend than she's ever had before."

They finished their heaping platefuls of pasta, and when Jillian said she was too full for dessert, Emil ordered two cappuccinos and a single order of chocolate mousse.

"It's delicious," the waiter told Jillian. "The house specialty. Sure you don't want one?"

"I'll taste his."

They sat for a long time over their cappuccino, and at Jillian's urging, Emil spoke about his son, Erin, explaining that he was in boarding school now and hoping to attend Princeton in the fall. Erin wanted to graduate early and spend spring semester backpacking through Europe with his girlfriend. Emil was in favor of all of it except having the girlfriend come along: he believed in setting moral standards for his son.

"If he's already sleeping with his girlfriend, your disapproval isn't going to stop him," Jillian said.

"True, but there's a greater moral issue to consider. What would you do if it were one of your daughters?"

Jillian smiled. "When I was young and single, I used to think that when I had children, I'd want them to be my friends and talk openly to me about their lives. I always figured it would be better for them to have their first sexual encounters at home than in the backseat of a car."

"And you still think that?"

"Actually I now think that part of the pleasure of a first sexual encounter is that it *is* in the backseat of a car."

Emil laughed. "So you like your sex when it's dangerous and illicit. That's good." He scooped up a bit of the delicate mousse and fluffy cream and leaned across the table, offering it to her.

"You must," he said. "It's pure ecstasy."

She licked the edge of the spoon and grinned at the tempting sweetness melting on her tongue.

"More?" he asked, and when she shook her head no, he said, "Don't be so cautious. You miss out on too many pleasures that way."

He paid the bill in cash, and they walked outside to the darkened street where they had parked. Emil helped Jillian into the car, then walked around to the driver's seat and slid in.

"Dinner was lovely," she said as he pulled the door shut.

In response he leaned over and kissed her, his lips catching the full softness of hers, brushing them with a gentle strength that spoke an unwillingness to let go.

She pulled away slightly with a quick intake of breath, caught off guard by the warmth of his presence and the unexpected force of her own longing. Emil touched her cheek softly and said, "I had to let you know, at last, how I feel." Then their lips met once more, lingering until Jillian again turned her head away, breathing deeply the air that was now filled with Emil.

He started the Porsche and drove quickly toward her hotel. Their talk was casual, as if the moment had never happened. Pulling up to the hotel, Emil started talking about the plans for shooting interviews with some of the other rock stars like Madonna and Mick Jagger who had agreed to be interviewed for the documentary on "The Secret Life of Rock and Roll."

"Did you get the shoot schedule?" Jillian asked Emil.

"I did, and it looks fine. But do you have any idea how all this is going to piece together?"

"I put a storyboard together last night and outlined a script that I think will work."

"Good. When can I see it?"

She glanced out the car window toward the softly lit lobby of the hotel, pleased that she had long ago decided to stop staying at the Beverly Hills Hotel. Her preference was a place that was equally expensive but more low-keyed, where she could actually get some work done; she left the see-and-be-seen detail to Keith, who couldn't understand wanting to be away from the heart of the Hollywood action.

"Right now if you feel like it. Come on in."

They abandoned the Porsche to the young valet standing gallantly by the door, dressed in a sharp hotel uniform that bore a striking resemblance to white tie and tails. As the valet got into the car, Jillian realized that the uniform was appropriate: drivers pulling up in fifty- or sixty-thousand-dollar automobiles wanted to think that their car was being handled by someone of their class.

Jillian stopped at the concierge desk to ask if anything had arrived for her. Glancing at a list in front of him, the concierge said, "Several things, and I had them all put on the desk in your suite, Ms. van Dorne. In fact, I believe you'll find three faxes and two Federal Express letters there."

She thanked him and walked toward the elevator with Emil, gratified again that it was not a hotel where anybody would be watching. Upstairs the maid had already turned her bed down for the night, and in the sitting room had left mints and a small bottle of cognac with two glasses. The desk was piled high with the urgent business correspondence that had arrived that day. Jillian leafed through it, then pulled the storyboard and script from the top drawer and handed them to Emil.

"Just one copy," she said. "Have a look."

He sat down on the sofa with the script, and Jillian stayed at the desk, going through the other reports and contracts that had been sent to her. One fax was from her secretary, listing the important phone messages that had come to Jillian's office that day, including calls from Drew Wilder, the president of the network, and Henry Munroe, the president of Wink Cola. Munroe had left a home phone number, and Jillian moved into the bedroom to call him from there. "So I won't bother you," she told Emil, and he nodded, too busy studying the script to look up.

Jillian chatted amiably with Munroe, who was glad to hear from her, and once she got a sense for why he had called, she reassured him that the footage they had for Annabelle would win viewers without being offensive. "It's still that image of youthful triumph we talked about over breakfast that morning at the Royalton," she assured him. "You could run it on The Family Channel if you want. It's going to be moralizing, not provocative." Even as she spoke, she wondered how news of the day's shoot had traveled so quickly. Instead of asking, she was charming and appeasing, and as a result he seemed to change his intentions halfway through the call.

"I was going to ask you if I could have one of my people at your edit session," Munroe said, "but maybe it won't be necessary."

"Let's both think about it," Jillian said pleasantly, resisting the temptation to tell him that a sponsor would be invited to the edit session only over her dead body. "Meantime, you have my assurances of good taste. Not to mention the fact that the network's standards and practices will approve everything we do."

Munroe laughed. "I trust your good taste better than theirs."

Jillian uttered a few more genial comments, repeated a funny remark that Keith had made to her, and amidst mutual laughter and pleasantries, told Munroe that she might even bring in the special under budget.

"You're a champ, Jillian," he said, won over yet again. "Let's plan to have dinner next time I'm in New York."

They hung up, and Jillian's smile turned to a scowl. She glared at the stylized phone as if it had done her a personal disservice. In the living room, Emil looked up in time to catch her expression, and striding across the long sitting room, he stood at the bedroom door.

"Problem?" he asked.

She shrugged, composing her face. "Not really. Munroe's happy again, but I get tired of stroking our sponsors."

He moved over to her and stood by the edge of the bed. Jillian started to get up uncertainly, but Emil sat next to her and said, "Poor Jillian. Always someone new for you to dazzle."

"I wish I could dazzle you," she said with a small smile, "but you see right through me."

"Right to your heart."

"Which is why I trust you."

"Then I hope it won't undermine your trust if I kiss you again." Not waiting for her to answer, he folded an arm loosely around her shoulders and pulled her close, leaning down to kiss her with a tender gesture that belied the force behind it.

This time the kiss didn't end.

Emil leaned back against the bed, pulling her toward him with his strong arms until she was almost on top of him, lying against his powerful chest, her hands touching his face. The heat of his body was warm against her, and his big, comforting hands stroked her back and shoulders, then slowly moved forward, touching her soft breasts. The gentle stroking became more insistent, and under her silk chemise, she felt her nipples getting harder from his attention. His hands slipped underneath to her smooth skin, and cupping her breasts, he brushed the nipples delicately, until her body began throbbing.

"God, you're gorgeous," he whispered, kissing her hair and burying his head in her neck. "You taste wonderful and you smell wonderful."

Pulling briefly away from her, he turned and slipped from the bed to kneel in front of her, his hands first at her thighs, then gliding back to touch her buttocks. When she started to protest in embarrassment, he kissed her knees, his lips grazing her soft skin, then he found her smooth belly and kissed it tenderly, over and over. His fingers returned to her breasts, and he lifted the chemise over her head so she was suddenly naked to the waist.

The phone rang then, and Jillian pulled back, looking from the phone to Emil; feeling exposed, she crossed her arms in front of her breasts and got up to answer it.

The concierge was on the line with a message from Jillian's office he had forgotten to give her.

When she hung up, Emil stood next to her and, taking her arms away from her breasts, he encircled each wrist with his fingers, then held them at her side. He looked longingly at the graceful body now revealed but said, "You can be saved by the bell if you want. I don't want to do anything unless you're comfortable."

For an answer she leaned over and kissed him sweetly on the lips. He released her hands and, reaching behind her, unzipped her skirt; the sibilance of metal against metal was seductive in the quiet room, and as the skirt snaked down her thighs, he held her tightly, slipping it off.

Dressed for the L.A. heat, she had on nothing underneath but a pair of scant lace panties, and as Emil hugged her close, his fingers dancing on her skin, her heart seemed to be beating violently against his.

"Come here," he said, and lying in his arms, she was awed by his strength, which pleased her even more than it frightened her. Almost naked, she felt vulnerable and suddenly timid. Then he pulled off his shirt and lay on top of her, grazing her breasts with his skin. She felt dwarfed by his strong shoulders and powerful chest. Though he didn't take off his jeans, she could feel him through them, large and manly. He kissed her again and again, leaning over to taste her neck, then, taking her eager nipples into his mouth, he played with them until her whole body begged for him.

"I wasn't expecting this," she whispered at one point. Still holding her, he pulled back and said, "I couldn't resist any longer."

She abandoned herself to him, enjoying the seductive movement of his body and following his lead. They touched and explored each other, stopping frequently to laugh and share stories. "I'm as eager to know your soul as your body," Emil said, but at last, impossibly aroused, he asked, "May I come into you?" Resistance weakened, wanting to feel his strength at her core, she sighed but said, "I'm not prepared for you."

"Ah, then I'm the better Boy Scout," he said, and slipping his wallet out of the jeans he still wore, he showed her the condom packet. "I'm almost afraid to ask how long you've been carrying that," she said, and kissing her nose, Emil said, "Put there just for you, so you needn't worry." They laughed together, and the sound of their voices joined in laughter was its own bond.

He pulled off his jeans then, revealing himself powerful underneath, and smiled at the gratified sigh she uttered at seeing him. She slid down his body, kissing him. Almost shyly she touched his cock and whispered, "You're so firm."

"Because I want you."

She was ready for him, wanting more, but he continued touching and kissing her until she murmured, "Come to me," and only then did he poise himself above her. Her body welcomed his immediately, and though she tried to restrain herself, she felt a sweet orgasm ripple through her. He sensed it and held her tightly until she caught her breath, then he began thrusting inside her again until she was moaning, her soft cries filling the room, and she came over and over, clinging to him as she did.

"I could do this with you all night," he said, hovering above her, whispering her name, and finally allowing his own release.

Sweaty and satisfied, they held each other for a long time, neither of them thinking of sleep. "It doesn't get much better than this," Jillian whispered, but Emil said, "I promise it will get better and better each time."

They dozed and woke again, and finally Emil got up to leave, whispering of his joy in her, his hope that she felt as good as he did. Wrapping her peach satin robe around herself, Jillian kissed him good-bye at the door, and when he was gone, she walked back to the living room and sat on the sofa for a long time.

■

Jillian slept only briefly, and waking up for some unclear reason, was startled to see that it was five in the morning. Calculating the three-hour time difference, she figured her children were getting ready for school. Quickly she dialed the number and, getting Marguerite, found that Mark wasn't home.

"Did he leave for the office already?" she asked.

"No, I'm afraid he didn't come home last night." Marguerite sounded embarrassed for her, so Jillian quickly said, "That's all right," and asked for the girls. Both of them were awake, and for the next half-hour, Jillian caught up on their worlds, sharing Eve's thrill in her discovery the previous day at nursery school that if she mixed blue and yellow paint she would get green, and Lila's disgust with a child who had thrown sand at her in the playground. Jillian said soothing words and sent hugs, admiring Lila's dismissive decision that "Kids can be silly sometimes," since her own instinct was more ferociously protective, and she would have liked to bury the child in the sand.

The girls told her what they had eaten for dinner and what they planned to eat for breakfast, and Eve discussed what she was going to wear to school. ("Is it okay to wear tights, Mommy? Marguerite says I should wear socks.") Jillian thought she could never get enough of the details of their lives, and they sounded so happy that Jillian suspected she missed them more than they missed her. They sent dozens of kisses across the phone, smacking into the air before they hung up so the children could go to school and Jillian could go back to sleep.

CHAPTER ELEVEN

K EITH Ross dove into the swimming pool at the Beverly Hills Hotel, feeling tremendously virtuous for having had nothing more than club soda to drink the night before. He swam thirty fast laps, then went back to his room to shower and call Jillian. At first it had irked him that she would never stay in the same hotel as he did, particularly when they were in Los Angeles. She claimed to like more out-of-the-way spots, but he couldn't imagine it and assumed that was her way of keeping their relationship professional. That way she never had to wander past the Polo Lounge and see him chatting up a starlet. He had the distinct feeling that Jillian really didn't want to know who was sharing his bed at different times. It worked out well for him, too, since if she were in the same hotel, they would probably have breakfast together, and he could think of more than one young woman who might see them together, read it wrong, and take umbrage.

Of course, there was always the possibility that Jillian was attracted to him and was putting herself out of temptation's way. Drying himself after his shower, he glanced in the mirror and had to admit that other possibilities were more likely. His new devotion to swimming was keeping him in good shape, but his body was still slight and his hair graying. Without the armor of his expensive suits and Hermes ties, he looked soft and—could he admit it?—no longer youthful. His only real sex appeal came from his career, not his

184

physique. His power mattered, particularly in L.A., where the greatest aphrodisiac was the ability to put someone on camera.

Keith tied a fluffy towel around his waist and decided that Jillian had too much power of her own to be interested in anyone else's. She had managed to set up a perfect life for herself—an exciting job that gave her creativity plenty of space to roam and also paid her generously enough that she could afford all the clothes and jewelry and pleasures that life offered. Sure, the job was stressful and at times overwhelming, but for Jillian all that was balanced out by the cozy family that she went home to at night, complete with supportive husband and charming little children. Jillian was the only person Keith knew who had no reason to screw around.

Keith lathered shaving cream on his face, then called Emil on the speakerphone, always eager to do more than one thing at a time. They discussed the day's plan while Keith shaved, combed his hair, and splashed on cologne. Hanging up, Keith next dialed Jillian to let her know that Drew Wilder wanted her in New York to talk about their special at the affiliates' meeting.

"So if it's all right with you, I'll let Emil and an associate producer go to London to shoot the local color on Annabelle. I don't really think you're needed, do you?"

"Not at all. Especially if it's going to interfere with the network meeting."

"I just spoke to Emil and told him you probably wouldn't go. He didn't sound very happy about it."

"I'm sure Emil will survive," she said icily. "I've already given him the script and the storyboards, and I imagine he can also express a little creative judgment of his own."

Keith laughed lazily. "Don't get in a snit about it, Jillian. Of course he'll be fine. He just happened to mention in passing that he wished you were joining him in London."

Jillian hung up and found that her hands were trembling slightly. Hearing Emil's name so early this morning was disconcerting at best. Just what had Emil said to Keith on the phone? It wasn't like him to indulge in locker-room talk, but then nothing had been happening in the past twelve hours the way it was supposed to.

People in television loved to point fingers, and if anything went

185

wrong with their special now, if it didn't attract high enough ratings, she would be the perfect target to blame.

The producer was screwing the director. What great gossip *that* was going to make.

There was a knock on the door, and she went to answer it. Probably the concierge with another fax for her. Or maybe Emil had sent flowers.

When she opened the door, she found Emil standing there, and he smiled gently at the shadow of surprise and embarrassment that crossed her face.

"A bad time for you?" he asked.

"Not at all. Come in."

He stepped in but said, "I'm just here for a moment. I wanted to know how you felt this morning."

Seeing him standing there, feeling him, strong and caring, she sensed her anxieties clash head-on with her affection. She wanted him again. But holding herself together, she said, "I enjoyed last night, Emil. Every minute."

He traced a finger around her lips, touching the center. "Sweet words said with ice. Tell me the truth."

She turned away from him and said quietly, "I'll be honest. I've spent the morning worrying. It felt so good to be with you last night, but I don't know where it will lead or what it means. And no matter how careful we are, I have the feeling that people are already gossiping about us."

"Who would gossip?"

"Who wouldn't, is more like it."

He shrugged and touched her shoulder. "Jillian, we know how we feel about each other, but nobody else does. And I would never mention it to anyone. Ever. Hurting you is the last thing I'd want to do. You must know that. Is there something else?"

"Of course not."

"You're going to New York today and not on to London with me, I hear."

"Yes—and I'm a little upset that you complained about that to Keith."

"I didn't complain. But Keith knows how much I rely on you, so

I said what I naturally would say—even if last night hadn't happened. You're being hypersensitive."

"Perhaps. I'm sorry."

Reaching for her hand, he scratched the palm lightly with his thumb. "I don't want you to have anything to be sorry about. I'm discreet—you know that. Even if I'm thinking of you every minute, I'll never call you at home or in any way disrupt your life. What we have is for us alone. It's not to hurt anyone else or amuse anyone else. I feel strongly about that."

And I feel strongly about you, she thought, but kept the sentiment to herself, aware that if any more emotion were spilled this morning, she would be mopping up all day. Emil leaned over to kiss her ear, tickling the edge with his tongue, and despite herself, she giggled. She turned to kiss him, glad to feel his arms around her again, his special strength. "You make me feel like an eighteen-year-old."

"That's what it's supposed to feel like. But leave the eighteen-year-old on the plane. Be you when you get home again. My great fear is that you'll decide that I am interfering too much in your life with your husband and children, and I'll lose you."

My husband didn't come home last night, she thought, but that wasn't news to share with Emil. Instead she said, "I called my girls early this morning. I miss them. They're such great kids."

"Mmn, and you're a very great woman." He smiled, his lips brushing gentle kisses on her forehead, his nose buried in her fragrant hair, indulging in its sweetness. "My lovely Jillian," he murmured. "You're a bundle of emotions this morning. I feel honored to be allowed to see you this way."

Nobody should see me this way, Jillian thought as they kissed good-bye, knowing they would be working together again in New York in just a few days. Emil left, and Jillian took a deep breath, making a conscious effort to put herself back in control. She made a few calls, wrapping up loose ends in L.A., and then she packed her carry-on suitcase and went down to the lobby. Her limousine was waiting, but it was too early to go to the airport, so she asked the driver to take her to Rodeo Drive. Mark's birthday was in a few days, and she hadn't had a chance to get him anything yet.

The traffic was terrible and while once that would have made her crazy, now she simply closed her eyes, aware of how tired she was. In front of them, an idling truck spewed fumes from its diesel engine, and Jillian thought about doing a special on pollution. She wanted to produce television shows that *mattered*; rock and roll was fine, but she was glad that there was going to be a message—of hope and help—for women.

By the time the driver pulled up at her favorite jewelry store on Rodeo Drive, he said, "I'll be waiting right here. We should probably leave for the airport in about twenty minutes."

It was still early enough that the boutiques on the street were uncrowded. At Fred Joaillier, an elegantly dressed woman greeted her pleasantly and asked if she could be of any help.

Jillian said she was looking for a man's watch.

"Do you have anything particular in mind?" the saleswoman asked, strolling over to an expansive display case.

"It's for my husband. His birthday." She laughed. "What else can I tell you?" *You see, he wasn't home last night, and I may be falling in love with someone else. But we have to keep up appearances, don't we?* "I want an everyday watch, and I guess it should be waterproof."

The saleswoman smiled dimly. "Perhaps a Piaget?"

"Probably too dressy," Jillian said. *This may be a gift of contrition rather than of love. We don't want to get carried away.* She peered into the glass display shelves while the saleswoman rattled keys and opened each case as if it were Fort Knox. She began arranging cards of black velvet to display the watches, but Jillian didn't have time and, pointing to one in the case that caught her eye, asked, "How much is this one?"

"Why don't you select a few and then we'll discuss price," the saleswoman suggested.

"I've selected this one."

"That is a Concorde. A pleasant watch, but without the prestige of some of the others I can show you."

"It looks functional. I like the style. How much is it?"

"Two thousand seven hundred fifty."

"Fine."

She took out her checkbook and scrawled the number, realizing it was extravagant but not really caring. The saleswoman looked at her in surprise. She had seen women spend hours in front of the watches. This transaction had taken less than five minutes.

Jillian waited for the package to be wrapped, then tucked it into her oversized Fendi pocketbook and dashed back to the limousine.

Later, when she was finally settled into her first-class seat on the plane headed back to New York, she wondered if she had been wrong to buy the gift. It was a lie, after all. A statement of love she didn't really feel like making. But so much else in their relationship was based on lies right now that she wasn't sure why a birthday gift should be any different.

Jillian got the telephone from the front of the airplane and called home. Eve, answering the phone, was thrilled to hear her mother's voice.

"Where are you, Mommy?" she asked.

"In the airplane, somewhere over Iowa, I think."

"Will you be home to have dinner with me?"

"Probably not, honey. But I should be home in time to kiss you good night."

"Good," Eve said, and she launched into an elaborate description of the pretty pictures she had made that morning at nursery school.

"They sound wonderful. I'm going to look at them the very first thing when I come into the house."

"Even before Lila's cow?"

"What's Lila's cow?"

"She made it in clay class, and Marguerite put it on the hall table so everyone can see it as soon as they come in. *And* Lila's at Cara's house having a playdate and I'm home playing all by myself." It wasn't easy being the younger sister.

"I'll look at Lila's cow *and* your pictures first thing, okay? And tell Lila that Mommy called while she was at her playdate. You can give her a kiss from me." Realizing that was too subtle for a three-year-old, Jillian added, "You both had special afternoons. Lila has a playdate, but you got to talk to Mommy."

"Goody-goody. I love you, Mommy."

"I love you, too, sweetheart."

As she carried the phone back to its stand at the front of the plane, Jillian noticed one or two of the other first-class passengers glancing curiously at her. The phones hadn't been installed for people who wanted to talk about cows and playdates, but Jillian couldn't think of a better use for them.

Back in her seat, Jillian pulled out the large pile of scripts she had brought along to read. But she couldn't concentrate. . . .

The blue sky and fluffy white clouds out the window made her feel strangely suspended; the flight was so smooth that they hardly seemed to be moving, and she had an image of herself floating between heaven and earth. There was a strange comfort in being in this in-between space where she didn't have to declare herself. If she could call to faraway New York from here, it seemed she should also be able to call her mother, who must be much closer. How nice it would be to call her and tell her about Emil, confide in the woman who had died when Jillian was eighteen but whose voice sounded loudly in her heart whenever there was a decision to be made.

Jillian's mother, Evelyn van Dorne, nee Evelyn Schott, was the most dazzling woman Jillian had ever seen. When she was a small child, people would tell Jillian how pretty she was, then quickly add, "You take after your mother. Lucky you." But Jillian grew up feeling pride rather than resentment for her mother, who had become a magazine cover girl when she was just sixteen. Those were the days when models were expected to end their careers long before the first wrinkle line appeared. Evelyn was a small-town girl with a sharp instinct for self-preservation, and even while she was being seduced by money and cameras, she decided to guarantee her future by marrying. Strauss van Dorne had inherited money from his family's shipping business and kept making more. He was a tall, severe-looking man with a rigid sensibility and a traditional view of the sexes. He wanted to get married. So at age twenty-two, the woman who *Vogue* had once described as "the toast of New York and Los Angeles, not to mention Paris, London, and Milan" decided to quit her job so she could devote herself to her husband and a future of having babies.

Evelyn took on her new role with a vengeance and did a fine job at it for many years. Less than a year after she got married, she gave birth to a sturdy son named Christopher, followed soon after by handsome Bentley, and then, after a few years' hiatus, her daughter Jillian. They were good and easy children who admired their mother and returned the comfortable love she showered on them; she enjoyed motherhood almost as much as she had enjoyed modeling. Where once she had collected photographs of herself shot around the world, Evelyn now collected the heart-shaped cards and lace-decorated pictures that her children loved to make for her. Strauss, in contrast, took his wife for granted, not realizing how much his dismissiveness hurt her. Because he considered raising the children her job, he paid little attention to any of them.

Evelyn accepted the terms of the unwritten family contract, getting enough satisfaction from the children to keep her feeling alive. But as the children grew older, her attention started to wander. She was proud of the fine young adults she had raised, but she was wise enough to understand that part of nurturing a child is letting go. It was time to focus on herself again, to fulfill some of the yearnings that were rising in her own heart.

If she closed her eyes now, Jillian could still remember the glow on her mother's face on her forty-second birthday, when with great exultation she described her plans to open her own modeling agency. She wanted to pick her life up again where she had left it nineteen years earlier. The boys were in college now and Jillian was in high school, and Evelyn wanted to know how she would feel about having a mother who did more than plan the best birthday celebrations and dinner parties in town.

"I wouldn't mind at all, Mom. I think it's nice," Jillian had said.

"Your father hates the idea," Evelyn had admitted. "He wants me at home. I want you to understand that he makes enough for both of us, but I'm doing this for reasons that have nothing to do with money."

"What are the reasons?"

"Being myself again. Having a passion in life again. When I was your age, I had a mental calendar for myself. Everything was carefully laid out—modeling, getting married, having babies. I've ripped off all the pages I had filled and still there's half my life left. How can I leave the rest of the pages blank?"

In the next months, those pages began to fill rapidly, and Jillian listened to her mother talk about the glorious satisfactions of work, the sense of herself as an individual that she was regaining after all the years as Mrs. Strauss van Dorne. With her partner Italo, a handsome and dashing man ten years her junior, Evelyn built the business steadily. Strauss, who had always seemed cold and distant to Jillian, seemed even more removed, but the connection between Evelyn and Jillian grew stronger and stronger. They became friends, each blooming into a new stage of womanhood. Evelyn gave her daughter a well-thumbed copy of *The Feminine Mystique,* and they read passages of it aloud to each other, joking that they were the only mother-daughter consciousness-raising group around. Jillian shared her mother's elation and the early joys of her liberation. As the modeling business kept getting busier, Jillian's father grew angrier and angrier.

One night when Evelyn came from her office at close to midnight, she had a fight with her husband that ended with Strauss storming from the house. After he left, Evelyn felt surprisingly calm and dry-eyed, but when she peeked into Jillian's room, she found her daughter sobbing in her bed. She went in quietly and sat on the edge of the bed, stroking Jillian's long hair, letting her cry.

"We want to please men, but first we have to please ourselves," Evelyn told her daughter quietly. "Life has to be lived with energy, not fear. If there's one lesson I can give you in your life, it's to find your own happiness."

"Could you be happy without Daddy?" Jillian had asked.

In the dark room, lit by a shadowy reflection from the full moon outside the window, Evelyn had nodded. "I'd like to have everything—and I'd like you to have everything—but if we can't, we have to learn how to make the right choices."

"Are you going to choose your business over Daddy?"

"It's not that simple." She gazed out the window, wondering if she should talk to her daughter about divorce and true love, explain how complicated life could be. But instead she realized that there *was* one simple denominator and she said, "If I'm pushed to a decision, I'm going to choose my own fulfillment, rather than his. Yes, I am." She began to talk then about her business and her future, and they sat together until almost dawn, dreaming and scheming and planning. Jillian sometimes thought she could remember every word of that conversation, of her mother's call for a life of passion.

The very next afternoon, the end of a strangely chilly October day, Evelyn came home with the news that her doctor thought she had a lump in her breast. Checking into the hospital the next week, she signed all the papers that said the doctors could do whatever they thought best. She went to surgery confident that everything would be fine and woke up from the anesthesia without her left breast. The doctors told her that they had performed a radical mastectomy—but didn't think they had been able to remove all the cancer cells.

Sitting in Evelyn's hospital room, Jillian had listened as the doctor placed the blame for the awful disease squarely on her mother's trembling shoulders. Evelyn had received silicone treatments during the earliest days of her modeling career to make herself one of the big-breasted beauties that were favored at the time. Now, according to the doctor, the silicone had masked the cancer for so many months that it had spread beyond the point where recovery was likely.

But Evelyn wasn't willing to give in to the disease. She went through chemotherapy and radiation treatments, losing her hair, her appetite, and her dignity, but refusing to quit. Sick most of the time, she sold the business to Italo, who visited her almost every day and flooded their house with flowers. Jillian stayed at her mother's bedside for hours at a time, listening to Evelyn tell and retell the saga of her life, trying to make sense of it all. Knowing she wouldn't be alive to see her daughter's achievements, Evelyn tried to give years of advice and encouragement, anticipating the problems that Jillian would face and giving her the words, the knowledge, that would help her cope. Jillian forgot how beautiful her mother had once been and thought only of how wise she had become.

Evelyn helped Jillian make the decision to attend UCLA and watched her get dressed in an aqua-blue gown underlayered with crinoline for her high-school senior prom. At the end of the dance, when her friends were heading for the prom-night ritual of an overnight at the beach, Jillian asked her date to bring her home so she could see her mother. They arrived in time to see Strauss van Dorne standing stoically at the front door, watching an ambulance driver removing Evelyn's covered form from the house.

I didn't ever want to stop crying, Jillian remembered. That was the night she suddenly understood that women were blamed for everything in life, even their own cancer. Silicone had masked

Evelyn's disease, and because of that, her daughter was supposed to understand that her mother deserved to die.

Her mother had dared to become the person she wanted to be, and she had been punished for that. *You die when you do something wrong.* In some deepest recess of her subconscious, Jillian believed that women who broke the rules, who played their own games and sought their own happiness, were made to suffer.

She conjured an image of her teenage self, lying in her soft and cozy bed, listening to her parents' angry voices the night that Strauss had slammed out of the house. For the first time, she remembered what she had long repressed—that it wasn't the business that had raised her father's fury, but something about Italo, something that the young Jillian hadn't understood but the grown woman could imagine.

Her mother had been so beautiful and determined—unwilling to give up anything in life, finally seeking what she deserved. And as Jillian thought about Emil, she tried not to remember that her mother was dead.

■

Emil returned to New York three days later with six cassettes of tape shot in London. All in all they'd shot over twenty hours of tape for what was to be a one-hour special, and the thought of editing it was overwhelming.

"That's why we have assistant directors," Emil said soothingly. "I'll have my a.d. screen and log every tape before we start editing. And I'll be right there editing with you."

He had phoned her in the office every day since their evening in Los Angeles, but she was so professional on the phone that it was hard to get a sense of how she felt.

Leaning across her desk, his voice low, he said, "I've done nothing but think about you since Los Angeles."

"Nice thoughts, I hope."

"The best. You're all I dreamed you would be."

She nodded, surprised by the catch in her throat that kept her from responding. Finally she said, "Do you have the editing schedule Liz typed up?"

He glanced at her, saw the suppressed emotion and decided not to pursue it. Instead he said, "I did look at the schedule, and I don't think a week is going to be enough editing time. Can you extend it to two weeks?"

"Unfortunately I can't. There's been so much publicity about the concert and the special that the network wants to air this fast. They've pushed up our air date, and I've got to get them a rough cut in a week. If we don't have enough days, we'll have to work nights."

"Well, then I'll see you on Monday. Ready to work hard. Unless you'd like to join me for dinner tonight."

She paused only briefly, then shook her head. "I really should get home." No need to explain that it was Mark's birthday.

"I understand. I'm flying to L.A. in the morning."

"And coming back on Sunday? That's a quick turnaround."

"We all struggle with our obligations, don't we."

Lila and Eve were waiting for her when her train pulled into the Melrose station, eager little faces beaming at her from the platform. She picked them up and hugged them, and the conductor, smiling at them from his open window as the train began to pull away again, sounded his horn in their honor. They grinned and waved.

"Daddy's not coming home for his birthday," Lila said to Jillian as they all piled into the Volvo.

"He's not?" She looked questioningly at Marguerite, who said, "Mr. Austin called a few minutes ago that he's going to be delayed tonight. He'll be very late, but he sends his love to everyone."

"Well, I'm sure he's disappointed," Jillian said, hearing the embarrassed sympathy in Marguerite's voice.

At home she saw just how hard the children had worked preparing for the birthday. A lopsided cake covered with M&Ms and edible glitter waited proudly in the kitchen; the dining room table was festooned with noisemakers and metallic streamers, and each place had been set with cheerful paper plates and party hats left over from the girls' own birthday parties. The glass serving table in the corner of the room was so crowded with pictures the girls had made and oversized packages they had wrapped in glittery paper that Jillian's dignified gift box was almost lost.

"What a wonderful celebration you'd planned," Jillian said.

"And now Daddy won't see any of it." Lila's eyes were misty, the surprise she had worked so hard to prepare spoiled. You bastard, Jillian thought. Ignore me if you want, but don't disappoint the children.

"What we should do," Jillian said decisively, "is leave all this just the way it is so Daddy can see it when he gets home, and then have a birthday breakfast for him tomorrow."

"With cake?" Eve asked.

"With cake. And tonight we'll go out to eat ourselves. A special girls' night out, okay?"

"Hooray!" said Lila, her mood immediately changing. "Where can we go?"

"Pete's Pizza! Pete's Pizza!" Eve said, doing a little dance in place.

"No, someplace fancier than that."

"The Melrose Diner?" ventured Lila.

"Great idea."

They left almost immediately, and the girls seemed to forget about Daddy as soon as they were seated at a booth in the diner—a former hamburger joint that had been refashioned as a Fifties diner, complete with a tiny jukebox at each booth. Lila asked for a quarter and picked a song by Madonna for background. Jillian was grateful that it wasn't Annabelle Fox.

"What did you two do today?" Jillian asked, and Eve immediately volunteered, "I played with Adam in the playground. Do you remember Adam?"

"Of course. Adam Homestead. We once met his mommy and daddy at a party. Weren't you going to marry him a while ago?"

"We *are* married," Eve asserted. "Adam's daddy is a lawyer, and Adam is going to be a lawyer, too. I'll be his secretary."

"Maybe you'll be a lawyer, too. His partner."

"No. He wants me to be his secretary."

Thinking of Walter and Lydia Homestead, Jillian wondered if children were doomed to re-create the lives of their parents. Years ago in college, she and her girlfriends used to tell one another that life would be easier for the next generation of girls. Well, the next generation was sitting in front of her, and she wasn't sure what had changed. I don't want them growing up to be little Annabelles, Jillian thought, and renewing her efforts to convince Eve that girls could do anything, she said, "It's usually more fun being the lawyer than the secretary. Maybe you and Adam could trade off."

Eve frowned, an intrinsic feminine knowledge telling her that would never work. But wanting to please her mother tonight, she offered, "Okay, Mommy, I'll be the lawyer, too. That way I can wear party dresses all the time."

"Girls don't have to be frilly to be successful," Jillian said, trying hard to follow the three-year-old reasoning.

"You wear pretty clothes to work."

"It's different. I'm not trying to play on monkey bars at recess. You should be able to run around as much as the boys do without worrying about your underpants showing." Even now Eve was wearing her pink-and-white eyelet party dress. The child's fascination with all things feminine baffled Jillian.

Eve shrugged. "I want to look like you instead of the other mothers," she said, and Jillian was startled to realize that to a small child, success made a woman glamorous. In Eve's eyes the real advantage of Jillian's job was that instead of wearing jeans and Reebok sneakers every day, she got to put on pretty clothes.

Lila ordered orange juice and shrimp cocktail—her idea of a sophisticated first course in a restaurant—and then took her turn expounding on what she'd done in school. There had been a class trip to the planetarium in the morning and a special painting project in the afternoon. Lila was doing so well with her piano lessons that she had been picked to perform in the school recital. "I might be a pianist when I grow up," Lila announced, "or maybe I'll be an astronomer."

"You could be both."

"Really?"

"Of course. It's fun to do more than one thing."

"Our mommy does lots of things," Eve piped in.

"That's right," Jillian said, hardly believing what a pleasure it was to sit with her daughters at dinner. "I have lots of jobs. One job is being a producer and one job is being a mommy."

"I hope I have enough money to get a job," Lila said, sounding worried.

"What do you mean?" A six-year-old's reasoning could be as puzzling as a three-year-old's.

"I hope I have enough money when I grow up so I can have a job." She said it with such surety that Jillian paused before saying, "Honey, you don't need money to get a job."

Lila sat back and looked at Jillian in bewilderment. "But you once said that poor people don't have jobs."

"That's right."

"So I want to have enough money to get one."

Suddenly understanding the child's confusion, Jillian smiled lovingly. "You make money when you have a job. The reason poor people don't have money is that they don't have jobs. It's not that they're too poor to get a job." Lila looked baffled, her six-year-old worldview shaken, and Jillian leaned over to hug her daughter tightly. Cause and effect were not easy to understand. Not easy at all.

■

Jillian arrived at Image Mix, an editing facility near Times Square, at eight o'clock on Monday morning and found Emil already there. Their editing studio was a small room crammed with monitors, huge control boards, and high-tech machines. The front of the room was given over to the expanse of editing equipment, and the editor, an intense man in his mid-twenties named Curt, sat in front of it like the pilot of a futuristic airplane. His swivel chair had wheels, and the Plexiglas strip running on the carpeting under the console allowed him to zip from one control to another with minimal effort.

Jillian had requested Curt since he was quick and smart and had a knack for making edits that seemed impossible. Long ago, Jillian had learned that a good editor could save endless time and aggravation. And at six hundred dollars a day for the edit studio, time was indeed money.

Curt said hello when Jillian walked in but didn't get up from the control panel he was adjusting. Jillian walked back to the long narrow table where Emil was sitting, three steps up from the control panel; it hovered above the machines, a perch for producers and directors that allowed them to look directly into the monitors. Emil stood up, offered a friendly kiss, and took her coat.

"You picked a great place," he said. "They already brought in breakfast."

Editing often went on for days at a time, so the best editing studios offered proper amenities. Behind their table, a leather sectional sofa surrounded a glass coffee table on which someone had put a big basket of muffins, bagels and jellies, various fruit juices, and a pot of coffee. Monitors jutted out from the walls at each end of the sofa, so it was possible to sit back for a moment without losing any editing time.

Five plush chairs were lined up in a row at the narrow table, and Emil sat down in the middle one. Jillian sat next to him, and he gave her a thick sheaf of papers.

"Editing notes from my assistant director," he explained. Each tape had a time code burned into it, and when the a.d. screened them, he wrote down each shot change and the time it appeared. That way they didn't have to waste time scanning through the tapes when they were using expensive editing facilities. The system was fully computerized, so they could tell the editor the time code they needed, and the right image would appear on the screen for editing.

It made things easier, but it was still a long process.

"Is your a.d. coming today?" Jillian asked.

"Of course."

"I have two assistant producers who'll be arriving soon, and Rob Daly is in from L.A. for a few days, and he wanted to be here, just for the experience. Keith will stop by in the afternoon."

"We'd better order extra lunch," Emil said cheerfully.

A graphics designer had already created an opening montage for the show, a forty-second extravaganza in black, white, and red for which Keith had paid twelve thousand dollars.

"You can start an edit master and lay that tape in at the top," Emil said to Curt. He pressed some buttons, and the montage appeared, full of brilliant special effects and clever electronic graphics.

"Is that from Double Digit Art?" he asked.

"It is," Jillian said. "Like it?"

"Just terrific. I love their stuff."

199

"Now all we have to do is match the style through the rest of the show edits."

"Sure thing."

He froze the monitors on the last image of the montage and put up one of the concert tapes that included the shot Emil had selected to start the body of the show. "How do you want to dissolve out of the montage?" Curt asked.

"Can we make the screen dissolve into black and white stars, then let them fall away and reveal Annabelle in close-up?"

Curt nodded and started to work. As he tried various effects, Emil watched closely, asking that the size and number of the stars be changed, that the dissolve out of the montage be slower and the dissolve into the opening shot be quicker.

"Let's start that close-up about fifteen frames earlier," he said, and when Curt previewed the edit, Emil asked, "Was that fifteen frames?"

"For God's sakes, you're talking about half a second," Jillian whispered. "Do you think anyone can possibly tell the difference?"

"I can tell," he said, strumming his fingers and waiting for Curt to check the computer readout.

"Sorry, Emil!" Curt called from the front of the room. "For some reason the machine did the edit without the extra fifteen frames. I'll try it again."

Emil winked at Jillian, and she laughed. "Okay, so you're perfect. Do you want me to leave and you can do this yourself?"

"Don't you dare." Under the table in the dim room he put his hand on her knee, then let it dally at the edge of her short skirt. "Have I mentioned that you have splendid thighs?" he whispered.

"No, and this isn't the time to mention it." But she smiled and didn't remove his hand.

By noon Keith and Rob and some of the others had arrived, but the edits were complicated, and after four hours' work, they had completed barely three minutes of the show.

"Editing is so tedious," Jillian said, suppressing a yawn.

"Go join Keith and the others in the back and have some lunch," Emil said.

"No thanks. I'd rather be close to you."

They finished for the evening at eight o'clock. Leaving the dark, windowless studio and walking outside to the street, which was bright with the glimmer of New York lights, Jillian felt strangely disoriented. Evening had settled in long ago. "We missed daylight altogether today," she said.

"And we'll miss it all week." Emil stretched his long body like a panther waking up from a nap. "A twelve-hour day of editing makes my head spin. How about going out to dinner on my expense account?" When she hesitated, he said, "Of course, there's always a back rub and room service instead."

"They both sound enticing," Jillian said, smiling, "but if I get on the train right now, I can be home in time to kiss my girls good night."

Emil sighed. "I feel comfortable competing against anything in your life except that. The girls win every time. Let me walk you over to Grand Central. Then I'll amuse myself tonight thinking about tomorrow, when I will again gaze longingly at you all day."

They worked furiously for the next two days, living in the darkness of the edit room, eating take-out Chinese food, and stealing private moments each evening to talk before Jillian got on the train.

When they finished editing Wednesday night, "The Secret Life of Rock and Roll" was barely beginning to take form.

"It's not going to get done in time," Jillian said despairingly.

"You guys want to crash this piece over the next few days?" Curt asked when they were leaving.

"Can you do that?" Jillian asked.

"Sure. Nobody else is scheduled in the editing rooms at night, so we can just stay here and get the damn thing done."

The next morning, Jillian packed a few things in her overnight bag and told Marguerite that she had no choice: she was going to stay in the city and work round-the-clock to get the show done.

"I'm sorry to leave you alone with the girls," Jillian said to Marguerite. "But I have to do this, and I don't know that Mark will be around much."

"Don't worry," Marguerite said generously. "The girls are so busy with school and soccer practice and birthday parties, they'll hardly be home anyway."

When Jillian got to the editing room, Keith was sitting next to Emil with a cigarette clenched between his teeth. The scene they had shot by the swimming pool with Annabelle and Denny was playing on three monitors, and it occurred to Jillian that Keith was seeing this part for the first time.

"Incredible," Keith said when the last shot flickered into blackness. "Let me see it again."

Emil's face tensed. "We don't have time to be screening tapes here, Keith. I'm sorry."

Keith ground out the cigarette and lit another one before the stub in the ashtray had stopped glowing. "It's my goddamn money and my goddamn show. Sorry to pull rank, but if I need to screen this fucking tape, I'm going to."

As the day continued, the tension got worse.

They had so much footage to choose from that the "truth" about Annabelle was going to be whatever they decided it was. A plucky, charming teenager preening backstage and swimming in her backyard pool? Or a weak, scared child being manipulated and abused by her manager-boyfriend?

They were playing with fire, and they knew it.

"This section starts after the fourth commercial," Curt called from his editor's seat. "I'm fading from commercial directly to the bumper. What's the first shot?"

"Go to 11:36:22 on the tape you're on now," Jillian said, looking at her notes. "When you get there, play it at half speed."

He pressed a few buttons, and they saw the blur on the monitor of the tape fast-forwarding. Suddenly it stopped on a close-up of Annabelle's face, streaked with terror, as Denny's huge hand moved toward her cheek in slow motion and slapped her with agonizing force. The close-up was so tight that you could see drops of water spurting from her hair as her neck twisted.

"About a twenty-frame freeze on the end, and then you're out of it," Jillian said. "The audio for it is the one Mark brought over yesterday that we just recorded. It's on audio tape six."

Curt popped in the cassette, and the room filled with the eerie sound of a well-known actress's voice.

"*Hitting . . . Violence . . . One big man . . . One small girl . . .*"

"Jesus Christ," Keith said.

202

They continued editing, Jillian calling for the shots and scenes she had already selected, making disparate elements come together to tell a story. Curt sat silent and sweating, previewing edits and abandoning them just as quickly when someone in the room wanted to try it another way.

At four o'clock the monitors went blank, as if they refused to go on in the overwrought atmosphere.

"Holy shit," Curt said.

Editors from other rooms, working on other shows, converged in the hall, each wondering what he had done wrong, and quickly realized that there had been a failure in the mainframe of the computer.

Unable to continue, Keith left the room to find a private phone; Jillian and Emil sat on the sofa, sipping coffee and waiting.

After nearly half an hour, Curt burst back into the room.

"The computer won't be back up until nine or ten tomorrow morning," he said. "But it looks like the memory hasn't been erased. We didn't lose anything we did today."

"Thank goodness for that," Emil said.

There was nothing to do but leave, and people began drifting out slowly. Jillian straightened out her notes and wandered outside with Emil.

"Where are you staying?" Jillian asked.

"The Waldorf-Astoria. Park Avenue and Fiftieth."

She laughed. "Did you know that's my old haunt?"

"No, but I hope it's your new haunt, too."

They nudged each other toward the hotel that Jillian had considered home for so many years and ambled through the gracious burgundy lobby. In the elevator, Emil pushed twenty-seven and said, "I got a suite for the week."

Perhaps in the hope that she would stay.

As he pushed open the door, Emil took the overnight bag she was carrying, tossed it in the closet, and reached for her.

"At last," he said, seizing her with a kiss that left her breathless.

He touched her brow with his index finger, felt the furrows there, and said, "You're tense. Is it from editing, or are you afraid of me?"

Laughing, she said, "A little of both."

"Well, I'll make sure you relax."

He slowly unbuttoned her billowy silk shirt, smiling at the glimpse of lace underneath. His touch sent a shiver through her. She brought her slim body closer to his, surprised by how much she wanted him.

They shed their clothes slowly, first her shirt, then his, her earrings and rings, his watch.

"You have perfect breasts," he told her, touching them appreciatively. "Have you always been such a sexy woman?"

"I only feel sexy with you," she said, and though he looked at her in disbelief, she meant it. Being with Emil made her feel as if she'd never had sex before. He was so confident and loving and sure—knowing how to please her and making it clear that though he wanted to possess her, he was willing to take his time.

"I'll bet every man who's ever met you wanted to make love with you."

"I don't know about that, but nobody has ever excited me the way you do." Since he was shirtless, she could admire his muscular chest and the smooth skin that had been burnished by the L.A. sun to a light tan. His jeans, still on, were unzipped at the top, and she could see where the tan line stopped.

Her skirt, his jeans, their underwear—the clothing scattered around the room as they reached for each other.

The front wall of the room was taken up by a long mirror, and she caught him glancing in it.

"We look wonderful together."

"I'd rather just look at you," she said, but she caught a glimpse of their pairing: she pale and slim, he dark and muscular, but still their bodies merging together so that they seemed an intricate puzzle, pieces of a whole.

"You're bashful," he said, noticing her turn quickly from the mirror, and when she nodded slightly, he said, "Then let's move away."

He led her to a thickly upholstered armchair in a dark corner of the room, urged her to sit, then kneeled on the footstool in front of it. They kissed, their tongues probing and eager, then he pushed her gently back into the chair and dropped his head to her thighs. For a moment she held her legs stiffly, but when he touched his tongue to her center, she felt her resistance melt. His tongue moved slowly, then finding the core of her rapture became more insistent. She tossed back her head, overcome by the heat coursing through her body and the startling sensations aroused by Emil teasing her most sensitive skin. She heard her own voice crying in pleasure, but it seemed distant; nothing was real but the throbbing bliss of her body. She whispered for him to stop, but he didn't—and so neither did she; waves of gratification rolled over her, each coming so quickly after the one before that she was unable to catch her breath. Her fingers were tingling and her thighs trembling, but Emil continued until she said, "Please, come inside me."

He pulled back slightly then, kissing the insides of her thighs and gently placing each leg over one arm of the chair. He held himself above her, and his cock seemed huge. But still he wasn't rushing, and he lowered himself tantalizingly close to her, rubbing his firm penis against her still-throbbing center; she wrapped her arms around his back and pulled him into her and then gasped at feeling him hard and deep inside her.

"My God," she whispered, and wrapped her legs around him, pulling herself closer, pulling Emil deeper, until feeling her body merged with his soul, wanting to hide inside him so they were one person, not two, she erupted in a final, overwhelming orgasm.

Letting himself go then, he unleashed the desire he had left unfulfilled through their days and nights of flirting. "Damn," he called softly as his sperm swept through his body and escaped. "Damn, damn. Oh God. Damn."

Opening his eyes, he found her smiling at him, and he said, "You're amazing." Then picking her up, he carried her to the bed. They kissed tenderly, and he didn't move from inside her. After a brief reprieve of talking and hugging, he was aroused again, his penis growing firm in her, flicking its need. She looked at him with surprised pleasure.

"You never stop," she whispered at one point.

"I can't get enough of you," he responded.

They began to make love again, and each time she felt sated, he would begin again, moving her easily to a new position, consuming her from front and behind, once looming powerfully over her on his knees until she was overwhelmed by the magic of his power.

Clinging to each other, they loved unceasingly; when they finally checked a watch, they found hours had gone by. They dozed off to sleep well past midnight, then in early morning they began again, just as eager now but pausing more to talk and reflect.

Not since Marina has it been like this, Emil thought. Not since the earliest days with Marina. And still this was better. He wanted to tell Jillian that he loved her but feared she would shrink from the words.

"You'd jump under the bed if I told you how much I care for you," Emil said.

"Tell me."

"Very, very much. No, more than that."

"That's very, very, *very* much," she said tenderly.

He pulled a sheet over them as they talked, forming a cozy womb, their own hiding place from the world. Her body felt stiff this morning from the hours of activity, her thighs ached from the luscious strain put on them in love, but neither of them wanted to stop. They clung to each other, Emil wanting to take her so forcefully that she could never leave him.

When they remembered to look at the clock, it was well after nine; the sun was straining through the chintz curtains in the room, and Jillian said reluctantly, "We should go." She moved gracefully from the bed to the bathroom and turned on the shower. Peeking out, she saw Emil standing nude by the television, an irresistible statue of power.

"Come join me?" she asked.

He chuckled. "If I do, we'll start again and never leave."

The heat of the water released the scents of love, of their mingling bodies, but refused to erase them. She washed carefully with the almond-scented soap he had left for her and wondered if her body had ever felt more used, more gloriously weary.

Stepping out of the shower, she heard Emil's voice and realized he was on the phone. One side of the conversation drifted toward her, and it was soon obvious that Keith was on the other end, calling from the edit studio, asking why Emil was late and wondering where the hell Jillian could be.

She waited until Emil hung up, then left the bathroom and walked naked to the closet to retrieve her clothes. Emil's eyes followed her, but she refused to turn around. By the time he had showered, she was fully dressed and sitting in an armchair, looking at a script.

"Go ahead on to the edit studio," Emil told her, rubbing his back with the towel. "We don't want to arrive together, anyway."

"Why not?" She put down the script and smiled seductively at him. "Are you ashamed to have been with me?"

Leaning over the chair, his face still wet from the shower, he kissed her and said, "You must be joking. I consider being with you one of the great achievements of my life. But I promised you discretion."

"I've decided to stop worrying about people gossiping," Jillian said. "What can anyone say that would hurt us?"

"You're married," Emil said gently. "I'm not going to ruin your family life. The only thing I want people to say about us is that we put out a damned great show."

"I hope it is," Jillian said.

"Are you worried?"

"A little."

"Don't be. It's a winner. I say it pulls a thirty-five share."

"You're an optimist."

"That's because I'm happy—and everything keeps going my way."

CHAPTER
TWELVE

W HAT a family I have. Thirty million people in America watched 'The Secret Life of Rock and Roll' last night, but my very own mother and brother missed it." Only half-joking, Keith shook his head and took a last sip of the kosher French wine Barney had brought for Shabbat. It wasn't bad—it tasted like an average French table wine—but it didn't seem to belong at this meal. They came to Lotte's house for tradition, and that meant kosher wine that was so sweet you could barely choke it down.

"But, Chaim, we already explained to you that—"

Keith raised his hand, stopping his mother in midsentence. "It's all right. I'm not hurt." He kissed his mother's hand. "But next time you have to be in shul when I have a big show on, would you make sure to take Denny Wright with you?" He drummed his fingers on the sheaf of legal documents that had been presented to him that afternoon, just a few hours after the Nielsen overnight ratings came out, showing that their special had won the night and buried the competition. A 42 share. It was incredible.

Everyone had liked it except Denny Wright—who had decided to sue.

"Amazing that he got those papers to you so fast," Barney said, eyeing the documents that he had perused before dinner. As usual, Glenda was working late. "I just don't see any lawyer taking on a libel suit at nine in the morning and having a marshall serve you those papers before noon. It virtually can't be done."

"So you think he saw the show before it aired?"

"I can't imagine anything else. But even if the papers have been sitting on some lawyer's desk for a couple of weeks, it's strange to serve them today. Normally, you'd wait a few days before charging that a client's reputation has been destroyed and they've suffered serious damages. The only point in doing it this fast, I guess, is to undermine the show."

While Keith was thinking about that, Lotte said, "What do you say we watch the tape now and have dessert afterwards?"

In the living room, Keith popped the tape into his mother's VCR. He liked it that Lotte Rossman was unfazed by VCRs, compact disc players, microwave ovens, or any other new technologies. She often said, as long as she was living, she was going to *live*, even if that meant pulling her chair very close to the television so she could see it and turning up the volume to a level that Keith found uncomfortable.

Once the familiar music that opened the show came on and Lotte was comfortably settled, Keith went back to the dining room to clear the table. He'd watched the show so many times now that, proud of it or not, he didn't think he could bear another viewing. But after loading the dishwasher and washing out the wineglasses, he went back to the living room in time to watch Annabelle walking nervously with Denny while the announcer's solemn voice talked about "the age-old problem of male violence, and the courage of this very young woman who had the spirit to fight back." The image dissolved then into a series of shots backstage at the New York concert with Denny yelling and threatening, then whisking Annabelle away when her set was over. Next came the frightening scenes from the Rumn Club and the house in Laurel Canyon, all carefully woven into a tapestry of terror. The segment reached its dramatic climax by the pool, and for what seemed like the hundredth time, Keith found himself clenching his fists in anxiety as the violence built. He heard Lotte breathe an inadvertent sigh of relief when the last violent scene dissolved to a shot of Annabelle, proud and spunky, singing "No More Teenage Virgins" at the Rumn Club.

"Many teenage girls lose their virginity before they lose their innocence," said the voice-over announcer. "Imagine how difficult it was for this young singer to confront the fact that the man she had been trusting with her life and career could be destroying both." Then a cut to a close-up of Annabelle singing onstage, dressed in a skimpy, sequined mini-dress and holding the microphone close to her mouth, her eyes closed as she emotionally belted out one of her hits.

> He said by loving me
> He'd set me free
> I'll give my lovin'
> But I'm keeping me.

In the context, the words of the popular song resounded with new meaning. Emil had played with special effects until, at the end of the song, the background dissolved, leaving Annabelle all alone on the screen, looking like a guileless child. Lotte sniffled, and Keith thought yet again just how much he admired Emil's ability to stir emotions with a camera.

"So what do you think?" he asked as the credits began to roll.

"Terrific show," Barney said, impressed. "And even though I see why Denny sued, I also think you have grounds to fight him."

"Never mind, of course he has grounds," Lotte said spiritedly. "What kind of crazy world is it that a man can go around beating up a poor girl, then sue because people find out what he's doing?"

"Very crazy," Keith said, "but it may at least turn out that she's not so poor. Her new manager is a guy named Artie Glenn, and he figures that Denny stole at least a million dollars from her. He's hired a lawyer to start litigation to get it back, and there's already been one emergency court order calling for Denny to turn over all the funds paid Annabelle for the New York concert and her week at the Rumn Club."

"He's probably spent it all already on drugs," Lotte said.

"I wouldn't doubt it, but he can't really plead poverty. Seems Denny is a vice-president in his father's real-estate business in London. The whole thing is disgusting. Denny could have been as rich as he wanted without bothering to enslave Annabelle. But I guess he didn't want to work in Daddy's business. He wanted some power of his own." Keith shook his head. "I used to think it was money that made the world go round, but I've changed my mind. It's power. Sex and power. Which in Denny Wright's case were probably the same thing."

"Denny Wright," said Barney suddenly. "Of course. He's part of the Wright Company in London, which is involved up to its ears with Austin Realty. Is that how you and Jillian made the connection with Annabelle in the first place?" When Keith nodded, Barney said, "The two companies—Austin and Wright—have a joint venture that's doing some consulting and construction in Eastern Europe. Could make them a fortune in the long haul."

"All legal?" Keith asked, joking.

Barney shrugged. "They're doing some fancy footwork. They've got one of those lawyers who manages to keep the first two layers of everything legal, and it's only when you dig to the third layer that you realize just how messy it really is. In fact, their lawyer—" Interrupting himself, Barney snapped his fingers and went into the dining room to pick up the legal papers Keith had left on the table. Coming back, he flipped to the last page and looking at the signature, offered a satisfied laugh. "C. Reilly is apparently Denny Wright's counsel. Cynthia Reilly. That's who I was just telling you about. She handles most of the complicated cases for Austin Realty, and she's masterminding the deal with Wright Company. Guess she took some time out to help Denny."

"That's strange." Keith lit a cigarette, and seeing the pained look on Lotte's face, immediately put it out again. Lotte's emphysema was about the only thing in the world that could keep him from smoking. "Do you think Cynthia Reilly doesn't realize that Mark Austin is married to Jillian?"

Barney shrugged and flipped through more pages. "It's possible. Jillian is specifically named in the suit, but she has a different last name than her husband. Maybe Ms. Reilly just never made the connection."

Keith tapped the floor with his foot, desperately wanting a smoke. "I wonder why Denny would use a woman lawyer, other than convenience. Jillian thinks he has a real problem with women. He hated her almost on sight, and she's convinced that it was misogyny that drove Denny to act the way he did with Annabelle."

Barney laughed. "Sounds like he'd get along fine with Cynthia. Tough as nails and a real user, too, from what I've heard. Maybe you could make a few delicate inquiries through Jillian about what's going on."

"That I'll definitely do." Then, changing the subject, he said, "I haven't told you about my newest project. We're just about ready to tape the pilot for our syndicated late-night talk show. There are no sure things in television, but this is about as sure as you can get. We've already got one of the biggest stations in Chicago behind us and interest from New York and L.A."

Lotte smiled at the news and, patting her hand, Keith added, "I'm going to have you on this one, Mom. No wheedling out this time. Once we get a go, we've got a hundred and ninety-five one-hour shows to tape."

"Ah, the truth comes," joked Lotte. "You want your old mother on just to fill time. Now, *that's* a reason I finally believe."

Both her sons laughed, and Barney asked Keith, "Who's your host?"

"Good question, because there are several of them. That's the original concept of the show. Instead of looking for a new Johnny Carson, we looked for a new idea, and we got it, so we're mixing some of the elements of the hot daytime shows—real people baring their souls—with nighttime entertainment. We do talk, we do singing, we do entertainment, we do controversy—and there's a host for each part. I got the two big contracts signed today. Tucker Fredericks is the talk host." Barney made a face that looked like he'd just bitten into a sour lemon, and Keith said, "I know he's a little overexposed lately on television, but he's handsome and smooth and the definition of professional. We needed somebody slick, because our singing co-host is anything but that. But getting her was the casting coup of the decade, if you ask me. We're expecting it to be all over the newspapers tomorrow."

Keith paused for so long that Lotte finally said, "Well, who is it?" Keith strummed his fingers against the velveteen slipcover on the sofa and said, "Annabelle Fox."

▬▬▬

Stroking Cynthia's thigh was Mark's definition of heaven. There was nothing else on earth that could arouse him that way, especially when she slid down on the bed just enough so that he was no longer caressing the thigh but fondling her between her legs, letting his hands slip around to feel her round, firm ass. He had never met a woman who enjoyed having her ass rubbed quite so much. Cynthia liked her sex straight, but she also liked it with variations, and at her urging, he tried positions he never would have dreamed of with Jillian.

Jillian. At the thought of her, his hand inadvertently paused in the circle it was describing on Cynthia's sloping hip, and he lost interest in the erection that had been trying to build under his trousers. He had ignored Jillian for so long now that she had stopped trying to get him back. On the nights Mark came home, there seemed to be an invisible barrier running down the middle of the bed; sometimes she still reached over to hold his hand, and when she did, he felt so guilty that he feigned sleep. But damn it if Jillian wasn't still *nice* to him. He thought of his birthday; he hadn't managed to get home until well past midnight when everyone in the house was asleep. But Jillian and the girls woke him early the next morning and dragged him downstairs for a delayed celebration, as if his delinquency the previous night didn't matter and they wanted to make up for what the family had missed. The dining room was decorated with crepe paper and balloons and the girls had presents for him and Jillian had an incredibly expensive watch that was so perfect he almost didn't know what to say. All the frivolity and familial affection made him feel good.

But not as good as he felt with Cynthia.

He'd intended to get home for his birthday, just stopping at Cynthia's for a drink after work. But she'd made it hard to leave, taking off her pretty robe as soon as he came in, displaying the black peek-a-boo bra and crotchless black lace panties that she was wearing. Just seeing her that way made him feel like a teenager, and he'd made love to her immediately, still standing by the door, losing himself inside her in seconds. On other nights he wasn't sure that she was totally pleased with his lovemaking; she would openly seduce him, then look at him in disappointment when they'd finished. On that birthday night it didn't matter, because Cynthia had more entertainment planned.

"Your birthday presents are really for us to share," she said, and he began unwrapping the small packages, starting with the love-massage cream that she poured over him and rubbed in gently until it began to feel warm on his skin; her cool tongue licked it away, generating its own kind of heat. He wanted to have her again right then, but she said, "You have more presents to open," and the next package had been edible undies, which she put on for him to taste. Neither of them tired of that for a long time, and before they did, she insisted on his opening the next gift, which was a vibrator with strange attachments. At first he couldn't fathom their use, but Cynthia seemed to know, and his using them brought her to such heights of pleasure that at first he felt inadequate for needing them, then proud that he could do that to any woman, no matter what it took.

"Now you're learning how to make love," Cynthia had said when she was finally sated. Then she'd asked him about his fantasies, and when he admitted that he didn't really have any, she asked, "Not even being dominated? Taken by a woman at gunpoint?" He pondered that and tossed it back to her.

"Is that one of your fantasies?" he'd asked.

"I grew up among military men, remember? There are all sorts of sexy things I imagine doing with my gun. It's a shame to have it just sitting in a drawer unused, don't you think?"

He hadn't been quite sure then what she had in mind and remembering the comment tonight made him want to ask all over again. Now the hesitation of his hand on her hip made Cynthia sit up. She had business on her mind instead of sex.

"I spoke to the D.A.'s office this morning," she said. "Our response to their inquiries seems to have satisfied everyone—at least for the time being. Your dad is very pleased."

"I'm glad. That reminds me—I understand you and Bill are talking about some change in your title?"

Cynthia tossed her head so that even in the low-lit apartment her pale red hair swirled around her like finespun cotton candy. "Don't you think I deserve a new title? Not to mention more compensation? I've been much more than legal counsel to Austin Realty."

"Certainly in my mind," he said, offering what he hoped was a wicked grin, but she just retorted, "And in your father's mind, too."

For a moment, he thought that she meant it as he had—*I'm more than legal counsel to your father*—and the thought sent him physically reeling, as if he had been hit in the jaw. Worst of all was that he didn't feel at all surprised. Bill would consider it his right to take Mark's woman, figuring that anything his son had acquired was simply through the forbearance of the father. Of course, there was another possibility, and pondering it, Mark couldn't decide if he felt better or worse. There was a chance that Bill had enjoyed Cynthia first—passing her on to Mark as casually as he turned over the various buildings that he was tired of managing.

While he worried about Bill's role, Cynthia said in her most executive tone, "I think Bill has finally come to respect the work that I do. He's never been very good at accepting women on a strictly professional basis. But maybe I've changed his mind."

The comment appeased Mark enough for him to promise his support for both the title change and the raise. Then, changing the subject, he said, "Remember how surprised you were to hear that your name doesn't get mentioned in our house? Well, it's been mentioned a lot lately."

He paused, hoping she would understand and respond immediately so that he didn't have to push the point, but instead she just looked at him with half-raised eyebrows. Plowing ahead, he explained, "We've been talking about you because of the lawsuit you brought on behalf of Denny Wright." Still she said nothing, so he sputtered, "That's my *wife* you're suing, you know."

This time she burst out laughing and leaned over to cup his cheek in her palm. "How devoted of you, darling. Protecting the little wife now, hmm? And I thought she was a big girl who could take care of herself."

"But she's still my *wife*." He wasn't sure why he repeated it except that the fact of their relationship was the whole point of his outrage. "You could have at least told me what you were doing." He said it firmly, and Cynthia looked at him with such contempt that he felt a burning in his heart; it was replaced almost immediately with the first click of divided loyalty to register in him in a long time.

Cynthia got up from the sofa and crossed over to sit in the armchair in the corner of the room. The message was unmistakable: *Stand up for your wife and you can't have me.*

"Look," Mark said, trying to regain his equilibrium. "Let's talk about this from a strictly professional position. You work for Austin Realty. Why would you be representing Denny Wright in bringing a libel suit against Keith Ross Productions for a show that has absolutely nothing to do with our company?"

"Are you now questioning my ability to represent Austin Realty?"

"Not at all." Remembering how good Cynthia was in a court-room, he realized that he didn't want to be debating her. "In fact, maybe I should just think of this as a free-lance project that you're doing on your own time."

"No, you shouldn't think of it that way at all. Look, Mark, we've got a problem with Denny Wright. A real problem." She said it conspiratorially, as if she had just decided to let him in on a secret that she'd been shielding him from all this time. "Denny is an angry young man since Annabelle turned against him, and he has two goals. The first is to get back at everyone associated with that television show. The second is to cause as much trouble as possible for his father. I met with Denny a few weeks ago to get his signature on that deal we're doing in Hungary"—she looked significantly at Mark—"and he wouldn't sign. Said he needed more information on what's really involved. I sent him a few papers, but the guy isn't a fool. A manipulator, yes, but not a fool. He shouldn't be underestimated."

"Has he signed now?"

"No, and he's starting to pry a lot deeper than he should. So, if you must know, I decided to try winning his trust. I gave him a preview a couple of weeks ago of the show your wife did on Annabelle, and he went crazy when he saw it. I told him that I'd help him out however he wanted as long as he didn't try to screw you or Austin Realty. And that's significant, because I have a feeling that Denny is close to knowing the one thing we *don't* want him to know. To put it bluntly, he mentioned that he was thinking about a vacation in the Cayman Islands."

"Jesus Christ. Does he know that we've set up a company there?"

"I'm not sure if he has any evidence, but he's clearly figured something out. We don't want him running to his daddy with it, do we?"

Mark wanted to curse and throw something across the room, but instead, trying to copy Cynthia's cynically optimistic tone, he said, "Even if Denny has it all figured out, why would he care? If he wants to cause trouble for his father, I'm on his side."

"More or less what I told him. But Denny needs a lot of blood to be satisfied lately, and if one of the Christians had to be thrown to the lions, I thought it might as well be your wife."

Showing more annoyance than he had intended, Mark said, "But why did you have to take the case? Libel and slander aren't even your field."

"If I didn't do it, he would have found some other lawyer to sue everyone in sight, including us for introducing him to Jillian. Remember that indemnification I told you to get from your wife? You never did it." She shook her head. "Sorry, darling, but you should listen to Cynthia. Otherwise I spend all my time cleaning up the messes you and Daddy make."

The sarcasm cut through him, and he sat quietly for a moment, trying to sort out what Cynthia had been saying. One comment jibed neatly with a question Jillian had raised, so he asked, "How were you able to give him a preview of the show?"

"On tape."

"Did you get it from me?"

"No, darling. I was in London and you were here, so I had my secretary call Jillian's secretary and ask that it be sent over. On behalf of you, of course."

"Goddamn it, Cynthia, you had no right to do that."

"I didn't?"

"No." He felt himself raging senselessly. "I'm still married to Jillian, and you don't have a right to interfere. You're a lawyer—so why don't you act like one instead of like a fucking undercover spy."

She sashayed across the room, pretending to adjust a shade but no doubt displaying the body that could be his.

"Such temper you've been showing lately. And nasty language. It's not like you. Maybe the tension is getting to be too much for you. Could be you're not cut out for intrigue."

"Maybe I'm not. At this point, I wouldn't mind just shutting down our offshore company and pretending it never existed."

"Too late for that. It's the major supplier of materials for that project in Hungary. Everyone's building in Hungary, of course. It's the best prospect in Eastern Europe. Half the materials are already being shipped. If the company disappears now, there are going to be a lot of questions."

"Fine. So we're in this up to our ears and we can't get out. That doesn't mean you have to make my life even more complicated by involving Jillian."

Cynthia shrugged. "If you wanted everything correct and above-board, you shouldn't have set up the company in the Cayman Islands. Because now it's not just you, me, and Jillian in a triangle. Now with the Austin-Wright deal, Denny, and the offshore company, we have a dozen triangles—and you're at the apex of all of them. Our job is to keep Denny from crossing the line and messing up everything we've put together."

■━━■

The phone rang so abruptly and unexpectedly that Jillian woke up and reached for it in one smooth motion, saying "Hello" almost before she was totally awake.

"Jillian? It's Annabelle. You've got to help me."

The clock radio next to Jillian's bed glowed neon green, casting a strange shadow over her hand. The numbers said 2:37, and it took Jillian a moment to realize it was the middle of the night. Next to her the bed was empty, the pillowcases crisp and untouched. Mark had taken to staying out this late almost every night, and about once a week not bothering to come home at all. No explanation and no discussion.

"What's going on, Annabelle?" Her still-numb brain registered that Annabelle was probably calling from Los Angeles, where it wasn't yet midnight.

"It's Denny. He just called sounding crazy, and he said he's going to kill me. That I've ruined him, and I deserve to suffer! He's here in Los Angeles, and he's bought a gun, and he said that if I don't start begging his forgiveness, he's going to use it." A muffled yelp escaped from her, a strange cry that was half fear and half sob.

"Are you alone?" Jillian asked.

"No, Rob is here, of course. We were in bed when Denny called. Rob just went to check all the locks on the house, and he told me to call you. I don't think Denny would come over tonight—but he said

218

on the phone that he's going to keep calling me until I beg his forgiveness and then he'll come back to me. If I don't do that . . ."—there was the muffled cry again—"he'll come over and kill me."

"God." Jillian was having trouble thinking clearly. *Where the hell is Mark this late? What does he do out every night?*

"I don't know if it was the show that set him off or what," Annabelle said. Worried, Jillian wondered if she was responsible for what was happening to Annabelle. Should she rush out to take care of her, just like she rushed home when her own children needed her?

"Have you spoken to Emil?" Jillian asked, and Annabelle said, "Not yet. I called you first because I'm scared."

"Then I'll come to L.A. tomorrow," Jillian said resolutely. "In the meantime I'll call Emil, because he's closer than I am and he should know what's happening."

"Call me back after you speak to him," Annabelle begged, and Jillian said simply, "Of course."

CHAPTER THIRTEEN

EMIL rushed over to Annabelle's house the moment he got Jillian's call, and when he rang the doorbell, Rob answered in jeans and a sweatshirt. Annabelle was just steps behind him in a white terry robe, panic inscribed on her face.

"Are you two okay?" Emil asked.

"Of course," Rob said with his usual bravado. "I've checked carefully, and everything is secure. Come on in."

They went to the living room and, looking around, Emil asked, "Do you think that the threats are real?" Neither of them answered immediately, so Emil said, "Maybe we should think about getting some bodyguards for Annabelle."

"Not necessary," Annabelle said. Her skin was pallid and her eyes were bleary from the tranquilizers she had obviously taken. "If Denny ever gets near me, I'll kill him myself. I swear I will. I'll go get myself a gun if I have to." In her anger, her cockney accent became more pronounced, and she sounded like a child of the streets rather than the hottest rock star on two continents.

Rob put an arm around her. "You're not getting a gun, and Denny's not going to hurt you. You know that. The guy gets drunk or stoned or high or whatever it is he does, and he starts making wild threats. We're not going to think about it."

Rob's comforting appeased Annabelle's anger but incited such an

220

outburst of hysteria that she buried her head in Rob's shoulder, sobbing and screaming.

"Why is Denny *doing* this? Denny never wanted to hurt me. He didn't. Maybe it's my fault. I hurt him."

"Of course it's not your fault. Denny hurt you. You didn't hurt Denny. And we're not going to let anything happen to you now." The words were as monotonous as a mantra and, as far as Emil could tell, had been repeated nearly as often. But they served their function of easing Annabelle's hysteria, and when Rob said something softly in her ear, she nodded and then ran from the room.

Shrugging, Rob turned to follow her, then said over his shoulder to Emil, "Stay here, if you don't mind. I'll be back."

Barely five minutes later, he returned without Annabelle, who had finally drifted off into an exhausted sleep.

"She's like a scared child," Rob said to Emil. "She needs me to lie with her until she falls asleep or else she has bad dreams."

Rob looked wan to Emil, his surfer's tan making the worry and fatigue in his face less obvious but not totally erasing it.

"Are you handling this okay?" Emil asked. Rob immediately answered, "Of course." Then seeing the deeper concern in Emil's face, he gestured toward the kitchen and asked, "Want to have a beer?"

"Sure."

Rob got two bottles of beer from the refrigerator, and even though Emil wasn't in the mood to drink, he took his, understanding that Rob wanted to talk and that man-talk wasn't possible without the right accoutrements. Guys talked over a beer. They talked in the locker room or the gym. But they didn't just sit down and have a heart-to-heart because their souls were aching.

While he downed his first beer, Rob talked mostly about football and whether or not the Rams had any chance of making it to the Super Bowl. Then he took another beer from the refrigerator and, sitting down again, said, "I'm in an odd position here."

"What's that?"

He chugged half the bottle, then said, "This whole relationship with Annabelle. I mean, I just kind of fell into it before I knew what was happening. She needed someone around, and that someone was me. Don't get me wrong, I like Annabelle. I really do. But I feel like a fraud acting like her boyfriend. I was planning to tell her all this once things settled down. But now . . ." He put the bottle to his mouth again but this time took only a small swallow.

"Now it looks like things will never settle down, is that it?" Emil asked.

"More or less. I can't walk out on her when Denny Wright is threatening her with a gun."

"No, you can't," Emil said simply.

Rob gave a half-laugh and said, "I suppose you think I'm crazy to be complaining. Here I am living with a hot rock star who loves sex and doesn't make too many demands, and I'm trying to figure how to get out."

"I don't think you're crazy at all," Emil said, "I think you know what you want—and that doesn't include using somebody else to get it."

Encouraged, Rob said earnestly, "I feel like I'm living someone else's life. Do you know what I mean? I don't mind helping Annabelle and giving her encouragement. And if I loved her, I wouldn't even mind having my career play second fiddle to hers. But we're not in love. I don't think she'd disagree with that. We're buddies who sleep together. Strange as it may sound, I'd rather be off building my own career and figuring out who I am. But the girl's been through so much, I don't want to wreck her in the process."

Emil sighed. "Relationships like this have a natural rhythm. If Annabelle's not in love either, she'll understand when it's time to change the terms and move on. Just let it happen naturally. You have kind instincts, Rob. You should follow them."

Finishing his beer, Rob fiddled with the bottle cap, then asked nervously, "Have I screwed myself with Jillian?"

"Why would you think that?"

"I figure I'm a laughingstock in the company. They ask me to help Annabelle and I end up practically moving in with her. I'm afraid Jillian won't take me seriously after this."

"No, Jillian understands that things happen," Emil said, getting up to leave. "No matter how much they overlap, work is work and your private life is private. Trust me, Jillian knows all about that."

■

Emil called Jillian before dawn to tell her things were under control and she didn't have to rush out to L.A.

"Perhaps I should anyway," she said. "Keith wants to tape the pilot for syndication almost immediately, and he needs me to work with Annabelle before we go into the studio." She told him the flight she was taking, and when he asked where she would be staying in L.A., she paused only briefly before answering, "The hotel where I always stay, of course."

When she got off the plane later that day, Jillian was only slightly surprised to find Emil waiting for her at the airport.

"Welcome to L.A.," he said, and drove her to her hotel. He parked the Porsche in front, and they sat talking for a long time, first about Annabelle and Denny, then about the more compelling subject of themselves. Finally she promised to see him later and went in to register; still he didn't leave. He stayed outside the hotel fiddling with the tools in his trunk and studying the maps in his glove compartment. In the midst of analyzing a map of downtown Boise, Idaho, he heard a knock on the passenger-side window and looked up as Jillian opened the door. Her suitcase was still in her hand, so he asked, "Any problem with getting a room?"

"No, I'm all checked in." But there was a look of sadness in her eyes that said she didn't want to go up to that room alone; no matter how luxurious it was, there was something she wanted other than an empty hotel room.

"Come on, get in," he said, and as she tossed her suitcase into the backseat, he suddenly understood what it meant for your heart to soar.

The sunroof was open and the Porsche was on the freeway before Jillian asked, "Where are we going?"

He had no idea, really. All that was driving him was the pleasure of their being together. But he said decisively, "I thought you'd come to my house," and as soon as the words were out, he realized that it was exactly what both of them wanted.

■

   The studio, Keith decided, was just the right size, and even though it was empty now, he could picture it with the "Wild Nights" set installed and a hundred eager audience members screaming their approval. He was glad to be shooting the pilot at WOJ in Chicago, particularly since it would save him so much money. Everything else about the show was wildly expensive. The set had cost more than it should have—he'd budgeted fifty thousand dollars and spent well over twice that to have an L.A. set designer come up with something original. Jillian had been disapproving—"This is a *pilot*," she had pointed out—but he was so sure that the show was going to be a hit in syndication that the extra money didn't matter.

   "So what do you think?" Barry Brunetti came striding into the studio and slapped Keith heartily on the back. "Is this a great place or what?"

   Deciding there was no point in showing too much immediate enthusiasm, Keith put one hand in his pocket and said, "It's fine. I don't think we'll have any major problems with the studio size."

   "Have you seen the control room yet?" Barry asked eagerly.

   "Yup, we went in there, and it's going to need a little rearranging, but it's not so bad that I'm going to lose sleep right away."

   Barry looked despairingly at the pretty young woman who had been showing Keith around, as if some failing in her touring abilities had caused Keith's lack of enthusiasm. This was the best studio in the whole damn station, probably the best in Chicago, and he couldn't believe that facilities in New York were so much better that Keith could be snubbing his nose at it. WOJ also provided private dressing rooms for the hosts, a green room for guests, access to hair and makeup facilities, and a spacious work area for the producers. What the hell else could he want?

   "Oh, one thing," Keith said. "I've been meaning to ask you if there's easy access to the studio."

   "Access?" Barry looked puzzled. "I don't know. I guess we've got whatever the law requires. Ramps and elevators and all that."

"That's good to hear," Keith said with a snort, "but I don't mean access for the handicapped—I mean for average people who'll be our audience. I've been in limousines since I got to Chicago, so I don't have a sense of the layout. Can people get here easily? Can a secretary slip over here when we're shooting?"

"Of course. We're minutes from downtown," Barry said. "And Chicago is teeming with doctors and psychologists and social workers, so when you're looking for experts for your talk panels, you won't even have to spring for airfare."

Keith shrugged. "I'm not as interested in experts as I used to be. People can get information in a magazine, but what they can't get is a sense of being connected to other people. The successful shows are video versions of gossiping over the back fence—a lot of average people sharing their experiences. Some of the talk is about wild experiences and some of it is pretty mundane advice, but that's the mixture people need and it's what we'll give 'em. People turn on the television at night to have something to listen to. Someone to talk to, even. Instead of friends, we now have talking furniture."

Barry laughed. "And on 'Wild Nights' we'll also have singing furniture. By the way, have you figured out your demographics? Who you think is going to be watching?"

Keith rolled his eyes. "When I was at the network, we thought we had a good grasp on demographics. Daytime viewers used to be women who were home ironing and cooking and bored to distraction. Late night was some mixture of kids in their twenties who think life starts at midnight and older insomniacs. Now I think that's all changed. The world has turned upside down, so that people have a hundred reasons for watching television late at night or during the day. On top of that, if people want to watch something, they tape it—no matter what time it's on."

Hoping he didn't sound sycophantic, Barry said, "That's why 'Wild Nights' is going to be such a success. It's a cross between Johnny Carson and 'Nightline'—only better. I wouldn't be surprised to hear about women taping it to watch at four o'clock the next day, instead of 'Donahue.'" He paused, and deciding it couldn't hurt to let Keith know that he traveled in the right circles, said, "Which reminds me. I was sitting next to Phil Donahue at a dinner a couple of months ago and he made the same point you did. He said that women don't always know who he is, but cab drivers recognize him. And waiters. And flight attendants and pilots. All the people who have flexible schedules and sometimes find themselves at home when the kids are in school and their wives are at work. It's too quiet and lonely at home, so they flip on Phil."

"Talking furniture," Keith repeated.

"But on your show you can get *intimate* with the furniture." Barry caught himself before he said *our* show. "Like having your best friends over for a chat."

Keith wasn't going to disagree with Barry since he thought "Wild Nights" would be a hit, too. "Viewers are always looking to make a connection with someone else," Keith said. "That's what we'll be all about."

"Getting Annabelle Fox was a nice move. People will tune in just because they've never heard her talk before."

"I hope she *does* talk," Keith said.

"It would be a real bummer if she didn't."

"Mmm. A real bummer."

■

Emil wiped the sweat off his brow and contemplated the barbell above him. He had just bench pressed the hundred-pound weight twenty-five times, which was part of his normal at-home workout, but he was feeling strong today, and he wondered how much more he could do. The long bar sat on its stand, a foot above his chest, daring him to try more. Curling his fingers firmly around the center of the bar, he closed his eyes and found himself thinking about last night.

Thinking about Jillian.

He saw her as if in a dream, hovering above him, her lips open slightly in pleasure, her head tossed back in the delight that he excited in her over and over. A dream—only it had been real. Her hips danced on his groin, and her fingers etched the lines of his powerful shoulders, stirring her blood so that he could sense the fire between her thighs. She had murmured, *You're so strong.* . . .

Eyes still closed, Emil pushed at the bar and raised it high, lowered it slowly to his chest, and pushed it up again, repeating the actions until he had pressed the weight thirty more times. There. He had done it now. He put the bar back carefully and sat up, surprised at how good he felt.

Was there anything that Jillian *couldn't* make him do? Any power she didn't give him? Emil moved over to the slant board and stretched out to start a set of sit-ups. Toes curled under the bar, he did fifty in record time and thought about doing fifty more.

It had been a long time since he had shared his house with anyone. Women occasionally spent the night, but that, of course, was different. For the last four days, since Jillian arrived in L.A., he had been able to open his bedroom closet and find it filled with Jillian's silk shirts and pastel blazers, their fresh scent making him think of all that was lovely in her. In the mornings, he loved to watch her in the shower, no less intent about washing her hair than she was about making the right editing decisions. Then she would jump out, dripping wet, and dab at herself with a towel before starting to get dressed.

"You never get quite dry," he said one morning, noticing that water droplets still gleamed on her shoulders even as she pulled on her pink panties.

"This is called air-drying," she joked. "I've done it all my life."

"Well, your life is changing now," he said, and taking the fluffy towel that she had tossed on the bed, caressed her shoulders until her skin was as smooth as a petal.

He longed for signs of domesticity—panty hose hanging in the shower or makeup left scattered around the bathroom—to prove to him that this was more than a brief fantasy. But she was neat and kept her items carefully contained. He put her toothbrush into the holder next to his, but her flowered cosmetics bag was stashed in the corner of the counter, a reminder that the arrangement was only temporary; at any moment her work in L.A. would be over, and she would pack up and return to husband and children, where she belonged.

No, she belongs here.

He had never seen her as relaxed as she'd been these last few days. One morning he'd slept late, and when he woke up, he was upset to find her gone; but a few minutes later, she returned, climbing back into bed with a tray of fresh-brewed coffee and the homemade muffins that she had made for breakfast.

"You shouldn't have to be in the kitchen," he said.

"I don't mind at all. I couldn't sleep, and you were so peaceful that I didn't want to wake you."

He kissed her on the ear before he bit into the warm muffin. "You're such a mix of bright ambition and traditional values—the ultimate career woman with a lot of old-fashioned twists. I'm at a loss to pin you down. Each minute I think I have it, you waft away, like a butterfly that refuses to stay still long enough to be put under a microscope."

"You don't really need a microscope to understand me," she said, smiling. "I'm a modern woman—and that means a woman conflicted."

"Am I part of the conflict?" When she didn't answer, he added, "I certainly hope so."

"Well then, I suppose." She picked at the edge of a muffin and finally put a piece of it into her mouth. A crumb remained at the corner of her lips, and he wanted to kiss it away. "The one thing I've learned and that I try to teach my daughters is that if you want your life to change, you have to do it yourself. Nobody is going to save you. Knights on white horses disappeared a long time ago."

"I'm in full agreement. What's the problem?"

She held the muffin in her hand, as if weighing it for lightness. "The problem is that I feel rescued by you. You answer all my needs. I hardly trust the way I feel."

He stroked her neck, the cleavage at her robe. "Please trust it, because I feel rescued by you, too. Men don't use those same words, I suppose, but we have the same fantasies. A woman who can make life bright again. Make you happy just to wake up and smell coffee and see the sun shining."

"That's how you feel with me?"

He looked at her, knowing that his eyes were filled with love. "That's how I feel every minute."

"I don't know what I've done to deserve you."

"You've just been you—that wonderful mixture of sweet woman

228

and powerful producer that I love so much. And I do love you. I hope that doesn't make your conflict even worse."

"I love you, too," she said. "Do you know that? I love you very much."

The words stopped him, and he put down his coffee cup so he could take her hand in both of his. Through all their nights of loving, she had never before said she loved him, and he felt that a giant step had just been taken, because he knew that Jillian van Dorne didn't use the words lightly.

■

Annabelle woke up with her heart racing and her head pounding and knew that she was going to die. She checked around the room to see if there were any signs of a tequila bash the night before; but no, those days were over. She woke Rob to tell him that she was going to die, but he was unshaken.

"You're not going to die," he said kindly, "you're just having a panic attack. Remember what the doctor said? Nobody has ever died of a panic attack."

"Maybe the doctor lied. Or maybe I'll be the first." Her heart was beating so fast that she was sure she couldn't stay alive. But Rob stroked her back and reminded her that twice in the past few days, they'd gone dashing over to the emergency room at Cedars-Sinai Hospital, and both times the doctors had called it a panic attack. In fact, Rob still had the pills that had worked so well the last time.

She took the pill Rob offered and held him tightly, and in an hour she was feeling much better. When he gently mentioned that he should go to work, she told him to go ahead, she'd be fine. Then she wandered around the house alone, trying to figure out what was happening to her.

Things were happening too fast, that was for sure. The concert and the television show and breaking up with Denny. Two of the guys in the band had quit out of loyalty to Denny, and even though she had replaced them easily enough it was a shock; her own backup boys thought she had done wrong. Now Artie Glenn had signed a contract for her to be the host of a television talk show. Sure, she was just supposed to be handling the music segments, but what did she know about hosting a talk show? Jillian and Emil had been convincing, and she *did* trust them, and Artie said it was going to be fine because they wouldn't let her get in over her head. But Artie was just her agent, and how could she know whether or not he really cared what she did? Jillian had spent the last few days with her, getting her prepared, but she was more nervous than ever.

Denny's threatening her with a gun had terrified her, and that's when these panic attacks had started. Much worse than anything she ever felt before a performance. Jillian made her report the threats to the police, but she realized it was a mistake because Denny called to say that he was only threatening her because he loved her. She had broken his heart by leaving, and he missed her so much that he was going mad. If she came back, nothing bad would ever happen.

"You can't listen to him," Jillian had warned. "He knows how to control you, and you just can't let him."

But Jillian was probably just angry about being dragged out to L.A. Plus Denny was suing her about the television special, and Jillian couldn't really be expected to understand Denny's sensitive nature.

Denny had been calling a lot lately, and though she didn't admit it to Rob or Jillian, she talked to him almost every day. Most of the time he screamed and ranted and threatened, but once he said, "Listen, dolly, nobody will ever love you the way I love you." It was that, rather than the wild ravings of the other conversations, that she remembered. No matter what else had happened, she had to believe that Denny really did love her. There were times that he could even be gentle, like the night after the New York concert when they'd gone back to their room instead of to the celebrity party; she was glad because that night even the sex had been good.

Reckless passion, that's what Denny had for her. A lust that made it impossible to keep himself in check. That's why he had threatened her with a gun and why he got too rough sometimes. Okay, *much* too rough. Running away from him after the scene at the Rumn Club had been right, because she had to teach him a lesson. But did she have to stay away forever?

Nobody will ever love you the way I love you.

Having Rob around was fine, but he was more of a friend than anything else. Jillian said it was nice to be with someone who didn't try to manipulate you, and Annabelle couldn't really explain to her how much she missed Denny. And there was this Cynthia woman Denny talked about all the time now. A lawyer in his father's firm or something like that, and he was going to trick her into cutting him into a deal that would make him millions. Sure it would screw his father, but what was wrong with that?

If Annabelle didn't do something soon, maybe Denny would fall in love with Cynthia. He liked women who made him rich.

What would be wrong with going over to see Denny? Annabelle felt she was a big girl now; she could take care of herself. If he did try to hurt her, she'd just walk away. Or she'd fight back if she had to, and she knew just how to do that. It was crazy never to see him again.

"Annabelle is wavering," Jillian told Emil. "All these weeks of being away from Denny, and she's forgotten some of the terror. Now she's decided that his threatening her with a gun was just another way of showing he loves her. I don't know how to keep her from going to see him."

"What do you think he'd do if she came to see him?"

"I don't really know, but I also don't think any of us want to find out."

Emil shrugged and watched Jillian as she folded her nightgown and put it into her suitcase. Tomorrow morning he would drive her to the airport, and even though he would be going to New York in another week, he didn't want her to leave. These few days together in his house had been too perfect. What was going to happen to them when reality interceded again and he was just one more element she had to balance in a schedule of husband and Keith and children and television shows?

He leaned over and put his arms around her shoulders. "Stop packing, okay? I don't want you to leave."

"I don't want to go either," she said simply. "But one thing is for sure. I'm not leaving you. I could never leave you."

They kissed for a long time, and when he felt the curves of her body, he wanted to wrap himself into her forever. Pausing for breath, they pulled apart briefly, and Jillian asked, "What time is it?"

"Almost ten o'clock."

"Then we'd better not get started or I'll never make it to my plane."

"I thought it wasn't until nine o'clock tomorrow morning."

"It's not," she said, smiling, and he realized that she was teasing him, poking gentle fun at his ability to go on and on all night with her.

"Would you rather that I devoted less time to loving every inch of your body?" he asked.

"Absolutely not. You arouse desires in me that I never knew I had. I love every minute of what you do."

"Well, then, come here, because I have only ten hours to enjoy you."

And ten hours won't be nearly enough, Emil thought late that night, when their lovemaking was only just beginning to slow. He loved the astonishment he saw in Jillian's eyes each time he brought her new pleasure. Sometimes she would whisper that she was thoroughly contented, but he still wouldn't stop. "There has to be one more tiny orgasm up there that we can find," he had whispered to her tonight, and though she had insisted that there wasn't, he had persisted until she was breathing deeply again, then gasping in satisfaction.

"How do you *do* that?" she asked when she had recovered, and her giggle touched him. Could it be that nobody had ever devoted himself to Jillian the way he did? Hard to believe. He wanted to spend forever making her happy.

Now Jillian was lying against his chest, her tongue making lazy circles at his neck as they talked languidly, too satisfied to continue their lovemaking but too in love to go to sleep.

"You're the most amazing lover I've ever met," Jillian said, kissing his ear. "Are you always this way with women?"

"What way?"

"Tireless and devoted."

"Of course." He rolled on top of her, teasing. "I keep any woman I can find locked in my bedroom for hours on end."

"No, I mean it." She stroked his chest, and her innocence touched him.

232

"The truth?" He moved next to her, turning serious now. "The truth is that it's different with you than it's ever been before. It isn't just sex that drives me, it's you. I couldn't be like this with any other woman. You send me to amazing heights."

Jillian turned over, her back to Emil, and curled into the concave space of his firm belly to rest; but he began to rub her back, then brought one arm around the curve of her waist and let his hands explore until they found her perfect nipples. Her buttocks, round and firm, rubbed gloriously against his penis, and he reached between her legs, stimulating her damp arousal.

The doorbell rang loudly.

"Damn."

Checking the clock, he saw it was two in the morning. He pulled away from Jillian, fearful that only an emergency would warrant a visit at this hour. As he moved to the edge of the bed, he glanced over at Jillian, who obviously had no such fears. She was lying dreamily on the pillows, not moving, waiting for the interruption to be over.

Pulling on a pair of jeans but nothing else, Emil left to check out the source of the disturbance.

A few moments later, he came back into the bedroom and clicked the door closed behind him. "I have some shocking news."

"My God, what is it?" Jillian sat up quickly, clutching the sheets to her body. He caught the look of alarm flashing in her eyes.

"There are two detectives at the door from the L.A. Police Department. Denny Wright was shot a few hours ago."

Her mouth opened, but no words came out. Then she whispered, "Denny Wright is dead?"

"Apparently shot with a handgun."

"My God. Where did it happen?"

"In the apartment he'd rented out here." Still bare-chested, Emil put his arm around her. "The detectives went looking for Annabelle immediately and found her at home with Rob. They're both being questioned, and she gave the police our names. They've already been to your hotel and know you're not there."

Jillian hesitated barely a second, then said, "Why did they go looking for Annabelle?"

"I have no idea. I guess she's a suspect."

233

"Annabelle kill Denny? No." She looked at him in disbelief. "It couldn't happen." Then running various scenarios through her quick mind, she said, "Could it have been self-defense?"

Stroking her cheek, Emil said, "You're asking more questions than I can answer. I have only the sketchiest details. But I repeat that the police know you're not at your hotel."

Jillian looked at him in surprise, as if suddenly understanding what he was saying. Then, with barely a pause, she said, "Well, go out and tell them I'm here, will you? What's the problem? I'll get dressed. You just tell them I'm here."

CHAPTER FOURTEEN

*T*HE policemen stayed for almost two hours. The two officers both remembered seeing "The Secret Life of Rock and Roll," and although they didn't come out and say so, they seemed to be working from the assumption that Annabelle Fox had finally struck back and killed her abusive boyfriend.

"Happening more and more," reported the older one, whose name tag said Captain Frank Murphy. "Can't say that I blame these girls. And juries are all finding them innocent, too."

Jillian wondered if Captain Murphy could be feigning sympathy in an effort to get her to say something incriminating. But in truth she had nothing to say. Sure, Annabelle had been talking about going to see Denny again, but Jillian had tried to talk her out of it, and as far as she knew, she had been successful. No reason to mention private conversations and remote possibilities.

"Let's talk about that television show you folks did," Captain Murphy said, after accepting the second cup of coffee that Jillian offered him. "Go through how you shot it and what you saw while you were doing it."

They talked for a long time about the show and Annabelle and Denny, and it occurred to Jillian that Annabelle might be having a similar conversation with the police officers in her own home. Thinking more about Annabelle than herself, Jillian said, "I'm beginning to feel that we should have a lawyer present for this discussion."

The policemen exchanged glances, and the younger, Officer William Reynolds, said, "That's of course your right, if you'd like. But this isn't a formal questioning. You're not suspects, and we're just talking to you by way of getting some background."

Still, Jillian excused herself and, after closing the bedroom door, called Artie Glenn. Awakened by her call, he swore softly to himself, then said, "Call Roger Simnowitz. Don't worry that it's the middle of the night. Our firm has him on retainer just for cases like this."

"For rock stars suspected of murdering their managers?" Jillian said sardonically. "I didn't realize it was such a common problem."

"Anytime you deal with rock stars you have problems." Artie sighed. "Murder is sometimes the least of it."

Though it was now almost three in the morning, Roger Simnowitz, one of the more successful defense lawyers in Los Angeles, sounded wide awake. In minutes he seemed to understand the full dimensions of the case and said his first priority was to talk to Annabelle.

"You and the director can use your own judgment about what you need to answer and what you don't," he said. "Stick to the facts and don't offer any opinions. But I'm worried about Annabelle. If the police caught her off guard, she's probably blabbing away, unrepresented. I want to get in touch with her immediately, then I'll get back to you."

Jillian gave him Annabelle's number, then sat huddled by the phone, as if she were already waiting for the jury to return with a verdict. From the living room, she could hear the low, rumbling voices of Emil and the police.

Even though she was expecting it, the jangling phone startled her, and she picked it up anxiously.

"No problem," Roger reported cheerily. "Annabelle got hysterical when the police told her about Denny, and she couldn't be questioned. That guy Rob you mentioned is with her now. She's been sedated, and the police will be back at seven in the morning. I'll be there, too."

For some reason, Jillian felt more vulnerable when she returned to the living room than she had before. Though she knew it was fake, she had been soothed by Captain Murphy's attitude of we're-all-just-chatting-over-coffee. But after talking to Simnowitz, she felt more on her guard.

In her absence Emil had told the police about some of the scenes between Denny and Annabelle that they had witnessed while shooting the special. Jillian quickly realized that he hadn't broken any new ground—snippets of every scene he described had appeared on the show. She wondered if the original tapes would be subpoenaed at some point. The police lingered over Emil's description of the scene by the pool and asked Jillian for more details.

"Annabelle never fought back or retaliated when Denny attacked her," Jillian said, sticking to the facts. Then, unable to resist, added, "She's simply not the type who would."

"That was powerful stuff you showed," Captain Murphy said, and it suddenly occurred to Jillian that every television station in the country was going to want to replay that pool footage on their six and eleven o'clock news reports. It would soon be as familiar to viewers as it was to Jillian, who had relived it, frame by frame, a hundred times in the edit suite. She made a mental note to call Liz as soon as the sun rose and prepare her for the barrage of calls they were likely to get this morning.

From the scenes in the television show, the policemen kept segueing to events of the last couple of days, but Jillian could honestly say that she had no reason to believe that Annabelle ever wanted to be near Denny again.

"She wouldn't have stopped by there last night for anything?" Officer Reynolds asked.

"I can't think of any reason why she would."

"Does she own a gun?"

"Not that I've ever seen or ever heard about."

Captain Murphy stretched and Jillian stood up, thinking the interview was over.

"I know you're tired, but just a couple more quick things," said Captain Murphy, leaning back in his chair. "I don't think we ever found out what Ms. van Dorne was doing here this evening. Or rather, I should say this morning."

Jillian and Emil looked at each other.

"We work very closely together," Emil said finally. "We're preparing to shoot a pilot in a few weeks, and there are a lot of production problems to handle."

"Do you always deal with production problems in the bedroom?"

Emil stood up. "If there's nothing else, Officers, we'll see you to the door."

The police officers stood up. "I think that does it." Then, turning to Jillian, Officer Reynolds said, "Anything your husband in New York could add to our investigation?"

"Nothing at all," Jillian said. "His work is quite apart from mine."

"I see that," Captain Murphy said, and with a leering glance, he picked up his hat and was gone.

By ten o'clock in the morning, Jillian and Emil had caught only the briefest nap. Having decided to delay her return to New York, Jillian sat in Emil's living room, gazing through the glass wall that offered an unobstructed view of Coldwater Canyon. The rocks took on an ethereal pink hue in the morning light; it had already turned into one of those rare L.A. days during which the sun shone brightly, undeflected by smog, and the gentle Santa Ana winds cleaned the air as efficiently as a scrub brush.

But it wasn't a bright day for Annabelle. She sat on a sofa across from Jillian, sobbing.

"I didn't do it, you know."

Surrounded by a pile of soggy tissues, Annabelle repeated her denial for at least the twentieth time. Her seven A.M. questioning by the police had been relatively brief, thanks to the presence of Roger Simnowitz, the attorney. Immediately afterward Annabelle had insisted on coming over to see Jillian and Emil—seeking comfort and succor, which is what they had offered. Roger's arrival a few minutes later, however, changed the tone of the conversation.

"You're not guilty. I take that as a given." Roger sat perched on the arm of the sofa, arms crossed, more prosecutor than friend as he looked down and questioned Annabelle. Years of courtroom experience had taught him to seek the position of power in any situation, even when talking to his own clients. He was wearing a well-tailored three-piece suit and neatly polished shoes, and his thick curly hair and dense black beard somehow seemed too hot for such a beautiful day.

He got up and, arms still folded, stood in front of the tremulous Annabelle.

"I believe you, but you have to understand what my associate just told me on the phone. The police have apparently found someone who claims to have seen you going into Denny's apartment last night. I just want to know whether or not that's true."

His manner was matter-of-fact, but Jillian winced. Never had Annabelle seemed more the waif than she did this morning. Dressed in a Lycra midriff top and neon biker's shorts, she looked like a child who couldn't possibly be held responsible for anything she did or said.

Roger's comment produced a fresh round of sobbing, and while Annabelle blew her nose loudly into another Kleenex, Roger rolled back and forth on the balls of his feet.

"Annabelle, I'm going to be blunt with you. You're in shock right now about Denny, and I understand that. But you also have to understand that the television special made by your friends here revealed so many things about you and Denny that no matter what you say now, a lot of people are going to draw their own conclusions. They've seen how Denny treated you, and they're completely sympathetic with anything you might have done."

"But I didn't do anything," Annabelle said stubbornly.

"Let's run through last night just one more time," Roger suggested.

"I've already told you," Annabelle said, sniffling. "Rob was out working on something for Keith until almost midnight." She had already repeated that several times this morning, along with the fact that she hadn't left the house all evening. She blew her nose loudly again, and said, "I went out once, at about eight o'clock."

"Where did you go?"

More sobbing, and then Annabelle hiccuped, "To Denny's."

"You did?" Jillian turned away from the window and looked at Annabelle in surprise.

"Yes, I did," Annabelle said defiantly. "He loved me, you know. Even with everything that happened, he loved me. But he said it wasn't a good night for us to be together, so I left. I didn't even get in the door."

"Did you have sex with him?" Roger asked, as if Annabelle hadn't uttered the last sentence.

"No, but I was going to meet him tonight. It was all arranged. I was going to see him tonight, but now I can't because he's dead and I didn't kill him."

Jillian looked at the girl carefully. There were no signs of injury, but Jillian knew that Denny had been a master at brutalizing Annabelle without it showing. Could it be that something really had happened between them last night and she had finally struck back? No; Annabelle insisted that she hadn't, and there was no reason yet not to believe her.

Trying to talk before another outbreak of hysteria, Roger asked, "Did Denny say why it wasn't a good night?"

Annabelle dabbed at her nose and rearranged herself on the sofa. "He was seeing someone about business," she said flatly.

"Who?" Roger asked.

"I have no idea."

Roger seemed to think about this new information for a moment, then said, "This might sound beside the point, but it's not, so I don't want you to take it wrong. Did you and Rob have sex after he came home last night?"

"No." Though not insulted by the question, Annabelle seemed embarrassed by her answer and quickly added, "I mean, we almost always have sex, but he'd just been home a few minutes when the police came by with the news about Denny."

She sniffled some more, and Roger began pacing.

"It's my policy to believe what clients tell me," he said, stopping in front of Annabelle. "However, I also know that people sometimes remember things a few days later that they don't remember in the initial shock of an event. Women who've been traumatized often have temporary amnesia. The mental defense systems kick in, and the event is so effectively blocked from your mind that you honestly don't know it occurred. That's why it's a good idea to collect all the evidence you can while it's still fresh."

"Like what?" Annabelle asked suspiciously.

Roger shrugged. "So many things. Let's imagine—and this is just imagining—that you went inside Denny's house last night after all, and when you did, he brandished that gun at you. Or he raped you at gunpoint, and you grabbed the gun and shot him. It's quite possible that you blocked that from your mind. But if you had a gynecological exam this morning and they found semen, it could be analyzed and used later in evidence. When a woman has been raped, a strong case can be made for shooting in self-defense, or justifiable homicide."

"But I wasn't raped," Annabelle said.

"If Denny was expecting a business associate last night, you never know when she or he arrived and what was seen," Roger added. "Think how quickly the police found a witness who saw you at the door."

Annabelle looked pleadingly at Jillian, who immediately got up and crossed the room to put a hand on her shoulder. "I think you're being a little too rough, Roger. Annabelle would remember if she had sex with Denny last night. Besides, she knows that she can be completely honest with us here. She's among friends. We all love her and believe in her."

"Of course," Roger said, "but from my long experience, I know that if you collect evidence early—with no fanfare, of course—you're sometimes in a much better position later on. The only purpose of an exam at this point would be—"

"I don't need a bloody exam!" Annabelle pounded the sofa, interrupting him, her eyes fiery red from both her endless crying and her rage. "Denny didn't rape me. Okay, maybe I was over there last night, but Denny wouldn't have raped me because he *loved* me. Don't you get it? He *loved* me."

■

In his office in Manhattan, Barney Rossman hung up the phone and immediately picked up the intercom to ask his assistant D.A. Margery Warren to come into his office. A moment later she appeared at his door, holding a stack of files. Her navy blue skirt was wrinkled and too long, and her loose cardigan sweater accentuated the fact that she needed to lose a few pounds. The gray Nike sneakers and ankle socks she wore with the outfit didn't do much to improve her overall appearance. Should he make a gentle suggestion sometime about how she could improve her dress? No, he decided, it wasn't his business; he had hired her for her brains, and she wasn't lacking in that category.

"Sit down, Margery," he said, gesturing to a chair. "I've just had an interesting call from the L.A. District Attorney. Denny Wright, the son of London's Kingsley Wright, was shot to death last night."

"I know, I heard it on my radio Walkman while I was coming to work this morning," she said, then added proudly, "I walk thirty-five blocks for exercise every morning before I allow myself to get on the train."

That explained the sneakers, at least, but choosing not to discuss her exercise plan, Barney said, "I didn't realize Denny Wright was important enough to make the news in New York."

"I'd imagine it's only because of that television special your brother did a few weeks ago," Margery said. "I'm sure you know that it got huge ratings and a lot of attention. I've seen newspaper columns about Denny and Annabelle, and they're a favorite subject on radio talk shows. I listen to those when I'm walking home," she added with a small smile.

"Well, whatever interest my brother roused in Annabelle isn't about to end. He's signed her to be one of the hosts on a new show he's shooting in a couple of weeks."

Margery nodded noncommittally, and he added, "I'll continue fielding the calls from L.A. for a while, but if the situation starts getting sticky for me, I might turn it all over to you."

"That's fine."

Margery seemed to be about to say something more, but Barney spoke first.

"From what I've heard from L.A., they're assuming that the killing is related to the public side of Denny's life—some fallout from rock and roll and drugs. They don't know much about his role in the Austin-Wright realty dealings, and I said you'd call with some background."

Margery thought for a moment and asked, "Any reason for me to clue them in on our investigation of Mark Austin?"

"I don't know. Why don't you give me an update."

She had a file on her lap, but she didn't bother to open it.

"There's a company in the Cayman Islands that's working as a major supplier for Austin-Wright. Nothing wrong with that except for the coincidence that Mark Austin may have some connection in the Cayman Islands. Unfortunately, I haven't yet been able to determine exactly what it is. All I know right now is that there've been an unusual number of transactions between his personal bank account in New York and an offshore account."

"In the Cayman Islands?" He was struggling to follow, and when she nodded, he said, "Any way Denny Wright could be involved with all that?"

"I just don't know. But it's a possibility."

———

Keith leaned back in his chair and ran his fingers lightly over his free-form, burled-wood desk. He'd always liked the feel of it: the smooth wood was soothing to his nerves. He thought of Jillian's teasing him about still having his California tree stump here in his New York office. Well, it was art, not a tree stump, so fuck Jillian.

No, he couldn't do that. Emil was already fucking her.

Looking for distraction, he spun his chair around to look out the window. Central Park seemed barren at this time of year; the trees had lost their leaves, and from this distance, he could make out only a few odd joggers making their way through the dusk. Gone were the late hours of sunshine and the crowds of bikers and nannies and babies in strollers who gave the park life in the summer. Maybe it was time to move back to L.A., where it was warm all the time.

And where Jillian and Emil were right now.

He turned back to his desk and opened the first file folder that he saw. Budgets for the pilot. Those needed his final approval, even though he noticed that Jillian had already initialed them. They were going ahead with the pilot; goddamn it, they were going ahead even if their co-host landed herself in jail.

But she wouldn't. From what Keith had heard, there wasn't a shred of evidence linking Annabelle Fox to Denny's death. And he was getting the news while it was still hot, because Barney had been speaking all day to the District Attorney in Los Angeles. Every time he called his brother, Barney explained that he wasn't going to pass along anything that might be confidential—but then he gave him the full report from L.A.

The worst news he'd heard in this whole awful day of bad news was about Jillian and Emil.

He'd spoken to each of them at least half-a-dozen times today, and not once did either of them deign to mention that they had been in bed together when the L.A. police knocked on Emil's door. No, that he had to hear from his brother Barney.

Keith pushed away the budgets and wandered over to his case of Emmy awards. Why the hell was he so angry about Jillian and Emil? So the producer was fucking the director. It wasn't the first time in the history of television that had happened. But Jillian was his partner. He trusted her to be on his side, and now if there were any problems, she'd be there upholding Emil's position even if it wasn't best for the production. The two of them could conspire against Keith and destroy his whole show.

Trying to calm down, he fumbled around the office for a cigarette, and finally finding one, lit it quickly and stood in the middle of the room, inhaling deeply. So much for his three-week attempt at quitting. He couldn't be expected not to smoke on a day like today, could he?

With the comfort of a cigarette in his mouth, he had to admit that his conspiracy theory was a lot of hogwash. Why would Emil want anything less than the best for the show? Why would Jillian? In some ways he should be grateful. If they were spending a lot of time together, they probably spent some of it talking about television.

Maybe he was just jealous.

Jillian was *his* find, *his* old friend. Talented, pretty, confident Jillian, whose life seemed to be in such perfect order that he wouldn't think of disrupting it with sexual advances. Well, Emil hadn't worried about that, and he'd gotten her into bed. Was she going to fall in love with him and leave her husband, or was this just a fling inspired by convenience and proximity?

It was none of his business.

Keith crossed over to his desk and quickly dialed Emil's number. Jillian answered the phone on two rings. After exchanging brief greetings, Keith asked, "Did you get Annabelle to the doctor for that exam the lawyer wanted?"

"No, she absolutely refused. Said it was a waste of time, and she'd know if Denny had raped her. She says she didn't have sex with him last night at all."

"Speaking of that," Keith said, but he stopped because the words about her being at Emil's house last night just wouldn't come. Maybe that was a conversation they needed to have in person. "I mean, speaking of last night, the L.A. District Attorney apparently told my brother that they have solid evidence that Denny was involved with drugs."

Jillian laughed. "I think anybody who ever met Denny could give that evidence."

"Well, they don't think it's a drug-related killing anyway."

"Because of the way it was done?"

"Right. A single bullet through the head with a thirty-eight–caliber bullet. Probably a small handgun. That's still confidential, by the way. The good news for Annabelle is that a single bullet isn't really the sign of a crime of passion either. Or even of self-defense. But that's not going to be enough to let her off the hook."

"So what's your best guess?"

"I don't have one," Keith admitted. "But from the calls I've gotten today, the New York tabloids are going to remind everyone that Denny had a libel suit pending against us."

Jillian thought about that for a moment, then said, "Well, you're in New York, so am I supposed to have killed Denny to prevent the libel suit?"

"I don't know," Keith said. "But I'll tell you this. It wouldn't have been the worst idea I ever heard."

■

Barry Brunetti was stuck in traffic on Lake Shore Drive when he heard the report on CBS Radio News. "*Dateline L.A.*," the announcer intoned. "*Denny Wright, the former manager of rock star Annabelle Fox, was found dead early this morning after an apparent shooting. Wright gained notoriety a few weeks ago when a CBS*

television special, 'The Secret Life of Rock and Roll,' revealed that he
was mistreating and physically abusing the young rock star. It's not
known if Annabelle—who is only eighteen—is a suspect in the murder."
There was a brief pause, and the announcer continued, *"Dateline*
Miami. The Coast Guard reports that marine life . . ."

Barry gripped the steering wheel with one hand and jiggled the
tuning buttons on the radio with the other. How in hell had he spent
a nine-hour day at the station and not heard about the murder? He
didn't exactly hang out in the newsroom these days, but *someone*
should have made sure the story got to him. Everyone at the station
knew about "Wild Nights" and knew that Annabelle was going to be
part of it. In his mind he ran through the various assistants he could
ream the next morning for falling down on the job and decided that all
of them—except the little blonde who was wearing the formfitting
green knit dress today—deserved his wrath.

Despite the traffic, Barry had fallen behind the car in front of him
by two full car lengths, and the driver in back of him was furiously
honking his horn. Barry raised his middle finger and shoved it angrily
out his window at the black Camaro. Nobody was going anywhere
right now anyway.

Several of the radio stations had hourly news reports, but it was
now six after the hour, and they were going back to music or talk. He
flicked again to the all-news station, but they were giving weather and
rush-hour traffic. *"On Lake Shore Drive, cars are bumper to bumper in*
the southbound lanes. . . ."

Paying more attention to the radio than to driving, Barry had
fallen back again and the Camaro driver started his irritating honking.
Ignoring him this time, Barry picked up his car phone to dial the
newsroom, but he couldn't get a dial tone. Shitty Chicago. So
small-town that they didn't have enough frequencies for all the cellular
phones that needed them. Well, he'd be on the coast soon enough.

Thinking about that, he felt a sudden flush rising to his face.
"Wild Nights" was going to be his ticket to the coast, and if anything
happened, he was going to be pissed. Damn it, he needed more details
about what was going on with Annabelle. With scarcely a thought, he
swung out of the left lane of traffic and went bumping through the
grassy central divider. Traffic in the other direction was flowing

quickly, and he had to wait a few moments before he could accelerate and break in, heading back to the station. He thought only briefly about the brunette who was waiting at a bar fifteen minutes away to have drinks with him. Well, if she wanted to have a date with Barry Brunetti, she'd just have to wait a little longer.

■

"So the bastard's dead." Cynthia smiled pleasantly at Mark. "Too bad it didn't happen a few days earlier. It would have saved me a trip. Twenty-four hours in L.A. and I spent most of my time at the airport."

"You never got to see Denny?" Mark felt a deep anxiety he couldn't shake, a nameless dread that was rattling him to the core. They were back in Cynthia's cozy apartment on Thirty-eighth Street, but Mark felt strangely as if someone were holding a rifle to his head. A fire blazed in Cynthia's fireplace, not a Duraflame log like everyone else in Manhattan used, but an honest-to-goodness, wood-burning fire that crackled and hissed. Cynthia could do that: create heat and light where there had been only a dark hole, control nature however she chose. So different from his own fumbling efforts to keep fires burning.

"You're not paying attention, darling. I said I never got to his apartment. I met him at a coffee shop that morning before he was killed, and we were going to meet the next morning to iron out the final details. But he was dead, so I came home."

"Did you find out what he knows about . . . our company?"

"Of course." Cynthia offered a lazy laugh. "We had that part all worked out in the morning. He'd figured out everything, but as we suspected, he didn't mind seeing his father's company being screwed. I offered him a cut of the offshore profits, and after that he agreed to everything else. It was quite easy. I managed it without even using all my powers of influence."

Again she laughed, and Mark said abruptly, "I'm not sure what that means."

She came close to him, extending a red-painted fingernail that she used to trace the worry lines on his face, curved moons extending from nose to mouth. "Don't tell me my darling is jealous of a dead man. Are you worried that I was planning to get on my knees in front of him?"

Her effrontery shocked him so that he pulled away and watched her sashay over to her steel-topped desk. Her briefcase had been tossed casually by the side of the desk, papers bulging above the opened zipper and an umbrella sticking out from the side pocket. It was the only indication that she was recently back from L.A.; all other baggage from the trip had been unpacked and tucked away. Cynthia's apartment bordered on the austere: white blinds and white walls, furniture that spoke of random acquisition rather than home. For a moment, he yearned for the comfortable haven Jillian had created, the sun-drenched rooms and cozy fabrics, the pictures of the children in ornate silver frames and the fresh flowers that burst from vases year round. Why did he never notice any of it when he was there?

Cynthia held out to him a file thick with papers, and he took it hesitantly. "All the releases and agreements that Denny signed that morning," she said. "Once we had settled the offshore matter, he didn't pay any attention to the details of the Austin-Wright deal."

"He was completely on our side?"

"Of course. I even got the price for his silence and signature down to a reasonable level. When I think of all that effort wasted—now that he's dead, we don't need any of it." She took the file back and made as if to toss it into the fireplace, but he grabbed her wrist, unsure if her action was serious or mere theatrics.

"Don't."

"Why not?"

"You may need it. To prove something."

With a shrug, she tossed the file on a table. "I should think you'd want it destroyed. That file also contains the papers he wanted filed against your wife. The libel suit was his new cause. He was going to pursue it to the end."

Mark opened the file and took out the Austin-Wright agreement, turned casually to the last pages where Denny's almost illegible scrawl had been left. Seeing the name gave him a strange sense of relief. So Cynthia was telling the truth and everything had been amicably handled many hours before Denny was killed. He turned to Cynthia, feeling suddenly freed.

"Jillian is staying out in Los Angeles an extra night because of this, you know. And I don't think I've had the chance to show you how much I missed you."

She leaned back, her bottom against the hard steel desk. "Come show me," she said, sultriness returning to her voice. "Better yet, Mr. Austin, come fuck me. Right here on the desk."

He hesitated, thinking more of the logistical difficulties than of whether he felt desire. She slid herself onto the desk and invited him to stand between her spread legs, his thighs pressed into the edge where steel met steel.

Pausing in their embrace, Mark said, "It's strange to think of your having coffee with Denny so soon before he was killed."

"Oh, really, darling?" Her cool hand slipped casually from the small of his back and moved idly between his thighs. "Do you think I did it?"

He heard the mocking amusement in her voice, but still he recoiled and said, "My God, of course not. I didn't mean that at all."

"Then what?" Still she was teasing him.

"Just that the only people I've ever known who've died have died of old age or cancer or some disease. I've never known anybody who was murdered. Of course, I never really met Denny, but you knew him and were with him—maybe even aroused his lust—then a few hours later, he was dead. It just all seems so strange to me. The arbitrariness of the world."

"Well, we met in a coffee shop, so he didn't die with the scent of me on his cock, if that's what you're wondering."

"No, it's not what I was wondering, but thank you for the reassurance. Are you aware that you're being crude tonight?"

"Maybe because you're so innocent." She stroked his face, the daggerlike nails again frightening him more than they seduced him. "I've known many people who were killed, so I don't find it quite as bizarre as you do. All the honorable military men I grew up with who were shot in various wars ended up just as dead as victims of street violence. I've never understood why some people exalt one and condemn the other. They're like kids making up rules with play guns—step over this line and you can kill the bad guys and win a

Purple Heart, but do the same thing on the other side of the line and go to jail."

As she talked, her fingers played at his groin, stroking and cajoling, and he realized with some embarrassment that his body wasn't responding. Rather than pleasure, he felt only the pain of the steel-edged desk cutting into his thighs; he shifted his position to relieve it and tried to concentrate on getting hard. But he felt nothing. They both stopped talking and concentrated on his groin, and the attention made it impossible for him to grow firm.

"Maybe a drink?" she asked. "Some wine or vodka to relax?"

"Yes, that would be fine." Even as he said it, he knew that nothing would help to arouse him tonight. He wasn't sure just why, but he knew it as surely as he knew that Denny Wright was dead.

CHAPTER FIFTEEN

A NNABELLE looked at Rob Daly with disgust and wondered why it had taken her so long to figure out that he didn't excite her as a lover. Sound asleep next to her, he was buried under the black satin sheets so that all she could see were his mop of blond hair and his pale blue nightshirt. A nightshirt! It used to make her laugh, but now she didn't find it funny. Who wanted to make love to a man in a nightshirt?

She missed Denny, longed for him now that he was gone. Sure, Denny had been too brutal and made her pleasure him whether she wanted to or not, but at least there was an electricity between them. Jillian said she was romanticizing their sex, and maybe she was, but in memory, she couldn't recall Denny's degradation of her as much as the occasional nights when he wasn't drugged and he wanted her to be happy. Then he could drive her wild, his own frenzy inciting hers, making her scream and come and scream some more.

Rob had all the traits she was supposed to want in a man—he was kind and funny and thoughtful, and when she said no to sex, he kissed her sweetly and rolled over and went to sleep. But all that made her feel scornful rather than loving. A man had to be a man, didn't he? Denny just took what a man wanted, and in retrospect how could she really fault him for that? Rob hadn't figured out that no didn't always mean no. Sometimes it meant come and seduce me, and sometimes it meant let's play a little game first, but it almost never meant absolutely no fucking. Rob just missed it.

251

Tonight she had been looking forward to having sex with Rob, but he had come home from work so exhausted that when he fell into bed, she just kissed him chastely and let him sleep. It didn't really matter, because she was tired of pursuing him; she needed a man who wanted her so passionately that nothing could get in the way.

Denny at least had loved her—more than anyone ever would, could she forget that?—and she had destroyed him. No matter how much she told herself otherwise, she was convinced that Denny was dead because she had deserted him. After all he'd done for her, after making her such a big star, she'd blown it all away because . . .

Sighing, she got out of bed, padded across the thick Chinese rug to the bathroom, and fished through the huge mirrored medicine cabinet for a pill. There were no Valium, but Rob had convinced the doctors in the emergency room to provide more of those little dolls that protected against panic attacks. Swallowing one without water, she struggled to get back her equilibrium.

Jillian had gone back to New York yesterday, after a week of holding Annabelle's hand and promising her that the police wouldn't hurt her. But Annabelle could imagine what she would say now.

Annabelle wasn't responsible for the end of the relationship with Denny—he had been the one who'd caused it. She had left Denny because he was *beating* her, tormenting and degrading her body and leaving her ego shattered on the floor. And he didn't care. If that was love, she could do without it, thank you. He'd had no right to want her back or even to think that he could get her back. Instead of being so anxious and scared now, she should just be grateful to have escaped with her own life intact.

That's what Jillian would tell her. But Annabelle didn't believe it.

The pill got caught somewhere in her throat, and she took a drink of water from the swan-necked faucet in the sink without even bothering with a cup. Who needed one. The brass faucets in this house probably cost more than her father had earned in a lifetime. The whole house fascinated her so much that Artie Glenn had suggested she buy it—something about tax deductions, he said—but the notion alarmed her. She didn't deserve to own a house with brass swans in the bathroom. Not after Denny. Not after all that had happened.

Just taking the pill made her feel calmer, even though she knew that it couldn't really be working yet. With new determination, she leaped onto the bed next to Rob, hoping to awaken him. When he didn't stir, she tugged at the covers and turned up the bedside light, then leaning close to him, muttered, "Rob, Rob," and finally, with her hand on his shoulder, a much louder, "Are you awake?"

He sat up and asked, "Are you okay?"

Suddenly, though she hadn't intended this at all, she started to cry.

"No, I'm not okay. I'm not okay at all. And you shouldn't be here, because you don't really love me."

Awake but not yet focused, he looked at her in bafflement. "What happened?"

"Denny is dead and I'm going to die and you don't love me." She heard the strange shrieking in her voice that was panic setting in. Maybe she just needed to take another pill so her heart would stop pounding and her breath would return.

"I care about you, Annabelle, I really do." He was wiping her tears and stroking her hair, caring for her like the good daddy she'd never had. "Please let me help you."

"I killed Denny."

Quite unexpectedly she was sobbing, and Rob was holding her, rocking her in his arms.

"You didn't kill Denny."

"I did, I did." She was tearing at Rob's nightshirt, trying to get to the chest underneath, wanting to feel a warm body pressed against her own. "I killed him."

"You miss Denny, I know that. Maybe you even still love him. But you didn't kill him, Annabelle."

"You don't know. You think I didn't kill him, but I left him and said bad things about him, and he's dead and I did it."

"You killed him in your heart, but not with a gun. Don't get yourself confused again. Evil thoughts don't shoot bullets. Somebody took a gun to Denny and ended his life, but it wasn't you."

"Then why do the police keep asking me questions? Why do reporters call at all hours wanting me to talk about killing Denny on television?"

"The world is interested in you, Annabelle. You're a big star. You sing gorgeous music and excite people, and they care about your life. That's the price of fame."

"No! They want me to talk on television, and I just won't do it. I'd probably faint or die. Which is what's going to happen when I try to do Jillian's show. It's the band that gets me through when I perform, and if I have to talk and there's no band, I can't do it."

"There won't be much talking. Jillian promised you that. Just introductions of guests and a couple of questions to them. They'll be your friends. Other musicians and all."

"But what about all these reporters and police who want me to talk about Denny?" She was rocking back and forth, losing her control.

"We've talked to the police time and again. They haven't bothered you in days. From what I understand, they're looking into other parts of Denny's life now."

"I won't talk about *anything*. I want to talk about Denny, but I can't. Why don't they get that? Why?" Hysteria was ripping through her, and she needed to come back to reality, shake the panic and pain. A different pain, that's what she needed, something to take her away from her thoughts. *Hit me, Rob. Hurt me.* But he wouldn't. No matter how much she begged, he wouldn't.

■

For the third time, Barney Rossman read over the memo that Margery Warren had prepared for him on Austin Realty's financial dealings. The last sentence informed him that her report "could point to only one obvious conclusion." Unfortunately, she hadn't been notably direct in pointing it out, and the conclusion wasn't obvious to him at all.

Flipping through the report again, he took in that Mark Austin had set up an offshore company in the Cayman Islands to ship supplies to the Wright-Austin joint venture in Eastern Europe. But, hell, that was legal, wasn't it? Financial management wasn't Barney's strength; he relied on his assistants to guide him in those matters. One reason he'd put Margery on this case was that he remembered she had degrees from Columbia in law *and* business—so she should be able to help him out. But apparently she didn't realize that he needed helping. He

254

smiled to himself, thinking that the Republican running against him in the last election should have made a campaign issue out of his degree in comparative literature from Amherst. Not much use for comp lit in the D.A.'s office.

The report said that Mark Austin was also investing heavily in certain Eastern European countries through the offshore business. Tax evasion? The whole point of an offshore company, as he understood it, was to avoid taxes or launder money. There was no indication that the Austins were linked to organized crime in New York, and you didn't launder money that you came by legally. But something was awry with Austin Realty.

He buzzed Margery Warren. They'd go over the report step by step.

Jillian assumed that the story about Denny's murder would hold less interest in New York than it did in Los Angeles, but as soon as she stepped off the plane at Kennedy Airport, she realized that she was wrong. Almost a week had passed since the killing, but the entire front page of one of the New York newspapers was a full-length picture of a dazed-looking Annabelle with the headline: SHE WAS THERE ON MURDER NIGHT!

At least it had taken the press a while to get hold of the information that Annabelle had admitted to her lawyer, Roger Simnowitz, the next morning.

But whatever suspicions were held by both press and police, Jillian was satisfied that there wasn't a shred of evidence linking Annabelle to the killing. Denny's own guns were found in a locked drawer in his apartment. Annabelle had never owned a gun and was terrified of all weapons. Jillian remembered taking her once into an avant-garde clothing store in SoHo where the salesgirls paraded through the store, modeling the clothes. One of the models was showing off a black leather bodysuit and carrying a starter's pistol for effect. Seeing it, Annabelle began trembling, and Jillian had to calm her down, explaining that the gun wasn't real and wouldn't be shot.

How could anybody possibly imagine Annabelle grabbing a gun and actually using it?

Annabelle had been hysterical for most of this last week, as frightened by police as she was of guns. But what did that prove? Absolutely nothing, except that policemen hadn't been friends in her childhood.

■

Jillian had been back in New York for just a few days when an eager producer from CBS called her one morning as soon as she stepped into her office.

"I'm not really in the mood to speak to anyone," Jillian told Liz grouchily.

"Do you want to call him back?" Liz asked.

"No, let me get it over with now."

The producer wanted to interview her for a segment they were doing on Denny's shooting for the morning news. Jillian declined to be interviewed, but the producer pressed, so Jillian pressed back.

"If you had any integrity at all, you'd not only forget about interviewing me, you'd forget about the whole segment," she told him heatedly. "Your viewers don't care about Denny Wright, they care about Annabelle Fox—and you and I both know that the only reason you're doing the story is to suggest a connection in the killing that just isn't there."

"We're not suggesting anything," the producer retorted, taking immediate umbrage. "We're reviewing the victim's life—and that, of course, includes Annabelle. At the moment the shooting is a mystery, and we understand that."

"Well, forget it. I'm not speaking for the record about Annabelle Fox or Denny Wright."

The producer backed down, no doubt realizing that even if he couldn't get Jillian to talk, he needed to be in her good graces to get the tape he wanted from "The Secret Life of Rock and Roll."

Maybe I won't even give him that, Jillian thought irritably. Keith Ross Productions owned the rights to all the footage, but their lawyers had advised them to provide it to news organizations for nothing more than an on-screen credit. They had done that endlessly—but how long was this going to continue? There was a strange dance going on. Reporters all seemed to be making assumptions about Annabelle's guilt—then coming out on her side. Fine to argue about an abused woman's right to strike back, but there was no evidence that Annabelle *had* struck back.

As she hung up, Jillian felt a knot of rage rising in her chest. It's not directed at that silly CBS producer, she told herself, but rationality held no sway this morning, when she was distraught and wanting vengeance on the world. Deciding to take action, she put in a call to Hale Areden, the president of the network news division, and got through almost immediately. He had little sympathy for Jillian's position and urged her to cooperate with the story that the morning show was trying to put together.

"You should be pleased with all the publicity," Areden told her. "Haven't you heard that the network is planning to repeat your 'Secret Life' special in a couple of weeks? Your ratings should be even better than the first time. Everyone's going to tune in out of curiosity."

"I'm not sure it's worth it."

"Not sure what's worth it?" Areden asked.

"Getting high ratings at an innocent woman's expense. People want to watch Denny beating up on Annabelle so they can imagine her turning around and shooting him. But there's something terribly unfair about being tried by the media when the police and courts haven't brought any charges at all."

"That's modern life," Areden said, as if he were explaining the world to an innocent. "The old joke about television says it's a tough job but somebody's got to do it. In this case, *somebody* is going to get high ratings from the Wright shooting, so it might as well be you. Relax and enjoy it."

"That's what you do when television is raping you and your friends, hmm? Thanks for the advice."

Jillian called their business manager to tell her to hold off on giving the CBS morning show rights to the footage.

"That may cause a legal problem since we've given it to all the other morning shows—not to mention a political problem since it's our own network," the business manager advised.

"They'll get it eventually," Jillian said, "but let's make them sweat for a while."

She was being childishly vindictive, and though she knew it, she didn't care. Back in the early days of her career, she had been a dispassionate executive, able to make decisions without much concern for the people who would be affected by them. What has changed? she wondered, propping her face in her hands and staring at the wall. Nothing about television and ratings seemed so desperately important anymore.

Jillian rubbed her temples, feeling a roaring headache attack her even at this hour. The day had started out badly and now it kept getting worse. Every instinct told her to take the day off and go home. Instead she stared despondently at the wall calendar. The twenty-seventh of the month, the day they would start to shoot "Wild Nights," was circled boldly in red—and the date seemed uncomfortably close. At least until then, she had to keep herself focused.

Finding a notebook, she slammed her desk drawer closed and went to the conference room, where the whole staff was gathered in a production meeting. At the last minute, the network had offered to run five full shows rather than a single pilot; the shows would be aired on the network-owned stations for five consecutive Mondays during the summer, and if the ratings were high, future success seemed almost guaranteed. The syndication deals were already lining up.

Keith was nervous—thinking and rethinking the content of the five shows. It was vintage Keith to make changes and get new ideas almost until the cameras were rolling. Normally Jillian didn't mind— his changes made shows better—but the deadline was pressing down on them, and she wasn't in the mood to humor Keith.

She wasn't in a mood to humor anyone.

Jillian interrupted Keith several times, even though she knew she was being rude, to suggest that they stop brainstorming and start making decisions. But he was busy rolling out new ideas, and by lunchtime the conference table was covered with stacks of books and magazines, newspaper clippings, and assorted notepads, scrap paper, and broken pencils.

They sent out for pizza—Keith's effort to keep everyone in the meeting during lunch—and Liz came in with a case of Wink Cola.

Jillian smiled seeing it. The morning after "The Secret Life of Rock and Roll" had first aired, Jillian had received a note from Henry Munroe, their sponsor and the president of Wink, which said, "*I'm sure you know how much we loved the show. You have won our complete loyalty, and we're taking no chances on losing yours.*" The note was vaguely baffling until a few minutes later, when workmen had appeared at her door wheeling hand trucks filled with Wink Cola. They kept coming and coming, filling Jillian's office and stacking up halfway down the hall to Keith's.

"Must be a lifetime supply," muttered one of the workmen as he unloaded the last case.

Henry Munroe had also agreed to be one of the sponsors of the pilot for "Wild Nights," and in unstated deference to him, there wasn't a Pepsi or Coke anywhere in the office.

While the staff took a brief break to consume pizza and soda, Jillian wandered to the front of the room, where a long Write 'n' Wipe board covered a large expanse of the wall. The board showed the working rundown for the shows. They should have been done by now—everything in place. And, in fact, they *had* been done a few weeks ago. But this was last-minute panic—rethinking and reshuffling. So much was riding on the show that they had to be perfect.

Black lines that had begun to swim in front of Jillian's eyes divided the hour-long shows into a melange of three- to six-minute segments. For quick recognition, they had written information about the musical numbers in orange, the talk segments in green, the entertainment segments in pink, and the Tough Talk—the controversial discussions—in yellow. Commercial breaks, identified in bold red, cut through the pastel board like gashes of blood. Though Jillian had already approved most of it, the plans spun in front of her eyes like a child's cut-glass kaleidoscope. Too complicated. Too many pieces that could change. Tucker hosting talk and Annabelle hosting music and a charming blond reporter from L.A. handling entertainment. How were they going to make it all work?

Keith was about to start the meeting again to continue brainstorming, when the middle-aged receptionist who had been with Keith for years appeared at the far door and called out in a loud voice, "Jillian, there's a call for you from Los Angeles! It's Emil." Jillian turned slowly, and the receptionist, mistaking the distracted look in Jillian's eyes for lack of recognition, added needlessly, "Emil the director. He said it was important, otherwise I wouldn't have bothered you."

Emil was directing the pilot for "Wild Nights," so it was reasonable that he call, but Jillian felt his name resonate in the room. She sensed Liz exchanging sidelong glances with another young assistant, both of them dropping their eyes when they thought she might be looking.

"Thank you, please transfer it to my office. I'll take it there."

Leaving the conference room, she saw Keith glaring at her from the head of the table. "You can get everyone started again, and I'll be back right after I take this call," she called to him without looking back.

She made herself walk rather than run to her office, not wanting her eagerness to give away anything that wasn't already known—but as she clicked her door shut, she was aware that her need for privacy would do just that. Theirs was typically an open-door office, but she couldn't bear any possibility of eavesdropping.

"I know I shouldn't be bothering you right now," Emil said almost immediately when she picked up the phone. "The receptionist said you were in a meeting."

"I was, but I'm glad to get out." Simply holding the phone, connecting again to Emil on the other end, made her feel calmer. "We're struggling through the rundown for the shows, and it's unnerving. Too much to do and too little time."

"Always the case, isn't it? I won't add to the burden. I just needed to hear your voice and tell you I love you. Can I call you later to talk?"

"No, talk to me now." There was an edge in his voice that made her suspect a serious agenda. "Anything happening I need to know about?"

"Yes." He paused briefly, then said calmly, "I just came back from two hours of talking to the L.A. police."

"Oh, no. What now?"

"Captain Murphy had requested that I speak to them again, so I went, accompanied by our lawyer friend Roger Simnowitz. Allegedly they wanted to run through every step of the taping of 'The Secret Life' to find out what I'd seen between Denny and Annabelle. But we'd done that the day after Denny was killed, so it wasn't clear to me what we were gaining by going through it again at this point. They also asked a lot of questions about you—or rather, the two of us together."

Jillian's throat was dry, but when she picked up the can of Diet Wink on her desk, she found it was empty. "What was the point of the questioning?" she asked, her voice hoarse.

"Grasping at straws, Roger thinks. It's been what—two weeks now since Denny was murdered? And they don't have anything. Our affair is at least something out of the ordinary. Of course, this is L.A., so I don't trust anybody's motives. I think the cops all work side jobs providing information to the gossip columnists in this town."

Jillian laughed but then said anxiously, "Will you tell me what they asked?"

"It was very basic. How long we've been together. Who knows about us. How it affected our relationship with Annabelle and Denny. Roger kept telling me that I could refuse to answer anything I wanted because it was all so irrelevant to the investigation. But I figured I'd appease their curiosity—if that's what it is—and keep you from being bothered."

"You're kind. Did you have the feeling that they were looking for something specific?"

"It wasn't clear. The police have apparently been talking to everyone, including some of the people in your husband's company. But Roger thinks the police are still convinced that Annabelle is behind it somehow and they're frustrated because she has stayed so low profile. No press releases about the murder. No interviews on Barbara Walters specials. Nothing. So they're looking for new angles to get to her. Roger also says that these fishing expeditions—his phrase, not mine—are what the L.A. police do in high-profile cases that they can't solve. If the press starts asking questions, they can at least say they've followed up on ninety-nine different leads, and toss the reporters a few tidbits."

"I don't think the press really needs any help," Jillian said. She told him about the segment that would be appearing on the CBS morning news and the network's plans to rerun their special.

"I mentioned all this to Keith this morning, and he's thrilled. He doesn't see any dark side at all. I'm beginning to feel like I'm the only one who takes murder seriously. Keith and the network guys are acting like the whole thing is some great publicity stunt that they're actually getting for free. Apparently, I'm seen as a bad sport, out to spoil their fun."

"You and Keith are at odds over this?" Emil asked.

"We're at odds over everything."

"Tell me."

"Not now, we're talking murder. You poor dear, having to put up with more questioning this morning. I'm sorry if I was responsible."

"Don't be silly—I only called because I thought you should know. But you sound unusually distraught—so now it's your turn to tell *me* what's happening."

"It's been a bad morning."

"I gathered that. Now tell me more."

She sighed. "You've had your own turmoil for the day. You don't need mine, too."

"Of course I do. I want to know everything about you—including your bad days."

She thought briefly of telling him that it was the call from CBS that was bothering her, but he knew her too well to buy that, and the need to share her despair was overwhelming. "Okay, here it is. I found a love letter this morning written to Mark. And it wasn't written by me."

"Not good," Emil said sympathetically.

"No," Jillian said. Then, embarrassed at having blurted out the problem, she said sassily, "But I suppose it's better than spending the morning with the L.A. police."

"Tell me the details," Emil said, ignoring her forced flippancy.

His intensity warmed her; she felt his concern pouring across the line.

"I don't know how to tell this story except chronologically, so here goes. After I dropped the girls off at school this morning, I swung by the dry cleaners before going to the train. There were a few of my things being cleaned and a couple of Mark's suits, so I picked them all up, and when I went to hang them in the car, I saw that pinned to the outside of the plastic bag was an envelope—the kind they use if you leave a pen or some money in your pocket, and they take it out before cleaning."

"An honest dry cleaner," Emil said.

"We have only the best in Melrose," Jillian agreed sarcastically. "Anyway, inside was what had been left in a pocket. And it wasn't my pocket, I can tell you. There was a note with Mark's name written on the outside in a very feminine scrawl. It was taped at the corners, as if it had been stuck up on a door."

"So you opened it."

"Of course I opened it."

"And?"

The thought of repeating the words on the note suddenly embarrassed her, so she said, "I can't remember it exactly."

"Give it to me as close as you can."

Fumbling in her top desk drawer, she found the crumpled note that she had hidden away; somehow reading it directly would require less emotion than recalling the gist. "Ready? I've got it right here." Taking a deep breath, she read: "'Mark, darling. Use your key and come in. I won't be back until late so take off *all* your clothes and crawl into bed. I'll have a surprise when I return. I love you always.' And it's signed, 'C.'"

"Ah."

His tone resonated sympathy rather than embarrassment, so she asked, "What do you think?"

"I think you should stop going to the dry cleaners."

"My husband is having an affair with a woman named 'C.'"

He paused, then said, "It's hard to find an alternative interpretation for that one, I'll admit. Do you think it's been going on a long time?"

"I'm not sure. I wasn't fully conscious of it, but I think I've known on some level for months."

"Is that why you got involved with me?"

"Of course not!" She said it too quickly and too loudly and felt unexpected tears springing to her eyes, her whole body shaking in distress. Emotion gripped her like a howling dog, and she added, "Maybe the tension at home made me open to you, but I didn't fall in love with you to wreak my revenge."

"You're crying."

"No I'm not." Then quickly, "Sorry—I *am* crying, and I don't know why."

"You're hurt," Emil said. "Your husband is having an affair, and it's painful."

His sympathy released the frozen well in her; sobs burbled to the surface, and she couldn't restrain them. As tears flooded down her face, she tried to cry silently, but little gasps of despair escaped across the phone line. Trying to control herself, she said, "I don't have a right to be upset about Mark, of course. So he's having an affair. Given the way you and I feel about each other, and after all we've done, you must think I'm a terrible hypocrite."

"No, I'm thinking how much I love you. And how I wish I were there to hold you right now."

"I love you, too."

The words were still in the air when her office door opened, and Liz peeked in. "Keith wants you," she mouthed.

Jillian said, "Excuse me," into the phone, and rubbing at her tear-smeared face, said, "What?"

"I'm sorry." Liz, clutching at the edge of the door, looked genuinely distraught. "Keith said to tell you he really needs you in the conference room as soon as you're through talking to Emil."

"Tell Keith I'll be there. When I've finished with the call and not before."

Liz closed the door, and Jillian said into the phone, "Keith is acting like a spoiled child now. He doesn't want me talking to you on his time."

"You have to talk to me. You're his producer and I'm his director."

"I know that."

"He's jealous."

"I figured that out, too."

"Let's talk business so he can't complain. How's the pilot?"

She knew Emil had changed the subject on purpose, giving her time to control herself. "We have all these widely varied hosts and segments, and I'm afraid it's becoming a mishmash. Keith thinks giving viewers a little of everything is wonderful—a glorious stew, he calls it. My fear is that if you mix meatballs and chocolate sauce, you lose the meat lovers as well as the chocolate lovers."

"What an unappetizing metaphor."

"It's meant to be."

"You think Keith is developing an unappetizing show?"

"It's hard to say if my real animosity is toward Keith or the show. Frankly I'm losing interest in both."

"I know how you feel, but stay cool. It doesn't get you anywhere to fight with Keith. Has he been giving you a hard time about . . . us?"

"No, in fact, he hasn't said a word to me about it, which I suppose qualifies in its own way as giving me a hard time, since it's obvious that he knows." She palmed the soda can, running her fingertip around the ragged metal at the opening; then, her voice softening, said, "I miss you."

"Well, good, because did I mention that I have urgent business in New York? I'm taking the overnight flight tonight and I'll be there at six tomorrow morning. Would you like to meet me for breakfast?"

"Of course. Where should we meet?"

"Why not make it easy and meet at my hotel. I think I'll stay at the Carlyle this time. Or maybe the St. Regis. Let me see about making a reservation, and I'll leave a discreet message with your receptionist so I don't have to disturb you—or rather disturb Keith—again."

"I thought you were shooting something in L.A. What's your urgent business in New York?"

"Seeing you. I can't think of any business more pressing. My shoot is finished, and there's far too much emotion burning between us to trust to the phone lines. Keith's switchboard will burst into flames if we continue this way, and he'll never forgive us."

"He probably won't forgive me now for missing so much of this meeting, but I really needed to talk to you. Thank you."

"Don't thank me. I love you, remember? I wish I could swoop you away from all this misery and make you happy, but for now all I can do is send you a big kiss and promise to see you tomorrow."

"Don't hang up." She clutched the phone, her love's umbilical cord, pained at the thought of having the nourishing connection cut.

"I'm glad to talk all day."

There was another knock, and this time the door didn't open until Jillian said, "Yes?" Liz, embarrassed by her mission, looked in and said, "Keith wants to know how much longer you'll be."

"Tell him I'm on my way."

Overhearing the exchange, Emil said, "You don't even sound angry."

The door closed firmly, and Jillian said, "No use blowing up at Liz. And frankly I'm not sure I even have that much emotion left for Keith. It's all directed elsewhere."

When she walked back into the conference room a few minutes later, her makeup was repaired and the telltale signs of crying were mostly expunged from her face; but Keith eyed her with an aggrieved haughtiness, as if he had heard the bedsprings creaking moments before she arrived. There was a generalized tension in the room that her presence did nothing to appease.

"So you're here. Good." Keith nodded at her as she sat down next to him. "We have a fabulous idea and need some information from you."

"What's the fabulous idea?"

"Before I tell you that, how about the information we need?" Jillian saw that the excited fire in Keith's eyes wasn't matched in the other faces around the table.

"Go ahead."

"The question on the table concerns Annabelle Fox. You know her better than anyone. In a nutshell—can she talk?"

"About what?"

Keith shifted in his seat, aware that everyone was watching him closely. "That's not the point. The question is—could she help host the Tough Talk segment of the show?"

Jillian looked around, wanting a hint as to where all this was heading. Not getting one, she said, "I don't think she'd be brilliant at it. I'd rather leave her handling the musical numbers. If you want her to be interviewed, let Tucker Fredericks do it."

Keith pursed his lips, then pushing on, said, "How about if the Tough Talk subject were a topic dear to her heart? Something that might inspire her to have a lot to say?"

266

"Maybe," Jillian said. "Maybe it could work. What's the subject?"

"Women who kill in self-defense."

Stunned, Jillian sat back, aware of both Keith's smug expression and the intense gazes of the writers and segment producers and assistants sitting around the table. *They're waiting for me to save them from Keith's exploitation.* She had the feeling that with one word of disapproval from her the room would erupt against Keith, but remembering Emil's warning about not fighting with Keith, she adopted a conciliatory tone and asked, "What's the focus going to be?"

She imagined a hissing around the table, air being let out of a collectively overinflated balloon.

"The focus goes wherever the guests take it," Keith said cheerfully. "We could have four women who killed husbands or lovers on the panel, and all they'd have to do is tell their stories. Then we'd have an expert to bring up the issue of killing abusive lovers and what abused women really can do. But it wouldn't be preachy, because we'd have the killers sitting right there. Compelling television, don't you think?"

Struggling to control herself, Jillian said, "I don't mean to sound jaded, but it's not exactly new. Abused women who've killed have been on talk shows before, and I have the feeling that most viewers know their stories by heart. Given the sheer volume of talk on television, the stakes have been raised."

"That's why we'd have Annabelle. She'd up the ante, wouldn't you say? By the way, it was Liz's idea." He smiled ingratiatingly at Liz, who looked up sharply.

"That's not fair, Keith!" Liz looked pleadingly at Jillian. "I had a whole list of ideas because Jillian told me to go through the newspapers looking for controversial subjects. I never thought of this in terms of Annabelle."

"But I did," Keith said, grinning. "What a team."

Liz looked at him in anger, then working up her nerve, said, "It's not fair to put Annabelle into a segment like that. It's exploiting her. She becomes guilty by proximity."

Keith laughed and Liz, reddening, continued. "Maybe that's not the right word, but you know what I mean. Rob will go nuts when he hears it."

"We're not doing this pilot to please Rob, we're doing it to get good ratings. And with Annabelle involved, people will watch, won't they?" Keith seemed positively merry. "Even if Annabelle doesn't make any personal comments at all, just having her there will send the ratings through the roof. We can do a killer advertising campaign, excuse the pun. The pilot will get such high numbers that we'll sell this sucker as a series in no time flat."

"It's going to sell anyway," Jillian said. "But while we're thinking about what to do with Annabelle, let's run through the rest of the show." Her simple diversion worked, and they went over the rest of the board; the colors blurred in front of her eyes, and Jillian tried to imagine what the show would be like when it was transformed from squares on a board to lights and music and talk and people. The tension in the room had evaporated into detachment; everyone seemed disappointed in Jillian's response, and their attention had wandered.

When the meeting broke up, Jillian followed Keith back to his office.

"So you liked my idea with Annabelle," Keith said, glancing through the messages that his secretary handed him as he walked by. "I'm glad. I knew you'd see it my way, but the kids in this office see you as some sort of demigod of good taste. The general feeling in the room was that you were going to go nuts at the suggestion."

"Instead I loved it."

Something in her tone made Keith stop on his way to his desk and turn around.

"Didn't you love it?"

Sitting down, Jillian drummed her fingers on the arms of the chair. "Come on, Keith, you know perfectly well what I think about this whole subject. It's awful and exploitative. I don't know why you even brought it up in front of me. You can't tie Annabelle to a show on women killers. She hasn't been accused of anything, and as far as we know, she hasn't done anything."

"I'm not looking for a confession."

"It doesn't matter. The implication is there. And regardless of what you and I decide, I can guarantee that Annabelle herself will refuse to appear."

"She'll do it if you tell her to, and you know that as well as I do."

When Jillian didn't respond, Keith dropped the pink message

notes on his desk and turned to her, his arms crossed like a shield in front of his chest. "You won't tell Annabelle to do this?"

"I won't. It's wrong and you know it. There has to come a point where people's lives count more than ratings, and I think we've reached it."

"Excuse me, but since when has Jillian van Dorne become the paradigm of television integrity? It seems to me that you were the one who arranged all the shenanigans for the 'Secret Life' special, and you didn't apologize when the ratings came in. Care to tell me what's different now?"

"There was nothing exploitative last time. Annabelle was in a jam, and we helped her out. Sure, it was good for the show, too, but I don't think I'll be damned in hell for helping an abused woman get out of her house. That time we helped each other. This time she'd be helping us by making a fool of herself."

"I don't believe I'm hearing this." Keith moved behind his desk, the boss trying to regain control of the situation. "This isn't the impression you gave in the conference room."

"Good, because I think the proper forum to talk about our disagreements is in private, don't you?"

"Not if it means that we waste an hour of a meeting and then we have to start all over again. Of course, you were too busy to be at most of that meeting anyway."

"I was at *all* of that meeting, Keith, except when I was on the phone with our director."

"Your director."

"My director? Just how is that?"

"Must I spell things out for you?"

"Yes, I'm afraid you must."

They glared at each other across the desk.

"I don't think you'll enjoy hearing my opinion of *your* director," Keith said petulantly.

"Correct me if I'm wrong," Jillian said primly, "but I believe you're still the executive making all the staffing decisions. You were eager to have Emil for the 'Secret Life' special, and I got him for you. Then you were desperate to have him direct this pilot, knowing he doesn't usually do such things, and I guaranteed that, too. So I'm not sure I understand your grievance."

As if he were claiming his territory and preparing to attack intruders, Keith spread his hands across the sculptured desk. Jillian could think only how ridiculous the desk seemed in this place, how false and pretentious. But pretense was their business, and it wasn't fair to hate Keith for having mastered the art of television.

"My grievance is simple, Jillian, and if you're going to goad me, I'm going to say it. I'm glad you got Emil to direct our shows, but I didn't realize the lengths you'd be willing to go to convince him. I don't like it that you're fucking Emil. I don't like it that everyone in the business knows about it either. I found out from my own brother, for God's sake."

He slapped his fist against the desk, but Jillian's only response was to raise an eyebrow and gaze at him imperiously. She could tell that the attitude disarmed him—he expected her wrath to match his own, probably assumed she would angrily rise to defend herself or burst into tears or go storming from the office. Instead she said, "I assume your brother has only the best sources."

"Well, yes, he does." He hesitated briefly, having assumed she understood Barney's source but worrying suddenly that he had gone too far. "You don't really need sources to gather the truth about you two—all you need are eyes. You're like magnets for each other. You can't stay apart. It's a bad atmosphere for the staff."

"Nobody had any idea about my relationship with Emil until the night Denny Wright was killed," Jillian said, "so I'll thank you not to start making accusations about the staff and my professionalism. If you have any problems with my work, let's discuss that straight out."

Softening slightly, he said, "Of course I don't have problems with that. You're the best, for chrissakes, and you know it."

"So my work is fine and we've created stellar shows—you, me, and Emil. But your brother tells you something and you turn against me, is that right?"

"Not exactly." His anger was thoroughly depleted now; he wanted the conversation to end quickly. "Look, Jillian, it's simple. However it is that we all know about you and Emil, we do know. As your friend, I'm worried about you and your marriage and your kids. I assume your husband doesn't know anything about this, and I doubt you want him to. As your partner, I'm worried about our image in the industry. That's all."

"I appreciate your concern, but I must say this whole conversation strikes me as oddly ill-timed. We began by talking about Annabelle, didn't we? You were trying to get me to agree to something that is both tasteless and immoral, and when I wouldn't say yes, you took a sharp turn to my relationship with Emil. Just what that relationship is, by the way, is none of your concern. You can think what you like, but don't use your opinions to blackmail me into doing something that I know to be wrong for us and wrong for the show."

Keith looked startled, his gray eyes opened into round O's on his face. "You're misinterpreting."

"Am I? I wonder, Keith. I really wonder."

Back in her own office, gathering her things to go home for the evening, Jillian's eye landed on the calendar again. The twenty-seventh loomed. She'd make it to the day they shot the pilot, no question about that. But she wasn't sure what she would do afterward.

CHAPTER SIXTEEN

MARK unstrapped the watch from his wrist and carefully laid it on the side of the sink, not trusting it to be as waterproof as claimed. It had been a long time since he'd given the girls a bath; tonight, when Jillian had called to say she'd be home late, he decided to come home early. The mushroom pizza he picked up on the way home from the train station was a hit: the girls treated him like a returning hero. Their childish ease was strangely comforting for him tonight, ameliorating the sense of terror that he couldn't otherwise shake.

God, it had been a stressful week. The police had been poking around their office for days, trying to get some information on the Denny Wright shooting. But nobody in their office knew anything. Sure, Denny was part of the Austin-Wright joint venture, but he was never involved in any way that mattered. At least, that was the party line. And Mark and Cynthia were the only ones who knew otherwise.

Damn, this killing had been inconvenient. Probably some druggie friend killed Denny over half an ounce of coke and the upshot was to focus police attention on their company. It wasn't fair. The police weren't likely to stumble across his offshore company, Cynthia insisted, because they weren't looking for anything like that.

And because it had nothing to do with what happened to Denny Wright.

Mark felt as if he had walked out to the edge of a cliff and put out one foot, believing that he could stay there forever while he decided whether or not to jump. But just when he decided he *shouldn't* jump and prepared to turn back, he discovered that the other foot had slipped.

That's where he was now—in the middle of the air, falling, and wanting to turn back.

What has happened to me? Mark wondered. The bathtub was full, and he was kneeling at the edge of the tub, his hands dangling into the bubbly water. The girls splashed and played with their tub toys, and their sweet laughter combined with the warmth of the water soothed him as a lullaby would. His thoughts floated away, and though his fingers were rooted in the bathtub, his mind wandered far— through London and Los Angeles into the hotels and apartments he had shared with Cynthia, the secrets they had shared in the grips of passion. Ah, the secrets.

"Daddy, want to hear a joke?" Lila's voice startled him, and he pulled himself back from his reveries, as disoriented as if an alarm clock had awakened him from a deep sleep. Focusing on where he was, he saw Lila sitting on her knees in the tub, her smooth belly dripping bubbles, the edges of her blond hair clumped together from the water.

"Of course. What's your joke?"

"What did the boy octopus say to the girl octopus?"

"I don't know, what?"

"I wanna hold your hand, hand, hand, hand, hand, hand, hand, hand."

She counted the "hands" on her fingers, and when she reached eight, he laughed, at least in part because it felt good to allow himself some relief from his torment. For once it was a joke he hadn't heard before, and he thought that the funniest part of it was realizing that "I wanna hold your hand" didn't mean anything to Lila. It wasn't a song, it wasn't the Beatles, it wasn't the Sixties—it was a phrase that made adults laugh for some unfathomable reason, and so she would use it again.

"I have a joke, too, Daddy." Eve stood up now, rounder than her sister, small dimples of baby fat still apparent on her thighs and in the gentle roundness of her tummy. He found her softness appealing and wondered why so many adult women detested their own flesh, looking at roundness on themselves with loathing. His daughters' bodies amazed him—they seemed so devoid of any semblance of female sexuality that it was hard to imagine the bald vaginas and flat breasts burgeoning into lushness. Little girls' bodies seemed unconnected to the mature forms. Not so little boys, whose genitals were fully formed, dangling proudly, even at birth. A few weeks earlier, neighbors of theirs had stopped by with their two sons, and all the children had played together until the boys announced that they had to pee. Rushing into the bathroom without closing the door, they had tugged at their pants and whipped out their penises, the older boy calling to his brother, "Come on, let's squirt these squirt guns!" There was an aggressive swagger to their sexuality, a pride in their genitals, that was common to boys but rare to find in women.

Though he had found it in Cynthia.

He tried to imagine Cynthia as a small girl, burrowing for a sexuality that was secret and guarded and certainly, in childhood, well hidden. However it was, that aggressive sexuality had emerged in her. And in the face of it, he himself had changed.

"Tell me your joke, Eve."

"Where does a sheep get a haircut?"

Eve looked at him with eyes so wide he thought he could dive into them, pale blue lakes that welcomed friends and strangers alike.

"I don't know. Where does a sheep get a haircut?"

"At the baa-baa shop!" She let out a three-year-old yelp of satisfaction, and again he laughed, mostly at the joy her young humor evoked. Her bountiful laughter rippled across the bathtub as light and translucent as the bubbles in the water.

"Are we funny, Daddy?" Eve asked.

"You're very funny," he said, and he had to get a grip on himself, look away for a moment, because the joy emanating from the two little girls was so strong that it almost overwhelmed him.

There was a knock on the door, and suddenly Jillian was in the room, smiling.

"Mommy! You're home!" Eve jumped up and down in the tub, and Lila, methodically soaping her washcloth, broke into a satisfied grin.

Jillian threw kisses to the girls and smiled at Mark, then asked, "How is everybody?"

"Bad," Lila said, smiling.

"Bad," Eve echoed happily.

"You don't look bad. In fact, you look very happy." She hung her suit jacket on a hook on the back of the door and rolled up her sleeves.

"Mommy, come here and I'll tell you the joke I just told Daddy." Lila sensed an important moment: both her parents in the room at the same time, an event that hadn't happened in ages, one that she must do everything to preserve.

"Let me go change my clothes," Jillian suggested, but Eve's sudden cry of "No, Mommy! Stay here!" seemed to change her mind, and Jillian knelt down next to Mark, her silky hose swooshing against the plush pink bathmat, her expensive designer skirt crushed against the porcelain tub.

Mark thought about the four of them in the small, steamy room, the girls' faces, rosy from the heat of the tub, gazing transfixedly at the sight of their parents, thigh-to-thigh, in front of them.

Eve reached a soapy hand out of the water to touch her mother's shimmering coral necklace. "Pretty," she said, and Jillian unwittingly pulled away, to protect herself from the splattering water. But she was a moment too late, and as the child touched the necklace, a shower of soapsuds slid down her satin blouse. Jillian looked briefly horrified, but before she could say a word, Eve cried tearfully, "I'm sorry, Mommy! I didn't mean to do that!"

Jillian said, "It's all right, sweetheart." Eve, sensitive to the happy moment she had just destroyed, began to sob, her mouth open like a hungry bird, wails of despair escaping.

As Jillian dabbed a towel at the blouse with little effect, Eve's sobs ricocheted off the marble walls, filling the room, until Jillian leaned over and put her arms around the wet, shaking child.

"Mommy, you'll get even wetter!" Lila cried, delighted.

"What's more important, a silly blouse or my little girl?" Jillian asked, holding Eve closer, feeling the child's wet hands gripping her back.

In a moment the sobbing slowed, and when Jillian pulled away, her blouse was decorated with wet handprints and soapsuds.

"Nothing a trip to the dry cleaner can't fix," Mark said, trying to sound cheerful, but Jillian looked at him sharply, as if he had just slapped her, and he was at a sudden loss for what to say.

■

The children were asleep. After the bath, Jillian had gone to Lila's room to read her a story and Mark had read to Eve; then they had switched for kisses, Mom and Dad passing each other in the darkened hallway like lovers soundlessly changing rooms, changing beds, in what seemed the middle of the night.

Now, though, it was barely ten o'clock, and Jillian stood at the island counter in the kitchen, spreading peanut butter on whole wheat bread so Lila's lunchbox would be packed in the morning. Ready to be added were a box of juice, an apple, and a heart-shaped note that said MOMMY LOVES LILA. Jillian insisted on making Lila's lunch each night, rather than leaving it for Marguerite. Each day at noontime, she felt a simple pleasure in knowing that Lila was thinking of her; though miles apart, their mother-daughter bond was unbroken as Lila read the note her mother had left.

Mark sat at the kitchen table, his back to Jillian, drinking a cup of coffee and flipping through a magazine. Jillian saw him profiled against the darkened skylight, only a hint of a moon gleaming through at this hour, the slivered crescent barely visible.

"Can it ever work again?"

Mark turned around at Jillian's soft words, saw his wife standing with the peanut butter knife poised in midair.

"Can what ever work?"

"Us. The marriage. Our family. Or is this it?"

"I don't know." Mark felt himself choking on the words. "It was nice tonight, wasn't it? A real family. The girls were great."

"The girls are always great," Jillian said curtly. "You're just not home to see them." Then, more kindly, "How was your day?"

"Fine, how was yours?"

"Fine. Anything special going on?"

"Not much. And you?"

"The usual."

They were as frightened of asking questions as they were of

answering them. Too much could be revealed if they spoke. Because she didn't want to give the details of her life, she couldn't risk asking about his. And what could he tell her, anyway? That he'd had—love? lunch? an orgy of passion?—with "C."

"The girls were happy to have both of us together tonight," Jillian said. "We haven't been a family in a long time."

"I guess they've missed it," Mark said. "To be honest, I have, too."

Jillian cut the peanut butter sandwich into quarters, wrapped them up, and put them into Lila's squishy pink Barbie-Loves-Ken lunchbox. Snapping the box shut, she finally looked at Mark and asked, "Have you really? I thought maybe you'd found other things that were of greater interest to your life right now."

When he didn't answer, she washed off the knife and plate she had used and put the peanut butter and bread back into the refrigerator. Chores done, she remained at the counter, leaning over so her elbows were propped on the cutting board and her chin cupped in the palm of her hand. Maybe it was time that they *did* speak bluntly, took a risk instead of continuing this strange minuet they danced, in which they stayed together and shared nothing but the music.

That thought lingered when Mark turned around in his seat and asked, "Do you still love me?" and instead of offering the glib "Yes, of course" that was expected, she leaned forward, balancing herself on elbows and the balls of her feet, and from that precarious position said, "It's hard to know, isn't it? You go along assuming that you love your husband and that your husband loves you, and then you realize that neither of you are acting like it at all."

Eyes cold, Mark asked, "Is that where we are?"

"It's a little hard to feel that we're basking in love here, wouldn't you say? It's also difficult for the girls, who know that something is wrong."

"Would it be better if we got a divorce?"

She took a deep breath, then asked, "Do you want that?"

"I don't know." He turned away from her again and dropped his head onto his hands. From across the room, Jillian could see his shoulders heaving and realized that he was shaking with emotion. Unexpectedly moved, she crossed over to him, touched his shoulders, and sat down next to him, holding his hand and rubbing his back.

When he raised his head, he was dry-eyed, but he gripped her arm tightly, holding her as if seeking sustenance in her closeness. "I've been having a bad time, and I know that you and the children have suffered from it. I'd say 'I'm sorry,' but that would imply that things will change, and I don't know if that's true."

His hands were cold and his speech left her chilled. "It will be hard to continue this way for much longer, I'm afraid," she said. He still held her hand, and with a touch of a smile she added, "You and I are masters at keeping up surface appearances, but it's just getting too hard, isn't it? Instead of feeling better when we're together, we demoralize each other. Home is supposed to be a haven in a heartless world, but our marriage is what's heartless now. All we do is hurt each other."

Vaguely surprised, Mark asked, "Have I been hurting you? For that I *can* say I'm sorry. I was aware of being unavailable, but not of inflicting pain."

"It's the same thing, isn't it? Making the other person feel unimportant and unworthy. Looking into their eyes and no longer seeing that glorious reflection of yourself."

"Reverend Paley," Mark said, knowing immediately what she meant.

"Reverend Paley," Jillian agreed. At their wedding ceremony, when Mark had looked at Jillian, he had been sure she was the most beautiful woman in the world, and Jillian had smiled at her soon-to-be-husband, knowing he was kind and caring and the finest man she had ever met. The minister had smiled at their enchantment with each other and said, "May you always see each other with the joy you have today. And may you always trust the glorious reflection of yourself that you see in the other's eyes, for it is both more true and more nourishing than the mundane view we each hold of ourselves."

The words had penetrated their wedding-day haze, and they had repeated them, in some form, to each other afterward.

"The dream is always that another person enhances you," Jillian said, "but I'm afraid we've gotten to the point of diminishing each other."

Something about the sentiment caused Mark to tremble visibly. "You've felt that from me, and I've felt it from you, too. Everything was fine and dandy in our lives when we got married, but bad times come, and I don't know if we can weather those anymore." He sat up straight, his lips tensed in an anxious line. "Want to know what I think about sometimes? Things in my business falling apart, and God knows that could happen. Sometimes it seems like half the businessmen I know have been indicted. Would you support me if there was the possibility of my going to jail? I don't see you sitting docilely in the courthouse behind me day after day and defending my innocence."

"Is that a serious possibility?"

He shrugged. "Anything is possible. You never know when the money will stop."

"You could never understand that I didn't marry you for money." She played with his fingernails, tapping the edges of her carefully tended nails against the rough edges of his. "I can make plenty of my own, thank you. But money is such a predictor of power and ego for you that you never understood that. I don't need money from you, I need love and attention. And those are in short supply."

"So you want out, is that it? Want someone who is more sympathetic and who offers a better reflection of yourself than I have allowed."

"You're saying that, I'm not." When he just shrugged, Jillian added, "You're having an affair."

It was a statement rather than a question, and as such he just nodded.

"You love her." This time the statement wasn't as quickly accepted.

"I don't know what I feel. More frightened than anything."

"Why should you feel frightened?"

For an answer he just looked away through the darkened windows in the kitchen where the shades had not been drawn, and in his face Jillian read a desperation that she hadn't seen before. He was frightened of something more than their marriage dissolving, but at the moment she couldn't imagine what it was, because it was hard to envision an event in their lives more distressing than that.

CHAPTER SEVENTEEN

*B*ARRY Brunetti handed the rundown that Keith had sent him for the pilot of "Wild Nights" to Garrett Jones, the best production manager he had at WOJ, and told him to let him know if there were any problems.

"So far everything has been smooth," Garrett said. "Keith Ross runs a very professional company."

Nodding his agreement, Barry asked, "When is the set arriving?"

"Sometime next week. I've allowed over a week for it to be installed, which I know is excessive, but the studio is free at that point, so I thought we might as well take advantage of it."

"Nice set, don't you think?"

Garrett grinned. "From the plans, I'd say it's a couple of hundred thousand dollars' worth of nice. That's why I'm taking special pains with it."

Garrett left and Barry went back to analyzing the rundown. Damn, he wanted this show to work. The police had been crawling all over the studio for the last week, looking for any dirt they could dig up on Annabelle and the murder of Denny Wright. But what did he know about anything connected to that? He'd never even met Annabelle, let alone Denny.

Barry had spent a lot more time worrying about Tucker Fredericks than worrying about the police. He thought that signing Tucker as one of the hosts was a mistake. The guy was too bland and predictable, and in television lately, bland and predictable seemed to be definitely out of style. Viewers liked wiseass black men who told dirty jokes or fat, nasty women who talked about their ovaries or overbearing white men who provoked fights on camera. Such was the taste of the American public. It wasn't a matter of going broke by overestimating it—the real problem was trying to understand it at all.

Keith insisted that Barry was wrong about Tucker—the show needed a stable influence, given the tumultuous personalities that were otherwise running it. They needed *someone* to counterbalance Annabelle Fox.

What a shame that Keith hadn't been able to convince Annabelle to do a talk segment on women who kill. Controversy was just what the show needed.

"Maybe *you* could convince her," Keith had suggested on the phone the other day.

"Why me?"

"Annabelle is a woman in need of a man, and you're *always* in need of a woman."

Ignoring the cynicism, Barry had asked, "What's her problem?"

"Her manager—or former manager—is dead. Her current bedmate wants to move out. She's scared and lonely and wants someone to run her life. I thought Jillian might do it, but she's otherwise occupied. Besides, she thinks Annabelle needs to stand on her own two feet and acquire some sense of independence so she isn't constantly bouncing from one man to another."

"Sounds right."

"No, sounds ridiculous. The girl is a rock star, not a Phi Beta Kappa feminist. When she's on the air, she needs a Tucker Fredericks type to keep her from floating into the ether. Off the air she needs a solid man to tell her what to do. Someone she can trust who won't take advantage of her. Her current bedmate gets high marks in the trust department, but he's not strong enough to handle her. She needs a station manager type, if you know what I mean."

Barry had just laughed, but now it made sense. Hell, if Annabelle was looking for a new love in her life, Barry Brunetti had more than enough qualifications. Maybe he should just call her and chat. There was definitely more than one way to end up in California.

To his surprise, getting through to Annabelle was easy. Keith had

281

supplied her home phone number, and Annabelle herself answered it on the second ring. Once he explained who he was—and that he was calling to help her prepare for "Wild Nights"—she was as eager as a puppy. She'd heard his name before from Emil and Keith and Jillian—the trusted triumvirate, he thought—and with almost no warm-up time, she talked to him like an old friend.

"I'm glad somebody is paying attention to how I'm going to do in this show," she said to him, her English accent far more pronounced than when she sang. "Jillian was out here a while ago to teach me how to read from a teleprompter and to know which camera to look into, but I'm still worried that when you get right down to it, I'll cause a disaster."

"That won't happen," Barry said reassuringly, "but if it would make you feel better to come out to the studio a week or so early, I'd be glad to give you all the personal help you need to feel more comfortable."

She didn't say anything, so he added, "Of course, you're probably too booked with concert dates."

"Not one," she said. "I'm just hanging out at my house with a boyfriend who can't wait to leave me and trying not to talk to the police and reporters who are now wondering why I *didn't* kill Denny."

Her openness appealed to him, and he laughed. After they talked casually for several more minutes, Barry said, "You know, we have a radio station here, WOJ-FM, that has a request hotline. I happened to notice on the tally sheet a couple of weeks ago that 'No More Teenage Virgins' was the most-requested song."

"Really? That song is as old as the hills."

"Just about a year or so, isn't it?" He didn't mention that her new notoriety as a suspected killer wasn't hurting her popularity. Again the strange fascinations of Americans.

"A year is *ancient*," Annabelle said, sounding every bit like the teenager that she was. "Artie Glenn says that I have to get out a new album soon, but without Denny around . . ." Her voice broke, and she finished bravely, "I just don't know how to do it myself."

"I'm sure Artie has the people who can produce it for you."

"A bunch of stuffed shirts who I don't like. Why should I do another record if it's not going to be fun? Denny used to say people could tell if you put love into your work, so we always got to the studio early and fucked on the floor of the sound stage." She giggled. "He called it fucking for fun and profit. A way to get me up for the recording session."

"Interesting," Barry said noncommittally. No use telling Annabelle what he thought of Denny Wright, but the story raised a number of possibilities in his head, all of which he immediately rejected. Only one comment seemed reasonable, so he said, "I know what you're going through. I used to produce records early in my career." No sense mentioning that it had been for his college frat band, Diamond Reo, named after the garbage trucks on campus; they gave the records away free at mixers to impress girls. "Of course, that was before I got into soap operas."

"You produced soap operas? I didn't know that."

A devotee, no doubt; she was clearly impressed.

Encouraged, Barry said, "'All My Love' mean anything to you?"

"You were responsible for *that?*" Her voice squealed to new heights, so he said, "Well, not responsible, exactly . . ." but the impression had been made. It was exactly the impression he'd wanted to give, but he suddenly hoped to God that Annabelle never mentioned it to Jillian.

"Well, gosh, maybe you can help me with my next record," Annabelle suggested excitedly.

Her naïveté astounded him; exploiting Annabelle would be so childishly easy that he couldn't go on with it. "Listen, we could talk about all that when you're in Chicago. Just tell me when you want to come, and I'll take care of everything—security, reservations, you name it."

"I'd come soon, but I hate hotels," Annabelle said flatly. "At least, I hate being *alone* in a hotel."

"I have a couple of extra bedrooms, if that would be better," Barry said.

"Sure sounds better," Annabelle replied, and as the conversation concluded, Barry wondered if it would really be as easy to score with Annabelle as she made it seem.

■

Emil and Jillian sat next to each other on a banquette near the back of the restaurant, facing out to the fake Italian fountain in the center of the room. They hadn't looked away from each other for the entire meal, so the splashing baroque angels interfered with neither their dinner nor their mutual fascination.

"Anybody walking in could tell we're lovers," Emil said, sipping his coffee.

"Why do you say that?"

"The way we look at each other. The way we sit with some part of our bodies constantly touching. We send off such electricity that I'll bet people have been feeling shocks as they eat their dinner."

"Do you mind?"

"I worry only for you. I don't want this to become more public than you intend."

Jillian laughed. "The L.A. police have made your months of discretion totally beside the point. I think the only one left who doesn't know about us is Mark."

"Why hasn't he found out?"

"Who would tell him? He doesn't know anyone who knows about us. He lives in another world and doesn't really care about mine." She didn't try to mask the bitterness in her voice, but looking at Emil, she felt a flood of warmth and added, "Anyway, I don't care who knows. I feel like I should be shouting about you from the rooftop, not trying to keep it a secret."

They held hands under the table.

"Run away with me."

"All right."

"No, I mean it."

"So do I."

Emil signaled the waitress to bring Jillian another cup of tea, then asked, "Where would you like to go?"

"Anywhere you say. A small Caribbean island, I should think, where nobody can find us. Though if you prefer a dreamy island in the Mediterranean, I won't quibble."

"No, I have something very different in mind." Her tone had been light and frothy, but he, feeling somber, didn't try to match it. "For you, our being together is only a fantasy. For me, the fantasy is that it could be a reality." When she started to respond, he put up a hand and said, "It's all right. You and Mark are staying together for the good of the children, as people used to say. I know that. I promised you at the beginning that I would never disturb your daughters' lives, and I won't."

"I have a feeling they're going to be disturbed anyway." He raised an eyebrow, so she said, "Emil, in case you haven't guessed it, the problem is more than Mark's affair. Or our affair, for that matter. Mark and I don't much love each other anymore. That's becoming clearer and clearer. We talked about divorce the other night. Life at home is not wonderful, and the only question is how long we'll hang on for the children."

"I'm sorry. I don't want things to be unhappy for you."

"It's not unhappy, really. But it does make me wonder what happens in life. I have vivid memories of the year after Lila was born, when I felt like the whole world was mine. I was still at CBS and I had my terrific daughter and my great job and Mark and I were in love with everything. It's funny, because I understood then how happy I was, and I used to tell myself to appreciate it because it might all fall apart, and I didn't want to look back and think, 'I was happy then, so why didn't I enjoy it?'"

"So you did enjoy it, and it fell apart anyway."

"But that's life, I think. Things change and the world moves on. Instead of regretting lost pleasure, you have to build your happiness anew."

"I don't dare ask if you envision our building that happiness together."

Jillian dabbled the tea strainer into the hot water that the waiter had brought, then squeezed a wedge of lemon and watched the juice dribble into the cup. "You don't have to ask. All you have to do is look at me to know that I want you more than I've wanted anything in a long time."

"I needed to hear you say that." They were sitting so close that he could feel the warmth of her breast against his arm when she turned slightly toward him. "It's hard for me to imagine that you could feel the way I do."

"More so. As my daughter would say, I love you more than you love me."

"Impossible." He sighed and then asked, "What do we do now?"

"Let's go back to your previous suggestion and run away together."

"I'm afraid we'd only get as far as Chicago before having to stop and shoot Keith's show. How's that going, by the way?"

"Not that well at the moment." The affection on Jillian's face soured at the mention of Keith's name. "At least, things aren't particularly cheerful between Keith and me. Annabelle wouldn't even talk to him about being in that segment on women who kill, and Keith is blaming it on me. I didn't even discuss it with Annabelle—I just mentioned it to her lawyer, who of course went crazy. But Keith is in a panic about 'Wild Nights,' and he wants to have someone handy to blame in case it fails. I'm the one, of course. He's also convinced that you and I are going to steal his best ideas and turn around and develop our own production company."

"Which wouldn't be a bad idea," Emil said coldly, his anger directed against the unseen Keith. "If he's so worried about my ethics, I'd be glad to bow out of this pilot and let him find another director."

"Don't you dare. If you go, I go, and while I'll probably be ready for that soon, I'm not at the moment." She recrossed her legs and played with the empty teacup, trying to contain her restlessness. "Maybe Mark was right all along and I never should have joined Keith's company. It strikes me sometimes now that I'm away from my children all day so that I can devote myself to what? The greater glory of Keith Ross Productions?"

"You're feeling terribly discouraged. I wish I knew how to change that."

"Advise me to quit my job."

"I can't do that. Despite it all, you love television, and if things don't work out with Keith, you'll go on to something better."

"Then I have another way for you to cheer me up." Her eyes sparkled. "You just have to say five little words. 'Leave Mark, come to me.' Whatever you think, I'd do it in a minute."

"Don't tempt me. You know how much I'd love to say those words. But you'd get halfway down the street and think, 'What am I doing to my daughters?' and you'd pull a U-turn and head right back."

"U-turns are all but impossible in New York."

He smiled at her teasing and, stroking her arm, said, "Our lives are getting complicated, don't you think? In a very odd way, I feel like I've betrayed you by caring so much about you. We were supposed to have a casual affair, not fall in love."

"No, that's not right, because I don't have casual affairs."

"You wanted to fall in love with me?"

"I didn't plan it. I planned my children, I planned my career, I planned my marriage, but I didn't plan on feeling this way about you."

"I'm surprised at the raw emotions I've touched in you. I hope it isn't too painful. Or frightening."

"Both of the above, but mostly surprising. The most organized woman in America finds her life in disarray because she wasn't counting on love. But it serves me right. My mother warned me."

"You mother is . . ."

"Passed away. Many years ago," Jillian said, completing his sentence. "But before she died, I was dating a boy she didn't like, and she told me to break up with him before I got too involved. I was thoroughly scornful and said, 'Mother, I'm not going to *marry* him,' and she said, 'How do you know? What if you fall in love?' I remember explaining to her that I wouldn't just fall in love, I would *decide* to be in love when the right person came along. She smiled at me and said, 'Sweetheart, if that's true and you choose a husband for all the right reasons, I hope you are also blessed with having a grand passion.'" Jillian paused and, looking at Emil, said, "So there it is. You're the grand passion my mother has sent as her blessing from heaven."

Clearing his throat, Emil asked, "Was your husband never a grand passion?"

"I guess Mark was the Strauss van Dorne of my life, though I didn't understand that at the time. We liked each other, and we built a family that matters a lot. But now it's unraveling, and frankly it scares me."

"And what do you propose to do?"

She smiled. "You're the one who's supposed to propose. Forcing me to make all those illegal U-turns and all that."

He leaned back. "I do have a proposal. My sister is getting married in Budapest the week after we shoot the pilot. I haven't been back in years, but given the new openness . . ." He gestured vaguely. "Why don't you come with me? Meet my family. See the country. There's an American stampede going on over there—Hungary has apparently become one of the main ports of entry into Eastern Europe. Hundreds of American corporations have set up joint ventures there, and there's billions of dollars being invested. Great liberal tax laws for foreign investors, so any money you make in Hungarian forints gets converted to dollars and sent home untouched."

"Sounds like you're thinking of staying," Jillian said, smiling.

He shrugged. "No, but I'm amazed how the world gets turned on its head. I once fled Hungary because of the repression, and now people are flocking there to make money." He reached for her hand. "Come with me."

"Can I think about it overnight?"

"As long as I can be with you while you're thinking."

▬▬▬

When Barney Rossman got home from the office a few minutes after midnight, his wife Glenda was lying in bed, keenly studying a pamphlet by the light of the high-intensity lamp on the night table. Barney kissed her perfunctorily and, pulling off his red striped tie, tossed it around the doorknob to his closet.

"What a day," he said, unbuttoning his shirt. "I think we've figured out all the ins and outs of the Austin Realty case."

"Really?" Glenda looked at him with interest and folded the pamphlet she had been reading around a finger, saving her place. "What have you come up with?"

He told her the details, keeping his own role as small as it truly had been. He knew he should be hugely grateful to Margery both for ferreting out the facts and for explaining them to him, but as with all truths, once it was recognized it seemed so blindingly clear that he couldn't imagine ever *not* understanding it.

"So what's next?" Glenda asked after listening to his narrative.

"I'm going to indict the bastard. I don't care that he's married to the estimable Jillian van Dorne or that she works for my goddamn brother. I'm sure he's a lovely man, but he happens to be breaking the law. Blatantly. Margery thinks Mark Austin knows that he's minutes from being indicted."

"Margery?"

"Assistant D.A. Warren, who's been handling the case." Maybe he hadn't given her quite as much credit as she deserved in telling the story to Glenda.

"Oh, yes, of course. I have trouble keeping them all straight. It sounds like the problem isn't limited to tax evasion anymore."

"Ah, would that it were. Then I could just turn it over to the IRS and forget about it." Barney slumped on the edge of the bed and retrieved the pajama bottoms that Glenda had neatly tucked under his pillow that morning. Pulling them on, he said, "But now that all this has come to light, what choice do I have?" She didn't answer, so he repeated, "I mean, what choices are there?"

"Probably none, I suppose."

The tone in her voice surprised him; she sounded so glum that he turned his full attention toward her for the first time that evening and finally noticed the title on the pamphlet she had been reading.

"'The Adoption Solution'?" He read it aloud as a question, then said, "What kind of solution is that?"

Sounding defensive, she said, "A reasonable one. Like you with the Austin case, I'm running out of choices. And I'm not just being morose. I saw Dr. Krevins this morning."

"The fertility specialist. Oh damn, honey, I forgot you were going again today." Being busy was no excuse. He felt miserable to have forgotten. "What did he say?"

"It's not hopeless, but it's not that good either." She outlined the clinical details: her blocked tubes and scarred ovaries, the endometriosis that hadn't responded well to treatment in the past. Barney's tests had all proven to be fine—good sperm count, okay motility. "The bottom line is that if you had a different wife, you'd have a baby by now."

"I don't want a different wife." He slipped under the covers next to her and, lying close, propped himself up on bent elbow. "But there are a lot of steps to consider before we get to adoption, aren't there?"

"Probably. Dr. Krevins described some of the in-vitro procedures to me, but I don't think I could stand it—spending all those months being consumed by the rhythm of your ovaries."

"But you like the idea of adopting?"

"I don't know." She started to cry very softly. "I'm sure you'd rather struggle and have a baby with your own genes, but it doesn't seem that important to me. There are so many babies in the world that we could help and love."

He dabbed at her tears and put his arms around her. "If you manage to keep your humanity in the D.A.'s office, you learn something about perspective. I spend all my time outwitting people who wanted something so desperately that they lost all sense of the meaning of life. Usually they want money or drugs or power so badly that morality loses all meaning. Sometimes I look around and I think, Why can't people just accept what they have?"

"There are some things that are hard to accept," Glenda said, quiet tears still dropping from her eyelashes. "Not having your own baby is one of them."

"Of course it's hard, but we're not going to let it destroy us. When I was growing up, my mother's favorite phrase was always 'Make the best of it.' It never made sense to me, because Lotte was also very ambitious for us. But it's slowly occurred to me that you *do* have to make the best of what you have. Happiness comes from knowing that you're making the most of the circumstances you're in right this moment."

He hugged her, and feeling her close against him, tried to imagine the small baby they would adopt. He was surprised at how easily he could accept the idea. Life required accommodation—adjustments to reality, a willingness to accept your lot and play by the rules.

Something Mark Austin hadn't done.

Stroking his wife's back and wanting to share his musings, Barney said, "I've probably spent altogether too much time thinking about Mark Austin these days, but he's taught me something. From the outside guys like him have everything—successful wife, beautiful kids, family money. But there's something inside that makes them so miserable, they step over the line. Eventually they have to pay for that. Mark's going to lose everything because he couldn't make the best of what he had."

"I hate to be learning a lesson from Mark Austin, but I get the point," Glenda said.

They kissed, and Barney wanted to make love to his wife, but there was something right tonight about just holding and feeling close. Lying on the pillow, his face pressed against hers, Barney said, "Right now I like the idea of adopting, but we'll talk more about it in the morning. The only thing I want you to know now is that I'll be happy with you whether or not we have a baby. We have each other, we care about what we're doing, and we have a good life. Let's remember all that when we're making our decision."

Snuggling close to him, she said, "Let's remember because Mark Austin forgot?"

Sighing, he said, "Mark Austin definitely forgot."

For a brief moment as she drove herself to Lila's school, Jillian had the sense that everything had returned to normal. On her way to this morning's teacher's conference, she had driven Mark to the train and kissed him good-bye just as the express to Manhattan pulled in to the Melrose station. He was dismayed not to be able to join her at the conference, but he had a pressing meeting in the city that couldn't be changed. Even *that* seemed normal. Tonight they would hold hands and talk about how proud they were of their children and of each other and life would simply go on.

I still want all that, Jillian thought as she walked up the deserted steps of the school at a few minutes before eight. Lila's teacher, Mrs. Lasky, met her promptly in the first-grade room and showed her the various murals Lila had helped create, the storybook she had written all by herself, and the arithmetic problems she had solved. In the curious way of devoted teachers, she seemed to be trying to impress Jillian with Lila's success. Perched on a small chair then, Jillian listened as Mrs. Lasky described Lila as bright, charming, determined, and a leader of the class. From what she had gathered from other mothers, Jillian decided that all teachers described all children as leaders in the class. It was, no doubt, what American parents most wanted to hear. Were Japanese children praised for being good listeners?

Mrs. Lasky's generous report was pleasing, and Jillian listened respectfully, all the time wondering why she was even having a conference—because what could this pleasant, middle-aged woman know about her daughter that wasn't already obvious to her?

"There is one issue I bring up reluctantly," Mrs. Lasky said, having run out of adjectives of praise and subtly changing her tone.

Suddenly alert, Jillian asked, "What's that?"

"Lila has been more . . . sensitive lately. Almost as if she were upset by something happening outside of school." She looked kindly but frankly at Jillian. "I've tried to find out gently what's bothering her. I thought it might be a change of nanny, or that you or your husband were traveling a good deal. But she has rejected all my guesses."

"Just how is she more sensitive?" Sitting up straight, Jillian wanted the information directly, without the careful cushioning Mrs. Lasky was preparing.

"It's mostly on social issues. This is an age when the boys and girls are reconsidering each other and they do silly things. They chase each other on the playground and try to kiss"—she laughed self-consciously, as if she were involved in the kissing rather than just reporting on it—"or they talk about getting married. Now, that might sound surprising—"

"Not at all," Jillian interrupted. "Our just-turned-four-year-old is already happily married."

"Then you know what goes on. The other day a little boy named Tommy told Lila that he wanted to marry her. The typical reaction is for the little girls to run away and say 'Yech!' which naturally increases the attention they get from the boys."

"Lila responded differently?" Jillian asked.

"She burst into tears and wouldn't stop. I finally brought her inside because I could see that she was embarrassed and just couldn't control herself. I held her for a while and kept asking what was wrong, and she began sobbing, 'I'll never marry anyone. Never ever. It's horrible to be married.' She kept repeating it over and over, and it took a good twenty minutes for her to calm down."

Her narrative finished, Mrs. Lasky saw the stunned expression on Jillian's face, and ever the first-grade teacher, she said, "Of course, Tommy is a sweet boy but a terrible tease, and she might have just been reacting to that."

"She never mentioned anything about the episode at home," Jillian said.

"Which is why I thought I'd tell you now." If Mrs. Lasky wanted to pry further, find out why Lila might think it so horrible to be married, she didn't show it; instead she invited Jillian over to the science corner to observe the nature objects Lila had collected.

I'll never marry anyone. Never ever. The words echoed in Jillian's mind as she looked at the charts and graphs that Lila had made and admired the frog that Lila had found on a nature hike way back in the fall and had managed to keep alive ever since.

How bad has our marriage been recently? Jillian wondered, looking at the frog. When had Lila started noticing?

When she left the conference a few minutes later, Jillian no longer felt that life had returned to normal. Instead she was convinced that it would never be normal again.

I'm getting too used to this apartment, Mark thought, looking around Cynthia's haven on Thirty-eighth Street. Too used to being here.

He heard the shower turn off in the bathroom, and from where he was sitting, imagined that he could smell the poof of violet powder settling over Cynthia as she dusted herself dry. Preparing for him. That was one of the differences between them—Cynthia liked to shower before they made love, and he liked to shower after; her preference meant that in a few minutes, he would be burying his head in that violet cloud, indulging in the ambrosial scents of her body and the damp sweetness that clung to her still-moist curves. The very thought of it so aroused him that without really planning it, he began walking toward the door of her bedroom, ready to take her without any further discussion.

What am I doing? he thought, his hand on the doorknob of her room. So many months ago, he had tried to end the affair, but something had brought him back; it hadn't worked to be away. What was it she had said that day he tried to end it? *Let's break up after we make love.*

Only Cynthia could say that. No matter what she did, he was drawn back to her, like a fly to honey.

Or a fly to manure, Jillian would surely say.

The door opened, and he was briefly stunned, because Cynthia had opened the door, not he, and was standing inches away from him. She asked, "Why are you suddenly afraid of me, darling? You seem to jump whenever I come to you."

"No, it's not you." But he backed away from her, returning to the living room, and said, "It's the business that's making me jumpy."

Sighing, she said, "It's not working out just right, is it? I thought I'd done everything possible and that the offshore company was as well protected as could be."

"But?"

"But it's not." She posed on the window seat, peeking through the blinds into the city night, then turning back to him said, "I can't take any blame, darling. I told you my opinion from the beginning, and when you went ahead anyway, I did everything I could to protect you. *More* than everything." Her glance was so ripe with meaning that he felt his chest pounding uncontrollably.

"Why did you do it?" he asked.

"No, the question is why did *you?*"

"All the obvious reasons that one takes risks, I suppose."

"They're never obvious." She played with the tie on her robe, knotting the silken rope around her waist, then loosening it again. For once it was a gesture without intended sexual overtones. "I assumed that you were trying to prove something, but I'm not sure if you were proving it to your father or to me."

Or to Jillian, Mark silently added. But that motive was so confused, even in his own head, that he focused on what was easier. "The son always needs to outshine the father, doesn't he? Do something to step out of the old man's shadow? My father made the deal with Wright, and I took it one step further, all the way to the Cayman Islands." Distracted, he flipped open the glossy photography book Cynthia had left on the coffee table and found himself staring at a picture of John Kennedy on a beach in Hyannisport. Slamming the book shut, he said, "Sometimes the only purpose of the game is to win the battle in the locker room, and that's what I did with my father. Is there any doubt now that my balls are bigger than his balls?"

Cynthia laughed harshly. "I'm certainly convinced," she said.

Mark wanted to ask if she had another way of knowing—and now was surely the time to inquire—but he couldn't bring himself to do it. Instead he asked, "What are your motives in all this?"

"I'm a good lawyer. I make the best of what's given to me."

"Nothing more personal than that?"

"Of course it's more personal." She moved over on the window seat, making room for him to sit down, but he ignored the obvious invitation and stood in front of her, hands in his pockets, rocking slightly back and forth on his heels.

"You and Bill are like a family to me. Bill is the kind and understanding father I always wanted to have when I was growing up." Then, looking at him significantly, she said, "You're the husband I've always wanted and still want now."

He should be erect, ready to make love to her; what could be more enticing than a woman who wanted him? The seductive swirl of her hips curved against the window appealed to him, but his body didn't stir.

Because she was lying.

He couldn't say how he knew that, but he sensed it deep in his bones. Cynthia was indeed in quest of something, but it wasn't a husband. It wasn't him. What frightened him most about this treacherous game was that he couldn't guess where it led. If she didn't want him, what was she seeking?

"You've really put yourself on the line with the Cayman Islands deal," he said. "I appreciate it."

"I wanted the money," she said simply.

"How much trouble can we get into?"

"It depends. I've played it carefully. Even when the stakes got big."

It was the opening he needed to broach his suspicions—vague and untested but gnawing at him. "Tell me about Denny Wright."

If Cynthia was surprised by the question, she didn't show it. Instead she said coolly, "A death nobody mourned, wouldn't you say?"

"And a murder without clues. Instinct says it was Annabelle Fox who did it, but with no evidence, she gets off with nothing but a cloud around her name. Given her profession, it's almost a glamorous cloud. And since all attention is focused in her direction—or, as a corollary, toward those involved in my wife's television show—other motives might slip by unnoticed."

Unfolding herself from the window seat, Cynthia asked, "Are you hungry?"

"Not very."

"Well, I am. Let's go to the kitchen, and I'll make some omelets."

He followed her to the kitchen.

"It was admirably planned," he said. "The timing was clever—again, so soon after the television show. And as far as the rest of the world knows, you were on Denny's side. Even I've seen the papers you signed as his legal counsel, representing him against my wife and all that—which makes you almost above suspicion. No reason your name should ever come up. And when it did, there wasn't a problem. The police found the papers Denny had signed for you that morning. Lots of people saw you and Denny in the coffee shop and saw him signing the papers. So Denny was on your side and on our side. In fact, you made the whole company look clean."

"The papers *were* signed. Everything was in order. You saw them yourself."

"Of course. And there's no way I would mention anything about the offshore deal because—well, what would be the point? I'm not trying to commit suicide."

She opened the refrigerator to take out a box of eggs, then hunted down a glass bowl and a long wooden spoon. "He was going to expose our offshore deal and maybe sink the whole company. What more can I tell you?"

"Nothing, because I understand. You wanted that deal more than life itself."

She cracked the eggs into the bowl and added a dash of salt, a few turns of the pepper grinder. Soon the viscous yellow mixture, frothy and pale yellow from her beating, slithered into the searingly hot pan.

Her coolness startled him and excited him, too. She had killed someone and wasn't suffering.

"It amazes me that you would do all this for the good of Austin Realty."

"You misunderstand. That's not what happened at all." Her face was slightly pink from the heat of the stove. The eggs burbled as she scooped them out of the pan and arranged them on stark-white porcelain dishes. "Why would I kill Denny when all the papers were signed?"

"All the papers for the Austin-Wright deal, yes—but there was no way to get him to sign a statement saying he wouldn't expose our escapade on the Cayman Islands. Not the kind of thing you'd put in writing."

"No, definitely not."

"You were going back to see him the next morning. Presumably with some payoff, though I never asked. Interesting that he died before that. And despite all your efforts, the offshore company will probably be exposed anyway. How's that for dramatic irony?"

"No irony at all, because it won't happen. Just like the scenario about my killing Denny never happened." Seeing the disbelief in his eyes, she laughed shortly and said, "Of course, if it is true, that's all the more reason you have for protecting me. The police get suspicious about me, and they'll learn a few too many things about your dealings, too." She carried the plates to the black glass dining table and gestured for him to sit down; the table was already set for two, with sterling silver flatware, crisply edged linen napkins, and glistening crystal.

"What about the other way around? The D.A.'s been prying pretty closely into my personal accounts."

She shrugged carelessly and said, "I agree that he knows more than he should. Some pesky lawyer from his office named Margery Warren has been making a lot of inquiries on the Cayman Islands. If they get a handle on it, maybe you'll be indicted, but we'll fight it, and

I'll bet we'll win. Anyway, the charges aren't so serious that there'll be a long sentence."

"*What?*" He stood up squawking, as if he had been shot by an arrow. The sudden movement jarred the table, and the crystal complained but didn't break. "Just what charges are we talking about?"

"I didn't mean to startle you. Please sit." When he did, she said, "I'm just projecting possibilities. You're the one suggesting something will happen, not me. Anyway, darling, don't take this so personally. We're all in this together."

But they weren't in this together at all. This dangerous deal had been his: not his father's, not Cynthia's, just his. Had that been his idea—his way of standing separate from his father? Or had it been subtly suggested to him by Cynthia? So far she had been sharing royally in the profits, but she would never have to share the blame.

Cynthia ate the last bit of eggs from her plate, then glanced at his food, which was untouched.

"Not hungry, darling?"

For an answer he took the plate of eggs and hurled it across the room. The porcelain splintered against the wall and tumbled down with the happy, jangling sound of ice crystals; the eggs splattered on the spotless floor.

The shocked expression on Cynthia's face was his only satisfaction in the day.

▬▬

He left the room to calm down for a few minutes, and when he came back, still seething, Cynthia leaned over. With her face barely an inch from his, the cool minty scent of her breath fogging his senses, she whispered, "Point one: I didn't kill Denny. Point two: The D.A.'s not at your door, and I don't know why you feel that he is."

And then she put her fingers on his groin, his anger exciting her, his rare outburst of violence making her nipples hard.

His rage was still as prominent as the smashed plate that lay untouched on the floor, but Cynthia opened her robe, and he succumbed. This time his anger went to his cock and made him hard immediately. They tumbled to the floor, and he took Cynthia with a force that seemed to surprise her, ramming himself into her without any thought of her pleasure—but in his furious pounding he heard her groans of satisfaction, and he exploded then with such intensity that he heard Cynthia scream. The sound seemed distant, a strange echo of almost-forgotten lust. After the exertion he dozed off to sleep, waking moments later when Cynthia stirred, and he was aware of a strange sensation in his left foot. Somehow they had rolled to the wall, and his foot had landed squarely in the pool of now-watery eggs. Shards of splintered porcelain clung to his soggy sock, and when he pulled it off, a sliver extruded from his flesh, ripping a fine line down the length of his foot. The sight of the blood frightened him, less from pain than as metaphor. He had fallen for a woman who was a master at drawing blood, and this time the blood was his.

Just as two weeks ago the blood had been Denny's.

"We're trapped in each other's lies," Mark told her after they made love, when they had moved to her bed and were lying together. "Tell me what happened in Los Angeles."

And to his surprise, Cynthia said, "I went back to see Denny that night. You were right. But I didn't kill him in cold blood, and I didn't kill him to protect our deal."

"Tell me." His voice was raw and ragged; maybe it would be better to believe Cynthia's earlier effortless lie—*Point one: I didn't kill Denny.*

"If I tell, we'll be bound to each other even tighter."

"Good." Her legs were wrapped around his, and he could feel the softness of her crotch tickling his limp penis. He wondered why there was so little emotion in her voice, why all the pain was coming from him.

"Denny and I had arranged to see each other that night, not the next morning. Denny was wired on coke when I came in—Annabelle had been there minutes before—and he seemed over the edge. He started ranting about fucking women wanting to destroy him, and he drew a gun on me, screaming that there was no deal unless we fucked."

"So you killed him instead of being raped."

But Cynthia said, "Not exactly. First I tried talking to him, but it was impossible. He grabbed for me, and he was a lot more powerful than he looked—so I decided to give in. Is that so awful? I could think of worse things in life than fucking Denny Wright. It was over in a minute and I thought he would be sane again, but instead he started ranting about all the things he was going to do to me, and how I was in his power now because of everything he knew. That's when I couldn't stand it anymore, and I picked up his gun and shot him. One shot. I wiped my fingerprints off everything and went through all the papers I could find to remove everything that might be incriminating. I cleaned the gun as well as I could and put it back in the drawer and locked it. His apartment had been walking distance from my hotel, so I walked back and that was that."

She seemed satisfied with the confession, and for some reason all Mark could do was laugh bitterly.

"I wish we had hidden our tracks to the Cayman Islands that well. Because the way things are looking right now, I'll end up in jail, and you won't."

"You won't end up in jail, darling. I won't let it happen."

"But there's a reason you're telling me this." He paused, suddenly understanding. "When the Cayman Islands story comes to light—and it's going to—you want to make sure I never mention your name. Right now you're clear on this murder. It looks like the police have investigated your visit to L.A. and moved on. But if there's a motive suddenly revealed, they'll go back and look a little closer. They'll realize that you killed because Denny was going to blackmail you."

"He raped me. That's when I killed him."

"Maybe when—but not why."

▬▬

A sacrificial lamb, Mark thought that night as he lay unsleeping in his own bed. Cynthia's confession had done its job—he would make sure to keep her name out of anything he could. What was the purpose of doing otherwise? Maybe his name was to be forever associated with stealing; he didn't want to be tinged by the murder, too. Jillian and the girls were going to be embarrassed enough when his illegal company came to light—no sense adding to their distress by letting the tabloids shout about his alliance with Cynthia.

It wouldn't help his case anyway.

His was the only name—and bank account—behind the Cayman Islands company that was supposedly shipping supplies to the Austin-Wright ventures. He was the one who had faked the receipts and bloated the expenses. For a while he had just planned to skim a couple of million off the top. But it had all been so easy that when Cynthia suggested they use the company to front other projects in Eastern Europe, he had agreed. And how much was on the line now? She had taken millions already and so had he.

He turned over restlessly in bed, already feeling the handcuffs at his wrists. The D.A. was closing in, no matter what Cynthia said this afternoon to appease him and convince him otherwise. Her confession was like a dream to him: he had heard the words, but he couldn't remember if they were really true. He was losing his grip on reality. Even in his own bed, he felt like an imposter.

It was late, but still he couldn't sleep, and when Jillian came into the room, his eyes were closed, but his heart was racing. Like a child practiced in the art of faking sleep, he squinted his eyes so tightly that he created a narrow slit through which he watched as Jillian changed out of her clothes, wandered into the bathroom, and finally slipped into bed. He hadn't moved, and he was sure that from the outside his eyes appeared closed—so he was startled when Jillian leaned over and, without bothering to whisper, asked, "Are you awake?"

He sat up, pretending that he had just been awakened, but knowing that the effort was weak.

"Hi. Did you just get in?"

"Yes. Do you feel like talking?"

He gestured to the bed, trying to make it clear that his first priority was sleeping, but she had something to say and would not be dissuaded.

"I'm going away for a few days."

"To Chicago?" Time for shooting the pilot was getting close, that much he knew, even though he hadn't paid much attention to the details.

"Yes, first to Chicago to shoot the pilot. Then immediately after that, I'm taking a personal trip. I need a few days away, to get perspective. Our director is a good friend of mine, and he's from

Budapest. He's going back for four or five days for his sister's wedding, and he's invited me to join him. I'd like to do that."

Her blunt honesty startled him. She could have said, "Yes, I'm going to Chicago for longer than I'd planned," or L.A., or anyplace where he wouldn't ask another question. If she worried about such egregious dissembling, she could have admitted to Budapest but claimed a work motive.

Like he always did.

"This director friend is . . . a man?"

"Yes."

He felt the blood rising to his head, pounding behind his eyes. He wanted to rage at her, kick her or throw her out of the bedroom, call her a whore and a slut and a bitch. But as he opened his mouth to shout at her, no sound would emerge.

Don't leave me right now. Don't let me leave you. I need you too much right now.

"I don't want to lie to you, Mark. I got points the other day for being the aggrieved spouse, but I don't quite deserve them. You brought up the subject of divorce, and I think we have to face it. Being together isn't helping the children anymore. I suspect Lila understands more than we do about what's going on."

Mention of the child reminded him of an almost-forgotten obligation, and trying to shake off the anchor of fear that had been lodged in him all day, he struggled to surface in reality. To end this day of thinking about murder and rape and jail, he said, "Oh, yes, you had the conference this morning with her teacher. How did it go?"

"Do you really care? Did you call at any point today to find out?"

"I was busy."

"Of course you were busy, and I get busy, too. Maybe too busy. But once you can't find time to care anymore, there's something wrong with your life. And I think there's something wrong with ours."

"You want me to leave right now?" He got out of bed and stood over her. Mixed into his anger was the knowledge of Jillian's kindness. She would say, "No, of course not, get back into bed," and he would storm and rage, but then, in fact, he *would* get into bed and life would go on. Despite his fury, that's all he wanted right now: for life to go on.

302

"I've been trying so hard to do what's right," Jillian said, "but it doesn't seem right anymore. Maybe it *is* best if you leave."

She didn't say it harshly or even coldly but stated it as a matter of fact. The feeling of helplessness that had been gnawing at him all day suddenly overwhelmed him; he was full of tantrums today, an angry child with nothing to do but throw his toys.

And that's what he did.

His fingers tingled as they smacked against the smooth, cool skin of Jillian's face. His hand seemed to move in slow motion, reaching out for the target he hadn't really planned to strike. But once he had done it, he was glad, because for that brief moment, he was in control. The clap of skin against skin was like a burst of thunder—loud and shocking, but, he thought, mostly harmless. Enough to frighten but not hurt, reassert his role as head of the family. But then Jillian rose from the bed, contempt rather than fear scrawled on her face.

"I vowed to myself a long time ago that I would never stay for a minute with a man who resorted to violence, and I won't."

Suddenly weeping, he said, "You never had any respect for me."

"I had great respect for you. In fact, the problem was probably that I held you in higher regard than you held yourself. But you've just destroyed that."

He searched her face for signs of his wrongdoing and saw only a slight stinging pink on her left cheek. That didn't seem to qualify as violence, but she said, "I want you to leave right now, Mark. There's nothing else left to say."

She disappeared into the small study off their bedroom, and he slumped to the edge of the bed, waiting for her to return. When she didn't come back immediately, he stood up and began to shove underwear, shaving equipment, and a fresh shirt into his briefcase.

What frightened him the most was knowing that if he left, he would be going to Cynthia.

*C*HAPTER *E*IGHTEEN

———— ▬ ————

S HOOTING the pilot for "Wild Nights" was just short of a nightmare.

Keith was in a frenzy for the whole week of rehearsing and shooting—yelling at the staff and second-guessing all the decisions that were made. Jillian worked hard to make sure the show ran smoothly but somehow felt distanced from it all. She had come back to television to produce shows that mattered—she would always believe that "The Secret Life" *had* mattered—and she didn't want to be part of the faking and dissembling that went into a late-night talk show. But there she was, convincing "real people" to appear by making promises that wouldn't be kept. Wheeling and dealing to get the best celebrities. Rehearsing and re-rehearsing segments that were meant to seem spontaneous. Talk television was by its very nature exploitative, and though Jillian knew she could do it well, she didn't have the heart for it anymore.

She still hadn't told Lila and Eve that Daddy wasn't going to be living with them anymore. It was too much for them to understand just when Mommy was going to Chicago for a week to shoot a show. So for the first time that Jillian could remember, she lied to the girls, explaining that Daddy was away working. Eve took the news in stride, not even asking when Daddy would return. Lila appeared stricken, a flash of worry streaking across her face, and it broke Jillian's heart to realize that there was nothing she could say to comfort the child. The truth was simply too painful. *Mommy and Daddy have filed separation papers. Your little world is about to turn upside down.*

Marguerite, as always, was calm and told Jillian not to worry—she would handle everything while Jillian was away. Grateful, Jillian promised to be back in a week. So much for the trip to Budapest. Fully aware of the irony of it all, Jillian told Emil that she couldn't join him in Budapest; now that the legal separation from her husband was in process, she couldn't be with her lover because she wanted to get back to the girls.

Though Jillian arrived in Chicago reluctantly and wanted to leave almost before she got off the plane, she got caught up immediately in the whirling chaos of production. The pressure seemed to be getting to Keith, who had lost sight of everything except ratings, and Jillian spent her first day in Chicago trading angry words with him and fighting to keep some integrity in the shows.

The only pleasant surprise in the week was Annabelle, who had arrived in Chicago a week before Jillian and seemed happier and more at ease than Jillian had ever seen her. During rehearsals she introduced the musical guests with aplomb and juiced up her own numbers with a new style that had an edge of sophistication. Unfortunately, Annabelle and Tucker Fredericks disliked each other immediately, and it was so apparent that Jillian urged Keith to give up all efforts to establish an on-air camaraderie between them. It didn't really matter, because Annabelle was so talkative and funny whenever the television lights turned on her that she didn't need Tucker propping her up. The first time Annabelle rehearsed one of her own numbers, she was so good that the crew gave her a standing ovation.

"Barry's been helping me," Annabelle told Jillian breathlessly after the number, when Jillian rushed over to give her a hug.

"Well, tell Barry he's doing a good job," Jillian said.

"Tell him yourself." A grinning Barry appeared between the two women and reached out to put an arm around each of them, but seemed to think better of it and just gave Annabelle a loving kiss.

"I may be helping, but you're great all by yourself," he told her. Then turning to Jillian, he added, "*She's* the one doing a good job."

"She certainly is," Jillian agreed. She had been surprised at first that Barry and Annabelle were so close, but she couldn't really complain. Annabelle looked happy. Barry had always loved glamour and excitement, and he seemed to live for television and success; his blatant ambition had dismayed Jillian when he was working for her on his first job, but she had to admit that he had grown up. Still ambitious but more comfortable with himself, he had worked hard to get to his current position—and he wasn't stopping there. His affection for Annabelle seemed genuine. Jillian assumed that their relationship had probably started as just one more business deal, but it had evolved into something exciting for both of them.

Annabelle's good spirits were a boon to the production, and despite Keith's unleashed temper, the shows were exciting. As the week went on, Jillian was convinced that "Wild Nights" was going to become a hit show.

But she didn't really care.

Just before the final day of shooting, Mark called, and taking advantage of the safety of the phone and their distance, he told her about an offshore company he'd set up a year earlier. His voice trembled when he described all the money he was making and how successful the endeavor had been; but then he broke down, and Jillian struggled to understand his garbled confession about needing to prove something and wanting to surpass his father. He had started the offshore company to skim profits from the joint venture his father had formed with Kingsley Wright, but it had gone beyond that into an international web of cheating and deceit. Someone else had been involved, a woman lawyer, and the illegal activities had been her idea, but Mark was going to take all the blame.

Finally he mentioned that he had spoken with his lawyer, and instead of waiting to be led away in handcuffs, he was going to turn himself in to the D.A. the next day.

Jillian was stunned. Listening to Mark over a pay phone, from the midst of the chaotic studio, she could barely comprehend what he was saying. Or what he wanted.

"Should I come home right now and try to help?" she asked.

"No. You can't help, and even if you could, I wouldn't want it."

The bitterness in his voice surprised her. She tried again. "I don't want to abandon you if you need me."

"It doesn't matter. The two of us are finished—I accept that, and

I'm not trying to change it. But I'd like to believe that you can protect the girls from being hurt by this."

"How should I do that?"

"I don't know. If there's a scandal, you can at least keep the girls from turning against me. I want them to grow up respecting their father."

He just assumed the girls would stay with her—there would be no custody battle—and even as she felt a flood of relief at that realization, there was an angry pounding in her head. You have to earn respect, she thought, but didn't say it because she had the vague sense that his illegal enterprise had been established in rebellion against her, too. Mark had been trying to surpass his father and surpass his wife, and in the process he had done nothing but destroy himself. His weakness suddenly embarrassed her. Had the strength she once attributed to him been only an illusion?

After wishing him well and again offering to help however she could, Jillian realized that if Mark had asked, she *would* have gone home, making one last effort to be by his side and save the family. But he didn't want her help or even her presence. The finality was somehow troubling. We women have trouble with endings, she thought, thinking of Annabelle and herself.

Annabelle, who was waiting for her when she got off the phone, needed help with an introduction. Jillian was distracted and felt a deep despair setting in, but there wasn't time to indulge it.

"I wish I could cheer you up, like you always cheered me," Annabelle told her when Jillian admitted having problems at home.

Struggling to maintain her spirits, Jillian said, "You *are* cheering me up. Just seeing how good you are on the show makes me feel better than anything. And seeing you happy and playful again with Barry reminds me that good things can come from bad."

They worked on the introduction until it read smoothly, and Annabelle left confidently for the set while Jillian dragged herself toward the control room. Emil was in the hallway, working with the cameramen on preparations for shooting the show, and when she saw him, Jillian interrupted to say, "As soon as you have a minute, Emil, I need a word with you."

He looked at her with concern but finished the briefing. The moment he was free, he came over and asked, "What is it? You look stricken."

She told him about the conversation with Mark; the timing was terrible—they were about to shoot a show—but she couldn't restrain herself. She had to get it out.

"My poor darling," Emil said. "How can I help you?"

"I'm not sure—it's really Mark who needs help."

"I don't care at all about Mark. What kind of man passes news like that on the phone? I'm sorry, darling, but I have no sympathy for him. He's caused you too much pain already."

"Well, I think there's going to be more pain. He didn't give me details, but I have the feeling that whatever is going on could land him in jail. I don't know how to deal with this."

They couldn't discuss it, because Keith came by then, hollering that it was time for the show to start.

"We'll talk after the show," Emil said, glancing at his watch.

Her usual seat in the control room was in the second row, next to Keith, but she couldn't bear that today, and not caring what anyone said, she pulled up a chair next to Emil in the front row that was usually reserved exclusively for the director and his assistants.

The show was beautiful, a high-tech effort that appealed to the audience and had an unmistakable verve and energy. But as Tucker Fredericks interviewed his first guest, Jillian realized that her mind was wandering. Lila and Eve would start their spring break from school in just a few days, and Jillian had a fantasy of swooping up her daughters and disappearing for a while, escaping the misery that Mark's situation would cause them.

While he surveyed the bank of monitors, instructed his four cameramen on the floor, and set up the shots for the next segment, Emil must have been pondering the same thing.

"Why don't you all come with me to Budapest?" Emil whispered to her amidst the commotion in the control room. On the center monitor they watched Annabelle preparing to shoot "Just Beginning Again"—a new song that she was singing for the first time on the show.

"I'd love to," Jillian whispered back, "but it might be a bit much."

"A bit much for you or them?"

"All of us."

"Not for me," Emil said. "If you're ready to make a commitment like that, I am, too."

The assistant director started the countdown from ten seconds, and Emil leaned forward and flicked on his microphone, telling the crew to take their positions again. When the show aired, they would just be coming back from a commercial. The stage manager called for quiet on the set, and at Emil's signal the lights faded up only slightly from black; the music started while the set was still so cloaked in darkness that it was difficult to make out the small figure of Annabelle. Rising from the gloom came the hauntingly sad opening bars of her new song, and Jillian caught her breath at the ethereal shots Emil created.

Suddenly the tempo of the music changed and the lights soared; on camera, Annabelle stripped off the drab black coatdress she was wearing, revealing a bodysuit in multicolored sequins. The colors bounced off the cameras in shockingly beautiful bursts of light, and Jillian watched as Emil kept Annabelle in a spotlight in the center of the shot while camera three trucked around her, catching her splendor from all angles. Her singing voice sounded fuller than usual—there was a womanliness to it that Jillian had never felt before.

> Once I was a scared young girl
> Life wasn't worth a damn
> I had to grow and have some faith
> In the woman that I am.

The music so filled the control room that the usual chatter and hysteria from the back row of producers stopped. Jillian felt an unexpected chill, and the tears that caught in her eyes weren't for Annabelle but for herself. Noticing, Emil cupped his fingers around Jillian's knee and held them there as the music picked up even more and Annabelle tossed back her head for the chorus.

> Just beginning again!
> Makin' life my friend!
> Just beginning again with a friend.

His attention on the four monitors, the lights, the band, and the signals his assistant director was sending him, Emil nonetheless leaned back and whispered to Jillian, "Will you all come with me?" and as the music ended and everyone on the set and in the control room broke into spontaneous applause, Jillian whispered back, "Why not?"

Mark stared into the night, across the empty bed he was supposed to be sharing with Cynthia. Where was she at two in the morning? Through all those nights that he had left her bed at this hour to sneak home to his wife, Cynthia had complained bitterly, enticing him to stay however she could. And now that he was here, that he had no place else to go, she was gone. Life was snaking around to bite him in the backside.

He turned over, feeling less anger than relief. She was giving him an excuse to do what he wanted, answer affirmatively the question that had been burbling in his head for more than a day now. *Do you turn in your lover to save your own ass?*

The gentleman in him understood that it wasn't right, wasn't even reasonable. He'd be giving them a much bigger fish than they had caught. But he'd been reading the newspapers carefully lately, and he was convinced that white-collar criminals were getting longer jail sentences than murderers.

Making a deal with the D.A. would no doubt put him at the center of a tumultuous scandal—he could imagine the newspaper headlines, the gossip columns, the tabloid television shows. But what did he have to lose anymore? Sure he'd be embarrassed—but at least he wouldn't be embarrassed behind bars.

Assistant D.A. Warren frowned across the desk at Barney Rossman.

"You're really letting him turn himself in?"

"Yes, tomorrow morning at nine o'clock. Right in this office.

And I repeat that I told him the press would not be informed ahead of time."

"I don't understand it, I must say. I think it's a case that should send a loud message—not one we should try to keep quiet."

Barney looked at her carefully, trying to decide why she looked so different. Something about her hair maybe, or her makeup; she was wearing pumps instead of sneakers, and while she hadn't graduated all the way to attractive, she certainly looked more presentable.

Ah, Barney thought suddenly, the television cameras. This is Margery's biggest case yet, and she wants to be prepared for reporters asking her questions.

He decided not to compliment her appearance; instead, he opened a file on his desk and began flipping through the pages. Impatient, Margery said, "May I be so bold as to ask if your decision on how to handle this has something to do with your brother? I mean, is Mark Austin getting special treatment out of deference to Keith and his production and Jillian and all that?"

Barney pushed back his chair and stood up abruptly. "You really should *not* ask something like that. It's rude and inappropriate. Also totally wrong."

Taken aback, Margery said, "I'm sorry. I just don't see why Mark Austin deserves the excessive respect you're giving him."

"Because there's a chance he'll give us something back. Did that ever occur to you?"

Surprised by his fervor, Margery sat back.

"I had a long conversation this morning with Austin's attorney. He believes that Mark Austin could lead us to Denny Wright's killer. They're talking about doing a deal, and the D.A. in Los Angeles has begged me to go ahead with it. Austin gives us his evidence in exchange for our dropping all charges. If that's where we're headed, it doesn't make much sense to blow up the arrest in the press, does it?"

Margery thought about it for a moment, then said, "Do you think he has evidence against Annabelle Fox?"

Barney seemed reluctant to answer but finally said, "Bring it closer to home, Margery. Do you think Mark Austin set up this whole offshore deal himself with all those bogus papers you found and the complicated legal maneuverings? You came up with everything except a partner for him.”

It took Margery Warren barely a beat before she said, “Shit, I missed it. His bombshell attorney—what the hell's her name? Cynthia Reilly.”

▬▬▬

They shot five shows in three days, and when they finished shooting, Jillian headed for the airport almost immediately, leaving the studio before the traditional break party even began. She didn't want wine, she didn't want congratulatory speeches—she just wanted to get home.

▬▬▬

“*Where* is Jillian?”

Annabelle Fox enjoyed the shocked look on Barry Brunetti's face as well as the sense she had, almost for the first time, of being at the center of events—able to report them, rather than being manipulated by them.

“Jillian is on her way to Budapest,” Annabelle repeated. “She's going with Emil.”

“What the hell is she going to do there?” The first “Wild Nights” show was airing that night on the network, and Barry couldn't imagine being anyplace except in front of his television. “Doesn't Jillian care about the show?”

“Of course she cares about it, but her part's finished, and she didn't want to sit around waiting for the ratings to come out. If they're good, Keith will just take all the credit, and if they're bad, she'll get all the blame.”

Barry laughed, then asked, “Did Jillian and Keith have a falling-out?” He didn't mean to be pumping Annabelle for information, but she seemed privy to *everything*. She was the one who had told him that the D.A. who arrested Jillian's husband was Keith's brother. It boggled the mind. The perfect Jillian van Dorne married to a criminal.

“I think Jillian and Keith aren't much talking to each other

312

because the whole thing is so sticky." She moved closer to him, rubbing her body against his. "But do we have to talk about Jillian?"

"No, of course not." He took her in his arms, pleased—and still surprised—was every time by how close he felt to her. After shooting "Wild Nights," Annabelle had gone home to Los Angeles for a week but had come back to him. Though she was young, he adored her—and wanted her. "Let's talk about us." He kissed her, touching her nymphlike body, her hungry mouth. Damn, he liked her. Since the day he met her, his eye had stopped wandering.

"Let's have sex." She purred the words into his ear.

"No." He held her tightly, kissing her full lips, then took her hand and led her to the bed. "Let's make love."

■

Margery walked unannounced into Barney's office and waited while he finished a telephone call.

"I just spoke to the D.A.'s office in Los Angeles," she told him when he hung up. "They're getting Cynthia Reilly's medical records. A judge ruled in their favor today."

"The blood spots in the apartment?"

She nodded vigorously. "Exactly." The night Denny was killed, the police found blood that wasn't his, tiny drops that seemed to come from nothing more dramatic than a cut on someone's hand. The fact that it hadn't matched Annabelle's blood type had given them reason to believe that maybe there was someone else involved, after all. Nobody, of course, had thought to check Cynthia Reilly's blood type until now.

"I look forward to hearing the results," Barney said. Mark Austin had provided evidence and testimony linking Cynthia Reilly to the illegal company in the Cayman Islands, which meant that there was a reason for her to kill Denny Wright. He also swore that she had confessed the murder to him, but without any other evidence, that wasn't going to stand up in court.

Margery didn't leave, so Barney said, "Even if it matches, it will only prove that she was in the apartment that night—not that she killed him."

"It's a start," Margery said and sighed. "They're going to get her—I can feel it. But I worked so hard figuring out the Austin case that it hurts to see the charges dropped. Even in favor of a murder conviction."

Barney shrugged. "Well, it's not clear to me at this point what's going to happen. But we've got some guilty people on our hooks now, and we can sit for a while and watch them squirm."

■

My own father, Mark thought, watching the eleven o'clock news. Shit, I'm a bigger fool than I ever thought. There on the screen was Bill Austin, holding Cynthia's elbow as he led her down the courthouse steps. When a reporter stuck a microphone in front of him, Bill Austin said, "I have great sympathy for my son, but I don't condone his making accusations against innocent people in order to excuse his own illegal activities."

The reporter seemed satisfied, and Cynthia, looking pale but as beautiful as ever, moved closer to Bill as they got into a waiting limousine and drove off.

What lies did Cynthia tell to get him behind her? Mark wondered. Or had he always been there, hovering in the background, unseen by Mark? He thought of picking up the phone and calling his father, telling him everything he knew about Cynthia, but he was sure it would do no good. Cynthia's spell was too powerful. Mark himself would have forgiven her everything if his back hadn't been against the wall. There was no other way out. His decision to make a deal with the D.A. appalled nobody so much as it did him. *Unchivalrous. Ungallant. Wretched.* He would forever be known as the man who turned in his lover to save his own neck. But there was a twist nobody knew. His lover was fucking his father.

You won this round, Bill, Mark thought, turning off the television. The stakes kept getting higher, and Bill kept winning. It was a shame, because Mark had really wanted to prove something this time—to Jillian and Bill. God knows he had tried, but it had backfired.

■

Emil was hugging the two people who were clearly his parents, clutching them and kissing them on both cheeks. Tears of pleasure streamed down his mother's cheeks, and even Emil's eyes glistened in the dim light of the room. The woman was younger than Jillian would have expected, a small, plump woman with porcelain-smooth skin and bright, twinkling eyes.

Suddenly remembering his manners, Emil said, "Mother, this is Jillian van Dorne." Shaking Jillian's hand, Mrs. Luvic used a few words of carefully pronounced English to apologize for not knowing her guest's language better.

"And this is my father. Papa, meet Jillian van Dorne."

He was a handsome man in his early sixties, as brawny as Emil but with graying hair and a less prosperous air. When he smiled at her, Jillian melted, seeing Emil in twenty years and liking the kind eyes and gentle wisdom she saw in his face.

She didn't know how long they had driven to get there, since both she and Emil had dozed in the back of the limousine most of the way from the airport, wakening now and then to check on the sleeping girls, whisper a few affectionate words, and drift off to sleep again. When they arrived it was very late, but his parents were waiting for them in a small sitting room off the lobby. The room, once elegant, now comfortably seedy, had a fire burning in the fireplace. Emil and Jillian carried Lila and Eve upstairs to a cozy bedroom, where they fell back to sleep almost immediately.

"Would you like sleep, too?" Mrs. Luvic asked, taking Jillian's hand when they came back to the sitting room.

"No, thank you. I had a lovely nap in the car. Why don't we talk for a while?"

Mrs. Luvic looked over at Emil, who translated, and hearing the words, his mother gestured generously around the room. "Please, please," she said. "Please sit down."

Mr. Luvic opened the doors of a heavy oak chest and pulled out a bottle that was unfamiliar to Jillian. He showed it to Emil, who laughed and offered to open it while his father got glasses.

"Tokaji Aszu," Emil said to Jillian, pouring the liquid into one of the gold-rimmed wineglasses that his father offered him. "It's a syrupy sweet wine that's been famous in these parts for generations. The sweetest is five *puttonyos,* and look what we have." He held up the bottle, pointing out the words to her.

They toasted each other in English and Hungarian, and clicking glasses, Jillian was warmed by the genuine family affection that was so apparent in the room. How had Emil been able to leave all this so many years before? Maybe in America he had found the freedom to pursue the creative interests that had been repressed at home, but where could he find the family comfort that he had left?

She sipped the drink, which tasted more like a bitter chocolate liqueur than like wine, and told Emil not to worry about translating.

"I'm happy just enjoying the atmosphere here," she told him when he turned to her one more time to try explaining what his parents had just said.

The conversation continued, and Jillian soon lost even the drift of it. But watching the warm interaction between Emil and his parents was enough. Without words, she appreciated what she could learn from body language: Mrs. Luvic leaned forward, listening avidly to her son; Mr. Luvic, sitting tall in a straight-backed chair, engaged his son with loving respect.

"There's an incredible amount of foreign investment going on in Budapest," Emil explained to Jillian a few minutes later, not wanting to exclude her from the conversation. "My parents have managed this hotel all their lives. The government seized it a long time ago and it was just recently restored to them. My parents are still amazed at having control over their lives again. Now they're thinking of taking some foreign money that's been offered and modernizing."

Jillian nodded politely, and when Emil went back to his conversation, she studied the antique Turkish clock standing in the corner. Its ticking was hypnotic, and she imagined that it had stood in the same place for hundreds of years.

The whole scene was so peacefully mesmerizing—the soothing chatter of a foreign language, the sweet wine, the very late hour—that she wondered if she would drift off to sleep again. And she might have, if she hadn't heard Emil's sharp intake of breath, seen his quick look toward her.

"Did you understand that?" he asked, turning toward her.

"No, I'm sorry. What?" She dragged her attention from the clock to Emil.

"My parents have had an offer to become partners in the hotel from a company in the Cayman Islands. They were leery until they learned that the company had supplied a large project being built in Hungary by an English construction company and an American real-estate concern. The deal is that my parents will send them a sum that's equivalent to about ten thousand dollars for supplies. They'll take care of the rest."

Emil asked something in Hungarian, and Mr. Luvic crossed the room to a rolltop desk. He pulled out some papers and handed them to Emil. Still floating from the sweet wine, Jillian watched Emil flip through the papers and then speak rapidly to his father.

"I asked him if he knows the name of the American behind the Cayman Islands company," Emil said, and his father's reply, though in English, wasn't completely understandable.

"Say it again?" Emil asked, and Mr. Luvic repeated the name slowly, so that even to Jillian it was clear: *Mark Austin*.

■

The sun sparkled through the trees, sending spiderweb-like shadows onto the ground as Jillian nibbled the last bit of the picnic cheese Mrs. Luvic had packed for their day's excursion. The fruit trees along the banks of the Danube were in full bloom, and in the distant hills, Jillian could see sheep grazing in the shade of thousand-year-old castles. Across the picnic blanket, Lila and Eve were sitting close to Emil, taking turns peering into his binoculars, trying to see if they could locate the exact spot where the generally eastward-flowing Danube made an elbow bend to become a southward-flowing water-way.

They had spent the morning in the small medieval city of Esztergom, wandering through the basilica that dominated the hills and admiring the thirteenth-century golden crosses and the royal drinking horns from the fifteenth century. To Jillian, so much tarnished decadence became dreary after a while; the remains of the royal palace seemed to her like a monument to waste. But to the children, it was like walking into a fairy tale.

In fact, Emil had made *all* of Hungary seem like a fairy tale. On the first day in Budapest, he had taken them to Gerbeaud on Vorosmarty Ter, one of the great confectioneries in the city.

"In the sixteenth century, this country was overrun by the Turks," Emil explained as the children shared a rich *dobos torte* and Jillian dipped into the bitter-chocolate shell of a *konyakos meggy*. "The Turks were Muslims, which means they couldn't drink alcohol. The story is that they came up with all these treats so that they could get drunk on the sugar."

Lila giggled and dropped her spoon. "Can you really get drunk on sugar?"

"I can," Jillian said. "In fact, I feel like I've been drunk since we first arrived here."

"Me, too," Lila said, going back to her torte. "Can we stay forever?"

Emil stood up. "Come on, everyone, shall we take a walk by the river?"

They wandered close to the bank, the children first holding Emil's hands, then running ahead.

"It's beautiful here," Jillian said, tossing back her head in the spring air. "So beautiful that it's hard to believe what this country has been through."

"Easier to believe when we're right in the city of Budapest, don't you think?"

"So much spoiled grandeur, you mean? It does make you imagine what a different world it would be if throughout history we spent our money on art and culture and life rather than war."

"You're right, of course, but I've begun to believe that war and violence are part of the human condition, almost impossible to erase. When we have powerful emotions, we are programmed to respond to them with our bodies. Emil loves Jillian, so he wants to have fabulous sex with her. Someone feels threatened by Denny Wright, so she kills him. It's part of being human. No, it's even more far-reaching than that. It's part of being an animal on this earth."

"I'll agree with the part about loving you and wanting to have fabulous sex with you," Jillian said, smiling, "but the rest I question. Killing isn't programmed into our genes." She looked over at Lila and Eve, scampering through the trees, laughing happily. Feeling herself tensing, Jillian said, "You must forgive me. I'm still not capable of discussing the subject of Denny Wright with any degree of rationality."

"I apologize for bringing it up." Emil squeezed her hand. "I was thinking in theoretical terms, not specific ones."

Jillian stopped for a moment to watch her daughters, feeling too shaky to continue their stroll.

She didn't want to think about the murky horrors at home—but she couldn't help herself. Turning to Emil, she said, "What happened with Mark and his female lawyer—who I can think of only as 'C'—is almost beyond my understanding. If Mark knew she killed Denny, why did he move in with her? And why turn on her now?"

"Self-preservation beats out love every time. At least for someone like Mark."

"At first I could almost forgive his illegal company. Maybe he and Cynthia were stealing profits from the Wright-Austin joint venture—but it seemed the kind of white-collar crime that doesn't hurt anybody. But when I realized that by merest coincidence he almost fleeced your parents . . ." She shrugged. "That doesn't seem so harmless anymore, does it?"

"At least it's over now," Emil said. "Whatever deals he makes with the various D.A.'s, his conning people has been stopped."

They walked along quietly for a while, listening only to Lila and Eve laughing and shrieking as they scampered by the river.

"Did I tell you that I spoke to Annabelle this morning?" Jillian asked after a while.

"No. What's going on?"

"She's happy as can be with Barry Brunetti, and everyone is in heaven because the premiere of 'Wild Nights' got incredible ratings. Keith has put it up for syndication, and the stations are grabbing it. He's going to make gobs of money."

"And you will, too," Emil offered.

"Something to look forward to," Jillian said, but her voice was brittle.

Emil took her hand—openly, because the children had begun to understand that they were in love—and asked, "You're not happy?"

"No." Jillian sighed. "I'd like to forget about producing television shows for a while. It all seems so terribly important when you're in the midst of it—worth the total attention of your life. But the moment you take one step back, you think, 'Why did I *care* so much?'"

"Because that's who you are," Emil said simply. "Jillian van Dorne is a woman of quiet passion. It's always people like Annabelle Fox or Denny Wright—and now I suppose Cynthia Reilly—who are called passionate because they parade their emotions like so many brass trumpets. But in the end, you wonder if there's anything other than their own emotional state that interests them. But you put passion into everything you do."

"Well, I'd like to be passionate about something other than ratings now—something that really matters." Leaning close, she whispered, "You matter to me. More than you can imagine."

"And you to me. I love you desperately, Jillian."

"And I love you." Gripping his hand tighter, she said, "Maybe working on the show will be bearable if we're doing it together."

"*Anything* would be bearable as long as we're together. But I think we need something else right now. Let the legal circus in New York and Los Angeles go on without you and stay here with me."

"Stay here?" She looked at him in surprise. "I didn't know you were planning that."

"I didn't either." He smiled. "I guess it's the voice of the Danube speaking. Many years ago I felt passionate hate for Hungary, and I put those feelings on film. And now being here with you, I feel new passion. We're wandering through a country that is struggling to restore its battered self-esteem—a scarred nation trying for a fresh face. Somewhere in there is a lesson for all of us, a message of hope and renewal."

"And you want to capture that on film," she said, understanding.

He put his arm around her. "If you'll do it with me. What could be better than creating a work of passion with the person you love? And for Lila and Eve, it will be better for them to be here—having the experiences of a lifetime—rather than back in New York, where there'll be pain and confusion and scandal."

"You're very convincing," Jillian said, feeling a sudden sweep of promise and hope. "Work that matters. A man I love. What more is there?"

"Very little," Emil said. "But just so you never have to worry about what you've left behind, I promise that we'll make our own wild nights."

ABOUT THE AUTHOR

Janice Kaplan graduated magna cum laude from Yale University in
1976 and received a fellowship to write her first book, *Women and
Sports*. She spent several years as a writer and producer at ABC-TV's
"Good Morning, America" and is currently producer of the syndicated
show "A Current Affair." She contributes regularly to numerous
national magazines including *Cosmopolitan* and was a contributing
editor at *Vogue*. The author of two young adult books and the novel
A Morning Affair, she lives outside New York with her husband and
their two young sons.